#15

NO

ST ERNAN'S BLUES

The Third Inspector Starrett Mystery

PREVIOUS TITLES

www.paulcharlesbook.com

PAUL CHARLES
ST ERNAN'S BLUES
An Inspector Starrett Mystery

Dufour Editions

First published in the United States of America, 2016
by Dufour Editions Inc., Chester Springs, Pennsylvania 19425

© Paul Charles, 2016

This is a work of fiction. Except for public figures, all characters
in this story are fictional, and any resemblance to anyone else
living or dead is purely coincidental.

ISBN 978-0-8023-1360-7

2 4 6 8 10 9 7 5 3 1

Jacket photo of St Ernans: John McIvor
Hand Holding Rosary Beads: Wavebreakmediamicro | Dreamstime.com

Library of Congress Cataloging-in-Publication Data

Names: Charles, Paul, 1949- author.
Title: St. Ernan's blues / by Paul Charles.
Description: First edition. | Chester Springs, Pennsylvania : Dufour
  Editions, 2016. | Series: An Inspector Starrett mystery ; 3
Identifiers: LCCN 2015045936| ISBN 9780802313607 (hardcover) | ISBN
  0802313604 (hardcover) | ISBN 9780802360311 (ebook : MOBI) | ISBN
  9780802360328 (ebook : EPUB)
Subjects: LCSH: Police--Ireland--Donegal (County)--Fiction. |
  Murder--Investigation--Fiction. | GSAFD: Mystery fiction.
Classification: LCC PR6053.H372145 S7 2016   DDC 823/.914--dc23

LC record available at http://lccn.loc.gov/2015045936

Printed and bound in the United States of America

Thanks are due and offered to: Andrew my father,
Christopher, Duncan, Larisa, Brad, Christina, Clair, Lucy,
The James Gang (John & James) Lindsey and Donegal's
fab four: Carmel, Maeve, Laura and Catherine.

This book is dedicated to the memory of Mr. S. Graham
a great man in a world of few great men.

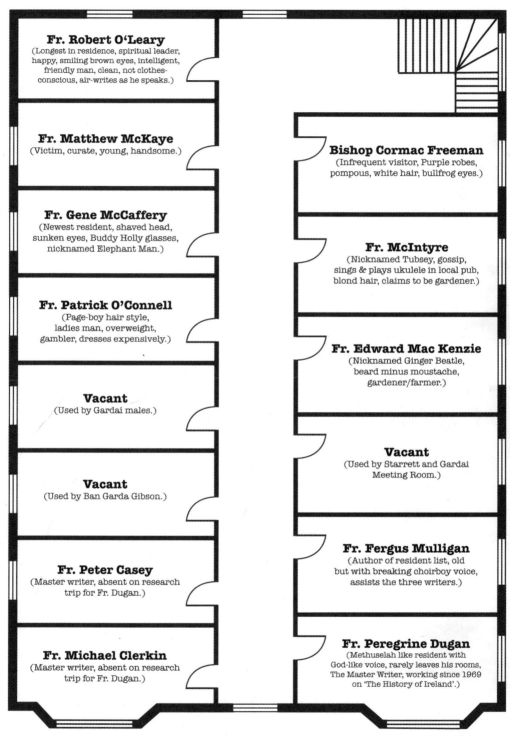

Fr. Robert O'Leary
(Longest in residence, spiritual leader,
happy, smiling brown eyes, intelligent,
friendly man, clean, not clothes-
conscious, air-writes as he speaks.)

Fr. Matthew McKaye
(Victim, curate, young, handsome.)

Fr. Gene McCaffery
(Newest resident, shaved head,
sunken eyes, Buddy Holly glasses,
nicknamed Elephant Man.)

Fr. Patrick O'Connell
(Page-boy hair style,
ladies man, overweight,
gambler, dresses expensively.)

Vacant
(Used by Gardaí males.)

Vacant
(Used by Ban Garda Gibson.)

Fr. Peter Casey
(Master writer, absent on research
trip for Fr. Dugan.)

Fr. Michael Clerkin
(Master writer, absent on research
trip for Fr. Dugan.)

Bishop Cormac Freeman
(Infrequent visitor, Purple robes,
pompous, white hair, bullfrog eyes.)

Fr. McIntyre
(Nicknamed Tubsey, gossip,
sings & plays ukulele in local pub,
blond hair, claims to be gardener.)

Fr. Edward Mac Kenzie
(Nicknamed Ginger Beatle,
beard minus moustache,
gardener/farmer.)

Vacant
(Used by Starrett and Gardai
Meeting Room.)

Fr. Fergus Mulligan
(Author of resident list, old
but with breaking choirboy voice,
assists the three writers.)

Fr. Peregrine Dugan
(Methuselah like resident with
God-like voice, rarely leaves his rooms,
The Master Writer, working since 1969
on 'The History of Ireland'.)

First Floor Plan for St Ernan's House, St Ernan's Island, Donegal, October 2015.

CHAPTER ONE

It started, as the majority of Starrett's cases did, with a knocking on a door.

This door, in itself, was strange. That perhaps should have been a tip-off to Starrett. Well, it wasn't really the door that was strange; it was more where it led you, or, perhaps even more intriguing, how it led you to where it led you.

The door was accessed by climbing fourteen heavily weathered concrete steps, passing through a deep arch, which Starrett noticed supported an overhead pathway. At the end of the darkened, murky, six-foot, damp-smelling vestibule was the wood-panelled, windowless door. The peeling and blistered, painted-white wood was broken only by a large black metallic handle, which also served as a knocker. Starrett's trio of loud knocks echoed off the water of the nearby Donegal Bay. The door was eventually opened by Garda Sgt Packie Garvey. Wordlessly, Garvey turned and led his superior up another fourteen steps. From the amount of autumn light beaming down, Starrett assumed they were entering a courtyard. Instead they ascended into a conservatory housing little more than the staircase exit and a passage to an open doorway, which he assessed to be the original external door to the house.

In the distance Inspector Starrett could hear members of his Gardaí Serious Crimes Unit, normally based a seventy-minute drive away at Ramelton Gardaí Station, efficiently going about their work. He assumed from the lack of banter that there was a corpse not too far away. If further proof were needed, his permanently bent right-hand forefinger was involuntarily twitching furiously away.

Starrett nodded silently to the left and right as he passed various members of his team. He proceeded down a narrow hallway that seemed to run the full length of the long house. The original architect of the grand building, the solitary house on St Ernan's Island, just outside Donegal Town, had cleverly disguised the need for a long corridor running the length of the house. He had prevented the corridor from appearing either too tall on one hand, or too claustrophobic on the other, by incorporating a catacomb effect to the passageway ceiling, which, at the same time, made it appear neither too low nor too high. Starrett clocked it as a very clever solution to an age-old problem.

As Garvey mutedly led him on and on, the eight rooms he passed – four on either side of the corridor – appeared, on brief glances, to be quite airy, furnished with antiques and smelling of fresh flowers and wood polish. The floor of the hallway was covered with a quilt of carpets, runners and rugs, all of which successfully served to dampen the sound of their shoes. At the far end, just beyond a grand wooden staircase, the hallway opened out, again on the right, into a book and painting-lined, panelled room with one of the most magnificent fireplaces Starrett had ever set his baby blues upon. If this was the anteroom, Starrett couldn't wait to see the main event.

His disappointment was obvious the second he looked to his left. The smaller part of the open-plan room was decorated and furnished like a kitchen-cum-dining room; the kitchen-cum-dining room of a beach bungalow. Just under the window, was a scene even more unsettling.

Slumped in a chair – matching the leather ones around the dining table – and the centre of attention for Dr Samantha Aljoe and two of her team was a man, who to Starrett's eyes looked too young to be the priest that his black clothes and white collar attested to.

So engrossed in her work was Dr Aljoe that she still hadn't acknowledged Starrett.

'What's all the commotion at the top of the staircase?' he asked, directing his question at Garvey.

Starrett's dulcet Donegal tones were enough to distract Aljoe, who turned from the corpse to face him. In one gloved hand she had a set of tweezers with what looked like a long strand of blond hair, and in the other a translucent evidence bag where she deposited the hair.

'Ah, Inspector Starrett,' she began, in her soft Home Counties voice and raising her eyes to the ceiling, 'that would be my fault. I'm afraid – in your absence and until as such times you arrived – I instructed your team to keep everyone upstairs and off the ground floor. I have to admit that I find Garda Romany Browne to be ever so cooperative these days.'

Then she rolled her eyes at him.

'Packie,' Starrett started, his eyes still fixed on the provocative Dr Aljoe, 'could you nip upstairs and offer young Garda Browne some of your own cooperation in helping him keep everyone quiet? I can't hear myself think with all this racket.'

Starrett was used to Samantha Aljoe's frivolous ways at the scenes of crimes. He knew it was her way of getting through it; only with such humour could she fully concentrate on her work.

'Who's your man?' he asked, nodding at the young priest in the chair.

'Ah, that would be Father Matthew,' a baritone voice behind him boomed in reply.

Alarm bells deep in Starrett's memory were now making an even bigger racket in his brain than the commotion upstairs. He involuntarily swung around in the direction of the voice only to discover the glaring bullfrog eyes that matched the perfect RTÉ delivery.

'Freeman…' he spluttered.

'And that would be Bishop Cormac Freeman to you, Inspector Starrett,' the white-haired, purple-robed Bishop replied curtly.

Dr Aljoe, her two assistants and Sgt Packie Garvey were glued to the floor in total disbelief as Starrett tore towards the portly member of the clergy.

He had only made it as far as securing two thumbs, seven perfect fingers and one bent one around the bishop's throat by the time Garvey and Aljoe were trying desperately to pull him off. They eventually succeeded, but only after Starrett had managed to rip Bishop Freeman's clerical collar from his neck and hurl it at his face in utter disgust.

CHAPTER TWO

As the badly shaken Bishop was led to safety by Garvey, Aljoe's eyes betrayed the 'what?' and the 'why?' in her mind.

Starrett muttered something that sounded like, 'What? Nothing…must have been a case of mistaken identity.'

'If that was mistaken identity, I'd hate to be around if you ever do meet the person you thought you were meeting.'

Starrett tried unsuccessfully to laugh it off and offered only, 'I'll let you finish up here, give me a shout when you're ready for me to take a look around.'

Aljoe continued to stare at him in disbelief before going back to her work, occasionally looking around and shaking her head.

Starrett left her to it and followed after Garvey's footsteps, which were heading in the direction of the racket upstairs.

He was worried that if he didn't get his emotions under control immediately he'd be tempted to break his one and only golden rule: never try to figure out who's committed the crime until you've first had a good look at all the evidence. He needed to avoid going down the 'who murdered Father Matthew' route, or, maybe more importantly, the, 'How did Father Freeman murder Father Matthew?' route.

He knew he needed to stop all such nonsense, especially now that Father Freeman was apparently Bishop Freeman. No, Starrett should be amassing as much information as possible and then following the evidence rather than allowing the evidence to follow his suspicions.

First to consider was Father Matthew. There was a fair to middling chance that somewhere in Matthew's past, in his life, there was a clue, a reason, a motive. So, Starrett thought, here we go, I'll make a start and go right back to the beginning and begin by questioning the available witnesses.

With every weary step up the circular oak stairs, the racket grew louder. But Starrett wasn't prepared for what was at the top of the staircase.

There, he was greeted by several priests; their long cassocks making them look more like penguins on speed than elite members of the clergy. On the other hand, the members of his gardai team seemed incapable of either controlling their wayward waddle or getting down to the work in hand – which was to start questioning these clergymen.

'Divide and conquer!' Starrett screamed internally. He wasn't sure if it was directed at himself and his threatening thoughts of Bishop Freeman, or the waddle of priests in front of him. Divide and conquer, indeed.

He pushed into the middle of them and held up his right hand. He didn't say a word, just held up his hand. Bit by bit the hustle and bustle died down. Starrett waited until there was complete silence before he dropped his hand again.

'Okay,' he announced, 'I'm sorry for your loss and I'm sorry for this disruption to your daily routine but I'm afraid you're going to have to bear with us as we go about our work.'

No audible response.

'What I need you to do now is to return to your rooms; one of my colleagues will accompany you and note your location. Then we'll come and get you when we're ready to talk to you.'

The detective wondered if his lack of energy had to do with it being September and the recent excuse for a summer hastily disappearing into the past.

'Okay,' he said at last, snapping himself into gear, 'who found the body?'

'That would have been Father Fergus Mulligan,' Sgt Packie Garvey volunteered, 'he's an Ulsterman, from the rich hills of Desertmartin.'

'Good on you Packie. Right, that's where I'll start then,' Starrett declared, as much to himself as anyone else. 'Please lead me to him.'

CHAPTER THREE

The first thing that shocked Starrett about Father Mulligan was how comfortable his rooms were. It wasn't exactly that he'd been expecting cold stone floors (very difficult to achieve on the first floor, as proven at the nearby Donegal Castle), white-washed walls, stained roll-out mattresses with horse-hair blankets and a tin plate in the corner with the remains of yesterday's bread and water. No, it wasn't that he was expecting exactly that, but at the same time, if that was what the Donegal detective had discovered he would have been less surprised than he currently was.

'Very comfortable quarters here, Father,' Starrett offered after Garvey made the introductions and left them. 'Bejeepers, sure this is as grand as any of the suites in Rathmullan House.'

'Yes I'd agree, detective,' Mulligan replied, looking around his room. 'Story has it that the previous owner, in order to pay for the upkeep and refurbishment, splashed out by converting St Ernan's to an upmarket hotel-cum-retreat. They even went as far as adding en suite bathrooms to each of the guest bedrooms. An earlier but inevitable recession put an end to his grand plan and the Church bought it from the bank.'

The priest looked like an overage choir boy and spoke like his voice had not long since broken. His thinning grey hair, reddish cheeks, lack of top gear in the movement department and the slight stooping of his tall, slim frame testified to the idea that he was most likely in his late sixties, maybe even early seventies. But he still had the number one quality present in all the better priests: a twinkle sparkling in his brown eyes.

'And what exactly is it that you do here?' Starrett asked, hoping to develop a conversational tone to the interview.

'Well, you've probably noticed that, with the exception of Father Matthew, God rest his soul,' the priest offered, pausing to cross himself, 'we're all, shall we say, past our prime. Maybe I'd also have to admit that we are, none of us, in the very best of health.'

'So St Ernan's is like a retirement home for the clergy?'

'Well, yes,' admitted Mulligan, if seemingly a little reluctantly, before continuing with further explanation. 'Those of us who have served God and the Church all our lives and have no remaining family members need to go somewhere when we can no longer serve our parish. I think, without exception, we'd all prefer to remain and serve in whatever way possible in our parishes but, shall we say, sadly the accommodation and resources are required for our replacements.'

'And Father Matthew?'

'Well, Father Matthew McKaye, God rest his soul, was sent here to look after us before being sent to his first parish.'

'How many of you live here?'

'Eleven, including Father Matthew,' the priest replied without hesitation, 'we can accommodate fourteen souls, the house has fourteen bedrooms in total. That's fourteen rooms and sixty sashed windows. I know this fact only because they all have to be cleaned.'

Starrett doubted if Father Mulligan cleaned even one of them.

'Including the bishop?'

'Why yes," the priest started, sounding unsure of himself. "Bishop Freeman is here infrequently.'

'So he's retired as well?' Starrett asked.

'No, no, he's ah, well, shall we say, he's still in active service for God but he keeps rooms here as a retreat.'

'Does he now,' Starrett said, not bothering to hide the fact that he wasn't asking a question and using the opportunity to take out his notebook. He scribbled down a few points before passing the notebook to the priest.

'Would you mind just jotting down the names of the residents here at St Ernan's please?'

The priest willingly obliged and a few minutes later returned the book with a list duly printed, rather than written, in neat, perfectly formed letters.

The full list read:

Father McIntyre
Father Gene McCafferty
Father Robert O'Leary
Father Edward McKenzie
Father Matthew McKaye (deceased)
Father Patrick O'Connell
Bishop Cormac Freeman (not a permanent resident)
Father Fergus Mulligan (author of list)
Father Peter Casey
Father Peregrine Dugan
Father Michael Clerkin
Mrs Eimear Robinson (housekeeper and cook, a
      Donegal Town resident)

'How long have you been here Father?' Starrett asked as he studied the list.

'I'm here six years in the middle of this October.'

'And the rest of the residents?'

'Father O'Leary would be here the longest. He moved in just over twelve years ago and oversaw the conversion of the property to our needs. Father Gene McCafferty would be our most recent resident, he moved in nearly two years ago in December. I remember it well because, shall I say, I felt very sad that he should have to leave his home in his parish coming up to Christmas.'

'I see from your list you also have a housekeeper and cook, a Mrs Eimear Robinson?'

'Yes, she's really the housekeeper and cleaner and she helps Father Matthew...sorry...of course, I should have said she helped Father Matthew with the cooking.'

'Was she helping him today?'

'No. Wednesday she's never in, she takes Wednesdays and Sundays off.'

Starrett walked around Father Mulligan's homely accommodation and stopped by the window. The room was towards the rear of the house and half the view was of the waters of Lough Eske and the other half of the trees that made up the rear of the island of St Ernan's.

The foliage looked like a giant green bird's nest had been plonked on top of the island. He could imagine the priest spending many a long hour enjoying this tranquil view. Starrett pulled himself away from the view and his mood and got back down to business.

'How long has Father Matthew been here?'

'He would have completed his service of one year at the end of this month. Then he'd have been off to his first parish and then we'd have had a replacement curate. October is always the replacement month.'

'Where was he from?' Starrett asked, taking a comfortable seat opposite the priest.

'He was from Sligo.'

'I see. Now, before you discovered Father Matthew, when was the last time you would have seen him?' Starrett continued, working his way through his important list.

'The funny thing was I saw him within the house just before and just after his death. Every day, mid-afternoon about 3:30, I go for a walk around the island by myself. At the far end of the island, just outside the line of the trees you see from here, there is a stone seat where I like to sit, enjoy the view of the water and beyond,' the priest said, glancing briefly up to the heavens before continuing. 'I meditate, say my prayers and give thanks. On my way out today I passed Father Matthew in the kitchen, peeling the potatoes for our evening meal.'

'And you discovered him when you returned from your walk around the island?'

'Yes in fact I did.'

'What time would that have been?' Starrett asked, totally intrigued with the priest's information.

'Around 5:30.'

'And did you notice anything different in the kitchen?' Starrett asked hopefully.

'Well, no. He was slumped in the leather dining chair near but not at the dining table. He looked very peaceful. In fact when I first came upon him I thought he'd fallen asleep. I called to him because his potatoes were boiling over. He didn't respond. I went over to him and as I got closer, I recognised immediately the look of death.'

'Did you touch the body?'

'No,' he replied automatically and instinctively paused and then qualified himself with, 'only to search for a pulse in his neck.'

'Then what did you do?'

'I went to the bishop's room, informed him and he rang the guards.'

'Did he go to the kitchen first to check Father Matthew himself?'

Father Mulligan thought for a few moments as though he was discovering something himself before offering, 'No. He went straight to the phone and called the guards.'

'Then what did he do?'

'He came back to the door, where I was standing, and told me the guards were on the way, then he instructed me to return to Father Matthew's remains and ensure no one touched anything until the guards arrived.'

'Was anyone else around when you returned to Father Matthew's remains?'

'No, he was still by himself, slumped in the chair.'

'So Father Matthew was by the sink the first time you saw him?'

'That is correct. As I said, he was peeling the potatoes.'

'Then when you came back in from your constitutional he was slumped in the chair and the potatoes were boiling over? And would you know exactly how long you'd been out?' Starrett continued, allowing himself to follow a natural flow.

'No more than two hours, but sometimes I just get lost in my thoughts and lose all track of time,' the priest replied.

'So what happened to the potatoes?'

'I took them off the boil?'

'And just left them there?'

'Yes,' the priest replied, his impatience growing, 'why is any of this important at a time like this?'

'Well, don't you see, people mostly behave due to instincts and their natural habits,' Starrett offered through a warm thoughtful smile, 'Like when I asked you had you touched anything else you said no, but just then you told me you turned the heat off the potatoes.'

'O-kay.'

'So I wonder, could there have been anything else you would have done without thinking?'

Father Mulligan looked like he was considering such possibilities. He grimaced gently, rubbed the back of his neck with his left hand and then the gentle stubble on his chin before saying, 'Well, I would have used the dish cloth to wrap it around the handle of the saucepan, but the usual one wasn't around so I undid the button on my shirt cuff, pulled it down and wrapped it around the handle of the potato pot to avoid burning my hands when I brought the potatoes over to the sink to drain them.'

He looked rather pleased that he'd been able to recall such details at will.

'Why would you have done that and not just turned the gas off under the pan?'

Again he thought for a few seconds before replying.

'Must have just been instincts, I guess.' The priest didn't seem satisfied with his own answer because he continued, 'shall we say, I acted on automatic pilot, the way I would normally have done and would have done dozens of times.'

'Okay. Okay, this is all good,' Starrett said in encouragement, 'it may seem unimportant just now but it could be vital.'

The priest nodded positively.

'Can we go back to the time you visited Bishop Freeman to advise him about Father Matthew?'

'Okay.'

'You said you told him you had found Father Matthew slumped in the chair. He rang the guards and he came back and advised you to make sure no one touched anything.'

'That would be correct.'

'He didn't discuss with you about ringing for a doctor or an ambulance?'

'No, but I'd advised him that Father Matthew had passed away.'

Starrett nodded 'okay' and said, 'and did you actually hear him speak to the guards on the phone?'

'No, I could hear him speaking but he wasn't talking loud enough for me to be able to make out what he was saying.'

'Okay,' Starrett sighed, 'that's nearly it for now but I do have one final question at this stage: do you have any idea where Father Matthew was going?'

'Heavens!' Mulligan said, so deadpan Starrett couldn't work out if he was joking or not.

'I meant more in the physical sense rather than the spiritual one. You know, which parish he would have gone to, had he lived?'

'Oh sorry, forgive me. Yes I do, as a matter of fact,' Mulligan replied in his breaking falsetto voice, 'Bishop Freeman had found a place for him in his parish.'

'Had he now,' Starrett said, showing he could do a bit of dead-panning himself when the mood took him, 'And tell me Father, where exactly would the bishop be in residence these days?'

'That would be in Salthill, just outside of Galway,' Father Fergus Mulligan, originally from Desertmartin, replied immediately, 'the bishop claims that the sea air is good for his health.'

I bet he does, Starrett thought as he said, 'Right Father, that'll do me for now. We'll talk again in the near future but in the meantime, if you have any more recollections from this afternoon please contact one of the members of the An Garda Síochána straight away.'

CHAPTER FOUR

Sergeant Garvey and Ban Garda Nuala Gibson were waiting for Inspector Starrett outside Father Mulligan's door.

'Yes,' Garvey said, literally the moment his boss appeared in the doorway. 'Dr Aljoe sent up a message to say she's just about finished downstairs and would like you to do your inspection before she removes the body back to the mortuary in Letterkenny.'

'Go and find Garda Pips O'Toole for me,' Starrett said, as he reached the bottom of the stairs and was in sure earshot of the aforementioned and naturally stunning Dr Aljoe.

'Who the feck is Pips O'Toole?' Gibson asked, shaking her head in a confident, "I'm not amused," manner. In a Ban Garda uniform it was difficult to look different enough to impress, not that she wanted to, but Gibson managed it quite simply with her snow, pure porcelain-like skin; sharp dark eyebrows; friendly, but reserved, brown eyes; blonde hair mostly tucked up into her standard issue hat and the most kissable lips this side of Scarlett Johansson.

'You know, yer man?' he replied. For his own personal reasons he wanted Gibson to be the one who'd take the bait.

'I don't know. Which man?'

'Yer man,' he barked impatiently and on seeing only puzzlement on both of their faces he continued, 'Romany Browne, of course.'

'Why not call him Romany Browne then?' Gibson asked innocently.

'Well, quite simply because you would imagine that someone called Romany Browne would have…you know, a full head of his own hair, perfectly chiselled features and a perfect body.'

'Not to mention his smiling eyes, perfect teeth, kind hands, good manners, fit physique–'

'Exactly, Ban Garda, exactly,' Starrett interrupted, faking impatience, 'which is why henceforth the rookie in question will be known as Pips O'Toole.'

"Let's just keep it simple sir, let's just call him by the name his mother and father chose to give him," Gibson said, making it clear it wasn't a question.

Not only was Nuala Gibson the Ban Garda in Starrett's squad but she was also the best friend of Maggie Keane, his girlfriend, so the matter was finally parked there and then.

Once the aforementioned Romany Browne turned up, Starrett completely ignored him while he instructed Gibson to team up with Sgt Packie Garvey to interview Father McIntyre up in his room. When they'd departed to do as bid, he nodded to Browne to follow him over to the grand fireplace, this time out of earshot of Dr Aljoe but still within her line of vision. He put his hand on Browne's shoulder and leaned in close to him and kept stealing glances of the glamorous Dr Samantha Aljoe. Eventually Browne couldn't help but steal glances of the pathologist as well.

By this point Dr Aljoe was eyeballing Starrett and Browne just as much as they were her.

Starrett braced himself for the corpse.

He walked around the kitchen-cum-dining-cum-grand-fireplace-cum-book area. He went to the sink and discovered on the worktop the large saucepan with the drained potatoes. He put on a pair of evidence gloves and found a fork in one of the drawers beneath. He discovered that the skins of the blues offered absolutely no resistance to his fork. These potatoes were well boiled. He made a note to check how long potatoes would have to boil to end up this soft. Starrett also couldn't find the missing kitchen towel that Father Mulligan had referred to. He picked up four pieces of two discarded opened Sweetex packets lying on the floor by Father Matthew's chair.

Aljoe clocked Starrett making his observations and remained schtum throughout the silent procedure.

Starrett eventually made his way to the body.

The first thing that struck him about Father Matthew was how handsome a man he had been. Starrett reckoned the priest would have been 25 years old, maybe 26 at the very most. Clean shaven, with well-groomed, jet black hair. With well-groomed hair in fact, fashioned in the style of Kirk Douglas. It certainly wouldn't have looked out of place on some of that generation of Hollywood actors. His eyebrows were perfectly formed. He wore flawlessly pressed black trousers, a black shirt (as would have been expected), but he broke with tradition by adding a very expensive looking pair of Nike trainers. Starrett figured it made sense; the priest was bound to be on his feet all day, but nonetheless, it still jarred Starrett a little.

Starrett sat down in the comfortable leather chair opposite Father Matthew and, with elbows resting on the arms of the chair, he clasped his hands together under his chin and stared at the remains of the priest. The young, handsome priest's eyes were shut, which only served to make his eyebrows appear all the more stunning. Starrett was thankful Father Matthew's eyes were shut; he was forever falling into a trance, induced by the strange spell of dead men's eyes. Father Mulligan was easily forgiven for mistaking his colleague for being asleep. Father Matthew really did look like he was sleeping, and peacefully at that. Could he really look so peaceful if he had experienced a violent or troubled passing? How had he died? Naturally? Starrett didn't think so; he looked too fit, too healthy, and too young for such a premature end. What had he done to get himself to the point where the breath was permanently stolen from his body? How had he met his end? What exactly had happened in the couple of hours or so between Father Mulligan going out for his constitutional and returning to the house again? Could Father Matthew have been accidently gassed? Nope, Father Mulligan had said he'd eventually turned off the gas under the boiling potatoes after he'd discovered the body, so the hungry, angry flame had devoured all of the available hissing gas supply.

He dared himself to put his gloved hand in a naked gas flame next time he saw one if it didn't believe it was angry. The detective knew he was getting nowhere with this.

The discomfort of the evidence gloves eventually shook Starrett out of his mood.

'What do you have for me Sam…sorry…Dr Aljoe?'

She fixed her eyes on him and dropped her head slightly, before shaking it and her mane vigorously. It looked like she had decided to avoid her usual approach of flirting as a way of dealing with the macabre situation she found herself in most days of her life.

'Well Starrett, come look at this,' she replied, as she walked over to Father Matthew and knelt down beside him.

Starrett did as he was bid and he was so close to her, the smell of her perfume distracted him from the inevitable rotten-apples smell of death – the same hypnotic bouquet that signalled the start of the inevitable decaying process of a human being. Her blue translucent scene-of-crime one-piece suit rustled as she swayed on her hunkers so she could position herself to cautiously lean across the body. Next she carefully lifted Father Matthew's right forefinger.

'What does that tell you, Inspector?'

'There's no dirt under his nails. He washed his hands properly?' Starrett offered, looking back at her, directly into her brown eyes.

'More?'

'He cut his nails regularly?'

'You're getting warmer, and all things considered quite warm for a man.'

'Thanks.'

'It wasn't a compliment,' she said, through one of her sweetest smiles.

'Thanks,' he repeated, 'and?'

'His nails; he'd had his nails professionally manicured and not only that, he'd had them done regularly.'

'Really?'

'Really Starrett.'

'Bejeepers. Samantha, colour me impressed, I'd never ever have picked that up. Shouldn't we ask the question: Why would a man manicure his nails?'

'That's not very 21st-century, Starrett. Haven't you heard? Some men take pride in their appearance nowadays. Some men want to look good for their partners.'

'Sure God was his partner'

'Oh goodness, I was so taken by his good looks I'd forgotten all about him being a priest,' she offered in a whisper, even though there was no one within earshot.

'And had you used the term "partner" instead of "wife" because you thought he was gay?'

'No, Starrett, I most certainly did not. I used the word "partner" as a term to suggest equality.'

'Right.'

'Well that's what I hope I meant,' she said, as she offered him one of her best 'but even if I didn't you'll still forgive me' smiles.

'Can I check his pockets now?'

'Yes of course, and then if I can borrow Romany Browne from you, we'll get the remains back to Letterkenny.'

'Sorry,' Starrett started, as he put his gloved hand into Father Matthew's right-hand pocket, 'but Pips O'Toole is otherwise engaged for the foreseeable future.'

He withdrew his hand with his bounty of a single unattached Yale key, an expensive looking set of Rosary beads in one side pocket and in the other side pocket he withdrew five twenty euro notes, three ten euro notes and three five euro notes, all folded neatly in descending order into a genuine silver money clip. In the single back pocket of the father's trousers was a perfectly folded cash receipt for a lunch for two in Blueberry Tea Room, Donegal for the Monday of that week.

Starrett searched the area for Father Matthew's jacket. He spotted one, hanging on a coat hook on the back door, which was perfectly in line with the corridor running down the length of the house. The jacket looked of an inferior quality to the priest's trousers and it had a pioneer pin on the right-hand lapel. Starrett took the jacket off the hook in order to go through the pockets, only to discover another jacket underneath. He searched the first jacket and surprisingly all of the pockets were empty. He took down the second jacket and noted immediately that it was a better-cut jacket and made of material identical to that of Father Matthew's trousers: it was clearly part of the same black suit. He replaced the first jacket, the one with the pioneer pin, on the hook, walked over to the worktop and, pocket by pocket, removed the contents of the second jacket on a cleared section of the worktop. He found nothing more than a pack of Kleenex tissues, a cinema stub for the Abbey Centre, Ballyshannon, a purple Liberty pen, some loose change and a couple of strips of a fresh mint chewing gum.

Aljoe passed little comment as Starrett continued his search.

'You've really got nothing else for me?' he said, as he placed all the contents of the jacket pockets into a separate evidence bag to the one he had used for the contents of the trouser pockets, before carefully labelling both of them.

'I have to admit that I haven't a clue how he died.'

They both hunkered down on either side of Father Matthew. She examined his hands closely again and then his face and neck, all his exposed skin in fact.

'I can also tell you that there are no needle puncture marks but, apart from that,' she said as she stood up, pulling off her gloves and removing her suit, using Starrett as a prop to lean on as she did so, 'I won't have anything else for you until I get him back to the morgue in Letterkenny.'

'Nothing else at all, doctor?'

'Just that he was healthy, died earlier this afternoon and I'd hazard a guess that he didn't die from natural causes.'

'I don't know why I even bother to come up any more, doctor. Sure, you've already got it all wrapped up. I could have saved myself the drive past Biddy's O'Barnes' and over the Blue Stack Mountains.'

'I'm not so sure of that, Starrett,' she replied, but didn't wait for his wise-crack before continuing, 'I'd say from your actions you'd have walked the whole way from Letterkenny, through the Barnesmore Gap, past the Blue Stack Mountains, and all in your bare feet for another chance to grab the bishop by the throat.'

'I'd forgotten all about that, doctor,' he claimed nonchalantly.

'I doubt that, Starrett, I doubt that very much.'

CHAPTER FIVE

Although Sergeant Packie Garvey had worked longer and closer with Inspector Starrett than Ban Garda Nuala Gibson, it was Gibson who seemed the most confident and the one who wanted to take the lead in the interview.

'I'm Father McIntyre but me enemies call me Tubsey,' was the slightly unorthodox introduction offered by the priest as he welcomed the two members of the Gardaí Serious Crimes Unit into his room.

Gibson introduced both herself and her colleague, responding positively to McIntyre's warm smile and strong, very strong, handshake.

The priest was probably in his early fifties, dressed in black chinos, black socks, and a black open-neck shirt. His head was shaved back and sides, but badly cropped on top with dyed blonde highlights. Gibson felt, and she would later relay this to Starrett in her report, that it looked inappropriate for a priest and certainly out of place on a man of his age. His clean-shaven skin enjoyed the red flush of a whiskey drinker.

McIntyre continued holding her hand in both of his and shaking it vigorously, like he was either trying really hard to make a connection or was just very nervous.

'Oh my goodness, I cannot believe what happened to our Father Matthew, I mean, it's terrible. What am I saying? Of course it's terrible. Do you know exactly what happened to him? I've been saying for ages we have to lock the front and back doors. Anyone could just wander in off the streets and murder us in our sleep! I shiver from head to toe when I think of it. These are desperate times we live in. Imagine being murdered just for a few spuds. It could have been any of us I suppose,' he gushed, with more than a slight hint of camp.

'So you think he was murdered?' Gibson asked, as she freed her hand and sat on one of the four seats around the priest's small pine dining table.

'Well, it's either that or one of us did it,' he announced confidently.

The priest instructed Garvey to sit at the table beside Gibson, then filled the thirsty silver electric kettle and switched it on.

'Don't be doing that on our account,' Gibson said, as the priest took out three mugs and a packet of Jacob's Kimberley biscuits.

'Forget on your account dear,' he tutted, 'I need an herbal tea to calm me nerves down; you can join in or not but I'd say by the look in your sergeant's eyes he's got his wee heart set on at least one of me bickies.'

'Oh go on then,' Gibson said, taking a tip out of Starrett's book of always trying to make these interviews less formal, more conversational.

McIntyre's attention was now focused entirely on Sgt Garvey.

'Oh my Go…' he started, raising his four outstretched and parted fingers to cover his mouth, 'goodness, you're not *the* Packie Garvey are you?'

'The very same man,' Gibson replied, on behalf of the modest hurling star.

'Donegal's finest on the hurling field – in me wee room? I just can't believe it! The fathers will never believe–'

Whatever Father McIntyre – or Tubsey, to his enemies – was about to say was loudly interrupted by the whistle of the boiling kettle peaking.

'You were saying that you thought it was either a stranger or one of the priests who did it then.'

'Slow down just a wee bit there, Ban Garda,' McIntyre said, stopping in his tea-preparing tracks, 'that's hardly what I meant. What I meant was that he was too young and too healthy to die naturally, although in all my days as a priest I've never actually witnessed what could be called a "natural death". I believe there's nothing more unnatural than dying.'

McIntyre continued making the tea, in silence. Gibson and Garvey followed suit.

'So how well did you know Father Matthew?' Gibson asked, as Father McIntyre brought the tea and the biscuits to the table.

'Coming up to a year now with the young curate' the priest started, 'sorry, I've just twigged, you asked me how well I'd known him and I answered you how long I'd known him.'

'No harm done,' Garvey said, making a rare contribution to the conversation, 'we'd have asked you that as well.'

'Well, you put ten men – eleven if you count the nights the bishop stays over – in a wee house and they're either going to get on like a house on fire or they're going to want to ki...strangle each other.'

'Sorry?' Gibson said, eyebrows rising.

'Whoops, that came out all wrong!' McIntyre apologised after the fact, 'of course, I didn't mean you'd actually want to strangle them in the literal sense.'

Then he paused, thought for a bit before mischievously adding, 'Well, on second thoughts someone clearly did. Whoops...me and me big mouth again!'

'So how well did you get on with Father Matthew then?'

'Well, you see, he worked for us, he and Mrs Eimear Robinson, looked after St Ernan's, took care of us all...'

It appeared that Father McIntyre felt that neither of the Gardaí was getting his drift so he continued with, 'I've always found it's much safer never to criticise your barber's wee hurling team, if you know what I mean?'

'The politer you are, the better the service?' Gibson offered, but couldn't help thinking that, by the state of the priest's hair, he must have done something drastically worse than slag off his barber's hurling team.

'Exactly!'

'Right,' Gibson said, while acknowledging that, between his supply of Kimberley biscuits, Garvey was making notes. 'So, how well did you know Father Matthew?'

'Oh yes, I never really answered that one, did I? I'll never get on the Graham Norton show now, will I?'

Gibson just stared at the priest.

'Ehm, let's see. Me dinner was always great and I would always offer him a wee compliment at that and things like that. But we'd never have deep conversations about the meaning of life or the state of the Roman Catholic Church in modern times. Neither he nor I would ever confide in each other. We'd never go to places together. Like for instance, every Sunday night I go down to Doran's, the wee pub, just off the Diamond in Donegal Town, and after a few wee drinks I'll take me turn at the mic and sing a few tunes. Look, we're talking more Val Doonican here than Bobbie Williams.'

'Robbie Williams?' Gibson offered, and then wished she hadn't.

'None of him either! No, as I said, just mostly Val and Jim Reeves,' McIntyre replied, missing her correction, 'but the point is he'd never ever been down to one of those sessions.'

'What did he do with himself?'

'I think he'd go around to Eimear Robinson's house quite a bit for meals and things. They seemed to get on very well.'

Gibson was unhappy at the amount of information she and Garvey were extracting but then she remembered Starrett advising her in a similar instance to be patient. Just keep talking. When you haven't something you can think of to ask them about the case, ask them about themselves. Starrett claimed that people just loved talking about themselves.

'How long have you been at St Ernan's?' Gibson asked, because that was exactly what she was wondering.

'I've been here just over four years,' McIntyre replied wistfully, 'the time has just flown by.'

'Why did you come here in the first place?' Garvey asked.

'I lost my faith, I didn't like what my church had become but at the same time I still wanted to be a priest, I enjoyed being a priest.'

'Surely if you lose your faith you can't remain a priest?' Garvey asked.

'Well, there's the thing,' McIntyre said, as he spooned his teabag around his mug a few times to try and revive a bit of the strength in his herbal tea. 'I enjoy the lifestyle. I enjoy helping people in a real way rather than trying to bring them spiritual enlightenment. This brought me into conflict with me superiors. I was confronted and asked to either change me tune or leave. I refused and so I was invited to move and see out me days here. I think the Church probably thought they were already fighting on too many fronts, as it were, and so if they could accommodate me here (in every sense of the word) it would mean I'd keep me mouth shut and so they'd save themselves yet another battle.'

'So what do you actually do here?' Gibson asked.

'Nothing.'

'Nothing?'

'Well, I mean, I don't have a role in the Catholic Church any more. We don't perform any services for the Church.'

'But they still provide food and board for you?' Garvey piped up again.

'Well yes – maybe you should consider it as one of the better pension plans.'

'Do you still get a wage?' Gibson asked, to satisfy her curiosity. The two things she wondered a lot about were, in order of priority, one, did the captain of teams in the English premier league get extra money for being captain and, two, how much were priests paid.

'I still get me eighteen thousand euro a year, tax-free,' McIntyre readily admitted. 'If I was still in my parish I would of course be paying taxes, but everyone here is deemed to be handicapped in one way or another so we don't qualify.'

Ban Garda Nuala Gibson figured that, plus food and board, it wasn't bad at all compared to her thirty-eight thousand euro, which was reduced to twenty-six-and-a-bit thousand euro after deductions. The two thousand-euro pay cut she and all public servants had suffered in the infamous 2010 budget had now been made good again with her annual increase, but it was still very difficult to make ends meet. She knew that these were not the thoughts Starrett (who she figured must be on about sixty-five to seventy thousand a year) would appreciate her having at this stage in an interview. Although, now she came to think about it, of course Father Matthew and his colleagues' financial situation could be relevant, very relevant to the investigation in fact.

'So how do you fill your days?' Gibson asked, trying to get back on track again.

'Oh you'd be surprised,' he started, seeming to be excited in the conversation for once, 'I, ah, well I run the wee gardens, you know. I produce enough vegetables to get us through the year and what excess we have we trade on for some basic provisions, just like they used to do in the olden days,' he concluded, rather proudly. 'We also sell some cakes and such like as well.'

'How well do the residents at St Ernan's get on?' Garvey asked.

'Well, I imagine they'll all have a wee chat with you about me so I'll return the compliment,' McIntyre declared. 'Let's see now, Father Matthew worked for us all and generally passed himself off with everyone and favoured no one in particular, although there are some among us who felt he might just have been a wee bit too preoccupied with his looks for a man of the cloth.

'Then there's Father Fergus Mulligan, a man without enemies but that sadly also means he's a man without friends.

'Father Robert O'Leary is a very nice wee man, and I mean genuinely a very nice man – he's been here the longest, the unspoken spiritual leader, a happy man.

'Father Gene McCafferty, he's the new boy and so we haven't really figured him out yet, but he's always walking around the island with his hands stuck deep in his pockets and his elbows sticking out by his sides like elephants ears. That is why he's called the Elephant Man; it's because of his elbows and not his looks, by the way.

'Father Edward McKenzie helps me out in the garden – bit of a comedian, he's also known as the Ginger Beatle but please believe me, not because of his looks. He's an Ulsterman and a good worker.

'Father Patrick O'Connell, now he's the sharpest dresser in St Ernan's. He's our public face as he accepts invitations to every official function in the diocese and has even been known to turn up at the opening of an envelope. He hangs around so much with the blue rinses I'm surprised some of it hasn't washed off into his own thatch. Wicked I know, but I'm having all of this month's fun in this single session.

'And then there are our three wise men: Father Peter Casey and Father Michael Clerkin. I don't know if both of them are tied to a vow of silence but they rarely leave their room and when they do, they never speak with anyone in sight of the rest of us. Father Mulligan always speaks on behalf of the three wise men.'

'You said three wise men but you've only mentioned two names,' Gibson said as Garvey wrote away furiously in his notebook.

'Excellent, well observed,' McIntyre said in praise before continuing, 'I was forgetting Father Peregrine Dugan, nickname the Master Writer. He has not been seen outside of his rooms since I arrived here something like four years ago. I've never even seen him or spoken to him.'

'Really?' Gibson said, echoing Garvey's apparent disbelief.

'Really! He's supposed to be writing a tome called The History of Ireland. Supposedly he spends every waking minute working on it. Father Casey reckons at last count they'd over two thousand pages between them. The remaining two wise men and Father Mulligan, bring him his food and his needs. Fathers Casey and Clerkin are frequently off on trips throughout Ireland, carrying out various research projects for the Master Writer. I believe at the moment that they are somewhere down around Youghal in County Cork. In their absence, Father Mulligan serves Father Peregrine Dugan and, as he's a scholar himself, he also works on the book. The four of them have their own wee enclave of rooms at the other end of the corridor on this floor. They're separated from the rest of us by the three empty rooms. I believe in the absence of tenants that they sequestered one of the vacant rooms for their mountains of files.'

Gibson couldn't help but wonder and be attracted to the theory that somewhere in those files lay the reason for Father Matthew McKaye's death. But that was going to have to wait.

'And that's your lot,' Father McIntyre offered in conclusion, as though he was signing off from a night's viewing on Ulster TV.

'Except for the bishop of course?' Gibson prompted, remembering vividly Starrett's reaction to the one in purple the second he saw him.

'He's not one of us, he doesn't live here,' McIntyre replied, somewhat coldly.

'But he stays here from time to time?' Gibson said, sensing the strangeness.

'He's not one of us,' McIntyre replied, with the definite air that this was where he wanted to park that particular part of the conversation.

As Gibson was indicating that she was ready to go, Garvey stared at her, his pen still poised about a quarter of an inch away from a fresh page of his notebook.

"Oh yes, Father," Gibson started, in a Columbo moment, "could you please tell us what you were doing between 15:30 and 17:30 this afternoon."

"That's easy," the priest replied immediately, "I was visiting Ballyshop, a supermarket down in Ballyshannon, they take some of our vegetables and pies and they'd fallen behind with their payments. I spent the afternoon convincing them that if they didn't keep up to date we'd have to move our business to somewhere like Quinns."

Father McIntyre plucked a business card from his inside pocket and as he wrote Ballyshop's details on the back he advised Garvey, for the benefit of his notebook, that he'd left for Ballyshannon just after lunch at three o'clock and arrived back at St Ernan's around twenty to six.

CHAPTER SIX

Meanwhile, Starrett was getting acquainted with the longest serving member of St Ernan's, Father Robert O'Leary.

Starrett took to the priest immediately. In a different life they could have been friends, possibly even good friends.

The priest was in his late sixties with greying, permanently unkempt, shortish black hair. He'd gentle, smiling brown eyes with a slim frame, probably, Starrett guessed, about five feet ten inches tall. He was wearing black, badly creased trousers, a crisp white-as-new collarless shirt, and when Starrett came calling into his room he was wearing black socks and a pair of red tartan carpet slippers. His room was very clean and benefitting immensely from American Arts and Crafts furniture, which was extremely well polished and looked like it might have been in St Ernan's since the house was built in the late 1820s. The floorboards were bare and varnished to match the furniture, which meant that Starrett's movements across the floor were as pronounced as a horse's hooves on a tarmac road.

Starrett was trying to pick his opening for the interview when O'Leary stole the initiative with: 'Before we start, I feel I should mention that we have a mutual acquaintance.'

'Oh?' Starrett replied, his interest piqued, a feeling he also acknowledged could be read as being a state of distraction.

'Yes indeed,' Father Robert O'Leary continued. 'I know Maggie Keane's brother-in-law.

'Oh, that would be Niall's brother?' Starrett replied, unsure of where this was going. The late husband of Starrett's now girlfriend had lost his lengthy battle with cancer a few years back, however Starrett still felt he was due the respect of aknowledging his Christian name.

'Yes, Eoin Keane – he'd have been a good deal older than Niall and I'd have played rugby with him when we were both at Queens,' O'Leary recited, as if reading from a book. He spoke very precisely and in a slightly higher register than Starrett had expected. The priest pressed his thumb and forefinger together, pulling his other three fingers into his fist. He lifted the resultant hand to his mouth level and moved it through the air together as if imitating the nib of a pen he was using to fluently write his spoken words. Starrett imagined the priest would have beautiful flowing handwriting.

'Yes, Maggie has mentioned Eoin quite a bit to me,' Starrett offered, 'they're very good friends but we've never actually met as of yet.'

'You knew her before she married Niall, didn't you?'

'Yes,' Starrett replied and for a brief moment it looked as if he was going to give the full explanation of his history with Maggie, but then he thought better of it and let the word hang solo in the air between them.

O'Leary's darting inquisitive eyes looked like they'd read the situation accurately and so he seemed content, as opposed to happy, to let that particular subject drop, at least for now.

Starrett imagined that O'Leary would also get around to raising the subject of his rather animated reaction to the bishop when he felt the time was right.

'So, this is all very sad with Father Matthew, isn't it?' the priest said, signalling that he too was ready to broach the topic they were both together to discuss.

'Very,' Starrett replied, taking out his leather-bound notebook and pen if only to acknowledge, from his side, that the interview had officially started. 'Tell me,' Starrett continued, picking his words carefully, 'when was the last time you'd seen Father Matthew alive?'

'Oh, that would have been today, earlier in the afternoon. I was in Donegal Town on business. I got back here around three o'clock and I nipped into the kitchen area on the way up to my room to pick up some choc bars and a cup of tea. Father Matthew was getting ready to start preparing for dinner.'

'Did you know Father Matthew very well?'

'Yes I did, as a matter of a fact,' O'Leary said, signing off another short sentence in the air.

'How so?' Starrett inquired, on a reply he'd originally thought to let go.

'Well, in point of fact, Father Matthew had lost his way and he'd come to me seeking instruction and we'd hit it off. He was a thoughtful and well-meaning, kind young man.'

'And you'd managed to gather him back into the flock as it were…' Starrett started, but struggled to find a conclusion which would not sound patronising.

'No,' Father O'Leary claimed, 'if anything I'd tried to convince him that he might be right; right, that is, to question the teachings of the Roman Catholic Church.'

'Really?'

'Why are you surprised at that, Inspector? I'm to believe that you yourself turned your back on the Church.'

'Maybe I'd incorrectly picked up the impression that Father Matthew was a happy priest,' Starrett replied, addressing only one half of the issues the priest raised.

'Well Starrett, as I always told my seniors when I first encountered my own personal doubts with the Church, no one wants to leave a blind shepherd attending the flock.'

'Yes,' Starrett offered, breaking into a grin. 'Why is it you are at St Ernan's?'

'Oh I'm too old to attend the flock nowadays,' O'Leary replied, using only his voice and not the sky-writing this time.

'But at the time you came here you would have been…'

'Fit for the lambs as well as the sheep?' the priest offered in assistance to Starrett's politeness.

'Well yes.'

'I'll be candid with you, Inspector, in the hope that it might make your investigation easier,' the priest said, through another warm smile. 'I felt embarrassed standing up behind the pulpit in front of a congregation. I was extremely annoyed by what some members of the clergy had managed to get away with. I was even more upset about what the Church was guilty of, in trying to cover up the trails of some of its members in order to keep them out of jail. Made me very concerned about how high up all this might go. I was disgusted, as in totally disgusted, at the amount of money they – the Church – was using to cover up this particular situation. I came to realise, as I stood in front of my congregation watching the collection plates being passed through the pews, that it was these people, my congregation, with their hard earned money who were paying once again for the crimes of our Church.'

Starrett was shocked by the priest's honesty.

'At the same time I'm still a believer, a committed Christian,' the priest said and started his sky-writing again during the word, 'believer'. 'I have my faith – I love my faith – and I could never just walk away from that. So my bishop allowed me to come here to see out my years, but only on the understanding I would help rid our beloved Church of this malignant cancer that threatens to destroy it as only a cancer can.'

'So you help those who have suffered at the hands–'

'No, I'm afraid that is not a quality I have and I continuously ask our Father for forgiveness for this personal fault of mine,' Father O'Leary admitted. 'No, what I can do, and what I seem to have been given the aptitude for, is to investigate those molesters accused of committing these atrocious…these crimes against mankind.'

'You'd call them molesters and not paedophiles?'

'Paedophiles suggests they molested only the very young, this we now know not to be true,' O'Leary replied clearly. 'But I'd like to return to my earlier point because I think it's very important and, as I mentioned, it is the single reason that I didn't leave my Church. It's not that just priests are molesters; it's more that some men who are priests – in the same way that some men who are lawyers, politicians, pop stars, actors, teachers or whomever – are molesters.'

'I'd agree with you.'

'But don't you see that may not be the popular belief?' the priest said, as he wrote his way through the air beside his mouth with an imaginary pen. 'I met a man recently, in point of fact, only today; he said at one point he was thinking, did men become priests so that they could abuse others, or did men become abusers because they are priests.'

'But, as you've just said, lawyers, politicians, pop stars, celebrities, teachers are also–'

'Yes, yes of course,' Father O'Leary interrupted, 'but we also have to consider the fact that all the celibacy we impose on young priests must result in frustration and man is already a weak being, as you and I know well.'

'Would you allow priests to marry?'

'I think part of the problem here is too many people express opinions when in point of fact they don't really have a full and proper understanding. I think there are now enough good people rising to a position of authority in the Church. I'm happy to wait until they reach their conclusions and announce their decisions and then hopefully we'll be compatible with the times we live in.'

'So,' Starrett said, drawing out the word, 'you said earlier that Father Matthew had lost his way...'

'Or words to that effect,' the priest said, through a forgiving smile.

'Or words to that effect,' Starrett conceded. 'Had anything happened to him? Or was he suffering doubts in his faith?'

'Father Matthew was young, good looking, he liked to look his best, but was he vain? No, I wouldn't have thought so. He was presentable and there is certainly nothing wrong in this day and age with our priests looking presentable rather than like an old fogey like myself.'

'Are you saying to me that he was attracting the attention of someone?'

'I think the best thing would be for you and me to have another chat about this when you've gathered some more information.'

'You're bound by the–' Starrett started, thinking he was realising what was happening.

'I'm not a practising priest, Starrett, but I still think it would be better if you and I chat when you've gathered some more information.'

'Okay, that seems fair,' Starrett said, thinking that he knew what the priest was getting at, i.e. Fr O'Leary wasn't going to break the confidence he'd had with a dead man. But if Starrett managed to gather enough relevant information, then the priest would be willing to discuss it.

'In the meantime, can we discuss your other work?'

'Are you 100 per cent sure a crime has been committed here, Inspector Starrett? Do you know how he died yet?'

'Fair play to you and good question, Father. In instances like this, where the deceased is young and apparently in very good health, we allow ourselves to, perhaps, err on the side of suspicion.'

'Just so you can get started while the trail is still hot?' the priest offered helpfully.

'Well yes,' Starrett replied, thankful for the understanding, 'obviously at this stage it's really a fact-finding mission.'

'Yes I understand fully, sometimes I have to start off one of my investigations in the same way.'

'I wanted to talk to you about your work,' Starrett started, picking his words very carefully. 'Could there be any chance that perhaps the subject of one of your investigations might be seeking vengeance?'

'No Inspector, not at all,' Father O'Leary replied to Starrett's confused look. 'In point of fact, all of my work is done in secret – the subjects of our investigations are not even aware we exist. There are several of us who conduct these investigations and then, when we conclude our inquiries, we pass our findings on to our superiors and they are the ones who would confront the subject, either directly or with the guards. It's really just a method we've come up with to protect those we are investigating – those who may be guilty of nothing more than being the victim of an angry, jealous heart.'

'Okay, I suppose that rules that out,' Starrett replied, wondering if in fact it did. Could Father Matthew McKaye really have lost his life just because the subject of one of Father O'Leary's investigations wanted to warn him off? Or could Father Matthew have been involved in one of Father O'Leary's cases more directly?

'Hopefully,' O'Leary replied, hands stationary.

'Yes," Starrett said, not in agreement but more as a stop-gap while he phrased his next question. "What were you doing this afternoon Father?'

The detective figured that keeping it general meant that, hopefully, no offense would be taken.

'I'd a working lunch in my room," the priest replied, clearly air-writing the word "room". 'I was reviewing and writing up all my case files until I was disturbed by the racket down stairs. That would have been sometime after five-thirty.'

'Any visitors?'

'No I always lock my door when I'm working on my cases.'

'Can I talk to you about your fellow residents?' Starrett asked.

'I wish you wouldn't.'

'Sorry?'

'I wish you wouldn't,' O'Leary repeated. 'I mean, I find talking about my fellow priests behind their backs to be in extremely bad taste. However, I do not feel that you will end up lacking in information on any of us. You will surely find those among us with willing words aplenty to spill at you from their tongues.'

Starrett would have liked to have continued talking with Father Robert O'Leary but he felt it would work to his benefit to play this particular hand to the priest's lead.

CHAPTER SEVEN

Talking about words spilling from a tongue, Gibson and Garvey were currently enjoying such a conversation with a very willing participant.

As Starrett was being escorted to examine Father Matthew's room by the accommodating Father O'Leary, the longest serving resident of the house, Gibson and Garvey were settling into the extremely comfortable rooms of Father Gene McCafferty, the newest resident.

Father McCafferty was heavy-set, with a shaved head, a white, unblemished full face, and sunken eyes behind Buddy Holly black-framed glasses and…yes, his elbows did stick out from his pockets like elephant's ears. He looked like he couldn't be much over fifty, which, apart from the deceased curate, seemed a wee bit young for the residents of St Ernan's. He walked around, elbows flapping like an off-duty vicar. He offered neither food nor beverage and seemed very keen to get straight down to proceedings. Gibson figured he was most likely working on the principle of the sooner they started, the sooner he'd finish.

'When was the last time you saw Father Matthew?' Gibson asked.

'At dinner-time yesterday.'

'How did he seem?'

'Same as usual.'

'Which was?' Gibson pushed.

'A bit like the cat that got the cream?'

'Pardon?' Gibson shook her head in shock. Even Packie looked up from his notebook.

'He was very pleased with himself,' Father McCafferty replied, still offering little.

'I mean, was there anything going on in the house that we should be aware of?' Gibson asked.

'No. Father Matthew, ehm, how should I put this,' McCafferty started, looking like he was going to be more generous with his words this time.

'Let's just say he loved to pass a mirror. He had the whitest, most perfect teeth ever witnessed outside a toothpaste advert. He worked out a lot, he kept himself fit. He was very tidy and clean and that worked to our advantage. The kitchen was always spotlessly clean.'

'Anything else?'

'Ehm, how should I put this,' McCafferty started, appearing to search for the words, 'let's just say I don't believe you'll find any sticky photographs in Father Matthew's room.'

'I beg your pardon?' Garvey offered, appearing embarrassed on Gibson's behalf.

'You heard me, Guard, and I'm certainly not going to draw you any pictures.'

'Sorry – I'm not following you?' Gibson said, still in disbelief.

McCafferty's only response was to laugh. He had a strange laugh which didn't really end, rather it just faded away.

Gibson decided it was best to move on. Ask something personal?

'We're told you're the most recent resident,' she started, as she formed a thought into a question. 'Where were you tending before here?'

'I was at St John the Baptist, in the Diocese of Cork and Ross,' he replied.

'And how long were you there?' Gibson asked.

'Two years.'

'And before that?'

'Ennis, at the Assumption of the Blessed Virgin Mary, in the Diocese of Killaloe.'

'And how long were you there?'

'Three years.'

'And were both moves due to promotion?'

'Promotion!? Promotion!?' the man of the cloth snapped. 'Please remember it's not a career we're talking about here, it's a vocation.'

'So were both changes in your vocational path as a result of an elevated degree of responsibility?' Gibson asked, this time more politely.

McCafferty looked like he was considering whether this was a compliment or an insult before forming a reply. 'Both moves were due entirely to jealousy,' he offered candidly. He punctuated his reply with his signature fade-out laugh, before concluding with, 'the jealousy of others, I hasten to add.'

'Surely that's a bit uncharitable?' Gibson offered gently.

McCafferty looked down his nose at the ban garda for quite a few seconds before he continued, 'Look, we're all the same – men, women, clergy, and lay people. We do what we have to do to survive. We do what we need to do to get through to the next day,' McCafferty stopped talking and just glared at her.

'Sorry, I'm still not really following you?' she replied, wondering if she'd done something to upset the priest.

'Look, let's just say that even Jesus of Nazareth felt the need, and this need was one of his first, most public acts, of overturning the tables and setting free the animals of the high priests who were money changers and moneylenders, who were charging extortionate rates to exchange money or to loan money to poor farmers so they could pay their taxes. As well as the moneylenders, there were the high priests trading goats, sheep, and doves to sacrifice for the Passover. Yes, he cracked his whip at all of them and shouted, 'Get out of here, how dare you turn my Father's house into a market!'

'So if I'm getting this right, you're suggesting all priests are…are what in fact?' Gibson stopped her question because she couldn't believe she was getting it correct.

'Look, we give our lives to the Church,' McCafferty said, through a large sigh, starting to sweat a little around his brow and on his top lip. 'We give up everything to serve God and then when the Church is done with us, they prefer we are the responsibility of our families. Yes, their priority is to cast us aside. But priests like me no longer have families, we can't go out and learn a different trade, we can't become minicab drivers overnight to pay our bills.'

'And so you?' Gibson asked, feeling she was on the verge of some kind of confession or other, but as to what the father was about to confess she still didn't have a clue.

'Look, I'm fifty-three years old, okay? I have a heart condition, okay? I was diagnosed with hypertension, you know, high blood pressure. So I had a procedure. I had open heart surgery where they took, in my case, five veins from my legs and chest and grafted them to the top of my heart and around to the bottom. What they did was to bypass the existing arteries that had failed.'

Gibson felt sorry for the priest and said as much.

'So while I'm recuperating I was in intensive care for three days and in the ward room for seven. After leaving hospital it took three months for my sternum, my chest bone, to knit back together and an additional year for my body to fully recover from the trauma of the operation. At the beginning of the procedure you have absolutely no concept of what you are about to go through, which in fact turns out to be your saving grace. You are overtaken by the whole event. Prayer brings you no comfort. You receive comfort only from your medication. You are on painkillers for the residual pain from the scar tissue alone. You're on six tablets for cholesterol, blood thinning to stop clotting, beta-blockers to slow your heart beat, gastro tablets to stop your stomach being irritated by the amount of drugs you are taking, and on and on it goes. I'd given my life to the Church; I did not give my life to Christ. I gave it to the Catholic Church. The Catholic Church does not pay for us to go on Bupa insurance so it was made clear to me that I'd be thrown to the mercy of my family if I didn't make a full enough recovery to continue to work for the Church. I told them I didn't have a family. They laughed at me and said, 'Of course you'll have some surviving family, somewhere in the world.'

'Right,' Gibson offered in sympathy, but she was still not really sure of the point he was trying to make.

'So I had to find a way to make a bit of money on the side. I figured as long as I wasn't hurting anyone.' McCafferty said, grinding his story to a full stop.

'And how did you make this money?' Gibson asked.

'That's not really important. Nothing illegal took place, I can assure you of that, but my newfound wealth did make me a target for my less well-off colleagues, and so I kept being moved on. By the strict rules of the church I shouldn't have been able to move from diocese to diocese, but enough to say that 'strings were pulled,' to accommodate my moves.'

'Was Father Matthew jealous of you?' Garvey said, sounding maybe just a wee bit too patronising to get away with it.

Father McCafferty looked at the sergeant as if to say, "you haven't been listening to me, have you?" He shook his head to the negative and said, 'I was not on Father Matthew's radar. I think you'll find that even at St Ernan's, most people are too busy looking after themselves to worry about anyone else.'

'Okay,' Gibson started, agreeing with her instincts not to pass judgment on Father McCafferty, at least not until a later date. 'Are you aware of anything Father Matthew was doing that might have landed him in trouble?'

'How should I put this,' McCafferty started through a smile, 'I did admit to you that others were jealous of me. Jealousy was never a sin of mine.'

'Can you please tell us what you were doing earlier today between the hours of 3:30 and 5:30?' Gibson asked.

'Ehm, how should I put this,' Father McCafferty said smugly, while blatantly ogling Ban Garda Nuala Gibson. 'Between those hours and more I was in a state of undress in the company of one of the county's most beautiful women.'

'And could you give me her name,' Gibson replied, without batting an eyelid.

'But, Ban Garda, you more than most should know that a gentleman never ever tells.'

'I'm sorry Father, but we do need to know her name so that we can talk to her and eliminate you from our inquiries,' Gibson continued, 'but I can assure you that we'll be very discreet.'

'But not nearly as discreet as I'm going to continue to be,' Father McCafferty said, with a degree of finality in his voice.

'I'm sorry Father, but we really do need to know where you were and who you were with,' Gibson pushed.

'How should I put this,' McCafferty said as he stood up, 'that's for me to know and you to find out.'

CHAPTER EIGHT

The first thing that hit Starrett when he was shown through to Father Matthew's room by Father Robert O'Leary was how small the room was.

'The smallest room in the house,' claimed O'Leary, raising his eyes to the ceiling. 'Not only that, but it is also the most sparsely furnished room in the house. You see, the rest of us have had to make our rooms our home, we're here for…well, we're here until we're called away. But in Father Matthew's case he's here for a minimum and a maximum of one year. He is clearly passing through and he's not interested in putting down any roots.'

'Or could it be that he's spiritual and was in no need of anything more?' Starrett said, voicing his thoughts.

'There's always the possibility of that,' O'Leary replied, looking to the heavens again.

The furniture consisted of a very basic single bed, with clean, expensive white cotton sheets. Starrett noted, a red, battered easy chair with three small blue cushions and a small varnished writing desk with a matching Captain's chair. The desk was clearly an antique and was in brilliant condition, looking like it had been cleaned and polished that very day. It had drawers down each side of the knee-well and a further bank of much smaller drawers stacked along the top rear of the writing surface, with lots of different nooks and crannies to store writing material, paper, envelopes, paper clips, an ink well, a pen pot, and a black marble ashtray. Father Matthew's further confirmation – if it was still needed – that he was on his way to somewhere and not required to put down roots was endorsed by the fact that there were no letters, or notes, or paper of any sort visible in any of the back ledges of the desk.

The walls were white and, maybe two or three years since, overdue a fresh coat. They were bare excepting for a large black and white photograph of JFK and RFK, nearly in silhouette, sitting on two beds in a hotel room, deep in conversation while presumably on the campaign trail, and a large (as in six-foot deep by three-foot wide) oak framed mirror, which was beside the door that led to the bathroom.

Starrett walked straight into the bathroom before he'd a chance to fully examine the bedroom. This was apparent from the fact that he totally missed the one remaining (and perhaps most important) piece of furniture. If he'd been asked about the omission he'd have put it down to being concerned that he wasn't going to get back to Ramelton in time to enjoy dinner with Maggie Keane and his newly inherited family of Moya and Katie Keane.

All such thoughts would have surely disappeared once he opened the medicine cabinet above the sink in the simple all-white bathroom. He had never seen as many male pampering products in his life. There, all neatly laid out with labels proudly to the fore, was: hair gel; hair tinting cream; scouring pads; cleansing creams; sun block; fake tan; a tub of Nivea cream; moisturiser; Gillette shaving cream; Crest 3DWhite teeth whitening strips; Nivea after-shave balm, to restore the skin after the wear and tear of razor blades; tweezers; toe- (and finger-) nail clippers; combs; one hair brush; and bath gel (he wondered why Father Matthew had no shower gel as the simple white bathroom suite housed only a shower and not a bath). There were two large boxes of Lemsip, one on top of each other. This surprised Starrett because the top box of Lemsip was still in its cellophane, the one underneath was minus cellophane and, if anything, appeared much more used. Surely the usual procedure would be to have the old box on top of the new, fresher box?

He reached into his pocket for a new pair of evidence gloves, which he quickly snapped on before gently lifting the top box of Lemsip. He wasn't able to remove the box completely because its exit was blocked by the shaving cream. So he lowered the sealed box of Lemsip back into its original position whereupon he removed the shaving cream, placed it on top of the white metallic medicine cabinet and then successfully removed the new box of Lemsip. The bottom box (the one without cellophane) was considerably lighter than the first one he'd removed.

'Bejeepers,' he couldn't help saying, but immediately regretted it and thought of Moya sending him up again, 'what have we here now?'

By this point he knew clearly what he had, but perhaps he wanted Father Robert O'Leary to give the discovery more credibility by being the one to discover it. Either way, he pointed the box out to the priest.

O'Leary very gingerly lifted a box, from within a box, with all the stage craft of David Copperfield.

The inner box was clearly emblazoned with the Durex logo.

And the shocks did not finish there. Once back in the bedroom, Father O'Leary showed Starrett that the oak framed mirror was in fact a door, which led into a reasonably sized wardrobe. He pulled on the string light for Starrett and both were shocked at the rows of expensive looking crisp shirts (white, blue, and blue with white stripes) three dark suits, several pairs of shoes, and (possibly) dozens of pairs of black and dark blue Armani boxer shorts.

'Well,' Father O'Leary began, his composure reappearing as they exited the wardrobe to return to the bedroom. 'I had been saving one wee bit of information for you to try and lighten things up a wee bit for all of us.'

'Oh?' Starrett said, thinking that surely there couldn't possibly be more.

'No, it's nothing really, but you know, this is the room in which previous owners found a packet of pen nibs, you know the pre-fountain-pen nibs, a nib on a stick affair, like the ones we learned to write with. Anyway they were addressed to John Hamilton, the man who built the house,' O'Leary offered, starting back up his sign-writing again.

Starrett's mind was still elsewhere.

'They were in the original packaging and addressed to John Hamilton.'

Starrett was close to the point of saying 'Oh that's nice', but luckily he resisted.

'They were never used and we kept them and the receipt, as passed on to us by the previous owner.'

This piqued Starrett's interest a little more. 'Oh really?' he offered, distracted somewhat by the previous findings in Father Matthew's rooms. 'Where are they now?'

'Just in front of you, Inspector Starrett,' Father O'Leary teased.

Starrett quickly glanced all around him. He couldn't spot anything that looked like he figured a pack of nibs would. 'They're where they've always been, Starrett; they're where the previous owner discovered them. They're in a secret compartment in the writing desk.'

The detective futtered around for a few moments whereupon Father O'Leary, who'd clearly lost his patience with this game of hide and seek, removed one of the little drawers on the rear stack, inserted his hand and flicked something, which caused a smaller drawer to spring out to the left. He put his hand in the newly released drawer and searched around for a few seconds.

'Well I'll be…'

'What's the matter father?' Starrett asked, troubled by the clear concern on the priest's face.

'Well, it's just that the St Ernan's heirloom seems to be missing.'

CHAPTER NINE

S tarrett knocked on the third door down on the opposite side to the
rooms of Father Matthew and Father O'Leary.

On being so ordered, he opened the door and entered to see a
priest apparently busy writing away at a desk by the window.

'Sorry to disturb you,' Starrett offered.

'Oh, it's quite all right, come on in,' Father McKenzie replied, 'I'm
just writing the words for a sermon that no one will hear.'

That's better, Starrett thought to himself, a priest who looks like a
priest.

In fact, Father Edward McKenzie looked like he might be straight
off the farm. He was strong enough and of sufficient straight spine to
be in his mid to late fifties. His clothes were ill-fitting, his shirt had
been stretched out from behind the safety of his thick, brown leather
belt, exposing a layer of excess fat, which Starrett predicted (to no one
but himself) would, in two or three dinners' time, block his belt from
view forever. His black clerical shirt had a few stains noticeable to the
naked eye and even more (quite a few more, Starrett guessed) that
weren't. His trousers were so wrinkled that they and the smoothing
iron had most definitely long since parted ways. He had a bushy, unkempt beard that looked like it was hiding a multitude of sins, if not
meals, in its midst. His eyes were ever so slightly bloodshot and his top
lip, for some reason or other, probably even unknown to himself, was
a hair-free zone. He'd a healthy head of hair (similar uncombed style
to his beard), a shade darker than his facial growth and his exposed
chin enjoyed a weather-beaten hue that would probably be classified
and labelled by Farrow & Ball as 'Farmer's Tan'.

For all of that, and maybe even because of all of that, he was a welcoming gentleman with a heart-warming smile and a strong handshake.

'I'm not great indoors,' Father McKenzie said, while still shaking Starrett's hand and sounding a little uneasy, 'would you mind if we went out and had our chat in what's left of the light? It can be quite magnificent at this time of the day on St Ernan's.'

'Count me in,' Starrett said, extracting his hand from McKenzie's grasp, reacquainting it with his colder partner and rubbing them both together furiously to share equality in temperature.

Father McKenzie lifted the Webley & Scott air rifle, which was just to the left of the back door on the way out.

Five minutes later they were passing a corrugated lean-to shed, which, due to the open front, Starrett could see was packed front to back, ground to corrugated tin roof with chopped logs. McKenzie freed four flat-ish and dry logs from the mountain and passed two of them to the detective to carry without any other word of instruction. To the other end of the woodshed was a series of mismatched stone outhouses, which looked like they might even pre-date the main house, and beyond that the rough gravelled ground rose sharply to the border of dense trees.

McKenzie led Starrett along a well-worn pathway, up to the crown of the hill and then down the other side. All the time they were covered by trees and their journey was monitored closely by what seemed like a battalion of rabbits. McKenzie popped off the rifle at a few of them, calling them rats with bigger ears as he did so. He missed every shot, either because he really wanted to, or, more likely, the task of carrying a couple of logs and shooting off a rifle at the same time was much too difficult to pull off. He didn't seem upset at his endeavours claiming, 'Oh well, it's pasta or pizza again tonight.'

Eventually they left the bunny boys in their wake at the tree border. It had been a ten-minute walk at the most but the change in scenery quite literally took Starrett's breath away. The priest showed Starrett to a primitive stone bench, similar to those the detective had spotted peppered along the pathway. He placed his two flat logs down on the bench, nodding at Starrett to do the same.

'The stones can get quite cold this time of year. Father O'Leary always warns me to be careful – cold surfaces can give you, give you…thingamabobs.'

'Yes, I think I know what you mean,' Starrett replied, finalising his own makeshift seating arrangement, 'the Unspeakables?'

'Yes, yes, that's them,' the priest said, before smiling largely, 'the Unspeakables.'

Starrett now realised why McKenzie wanted to get out of the house to this little oasis overlooking Donegal Bay. The water was glass calm, very inviting, but at the same time it looked as though it would freeze you to a permanent stillness. He figured that this was Father Edward McKenzie's way of escaping from the darkness descending furiously over the house; he certainly looked a lot more relaxed here, more at peace with himself.

'Is this your seat?' he asked, starting off gently.

'This is a place where all can go,' McKenzie replied immediately, 'but sadly few, other than Father O'Leary and myself, ever use it.'

'That's a shame,' Starrett replied earnestly, 'why do you think that is?'

'Oh, Father O'Leary says it's because we, mankind in general, just never learn. We've all been posted to St Ernan's at this stage in our lives because, you know, it wasn't working for us elsewhere and we're not so much being put out to pasture as maybe we're in danger of becoming the pasture.'

'Why are you at St Ernan's, Father?'

'Put quite simply, detective, because I'm a…a…whatdyamacallit?'

'An Unspeakable?' Starrett offered, trying to lighten the conversation somewhat.

'Well, that as well,' McKenzie said at the end of a fit of giggles, 'but not…I mean you know…yes, that's it, I'm a worker bee. Yes, I'm a worker bee and that's it, and when I'm left to do my work I'm totally fine. But when I have to lead or take responsibility for something I grow clumsy, I spill things, I break things and my tongue gets tied and I can't speak and then I go into one of my turns.'

'But you're okay while you're in here?' Starrett asked quietly.

'Oh yes, of course, I'm fine here. I love it here.'

'What do you do here?' Starrett continued.

'I have my garden patch back up by the house,' McKenzie replied, brightening up somewhat. 'It's just on the other side of those stone outhouses – I'll show them to you when we go back in.'

'So did Father Matthew ever come out here?'

'You know, I don't believe he did, he was always in a hurry, that boy.

He'd no time for peace and tranquillity. No, no, life had him by the…by the…you know, the whatsits?'

'The short and curlies?' Starrett offered helpfully, seeing a pattern emerging here, where Father McKenzie had been programmed away from rude words and taught new ones, and he'd obviously forgotten all the rude words the new ones were hiding.

'Oh yes,' he said, looking like a schoolboy sitting next to the boy who'd been caught smoking. 'That's it. Father Matthew was always running somewhere, or going somewhere, or coming from somewhere. He's so ambitious he'll either be the Pope or a criminal…oh sorry, sorry…I'm so sorry…he's never going to be either now.'

'Did you know him well?'

'He'd no time for me,' McKenzie said, without an ounce of bitterness. 'I wasn't his type. Don't get me wrong, Inspector, we never had any issues, no words to regret. You know, back on my father's farm he, my father, always used to say that the horses will never socialise with the goats. They've both got four legs but that's where the similarity ends.'

'Did anyone have regrettable words with Father Matthew?' Starrett asked, finding himself involuntarily staring at McKenzie's beard. He was trying to imagine how the natural lifetime growth of thirty feet of ginger beard would look if it was trailing behind the priest. Not a pretty picture, he felt, even for the Guinness Book of Records. On the other hand, a Guinness was the perfect picture to conjure up at this stage in the investigation.

'You know, I'd hear bits of gossip around the house now and again, but Father O'Leary says that gossip won't help feed and clothe the poor, so I always let it come in one door and kick it straight right out the other before it had a chance to get it's bearings,' McKenzie said, looking like he was rather pleased that he'd remembered O'Leary's quote.

'Okay,' Starrett said, conceding that one for now, 'but tell me this, Father: in your travels, did you ever come across anyone who looked like they wished harm on Father Matthew?'

'Never,' McKenzie offered after a delay.

Starrett noted the priest's eyes and furrowed brow contradicted his negative response.

Completely out of the blue McKenzie volunteered that he'd been working in his garden all afternoon. On the way back to the house

they stopped off at McKenzie's garden 'patch'. Starrett had been expecting more of an allotment-sized garden parcel, but the priest had
cultivated a very large chunk of land and had neat row upon row of
vegetables, protected all around by a waist-high, dense privet hedge.
All of this was lined on the interior with small gauge chicken wire,
used in this case not to keep the chickens in but the rabbits out.

As though reading Starrett's mind, McKenzie explained in great detail how he had also installed the chicken wire three-foot subterranean.

Starrett was clearly impressed with McKenzie's fine work but he also
must have looked shocked that the priest had managed to pull it off.

McKenzie started to laugh, quietly at first and then gradually it
grew until tears were rolling down his cheeks.

'Sorry, what?' the detective asked, joining in with the infectious
laughter.

'No, no, it's nothing!'

'Sorry?'

'Well, the look of you there, your face, your surprise at my garden
– it just reminded me of a story about the ex-president, Mrs Mary
Robinson. She once visited this home where the inhabitants were, shall
we say, a bit more restrained in their surroundings than we are.'

'Like a prison?' Starrett offered.

'Maybe more like an open prison, where the patients suffer from
personal problems more than the criminal type of problems, but either
way, they certainly were not allowed out. Anyway, Mary Robinson
wanders around the grounds, having her wee chat with this one and
that one, and she comes across this gardener and he's grown the most
beautiful flowers the president has ever seen and before she knows it
she's deep in conversation with him, discussing all topics under the
sun. The gardener picks a large bunch of flowers, which he presents to
the president and she's completely overwhelmed by both the gardener
and his beautiful flowers. She takes the gardener to one side and says,
'Look, I know you're meant to be in here indefinitely but after our
chat and your wonderful garden, there's clearly been some mistake
and I think I'm going to recommend to the warden that you're let out
immediately so you can come work at our palace.' One of her aides
takes the gardener's details and all is well and several minutes later, just
as the president is about to leave the garden, this brick comes flying
through the air and bounces off the back of the president's head. The
thrower of the brick turns out to be the gardener, who shouts, in the

direction of the fallen president, 'Now don't forget to get me out of here, you hear?'

McKenzie started his hearty laughing again. Starrett, too, started to laugh but then his laughter gradually changed until he reached the point, close to inconsolable, where he hoped that McKenzie wouldn't twig that the Donegal detective's tears were not the tears of laughter.

CHAPTER TEN

It was taking longer than Starrett expected to question everyone who had been in the house at the time of Father Matthew's death. He was concerned about whether he'd conclude all the interviews before the end of the day; Starrett's team was rather thin on the ground, what with all the recent cuts in the public services. So thin on the ground, in fact, that the only member of the Gardaí on duty thirty-seven miles away back in Tower House, the Gardaí Station in Gamble Square, in Ramelton, was Francis Casey. Francis Casey, Starrett knew, would be fretting not so much about the fact that Nuala Gibson was a seventy-minute drive away from him, but more that she was (currently) only a few seconds' walk away from Romany Browne.

There were at least two more people who needed to be interviewed. The first was Father Patrick O'Connell, and Gibson and Garvey were currently in session with him. The second was the Master Writer, Father Peregrine Dugan. Father O'Leary had introduced Starrett to Father Peregrine Dugan after the detective had concluded his inspection of Father Matthew's room and made his shock discoveries. Dugan assured Starrett that he hadn't been out of his room, had never in fact met Father Matthew (Father O'Leary confirmed both these facts) but, more importantly, he was just about to retire for the evening and wanted the interview postponed until the following morning. In light of the priest's senior years (82 at next birthday), and in the spirit of the level of cooperation he sought, the detective thought it was not an unreasonable request.

This just left Bishop Cormac Freeman, and Freeman was another kettle of nettles altogether. In fact, the bishop was currently being monitored in his room by Garda Romany Browne. He wasn't under, what you would call house arrest, but Starrett had stated it was important that he be kept under observation, and that as soon as Gibson and Garvey had finished their interview with O'Connell, Garvey would spend the night on shifts with Browne outside the bishop's room, while Gibson and Starrett nipped back to Ramelton. On the journey, Gibson could bring Starrett up to speed on the Father Patrick O'Connell interview. Besides, the bishop's restriction to quarters was sure to make him a little crazed, which was kind of the point, as it would make for a good interview the following morning.

On top of which, Francis Casey would enjoy a lot more settled a sleep. Given he was Starrett's top IT man – actually, Starrett's only IT man – it was imperative that he got his proper sleep. And on top of that, on top of all of that, Starrett would get back to Ramelton, Donegal's Holy See, to see Maggie Keane, who was proving to be a bit of a stickler for 'family time.'

Which was how, twenty-three minutes later, Ban Garda Nuala Gibson and Inspector Starrett where speeding up the N15, Gibson at the wheel of Starrett's BMW and reciting in great detail – for she knew that is exactly the way her superior liked his information – the fruits of her and Garvey's interview with Father Patrick O'Connell.

The door to Father Patrick 'Please, call me Pat' O'Connell's rooms was fourth down on the left-hand side of the house, the same side as Fathers O'Leary, McKaye, McCafferty and the absent Fathers Casey and Clerkin.

Father Pat spent the entire interview acting as if national hurling hero Sgt Packie Garvey didn't exist and instead focused all of his attention on Starrett's current narrator, Ban Garda Nuala Gibson. Gibson further felt that should Father Pat not have been wearing a very expensive dark blue suit with snow-white clerical collar, she would have considered him to be a ridiculous flirt. She further admitted to being very happy that she'd been accompanied by Garvey.

Father Pat's rooms were the same size and layout as both Fathers Mulligan McIntyre – a.k.a Tubsey the gossip - on the opposite side of the corridor, and McCafferty's, on the same but separating Father Pat from the rooms of the deceased Father Matthew McKaye. However, for a man who was clearly preoccupied with his own personal turn-out, his personal living space was a lot more throughother. Father O'Connell might not be as vain as Father Matthew had been, but that may have had something to do with the fact that his Maker hadn't been as generous to him when looks were being dished out. The priest looked like he was bursting out of his face, as though his features would soon explode beyond recognition. His skin was red and shiny, while his stubby hands had more of a purple hue and very unsmooth. Father Pat, Gibson felt, wasn't doing himself any favours with his pageboy, John Denver-style haircut. She couldn't be sure, but she felt the intensity of the blackness of his hair might have been aided by a bottle. It was maybe uncharitable to have such a thought, but Father Pat's uncouth undercurrents had brought out the worst in her.

'So, what you're trying to tell me,' Starrett offered, from the comfort of the passenger's seat, 'is that Garda Francis has no need to worry?'

'Well, at least not about Father Pat,' Gibson replied, before continuing with the details of the interview.

As near as Gibson could remember she, recalled verbatim (excepting, of course, a few interruptions from her passenger and boss Inspector Starrett) the interview with the boorish Father.

'Did you know Father Matthew very well?' Gibson had asked, as Packie drew out his notebook and pen again to record the proceedings for both the record and Inspector Starrett.

'Did I know him very well,' Father Pat began, breathlessly, 'well…well, as well as a man of my age can know somebody who may be as much as forty years his junior.'

'How was he?'

'How was he?' Father Pat posted, 'I'd say the best word to describe Father Matthew would be "confused".'

'Confused about his faith?' Gibson shot back.

'Well, in a way I suppose that's what I mean.'

'Sorry?'

'Look, as I was saying, he was young; it's a very confusing time. At that stage in your life, you know, when you've just crossed the threshold of the Church, that's when it starts to dawn on you exactly just how big a commitment you have made. I mean, there really is no hiding place.'

'Why do you say that?' Gibson asked, regretting her interruption while at the same time feeling it was called for.

'Well, basically you have two options. Option A, you stay with the Church or, option B, you walk away. Either path pretty much dominates the remainder of your life. So, as I was about to say, the upshot of this is that you start to doubt everything, and so a by-product of that is you can't but fail to doubt your own beliefs.'

'Did you discuss this with him in detail?'

'Did I discuss this with him,' the priest wheezed, 'no, certainly not, but I'd been there and, as they say, I'd bought the T-shirt. I knew exactly what was going on,' he replied, in his slow Castlebar drawl.

'Could you explain to us exactly what it was that Father Matthew was going through?' Gibson asked. 'It could be very useful to us.'

'Well, I can only tell you a bit about my own experiences and I believe, as I have said, I think he would have shared quite a few of them.'

'Go on?' Gibson prompted, when it sounded like the priest had reached a premature full stop.

'Okay, from my side, you have to realise that my family had always planned this life, or should I say, this vocation for me. I'll also admit quite freely that I never fought them on it because I didn't exactly have a Plan B waiting in the wings.' The priest paused for a moment or two, clearly deep in thought, before continuing. 'As a young man, the two things that ran my life were dancing and Gaelic football. I'm not for one moment claiming that I could have been a player, but I did seem to have the knack for reading the game well and spotting great players. I could tell which teams were going to win their matches from seeing their form only a few times. You know, seeing if the players wanted to win as a team or were in search of individual glory. I got it down to a fine art and at one point I was successfully predicting eight out of ten match results. I got on Radio Eireann – my friend's uncle, Tony Boland, worked there. Well, wouldn't you just know it but on that particular night I got both results wrong and ended any chance of a career on the radio. I enjoyed it, but I never felt that I could make a living from it.'

'And the dancing?' Gibson promoted, sensing a dead end looming.

'No…you…sorry, you misunderstood me, I didn't mean that I went dancing.' The horror in Father Pat's eyes betrayed how unattractive a prospective that notion was. 'I ran the dances – you know, with the showbands. I would have been seventeen when I started. I prompted the Royal Showband, they were from Waterford, you know, on a New Year's Eve dance and I made more money on that one night than my father did in an entire year.'

'How did your family feel about that?' Packie asked.

'How did my family feel about that,' Father Pat offered expansively, 'I'll tell you how my family felt about that: my father felt it was just a form of gambling, but instead of gambling on the gee-gees, he claimed I was betting on the showbands. I remember that New Year's Day just like it was yesterday, and I was very proud when I told him how much I'd made with my endeavours. Of course, I'd expected him to be impressed.'

'And was he?' Gibson asked, when Father Pat seemed reluctant to elaborate.

'Well, all he said was, "Be careful, Patrick, and remember that the Devil always arrives with the biggest cheque."'

'So you didn't keep working with the showbands?'

Father Pat locked and primed his right-hand forefinger behind his thumb and flicked his starched white clerical collar before saying, 'Clearly not. But I can't help wondering that if I had kept it up, you know, the auld promoting, by this point I might be the one promoting Bruce Springsteen, Garth Brooks, U2, or Neil Diamond down at Croke Park in Dublin.'

'Would you never run any dances just for the Church?' Packie asked.

'You know, we're all the same, when we're young – we're all seeking something out, trying to find something we're good at. You know, as I'm always saying, anything, anything at all will do. It doesn't matter how bizarre it might be. It just matters that you excel at this one thing in order that you may become your own person. With me, I tried the dancing, I tried the high jump, the guitar, the bagpipes, cross-country running and, as I said, I even tried being a Gaelic football expert. I don't know what Father Matthew tried to excel at, but I would bet you that if he was here today he would give you a list just as long and just as bizarre as mine. And then we both found something we could do, something we thought we wanted to do or, as in my case, something I knew my family wanted me to do. Maybe, even, it was something we thought we should do, and that's how we ended up serving our Father.'

'And do you ever regret it?' Gibson asked, trying to take him back to the ground she felt she'd lost with her previous, stupid question.

'Ah no, that wouldn't be my biggest regret,' Father Pat admitted solemnly.

'What would your biggest regret be?' Gibson asked, chancing her arm, or maybe even the both of them.

Father Pat hiked up his knee and clasped his hands around it. Gibson guessed he was suffering from cramp. With his knees permanently parted while in a seated position he looked like he was prised to rise up from his seat at the first opportunity afforded him by the two Gardaí.

'I'm beginning to feel I'm on the other side of the confessional box,' he acknowledged, 'but I will admit that yes, I did taste true love once, but only briefly. Still, I always felt it was enough to enable me to give council to others who were troubled by matters of the heart.'

'Such as Father Matthew, for instance?'

'Are you sure it's the An Garda Síochána you work for and not the Irish Daily Mirror?' Father Pat said, with a laugh flat enough to dismiss Gibson's question.

'No, no, sorry, I didn't mean it like that,' Gibson protested, 'I meant, was that what was troubling him?'

'All I can tell you is that I once was a youth, a youth who was inclined to ramble. I was running around all the time, chasing stuff and trying to get to somewhere I knew not where, but in the end it didn't matter. The only thing that really matters in your life's journey is the scenery along the way, because, as the boyo downstairs has just proven, the destination leaves a lot to be desired.'

'You said earlier that you once tasted true love; has the loss of the love–' Gibson, who'd started off so well, lost her nerve and stuttered to a stop.

'Has the loss of love, what? Ruined my life, was that going to be your question?'

Before Gibson had a chance to either protest or respond Father Pat continued immediately with, 'Before you grow too preoccupied with this topic I would caution you to please remember that in your life you spend more of your time eating, sleeping, walking, talking, dressing, thinking, washing dishes, working, having your hair cut, reading, listening to music, driving, cutting the hedge, mowing the lawn, cooking, studying, or even praying than you do making love.'

'And your point?'

'My point is that the enjoyment is not dependent on how much you do it, or did it.'

'Tell me Father, how long have you been a resident at St Ernan's now?'

'Aye, at least that's an easier one. I'm coming up to five years this Christmas,' he replied in a matter of fact tone and sounding like he knew what the next question was going to be.

'And why did you move here?'

'And why did I move here,' Father Pat said repeating Gibson's question, kind of proving that he did know what the next question was going to be. 'I'll tell you exactly why I moved here.'

Gibson nodded like a chess player does when they're not so much proud of their own move as they are impatient to see how their opponent responds.

'I was disciplined by my last church,' he admitted, but went no further.

'Why were you disciplined, Father?' Gibson asked.

'Why was I disciplined,' Father Pat said and continued immediately without waiting for Gibson to confirm her question, 'I had an inappropriate relationship with one of my parishioners. She was a married woman.'

Gibson figured from Garvey's body language that the priest had just cleared up one of the sergeant's own questions.

'I mean, of course her husband had left the family home,' the priest continued, suggesting that cheating was not as big a sin as committing adultery. 'I realise now she just wanted some company while I wanted…I wanted to feel that I was still attractive to women.'

Gibson couldn't help it but her first thought at that point was, "how could anyone be attracted to you?" She felt bad at having such an uncharitable thought and she apologised under her breath, and admitted the same to Starrett at this point in her recalling the interview.

Starrett remained non-judgemental.

'You know,' he offered, 'we're all the same really and the difficulty I find is that we can all, and I do mean all of us, be very disparaging about other people's looks. We're certainly by nature more fussy than we have a right to be. But at the same time we should know from even just the briefest of glimpses in the mirror that we have absolutely no say whatsoever in how we look. I mean, yes, of course we can present ourselves in the best possible light, with clothes, grooming and cleanliness, but beneath it all, we are, each of us, what we are and we can do nothing about it.'

'Yes!' Gibson agreed, 'and even those most elusive, truly beautiful members of the species will still give themselves a hard time over what they consider to be troubling anatomical features.'

They both pondered on Gibson's reply for quite some moments and several hypnotic swishes of the windscreen wipers, which were having to work overtime on the return journey.

Starrett liked working with Ban Garda Nuala Gibson. She was bright. She understood things quickly. She was respectful while at the same time always prepared to be honest about her opinions and theories with Starrett. The Ban Garda was great company and – mostly likely due to their different relationships with Maggie Keane - there were never any undercurrents in their dealings with each other. Gibson had known Maggie for nearly as long as Starrett had, but due to his 'lost years' had got to know her better. Starrett frequently wondered if Ban Garda Gibson had ever counselled Maggie Keane when Starrett was trying desperately to re-kindle his relationship with his first love. Starrett had never asked either Maggie or Gibson if they'd ever discussed him during this troubled phase in all their lives. Gibson was confident enough and professional enough not to discuss this topic with Starrett. Equally it has to be said that Maggie, for her part, never discussed any confidential issues about Gibson with Starrett, proving not that they were her equal best friends, but more that she was an equal friend to both of them. Starrett felt the only slight disadvantage to working with Ban Garda Nuala Gibson was that he would never trust her with his private stash of cigarettes the way he did with say Garda Sgt Packie Garvey, for fear that the news of his 'dreadful habit' would get back to Maggie Keane.

'So, getting back to Father Pat,' Starrett asked, 'did he tell you any more about his inappropriate behaviour and if in fact he was talking about mental, spiritual, or physically inappropriate behaviour?'

'Oh Starrett, I do wish you hadn't shared that one with me quite so vividly,' Gibson groaned, before continuing further details of her interview with the priest. 'Well, I asked him whether the husband found out.'

'If only,' Father Pat had replied.

'Sorry?!' Gibson said.

'Well, if it had been the husband, it would have been fine.'

'Sorry?' she'd asked again, still unsure of what he meant.

'Well, don't you see, if it had been the husband it would have been fine because apparently he was reportedly happy to be out of the picture,' the priest admitted, now starting to sound like he was enjoying himself. 'No, it was someone worse than a husband.'

'Who, for heaven's sake?' Gibson asked, fearing the worst.

'It was another parishioner who, I'm led to believe had set her sights on me. When I made it clear that I wasn't interested, by ignoring her, she went straight to my Bishop and made an official complaint about my behaviour.'

'Did she claim you'd slept with the married woman?' Gibson asked, still not seeing what this was all about.

'No, she couldn't – we hadn't…we had achieved only what I believe the youth of today class as getting to first base.'

'I think you'll find the youth of today now class that as "sucking face",' Gibson advised the priest, 'I believe it was my generation who referred to it as "getting to first base".'

'Right, okay, thanks for clearing that up for me,' the priest said, looking like he'd wished she hadn't.

'So you're telling me you were disciplined and sent here for kissing a married, but separated, woman?'

'Well, as I say, if you're going to be candid, be candid,' Father Pat started and seemed somewhat reluctant to continue, 'in fairness to the bishop, it wasn't the first complaint against me.'

'Oh,' Gibson said, 'you'd done it before?'

'Ehm yes, actually.'

'How many times?'

'How many times?' the priest replied, only this time he did deliver it as a question.

'Yes,' Gibson confirmed, 'how many times?'

'Quite a few,' the priest admitted.

'Define "quite a few" for me please?'

'With that particular Bishop, twenty-eight complaints.'

'And all the complaints were just about kissing?'

'No, in fact several of them were about more, quite a bit more in fact…'

'Okay, okay,' Gibson said, feeling a very strong necessity to cut him off at the pass, 'I think I get the picture.'

The room was silent apart from Garvey's squeaky pen.

'And with other bishops,' Gibson asked, because she felt she must, although she was dreading the answer.

'Oh,' Father Pat said, preparing to save her the gory details, 'let's just say they'd enough on me to have me expelled to St Ernan's for the remainder of my natural.'

'Do each of the residents know why the others are in here?' she asked, drawing a line under that particular topic.

'I believe we all hide behind the "health issues" flag while at the same time we all know we are here due to our own…our own…'

'Transgressions,' Packie Garvey offered helpfully.

'Yes indeed, transgressions covers it,' Father Pat acknowledged, but at the same time he refused to take his eyes away from Gibson. 'So there is a very good chance our fellow residents also have some skeletons in their own cupboards.'

'Or genuine health issues,' the public-spirited hurling champion added.

'Or, as you say, health issues.'

'Final question, Father O'Connell,' Gibson said confidently, 'what were you doing between the hours of 5:30 and 7:30 earlier today?'

'What was I doing between 5:30 and 7:30 today,' the priest said, looking like he wanted to look like he hadn't been expecting that particular question. 'Ah, let me see now…if it was last week or even last month it would be easier,' Father Pat O'Connell said and then paused.

Gibson wondered if the priest really thought that was an acceptable answer, or was he perhaps trawling through his memory banks to recall what he'd been doing less than a day before?

She nodded her head towards him once in an 'And?' kind of moment.

'Today. Yes, well now, let me see, but yes of course, I had lunch with a dear friend of mine, Edwina Uppleby. Yes, that's it, how could I have forgotten lunch with Edwina? She's such great craic and she doesn't even know it.'

'So what time did you meet up?' Gibson asked, as Packie completed writing Edwina Uppleby's name in his notebook.

'She picked me up by the Craft Village Shop, back out on the main road. It's very inconvenient for me but she just absolutely refuses to come in here, said she'd a bad experience here years ago, something about a bad choice of man. Edwina has always made bad choices with her men,' he tutted and then nearly tripped over himself to add, 'present company excluded, of course.'

'And the time she picked you up?' Gibson asked, all but sighing.

'Just after twelve o'clock. We were meant to meet at noon but I don't think she actually arrived until ten past.'

'What does Mrs Uppleby do?' Packie asked, because he knew that would be the first question Starrett would ask.

'Miss Uppleby.'

'Sorry,' Packie said, 'what does Miss Uppleby do?'

'What does she do?' Father Pat tried attempting a smile, which was a difficult manoeuvre to pull off with his over-blown features. 'I find women who "do lunch",' and Father Pat paused to give the words 'do' and 'lunch' quotation marks with two fingers of each hand, 'and we're talking at the very, very least two-hour lunches, rarely ever are in the employ of anyone. No, I believe Edwina benefited from parents – GRTS – who knew the pleasure and advantage of what is now distastefully referred to as "old money".'

'GRTS?' Gibson asked, in a bemused, head-shaking manner.

'God Rest Their Souls.'

'Oh yes, of course. So what time did you finish your lunch?'

'What time did we conclude our lunch...I'm afraid that would have been much closer to tea time.'

'Am...how close to tea time?' Gibson persisted.

'I believe we left the restaurant at 5:15,' the priest admitted as he crunched up his face in a "weren't we naughty" pose. On a teenage girl, such a pose is quite endearing but on a member of the clergy it proved to be an extremely hideous sham.

'Okay,' Gibson said, realising it was important to pay attention to even the most boring answers for Starrett's claim of 'statements hidden within'. 'What time did you get back to St Ernan's?'

'She dropped me off in Donegal Town, just outside Abbey Hotel,' the priest replied, 'I nipped in there, had a collision with an old chum from Queens, had another wee pint of Guinness with him and ordered a taxi.'

'And?'

'And I got back here at about 7:40, when your brigade were in full flow.'

'And?'

'Oh please, surely not another final question!' he said with great theatre, but at least he had the good grace to visually apologise.

'You still didn't tell me where you'd your lunch?' Gibson pleaded.

'Oh yes, of course, how remiss of me. We dined in the elegance and five-star luxury that is known as Lough Eske Castle.'

CHAPTER ELEVEN

By this point in her recalling the interview, coincidentally, Starrett and Gibson had reached Maggie Keane's house, which also happened to be Starrett's current residence.

Starrett felt nervous as he walked up the gravel pathway to her amazing home, a fair size but still – thanks to Maggie Keane – a cosy Georgian house on the Shore Road, in Ramelton.

Since Starrett had moved in, Maggie had gone out of her way to make him feel comfortable, even to the extent of giving him a room. The room in question was, in real estate terms, a prime location; it was the ground floor right-hand room, which enjoyed a spectacular view of the Leannon River where it fed Lough Swilly, which, in turn, flowed into the North Atlantic Ocean with the magnificent Inch Island on the other side. Maggie offered this room for his exclusive use as a study, thinking space, snooker room, or for whatever he wanted to use it. Starrett claimed he was very happy, as in very happy with their current arrangements, that is to say, he sharing Maggie's bedroom, but she did insist that he also needed some private space. Starrett figured Maggie was partly trying to get over the clichéd hurdle of one partner moving into a space that had been inhabited for quite some time by the other. Perhaps, he thought, she wanted him to have a space he could take visitors, who were calling on Gardaí business. Her endgame might even have been to try to contain this sometimes unsavoury business and perhaps maybe spare the rest of the house from it. As such, she encouraged him to decorate and furnish the room himself. Starrett felt she genuinely meant it, but equally he knew that she couldn't have possibly been happier than when he'd enlisted the help of her daughters Moya and Katie in his endeavours. For all of this, the room had still turned out to be rather masculine, with red painted walls, dim lights, lots of reading lamps, lots of small tables, but no desk, several reading chairs arced around the fireplace and book-shelves lined with most of Starrett's collection and all of Moya and Katie's dead father's books.

Whenever the detective was in residence, Moya had taken to knocking on the study door, even though it was always open, and ask-ing if she could join him. Always encouraged by Starrett, she would come in and sit down, quiet as a mouse, either to finish off homework or read one of her books.

On this particular evening, Maggie sensed there was something wrong with the detective the moment he walked into the house. He didn't deny it; he just casually said he didn't want to talk about it. She told him that was fine; he could do so when he wanted to.

'Okay,' she said, a little wavering in her voice, 'I'm not having much luck with my massage tonight. I've one other thing I can try if you want?'

'Anything as long as I can avoid the cigarettes,' Starrett replied, having long since come to the conclusion that smoking for all the bad-ness it did to your body long term, also had a few – well, at least one – relieving by-product.

She took him by the hand, led him to their bedroom, took him to bed and shifted him.

'A kiss always says what talking can't,' Maggie said, as they both sank into their respective lush pillows after the event.

Starrett was miles away when she said it. Their making love wasn't a regular occurrence so it was all the more special an experience when-ever it did happen, which he figured was the object of her exercise. That is to say, making what they had something special, random, tribal even. Starrett stopped himself there for a second; did he really mean tribal? He didn't think so; he wasn't going to share Maggie Keane with anyone now that he'd won her back. He knew her desire to avoid mak-ing sex into a routine activity was based on her need for both of them to retain some of their mystery for each other, physically, mentally, and sexually speaking. She had once told him in passing that the mystery of a romance can be ruined by the familiarity of a relationship.

He remembered being obsessed with her from the first time he'd seen her, when they were both teenagers.

He wanted to remember, to recall exactly what he had felt the very first moment he had set eyes on her. If he'd recorded it on video he'd surely have worn the tape out by this stage. This stage being the stage where all he dreamt of happening and wished to happen had happened. But more than anything, he needed to remember the feeling of complete and utter desperation he had experienced when there'd been a chance his relationship with Maggie Keane might not have developed as it subsequently had. Remembering that feeling was all it took to ensure that he would never, ever take her for granted.

In his youth, Starrett would often go for a walk up the town just on the off chance of seeing her by accident, or perhaps coming across her without her actually knowing he was there, just so that he could look at her; just looking at her was bliss and more than enough for the young Starrett. He knew, of course, that he wasn't just looking at her, rather he was staring at her, drinking in the vision of her, trying to embrace the pleasure of her beauty. He figured you looked at someone differently when you knew, they knew, you were looking at them, or even when you were looking at each other. When they were oblivious to the looking, or they didn't even know you, you could get away with staring. Yes, just staring at the object of your affections, drinking in this thing of magnificent beauty. He had never in his life – not on the telly, or in the movies, or in a magazine or even first hand – witnessed anyone with the beauty of Maggie. He knew if he ever admitted that to her he'd be out on his ear.

Starrett found himself wondering a lot about the idea of beauty; he accepted it was directly, or indirectly, behind quite a few of the serious crimes he and his team were called upon to investigate.

But what is beauty? How does it change?

A cut?

A scar?

A missing eye?

A missing breast?

A missing limb?

Through the ageing process?

He looked at Maggie, lying beside him; she wasn't exactly sleeping but she was in some sort of slumber land, enjoying her own space. She hadn't been affected by any of the above misfortunes and, in fact, if anything the ageing process had made her even more beautiful.

He stared at her face now, like he used to do as a teenager; she was oblivious to his looking, so he could really look, and what he saw at that moment made his heart skip a beat and brought a tear to his eye.

He wondered how men and women come to pick each other. Do they have any say in the matter?

For them, they had first become 'friends', through a mutual friend. How they'd hang out together, way, way before he'd the nerve to chance his arm (for that's what his first overture was, an arm around her neck). They both enjoyed each other's company and she'd admitted to him recently that she'd never, ever considered having anyone else as a boyfriend. She just knew they would be together. She also admitted that she'd waited patiently for it to happen because she accepted that, at first, she was most certainly too young, even though some of her friends of a similar age were already boasting about allowing their boyfriends to get to second base. But Maggie didn't want an immature and doomed relationship with him; no, she didn't want that to happen with her best friend, Starrett. Equally she knew how hurt he would have been if she'd tried to get experience elsewhere. So she'd snuggled closer to him when he'd first been brave enough to put his arm around her shoulders. A few months later they were holding hands. Six months after they'd shared their first intimate moment, they enjoyed their first real kiss.

Starrett knew, and admitted as much to Maggie, that it had been her looks that had first caught his attention. That impossible-to-ignore both girlish and womanly look of hers, the lopsided grin with her kooky, chipped front tooth, that made her self-conscious about breaking into a full blown smile. Her black, unruly hair that started each day styled and sophisticated yet always ended each and every day with various breakaway curls being realigned and redesigned and tucked here and there, behind an ear or re-clipped just about anywhere. The same mane of hair that helped transform the Maggie he'd become reacquainted with in the bedroom, to a wanton, sensual and, not to mention, hungry lover.

But back when they'd first started their relationship, the fact that they'd first become good friends and he'd genuinely liked her was also the reason behind his suffering endless sleepless nights worrying that he'd lose her to an older boy. He knew more than any of those who came chasing, and were thankfully kicked into touch, exactly how special

Maggie was. Equally, he knew how bad it felt to be shot down by a girl, and sometimes the girl he'd been shot down by had been Maggie. He remembered how some girls would even invite you out, only to say 'no'. And you would know for certain that they were going to either shoot you down or drop you, but you'd still go, just so you could be close to them for the final time when they uttered the heart-breaking 'no'. Maggie had recently claimed she'd said 'no' to him just to be sure.

Yes, Starrett knew for a fact that Maggie Keane was genuinely beautiful, but what was it about beauty that worked so? Why did he hurt deep in the pit of his stomach whenever he couldn't see her? Once again he considered what it was that pulls a man and a woman together? Do either really have any say in this magical process? What is a good look? Is it the look from someone who is appealing only to a certain individual, or is it the germ of attraction, set in motion by the hint we see, or think we see, of that individual's spirit? Is that why someone – such as Dr Samantha Aljoe, who had the ability to smile sincerely, yet effortlessly – tend to be more attractive? Starrett was most certainly attracted to a heart-warming smile, but yet it was Maggie's flawed smile that hooked him like no other ever had.

One of the many things Starrett loved about Maggie Keane was that she was great fun; she'd always enjoyed a keen sense of humour and a sharp mind. Plus, of course, the aforementioned stunning looks – there was quite simply no other way to describe her. On top of all of that, he wanted to do naughty things with her, but the most appealing thing of all was that she actually encouraged him to do just so. Maggie had always whispered to Starrett. A lot. Not in an 'I don't want anyone else to hear this' kind of way, for in fact she rarely ever whispered to him while they were in company. No, her whispering was more special than that, an intimate language between the two of them and no one else. Starrett in his AM (After Maggie) dating days, would come across girls who would make love to people they didn't actually love, yet in some instances they would not make love to people they claimed truly to love. Maggie Keane suffered from no such hang-up.

The thing Starrett found interesting about love was that you couldn't make yourself love someone, nor could you make someone love you. But the saddest thing of all is that you couldn't make yourself not love someone; you couldn't choose who you loved.

So, taking all of this into consideration, why had it all gone wrong?

To this day it was the one question he'd continually asked himself and, to this day, he'd never been able to come up with an acceptable answer.

Maggie and Starrett had dated through college, growing closer all the time, but not that close. Then he'd made a decision, a life-changing decision, for them both. The only problem was that he hadn't bothered to tell her about it.

They went out for what he had planned would be their last time together.

She'd interpreted his 'distance' as a sign he was about to split up with her. She'd felt, she'd recently claimed, with all her heart and soul that she didn't want to lose him to anyone else. If they could just stay together through the troubled times, at the end of college they'd be okay, they'd make it as a couple. And Maggie had wanted to make it with Starrett, to be with him forever, and so she had seduced him to keep him.

After the seduction, Starrett was even more guilt-ridden. He couldn't tell her then what had been on his mind, about his plan.

The following morning he caught the coach down to Armagh, to train to be a priest, and he didn't see Maggie again for another twenty years. In those twenty years Starrett had left the seminary – not too long after his and Maggie's last night together, in fact – moved to London, got involved (eventually as a partner) in a highly successful classic car company, moved back to Ramelton fifteen years later and, thanks to his father's friend, Major Newton Cunningham, had joined the gardaí.

In those same years, Maggie had married Niall Keane and had birthed three children, the first a boy called Joe – who Starrett had recently learned was his son– and the second and third, Moya and Katie, both daughters with Niall. Niall had died following a brave fight with a vicious cancer, which had spread its malevolent tentacles throughout his body before it had even been diagnosed.

Until recently, Starrett had been oblivious to most of the details of Maggie's life, but the two of them had met up again a few years before. And, after some time, she'd told him that Joe was his son.

He'd apologised as best he knew how, offered not to bother her any more. As an act of penance he would leave her alone forever. But she said she had totally forgiven him. She'd also gone to the trouble of warning him it would probably take him a lot more time to forgive himself.

Two years later, he was still working on that one.

Now here he was, living with Maggie Keane, and everything was working out great. He knew that things never stayed the same, yet he was still so annoyed when they didn't.

Starrett allowed Maggie to wrap herself around him; she wasn't as sleepy as he'd thought. She made her way to his ear and whispered to him.

'The last time was for you, to bring you away from your work and back to me. This time is for me.'

Twenty-eight minutes later they had collapsed in a heap of sheets and sweat. Being careful not to disentangle from her, he covered the both of them with the sheet and a blanket, which he'd awkwardly rescued from the floor.

Just as he thought Maggie Keane was about to fall asleep he heard her whisper.

'The terrible thing that happened to you, that you said we'd be able to talk about one day – has it come back?'

'The very same Maggie, the very same.'

'Starrett, please remember that no matter what it was, no matter what else you had to do, this time you're not alone.'

CHAPTER TWELVE

DAY TWO: THURSDAY

First thing the following morning, Gibson picked Starrett up – she'd borrowed his car overnight – and the idea was to take him to see his boss, Major Newton Cunningham, at his house out on the Ramelton to Rathmullan Road. Starrett felt, because of Bishop Freeman's involvement in the case, it was imperative that he briefed the Major on his findings thus far. Starrett knew that, aside from the Major's usual canny overview on all of his cases, he would be invaluable in dealing with the politics on this particular one.

The Major's current wife – his own affectionate way of describing his long-standing and only wife – came out to the car as soon as they drove into the drive of the unique-for-these-parts American log-cabin-influenced, waterside property.

She seemed a little upset, but for all of that she held her usual dignified pose as she advised Starrett and Gibson that the Major was 'not himself at the moment', and had requested she allow him to sleep in this morning. She assured Starrett that, in the Major's words, 'it was nothing', and he'd be fit as a fiddle when he woke up. Starrett said his business with the Major would keep till later in the day. He offered his services for shopping purposes, or perhaps even getting a doctor to his senior.

'As you know better than I, Starrett, if I did anything as rash as that he'd consider it grounds to commence divorce proceedings,' she said, not quite hitting the humour she'd been aiming for.

Starrett laughed and after promising to return to visit the Major on his way back from Donegal Town, he and Gibson set off to Steve's Café for their morning fortifier. The usual crew of builders, farmers and malingerers, at various stages of breaking their overnight fasts, were present, silently nodding to each newcomer. Starrett ordered well but ate meagrely, while Gibson was content with her usual tea and toast. Starrett didn't even take his usual pleasure from hearing Brendan Quinn via Highland Radio, as broadcast to the diners in Steve's. But he did feel good after his evening with Maggie. She and the home life she afforded him, and the fact that he was no longer alone, made the dark clouds appear less bleak. However, he was definitely troubled about not being able to talk to the Major. His boss was always a reliable sounding board and a great listener. After his evening with Maggie Keane, he knew he'd be able to go about the investigation in a professional manner, deal with it as it came along. The only thing niggling him was his potential conflict of interest, and he'd hoped the Major would've noted his concern, cautioned him, and told him to get on with it, but, without that safety net, he needed to be careful and work this case by the book. Not that he knew of any other way to work a case, of course, but he still felt he needed to mentally red flag the issue.

It was a beautiful autumnal morning as they drove to Letterkenny, past Locky Morris' exceptional telegraph pole sculpture – probably more of an installation than a sculpture, Starrett figured, but a phenomenal piece of work nonetheless – out the other side of the sculpture, up the steep Ballybofey Road, eventually through Ballybofey on the south bank of the River Finn, home to McElhinney's Stores (the plural is essential) and Finn Harps football team. Pretty soon they were out into the beautiful hilly countryside again, then through the Barnesmore Gap, passing Biddy's O'Barnes, the 200-year-old pub, where nothing was as old as the flagstones but the vegetable soup was always second to none. Next they followed the cold River Eske (to their right), which fed Lake Eske, just below the spectacular Blue Stack Mountains.

They were making good time up to that point then they hit Donegal Town, famous for its congested streets. Situated right at the mouth of the River Eske in Donegal Bay, Donegal Town or Fort of The Foreigners, was the town that gave its name to the county.

Starrett grew edgy at their lack of movement. They'd a lot to do and although it was still only 8:40 in the morning, he always liked to get a break on both the day and the case. Soon, but not soon enough, they were through to the south of Donegal Town and on to the old Ballyshannon Road. Ballyshannon was the home of Rory Gallagher and Starrett could never pass a road sign for the town without remembering one of the greatest live artists he'd ever had the pleasure of listening to and watching.

They took a quick right turn, very easy to miss, a couple of miles south of Donegal Town, just after they passed the Donegal Craft Village Shop off the new (ish) bypass, on the lazy road to Lagney. Eventually, up that minor road, they came to the causeway, which took them across to St Ernan's Island.

The wee island was originally owned by the Hamilton Family. John Hamilton was born in Dublin in 1800 (Starrett would readily admit he knew this only because he had Katie Keane, all of thirteen, Google it for him the previous night). Hamilton had picked St Ernan's as the site on which to build a home. The family had originally leased land in nearby Ballintra from Dublin's Trinity College, but John's wife was poorly and they reckoned she'd benefit from St Ernan's sea air. So in 1824, work commenced on converting the house on the island into what was to become a historic mansion, with stables, a coach house, and various outhouses.

The biggest challenge facing John Hamilton was not so much the refurbishment of the property, but more the building of the access out to it. Previously, access to the island could be gained only by rowing a boat or wading out in low tide in Wellingtons. Hamilton's plan, after he'd completed work on the house therefore, was to connect the island to the shore with a causeway. The difficulty came not from the construction of said causeway, but from the tides – the first attempt was washed away before work was completed. In a time when landlords were both hated and feared by their tenants in equal measure – such as was the case with John George Adair and the Earl of Leitrim – John Hamilton's consideration and support of his loyal tenants during the famine was repaid in spades when they all turned out in the dead of night to help him make another attempt at the causeway. It proved to be one monumental fight, humans against the elements. This time the tenants, from both sides of the religious divide and working for only food and drink, laboured wearily through the night and against the tides, successfully completing the construction, which still stands today as a lasting testament to the unbreakable bond not just between the island and the mainland but, more importantly, between this land owner and his tenants.

Starrett was greatly amused by the fact that on the morning after work was completed on the causeway, not one tenant would stand up and admit he'd been involved in the nocturnal goings on, and not for the reason that, even under the cloak of darkness, they didn't like to admit they were happy to work with their fellow men, but that, in the cold, bigoted light of day, they were somewhat reluctant to admit to working with anyone other than their fellow pew-dwellers. The church has always tried to exercise a strong hold over its congregation but, then as now, good neighbourly conduct trumped bigotry every time.

John Hamilton was heard exclaiming, 'Well, if none of you men did this wonderful work, the causeway must have been built by the Leprechauns.'

Starrett took great comfort from the fact that the story had lasted for nearly 190 years, so the owner must indeed have been as good as legend portrayed him to be, if only because the story was carried first by folklore and now by the current digital media. For the first time since he'd come into contact with Father Freeman on this case (he never would accept that he'd been ordained a bishop), he accepted that quite clearly some men are capable of doing good in the world.

They drove over the narrow ancient causeway, passing to the right of the sugar-pink St Ernan's house and up pretty close to the back door.

'What a great day to change a five punt note,' Starrett declared, as he exited the ancient BWM, while exercising his fingers.

Upon their arrival, Packie Garvey reported that he and Romany Browne had watched Bishop Freeman's room all night. Father Mc-Cafferty had visited the bishop's room once, at 21:33, staying that time for seven minutes, and had returned for a second time, at 21:55, with a tray of food of mostly cold cuts, apple pie, ice cream and tea.

After digesting the update, Starrett shocked Garvey, Browne, and Gibson when next he instructed both Garvey and Gibson to interview the bishop, and immediately. As both Ban Garda and Sergeant scooted off to the bishop's room with the air of a pair of bemused twins, Starrett then instructed Browne to lay his hands on some of the same supply of potatoes – the aforementioned blues, as originally used by Father Matthew – and time how long it took to boil the potatoes until they passed the fork test. He also asked the garda to repeat the experiment, but the second time to take the potatoes off the boil for fifteen minutes, and then to put them back on the heat and bring them back to boiling point until they, again, passed the fork test. That way, they could compare the net timings.

'What's the fork test?' Garda Romany Browne asked.

'Have you never seen your mum boil potatoes?'

'No.'

'Really?'

'Really,' Browne replied, looking genuinely bewildered. 'Someone always cooked our food. I–'

Browne looked for a moment like he was going to develop the dialogue into a non-work related conversation for the first time ever. Starrett felt for him at that moment, and he knew it was mainly due to his own son, Joe, whom he'd only recently come into contact with after sadly being totally unaware of his existence for the first twenty years of his life. Joe Keane was at University now and so Starrett felt he never saw him nor conversed with him as much as he would have liked to. Romany Browne had an additional problem to Joe, though. Not only was he fatherless – in his case his father, a very good friend of the Major, had been killed in action – but he also had movie star looks. Starrett knew however that the closest Mr Browne was going to get to Hollywood was if he were ever to visit Country Antrim and drop an 'L' on the way. Mind you, Dr Aljoe seemed to be paying him very close attention at the moment, so there were clearly certain advantages.

'As I see it, Romany,' Starrett started, addressing the young Gardai officer for the first time by his Christian name, 'the main problem with someone who wears glasses is that picking a new pair of glasses is always extremely difficult...because, when you're trying them on, you can never really see how they look – this would account for so many people wearing inappropriately framed glasses.'

'In other words, you don't need to be able to do everything yourself?' Browne offered confidently, after risking a fissure across his sculptured looks with a hearty laugh.

'Exactly. And always find someone who knows how to do the things you don't.'

'So how do you tell if your potatoes are properly boiled?' Browne asked.

'Okay,' Starrett began, feeling they were getting somewhere, 'you stick a fork into the potato – never a knife, always a fork – and lift said potato out of the boiling water using the fork, and if the potato slides off the fork back into the water it means they're properly boiled.'

Inspector Starrett then left Browne, who was trying desperately to commit the steps of the fork test to memory, to collect Father Robert O'Leary, whereupon both of them walked to the other end of the corridor, to the last room, on the opposite side of the building as O'Leary's, that is to say the front of St Ernan's. The permanent resident of said room was a certain Father Peregrine Dugan.

* * *

Starrett didn't know whether or not he'd already formed an opinion of Father Peregrine Dugan due to the fact that he'd recently been told on two separate occasions that the elder priest was: a) very intelligent and b) (reportedly) never left his room. If he had been expecting Old Father Time he didn't show it in the slightest when Father O'Leary introduced them both to a tidy but book-crammed room. What wall space wasn't covered by shelves, books, and a very large map of the island of Ireland was stacked chest-high with files. There was neither a computer nor typewriter in sight, just a tidy mahogany desk placed against the window, which afforded him a great view of the causeway leading back to the mainland. Consequently it meant Father Dugan could easily monitor all arrivals and departures from the house.

On his desk was a clean jam-jar packed with pens and pencils. Also on the desk – back and centre – was a Roberts Radio, while a clean stack of fresh loose-leaf paper was on the left-hand side and a larger stack on the right, that one betraying neat and beautiful handwriting. To the right of the radio was a box file about a foot deep with the neat black felt tip legend 'Death by Google'.

To Dugan's appearance: the priest wasn't exactly slim but he did obey one of the two golden rules for older men, and that was to never, ever wear tight trousers (the other one being never dress with your shirt worn outside your trousers). The Methuselah-aged priest was dressed in the pressed trousers of a suit, a black shirt, clerical collar and a grey pocketed and buttoned up cardigan, and (for someone who didn't go out much) he wore a pair of black leather, well-polished sensible shoes. He enjoyed a full head of healthy shoulder-length grey hair, was clean shaven and his skin was the white of milk, or rather the colour of skin continuously deprived of daylight. He'd watery eyes and had been cursed with a very large nose. When he spoke, he betrayed a lifetime of poor dental care and his words appeared to escape from the darkness of the cave that was his mouth. Starrett felt that most people with bad teeth appeared to mutter quite a bit as a way, no doubt, of hiding their decaying molars. But not so with Father Dugan, no, he spoke with what Starrett could only describe as the voice of God. Mind you, it wasn't that he was loud, more that his clear baritone delivery filled the entire room.

'I understand you're writing the history of Ireland,' Starrett said, when the introductions were completed.

'Oh, the history of Ireland has already been written, Inspector,' he declared, in a voice that threatened to move Starrett's bowels, 'we're just trying to record it for future scholars.'

Right, Starrett thought, that's me properly told off. He conceded (to himself) that it perhaps wasn't his best ever start to an interview.

'I was telling you why Inspector Starrett was here,' Father O'Leary offered, coming to Starrett's rescue.

'Oh yes,' Father Dugan replied, blinking his eyes furiously to try and remove the excess moisture from them, 'Father…Father…'

'Young Father Matthew McKaye,' O'Leary offered, good humouredly.

'Yes, Father Matthew – isn't he one of the bishop's protégés?'

'I believe there was talk of Father Matthew eventually going to the bishop's Cathedral in Galway, yes,' O'Leary replied.

'Would Bishop Freeman usually take the young curates from St Ernan's down to Galway?' Starrett asked, finding his way back into the interview.

'I wouldn't have a clue,' Dugan replied, while staring watery-eyed at O'Leary.

'Not normally, no,' O'Leary said.

'Had it ever happened before?' Starrett asked.

'I don't think so, but that would be a better question for the bishop. Let's just say that he would have a certain amount of clout along the well hidden corridors of power,' O'Leary said, and then something seemed to click with him, as though he realised what was happening and as he made for the door he added, 'Inspector, I've a few things I need to attend to and so I'll leave you in the very capable hands of Father Dugan.'

Starrett breathed a huge sigh of relief; perhaps now the interview could start proper. He knew that, with the priest reportedly room-bound, it was unlikely he'd get much information out of him regarding Father Matthew. But, equally, Starrett hoped that Father Dugan might know more than most about the behind-the-scenes stories; if he did, and at his age, he probably wouldn't mind spilling the beans.

'It's a shame Father Matthew's life was so short,' Starrett said, because that's what he was thinking and it was as good a place as any to try and manoeuvre the conversation back to the deceased priest.

'People often say that; that a life was so short, or something similar, but the reality is a life is but a life, it can neither be longer nor shorter than it was meant to be.'

'Well, relative to other lives, then, he had a short life.'

'That's certainly a different perspective on the subject and one I wouldn't disagree with,' Dugan replied.

'So you think–'

'I think we're all in a queue, waiting to die,' Dugan said, cutting off all potential avenues of small talk.

Dugan seemed bemused by Starrett blatantly and defiantly rolling his eyes. 'So you think we're worth more?' he asked, opening up one of the avenues he'd seemed so insistent on closing a few seconds earlier.

'I'm not sure,' Starrett admitted, 'it was more that I was very surprised to hear a man of the cloth make such a statement.'

Dugan sat down at his desk and swivelled round to face Starrett, before inviting the detective to take the one other comfortable seat in the room, a modern, dark leather bucket seat. He took a crumpled up tissue out of his cardigan pocket and rubbed his large nose a few times and replaced the tissue – crumpled to the nth degree now – into the opposite pocket from which he had taken it.

'Tell me this, Inspector,' Dugan began, 'do you believe in...but listen, you're not here to debate religious philosophy.'

'No, of course not, but I merely meant that life, or the length of life is long, or short, but only when compared to other lives. For instance, the average male in this neck of the woods will live to be seventy-nine years old, so compared to that, one could say that Father Matthew had a very short life. But, as you say, that's not what we're here to discuss. How long have you been a resident at St Ernan's?'

Father Dugan smiled, conceding something, though Starrett knew not what.

'I've been here for nine years now, Inspector.'

'And where were you before that?'

'I was overseas, in the Philippines, from 1973 until 2004. They brought me back here just after my 73rd birthday. The Mission needed the energy of a much younger man to do their work. I'd been working on my History of Ireland project since 1969 and I have to think someone up there – I'm talking about Armagh and not Heaven here, by the way – thought they would let me see out my days here at St Ernan's so that I could finish my life's work.'

'They encourage you then?'

'Unofficially Inspector, unofficially, and I've been lucky enough while here to have been joined by Fathers Casey, Clerkin, and Mulligan in helping me with invaluable research and with, of course, typing it all up onto the computer.'

'You've been working on this for nearly forty years?' Starrett asked in disbelief, belatedly doing the sums.

'Yes, but not every day of course and for the first twenty-odd years it was much more of a research project. I must say, it finally started to make some sense about a year after I came here. That's when I finally started to get a shape to it that I was happy with.'

'So how long to go until you're finished, then?'

'Well Inspector, funny you should ask that particular question because I was hoping to finish it this morning and then Father O'Leary advised me I had to sit with you.'

Starrett was formulating his next question on the back of what had really only been a polite interlude to segue the interview back to meatier stuff.

'Well. Okay. Wait! What?' Starrett said, eventually catching up with his brain's information processing plant.

'No, sorry, sorry, please forgive an old man his infantile sense of humour,' Dugan's baritone boomed all over the room and, Starrett feared, over the entire house, 'I was only codding you on, maybe to see if you were really listening.'

'You got me well and truly there, Father,' Starrett admitted.

'Well not quite,' Dugan chuckled.

Up to that exact moment Starrett had never imagined what God would sound like, not when he laughed but if in fact he laughed at all, that is, of course, assuming mere mortals were allowed to hear him. For that matter he'd never before considered God having a sense of humour. He'd always, due to his disbelief – lack of faith, if you will – pictured God as a Marvel-type character who would have benefited, just like Superman and Batman, from a Hollywood makeover. If religion and God were presented in such a manner, would it be easier for the next generation to accept Him?

Starrett was still regrouping from the priest's stab at humour when he eventually managed to get one of his key questions introduced and on to the record, 'Did you by any chance notice who travelled over the causeway in either direction yesterday afternoon, between say 15:30 and 17:30?'

'You know, Inspector, when I'm working I'm really in a state, like an elevated state. It's why I enjoy my work so much – it takes me somewhere. I'll tell you this, I've spent entire days in here happily working away and completely unaware when dawn concludes and dusk begins. The only signal I have is later in the day my frail body starts to betray me and whereas the spirit is always, but always, willing, the body is too weak to do its bidding.'

'You saw nothing unusual then?' Starrett asked, clearly disappointed.

'At this distance all priests would look the same to me,' Dugan admitted. Then as an afterthought, 'and yesterday was Mrs Robinson's day off, I believe, so there'd have been no variety in costume.'

'Would most people not arrive and depart by car?'

'Well, Mrs Robinson usually arrives by bicycle, yes, by bicycle, unless it's raining in which case her sister usually brings her across by motorcar.'

'But I thought you said your eyes–'

'Yes of course, good point,' Father Dugan started, feigning being impressed, Starrett felt. 'Well, firstly, there are not so many females crossing our causeway on a bicycle and secondly, Mrs Robinson's sister always uses her husband's car: it's red, very small and makes a bigger racket than the walls of Jericho collapsing.'

Starrett had never really thought about the boy racers who plagued many a Donegal village late at night, burning rubber as they attempted to deposit giant black donuts on the tarmac, as being married men, but then he accepted that there was nothing to say that a girl couldn't also be a petrol head.

'Do you really never leave your room?'

'Let's put it like this, Inspector, just like this; sometimes when you have a reputation for doing something, like never leaving your room, for instance, well, you do find that it gets you out of lots of boring invitations and chores and as I've said, I've a lot to do with the time I've left. I also find that the important thing is not whether or not you leave your room, but that one ensures that one is never seen out, to never be seen out.'

'But you were here yesterday afternoon?'

'On that occasion I was definitely here, here in my room,' the old priest replied.

'Could you do me a favour, Father?'

'I'd like to try.'

'When you get a moment and your head is clear, could you please think back to yesterday afternoon and have a good think about who travelled over the causeway yesterday?'

'I'll be happy to give it a try.'

'I just find that if I focus on something, while at the same time taking pressure off myself, I find I know more, or I've picked up more than I thought I did,' Starrett offered, as his departing shot. He needn't have bothered: Father Dugan was already mentally back into the pages of his book.

Chapter Thirteen

The first thing that surprised Gibson about Bishop Cormac Freeman was his glaring green, bullfrog eyes. To Gibson and Garvey
– and they discussed this point at length after their interview – Freeman looked more Friar Tuck than Roman Catholic Bishop, even right
up to the bit of circular red skin at his crown, which shone through his
rowdy white thatch like a stop light on a snowy night. He was about
five foot ten, quite tall for his girth.

The second thing that surprised Gibson was how nice Freeman appeared and how well-mannered he was with them both, particularly towards her.

'You're both very welcome, come on in here and sit down,' he ordered them both when they showed up at his door. He shook their
hands furiously as he led them into his temporary quarters. 'I've been
expecting you and so tea and coffee will be with us presently. Our
budget might even extend to an auld Danish or two.'

His room, directly across the landing from Father Matthew McK-
aye's final dwelling on this earth, was a bit throughother, Gibson
noted. There were expensive looking ecclesiastical garments draped
over all manner of furniture.

By way of explanation he offered, 'I'm not used to living in such a
small melody of rooms and, to add insult to injury, Commander Starrett has, I believe, issued orders restricting my movements for the foreseeable future.'

'Inspector Starrett,' Gibson corrected.

'Oh, I thought he would have been a lot further up the totem pole
by now,' the bishop said sweetly.

'We don't actually have a rank of Commander,' Sergeant Garvey returned, even sweeter. 'Inspector Starrett's preference is for the pure detective work of his current rank rather than the more administrative chores of the senior ranks.'

'Inspector Starrett is rated as being one of the best detectives in the country,' Gibson added, proving she, too, was singing from the same hymn sheet as her colleague.

'Yes, so I've come to understand,' Freeman replied, as a knock came on the door. 'Enter,' the bishop ordered, in an altogether differ-ent tone.

Father Fergus Mulligan was doing the honours and seemed very happy to escape the room without question or verse.

Bishop Freeman played mammy and once said chores were done, he went to offer the plate of Danish's around. 'Ah,' he said as he picked up one of the pastries and dropped it immediately as though it was a steaming deposit usually reserved for pavement, 'I didn't realise that my description of "auld" was going to be taken quite so literally.'

Garvey looked disappointed.

'Not to worry,' Freeman declared, 'let's see what I've got stored away in my private stash.'

He disappeared into his bedroom and returned with a fresh packet of Jacob's chocolate-coated Kimberley biscuits.

At that point, Gibson thought, Garvey most likely would have let the bishop get away with murder. Time to get on with the interview, she felt, there was just too much love in the room.

'So Bishop Freeman,' Gibson began, as Garvey licked his lips, wiped his fingers in the napkin provided and finally armed himself with his pen and notebook, primed to commence taking notes, 'you split your time between here and Galway we understand?'

Freeman took but a brief moment, a very brief moment, to study the ban garda. He hadn't himself taken a biscuit as yet but looked very alarmed when both Gibson and Garvey went in for seconds.

'Yes, don't you see, I travel a lot for my work, for my flock as it were, and I do feel that to do one's best work, one does need to find a way of recharging the auld batteries.'

Garvey stared at the delicious Jacob's biscuits.

'When did you arrive for this visit?' Gibson asked.

'I got here very late on Sunday night,' Freeman replied. 'I visited Sligo on the way.'

'What were you in Sligo for?'

'Visiting a colleague…' he replied, looking a little perturbed that she would ask such a question.

'Church business?'

'All of my business is my Father's business,' the bishop replied.

Gibson was tempted to say that surely the Sabbath was the hallowed day of rest but she resisted, wondering instead what the bishop had done to Starrett to warrant the (seemingly) unprovoked attack the previous day. Could Starrett's history with the bishop be the reason she and Gibson were conducting such an important interview? She really felt like asking Freeman why Starrett had attacked him.

'When did you last see Father Matthew?' she asked instead.

'I took him into Donegal Town, to The Blueberry, for lunch,' the bishop replied, appearing to mentally take himself back to that time and place. 'To be honest with you I'd have preferred to have gone to the Abbey Hotel like I'd been doing for years, but Father Matthew insisted on The Blueberry – it's a much younger place and he knew the owners, Brian and Ruperta. They're a very nice couple and Brian summoned Ruperta to come out from the kitchen when we sat down. It's a nice dining area, marvellous really – don't get me wrong, but you couldn't hear yourself think and we were right in the middle of the crowd.'

'How did he seem?'

'He was full of the joys of spring. Father Matthew wasn't a spectator. He liked to get stuck into life. He'd lots of friends around here.'

'Did he voice any concern or worries to you?' Gibson asked.

'Look, you're going to find this out anyway so maybe I should be the one to tell you,' the bishop offered, looking to Gibson like he was faking a bit of concern of his own, 'Father Matthew was at the point where he…where he…how should I put this…where he was wondering if he'd made the correct decision about joining the priesthood.'

'Really?'

'Yes, ehm…' the bishop continued and distracted himself by looking out at the still mid-morning water. 'Father Matthew, well he was young you know…and maybe he was just attracted to the uniform?'

'Sorry?'

'Well, it happens a lot you know.'

'You're surely not claiming that he became a priest just so that he could wear a black suit, black shirt, and clerical collar?' Gibson said, in clear disbelief.

'I was speaking in symbolic terms, not material, my dear,' the bishop pronounced. 'You see, it's important to note that Father Matthew was himself an orphan and had been in various homes over his lifetime without actually benefiting from having a true home. And so, don't you see, the priesthood and all it entails offered a spiritual home as well as a physical one.'

Gibson reckoned that made sense.

'But then people who come to us for such reasons realise there is a price to pay,' the bishop continued, clearly feeling the need to explain himself. 'But, don't you see, the price to pay only affects those of us who are not here first and foremost to serve our Father in Heaven but those of us who, as I was trying to say, are attracted to the lifestyle.'

'Was Father Matthew thinking of leaving the Church?' Gibson asked.

'Good heavens, no! Usually people only leave the Church when they think they have somewhere better to go.'

'Interesting,' Gibson said. 'Did Father Matthew ever discuss this subject with you in detail?'

'No, not really. It is said our Father spoke to us in parables which were Earthly stories with heavenly meanings, but Father Matthew spoke in codes; Earthly stories with oblique meanings. For instance, when he said how much he enjoyed going around to Eimear Robinson's house for Sunday lunch, how all the family got together and there was great craic around the table, what he was really saying was how St Ernan's was not providing him with the family support structure he thought he had bought into.'

'Eimear is the…' Gibson started.

'Mrs Robinson is the housekeeper here at St Ernan's,' the bishop offered, concluding Gibson's sentence for her.

'And she lives?' Garvey asked, pen primed at the ready for the answer.

'Somewhere in Donegal Town, I believe,' the bishop replied, 'Father O'Leary would be able to furnish you with the address. She's one of those incredible salt-of-the-earth women, and St Ernan's is very lucky to have her.'

'Sorry,' Gibson said hesitantly, 'and I'm really not meaning to insult anyone here but just so I have this 100 per cent clear in my mind, you're not suggesting that Father Matthew and Mrs Robinson were having an…'

'An affair?' the bishop asked and burst into a fit of laugher, 'why good heavens no, not at all!' He looked like he was going to offer further explanation but then seemed to think better of it.

'Okay, I just wanted to be clear,' Gibson said. 'So, let's go back to your lunch. Would it be usual for a visiting Bishop to go to lunch with a curate?'

This question seemed to achieve some kind of direct hit because the bishop immediately grew crimson. His already bulging eyes looked like they could pop out of their sockets at any second. He raised his hands in front of him and looked for a second as if he might break into prayer but instead he started to rub them together, as if trying to generate heat.

After a moment, he appeared to regain his composure and paused further to refresh everyone's coffee cups before saying, 'So, you caught me unawares there and I'm sorry, but for the first time I realise how sordid this is all going to get. You're going to go chasing for motives and suspects and in the meantime everyone is going to believe the worst of everyone involved and Father Matthew's name and our names are going to be dragged through the mud until you come up with the real reason for his murder.'

'Have you any ideas at all who would want to murder Father Matthew?'

'Is it definitely murder?' the bishop asked.

'We're treating it as suspicious until such time as the autopsy is completed,' Gibson replied.

The bishop rubbed the back of his neck and scrunched up his face.

'Sorry, but you never answered my question: have you any idea who might have had a reason to murder Father Matthew?'

'I really wouldn't know where to start to answer your question,' the bishop replied.

'Okay, well let's explore your theory that Father Matthew was dissatisfied with the priesthood?'

'We are certainly not in the habit of assassinating priests who wish to leave our ranks,' Bishop Freeman replied.

'Could there be any other reason, apart from that which we've discussed, why Father Matthew wished to leave the priesthood?' Gibson asked, trying desperately hard to give the interview the kick up the backside it so badly needed.

'For instance?'

'For instance,' Gibson puffed impatiently, 'for instance, money problems, woman problems, man problems, drug problems – for instance, Father Matthew becoming aware of something he wasn't meant to be aware of?'

'What, like all the priests in St Ernan's were running a crack house? Ban Garda, this is Donegal Town, not the Bronx, nor even Brixton for that matter,' the bishop chastised.

'Like he was being blackmailed,' Gibson continued unperturbed, 'or like he was blackmailing someone?'

The bishop laughed.

'Can you tell me, Bishop Freeman, what you were doing between the hours of 3:30 and 5:30 yesterday afternoon?'

'Ah, the scorpion question.'

'Sorry?' Gibson said.

'The sting in the tail of the interview,' the bishop replied.

'Well?'

'Well, as it happens, after the aforementioned lunch with Father Matthew, I stayed in Donegal Town, you know, I wandered around. I went to the castle to see if the roof had been returned yet–'

'Sorry?' Garvey said, looking up from his notebook for the first time in ages. If there was such a thing as an all-American man then Packie Garvey would most certainly have qualified as the all-Donegal man. He looked healthy, was in great shape and clean shaven, and had tidy dark brown bordering on black hair and reddish cheeks. But both physically and visually he was still a work in progress, when in twenty years' time he would mature into his prime.

'Oh, the wee castle we have in town doesn't have a roof and the story goes that when a captain, a man by the name of Basil Brooke, was leaving for Fermanagh, he either destroyed the roof or took it with him, preventing others from using the castle. So we're all still waiting – since the early 1800s – for Captain Brooke to return the roof of our wee castle. Mind you, in their defence the Brookes' always maintained that it was the O'Donnell clan who wrecked the castle before the English moved in and granted all of Donegal, including the castle, to Brooke. It also has to be said that the captain did a wonderful job of refurbishing and remodelling the castle while planning the original layout of the town, including our famous Donegal Town square, a.k.a The Diamond. They say there is a tunnel from the castle to...'

'Right,' Gibson sighed, drawing out the word as long as good manners would permit and pretending she hadn't heard Freeman's previous few words, 'all very interesting but I still need to know what you were doing between 3:30 and 5:30 p.m. yesterday please?'

'Yes sorry, I knew there was a point to this somewhere,' Freeman began. 'So, I was wandering around Donegal Town and I got back here about…well, just shortly after Inspector Starrett arrived and all hell was breaking loose.'

'Did you visit anywhere else? Did you meet anyone, bump into anyone?'

'In all seriousness I did wander around the castle. For ages. I find it very spiritual there. Very uplifting. No, I didn't collide with anyone I knew. I visited the book store up in the square.'

'Did you purchase anything on your travels?'

'No, not a single item,' the bishop offered with a tone of finality.

'I expect Inspector Starrett will want to talk to you presently,' Gibson said in conclusion.

'I expect he will,' Bishop Cormac Freeman said, rising from his seat in all his finery, 'I expect he will.'

* * *

'Well now, the words of a bishop,' Garvey declared, tapping his notebook before putting it away in the breast pocket of his uniform jacket, 'I've never heard a man say so much without actually saying a single thing.'

CHAPTER FOURTEEN

Garvey checked his mobile to discover five missed calls, all from Garda Francis Casey.

He returned the calls immediately, spoke a few words, and went off in search of Inspector Starrett, who he found down in the kitchen area alone with his thoughts.

'Garda Casey on the mobile, Sir – he says he's got something good for you,' and he switched his phone to hands-free mode.

'Francis, what do you have for me?' Starrett said, not quite exactly snapping his sergeant's iPhone 5 but asking his question before he was in full possession of the thing, which he proceeded to hold as delicately as if it was an ice-cream slider and he was considering how to accomplish his first lick.

'Okay. Fr. Gene McCafferty claimed that his previous two cathedrals had been at St John the Baptist, in Cork, in the Diocese of Cork and Ross, to be exact' Casey started, without any preamble. 'But Cork only has two cathedrals: a St Mary's and a St Anne's. What I'm saying is that there is no such cathedral as St John the Baptist in Cork, but this was a simple lie that any clergy would pick up on. So why tell it?'

'To buy himself some time?' Starrett offered.

'And...' Casey continued, not quite confirming that he agreed with his superior. '...and before Cork, Father McCafferty claimed he was at The Assumption of the Blessed Virgin Mary in Ennis, in the Diocese of Killaloe. But Ennis only has a St Peter and a St Paul.'

'So he's clearly trying to hide his past, but why? And why not so cleverly?' Garvey offered.

'Maybe he thinks that because he's a priest we, the Gardaí, won't question what he tells us and he'll cover up what he wants to cover up,'

Starrett said, looking at the mobile instrument of communication as if expecting the phone itself to formulate an answer.

'Maybe it was the best he could come up with on the spur of the moment?' Francis Casey suggested.

'So should we question him next?' Garvey asked.

'And blow Francis' great work? No, I don't think we need to tip Father McCafferty off just yet that we're on to him. Francis, why don't you do a bit more digging and find out where he was really stationed for his previous two posts, and then contact both of those fine establishments and discover what it is exactly he's trying to hide. This way, the next time we speak to Donegal's answer to Buddy Holly, we'll hopefully have the upper hand.'

'Grand,' Garvey and Casey said in unison.

'Excellent work, Francis,' Starrett said, as he handed the mobile back to Garvey, and after his sergeant had disconnected he asked him, 'How many ciggies do I have left, Packie?'

'Ah Starrett,' Garvey protested, 'I'm going to get it in the ear from *both* Maggie Keane and Gibson.'

'Ah, they'll never know – I haven't had one for ages and, as you know, I do me best thinking when I'm puffing on an auld Lucifer stick.'

Starrett was in fine form now, the investigation was up and running, things weren't exactly falling into place but at least they were falling. He just had to make sense of all the leads, if, in fact, any were leads. But the thing he was most happy about was that the case was distracting him enough for him to have lost his preoccupation with Bishop Freeman. That had been his one fear about working on this case: the worry that Freeman might affect his ability to do his work properly. At the same time, just because he was prejudiced against the Bishop didn't necessarily mean that the Bishop didn't do it.

CHAPTER FIFTEEN

Starrett next took a call, also on Garvey's iPhone 5, from the always vivacious and occasionally flirtatious Dr Samantha Aljoe.

'Good morning Starrett, how are you getting on up there?'

'Down here,' Starrett corrected, 'we're south of you.'

'Really? Okay, if you say so,' she continued, sounding somewhat amused. 'How are you getting on down there?'

'Slowly, but in the meantime, have you wrapped the case up for us yet?' he replied, only half joking.

'Well, funny you should say that but I do believe I have something very interesting for you.'

'Goodness Sam, I'm thinking of getting one of these things permanently grafted onto my ear!'

'Sorry?'

'No, it's that I've just, only a few minutes ago, taken a call, also on Packie's mobile, which produced some interesting information as well.'

'Oh right, but you'll never guess my information.'

Then there was nothing but electronic static on the phone. At first Starrett thought they'd lost the connection. Then he thought she was just leaving him a space to comment on her last sentence, but before he'd a chance to react she started to talk again.

'Our Father Matthew McKaye was murdered all right.'

'Really?'

'"Really?" Rather than "Bejeepers", Starrett?'

'Oh you noticed,' Starrett began, sensing the doctor's usual need to mix things up between the lighter things in life and the much heavier topic of her recent examinations into the cause of death of a human being. 'It's just that…ah…Maggie Keane's youngest daughter, Moya,

has recently been sending me up a bit about my overuse of that particular word. So I'm consciously trying to avoid it where possible.'

'O-kay,' Aljoe replied, giving nothing away. 'Father Matthew was
shot in the brain.'

'Be feckin' jeepers!'

'That's more like my old Starrett.'

'But hauld your horses a bit there, Sam, when you examined the
body, you found no marks and certainly no gunshot wounds?'

'And that, too, is correct, except for one small hole hidden by the
hairline on the back of his head, more like the neck.'

'And traces of blood?' Starrett asked.

'None,' she claimed, 'none at all, but one of two things could have
happened. Death would have been pretty immediate and so the heart
would have stopped pumping blood in almost the same second.
Nonetheless, even in these instances there's usually a little trickle of
blood that leaks from the wound. So if the latter was the case, then
maybe our murderer knew exactly what he or she was doing and
wiped the blood away in the hope of hiding the wound.'

'But hang on a minute – a bullet to the brain? Surely there should
have been blood all over the place?'

'Oh didn't I tell you?' she started coyly. 'There wasn't a bullet.'

'Sorry, this must be a bad line, Sam, I'm sure you just said that
there wasn't a bullet, but just a few seconds before that you said he'd
been shot?'

'Both are correct Starrett. He was shot but I didn't find a bullet in
him.'

'The JFK magic bullet, which bounced all around the insides of
both President Kennedy and Governor Connolly and was never located, strikes again?'

'More magic than that, Inspector – we have no bullet and neither
do we have an exit wound.'

'But surely that really is impossible?'

'I have an entry mark, I have a route of trajectory, and I have witnessed and examined all the damage caused along the way but…I do
not have a bullet.'

'Nor an exit wound?'

'Nor an exit wound.'

'Bejeepers,' Starrett hissed involuntarily.

He advised Samantha to keep this information under her hat but as he was doing so he realised he didn't really need to – she was the mistress of discretion. On top of which, he'd never seen her wear a hat. He also needed to find a way of getting Bishop Freeman off St Ernan's Island as soon as humanly possible. In honour of his history with the bishop, he just might bypass the human route.

CHAPTER SIXTEEN

By this point – mid-morning on the Thursday – and thanks to Father Robert O'Leary, Starrett and his team had been assigned three sets of rooms in St Ernan's, from which to work. Starrett had the room between Father Edward McKenzie (the ginger haired gardener) and Father Fergus Mulligan (the priest with tidy handwriting, who had compiled the original list of priests for Starrett and also assisted Father Dugan's trio with the massive writing project). The Ramelton Serious Crimes Unit also had access to the two rooms directly across the landing from the inspector. Starrett had advised Father O'Leary that two sets of rooms would suffice but the priest had insisted they might want the three, if only to give Ban Garda Nuala Gibson some privacy should they need to stay overnight.

Starrett figured that with the long drive to Ramelton, and back again in the morning, it might be an idea to stay over himself. Then he remembered he'd promised to visit Major Newton Cunningham at the end of the day, to see how he was doing and also to update him on the bishop Cormac Freeman situation and the potential conflict of interest there. He also really needed to drop in on Dr Aljoe and get the full SP on the mysterious, yet absent, bullet.

After they'd all decamped to their various suites (Gibson in the room across the landing from Starrett, and the boys between Gibson and Father Pat's room), they then met up in the boys' (Packie and Browne's) room, which was going to serve as the general meeting room for the time being.

Starrett was thinking of having a catch-up debrief but then decided against it, feeling that fact-collecting, rather than discussing, was much more important at this point. So he sent Packie and Pips (which Starrett felt had a certain Cagney and Lacey ring to it) to get on the phones with Francis Casey and assist him in his efforts to uncover just why Father Gene McCafferty had been lying about his previous appointments. Then they could interview McCafferty with better information in their arsenal.

Romany Browne passed over to Starrett a page that he said contained the results of his boiled potatoes experiment, and the inspector offered his thanks as he folded the sheet and slipped it into the inside pocket of his blue, zip-up, hooded windbreaker. He and Gibson, he explained, would negotiate the heavy traffic while they nipped into Donegal Town to visit Mrs Eimear Robinson, the housekeeper of St Ernan's. Father O'Leary had kindly furnished him with her address.

* * *

Mrs Eimear Robinson lived the life of a wife and mother trying hard to get by, with little or no time (nor energy) to entertain the big thoughts of life, such as why are we here? Or even, why, how, and whether we're to be taken from here. No, her concerns, 365 days of the year, were to do with ensuring her daughters, sixteen-year-old Julia and eighteen-year-old Jessica (named after Julia Roberts and Jessica Lange respectively, Eimear's two favourite actresses – they'd have been called Al and Kevin should they have been boys), grew up to have the opportunities she'd never enjoyed. She'd also successfully planned to ensure she'd never have more than two children.

Mrs Robinson knew that her husband didn't love her and she was almost certain she didn't love him. She accepted that most likely both facts were related. She also realised their complicated situation had a lot to do with the fact that she discovered he'd cheated on her nearly twenty years ago, when she was pregnant with Jessica. She'd also discovered that 'forgiving' someone didn't fully take into account the fact that when someone cheats on you, no matter how much you don't want to entertain the thought, you are forever doomed to be waiting around for the next time. She often wondered if her husband worried about the possibility of her cheating on him, if only to get her own back. Yes, it was nearly twenty years and counting since Mr Robinson had cheated on Mrs Robinson, but ensuring her daughters did well meant, she believed, bringing them up in a secure, stable family environment. So her husband hadn't been kicked out, hadn't been given the cold shoulder, no, far from it in fact: he'd been borne another daughter by Eimear, and all so that they – the two daughters – would grow up enjoying life, well fed, properly clothed, sufficiently housed, genuinely loved, and content and secure in an apparently happy family.

Eimear Robinson was a brunette, but Starrett couldn't figure out if she was a blonde hiding as a brunette or vice versa. He thought he knew what he meant by that, but when he ran the thought around his head a bit he wasn't so sure. If she were a genuine brunette and she'd dyed her hair blonde, was there still a chance she was a brunette hiding behind being a blonde? Starrett thought so, but wasn't sure it would stand up in court, or even if it would need to. She wore little make-up but what she did wear she used effectively. She'd an infectious smile and she engaged Starrett directly with her brown eyes. He thought that, most likely, Eimear Robinson had never flirted once in her entire life. She was slim, but not thin. Her hair was pulled back into a long pony-tail and try though he might, Starrett could not for the life of him see one dark root showing through. She was dressed straight from Dunnes and looked great in her around-the-house dark, tight-fitting slacks, all-white trainers and the collar of a white shirt or blouse showing over a dark blue, thick woollen jumper.

The Robinson's house was a new-build, a detached one-and-a-half story bungalow, popular in rural Donegal. In certain areas, the planner, for some reason or another, would only grant planning permission for one-storey houses. Most people got around this, even during the building stage, by adding two, sometimes even three, bedrooms and a bathroom up in the roof space, and lighting them with a dormer window or two on the rear of the roof; that is to say, not visible to the road, or the planners should they ever go out for a wee trip to inspect or check their rulings. The house was outside Donegal Town, on the road to Ramelton, and was in a compound with three other similarly styled houses. The house was so new that Eimear still had her snag list stuck to the fridge door. Starrett noted they were down as far as item number 26 – 'drawers getting snagged on rough wood of drawers' – a lingerie hitch the carpenter would have to deal with, and they were not even halfway through their list of snags yet. But for all of that, Eimear Robinson had already created a wonderfully comfortable and homely house, and she invited Starrett and Packie to sit down at the pine table in the uncluttered dining area (which partnered up seamlessly with the functional and modern kitchen) while she made them coffee. She also produced a couple of generous hot slices of freshly baked apple pie (the produce of St Ernan's, she claimed), garnished with a couple of scoops (each) of Ben & Jerry's Chunky Monkey ice cream, which Starrett was convinced was so addictive, people should require a licence to sell it. The ice cream, in fact rendered him at a loss for words. As his eyes rolled in ecstasy, Sgt Packie Garvey started off the proceedings.

'When was the last time you were up at St Ernan's?' he asked, as she milked their coffees.

'You know, I still can't believe it...' Eimear Robinson replied, totally ignoring Packie's question and seeming to grow tongue-tied with emotion. Her nostrils started to quiver, which was a sure sign to Starrett that tears would soon be galloping down the same pathway.

The St Ernan's housekeeper was the first person who'd shed a tear for Father Matthew McKaye. Starrett just stared at her, assessing the impact of this fact.

Eimear grew aware of the inspector's staring and he noticed her pick herself up and gather herself together.

'Sorry,' she started, 'it was just the way you asked your question, you didn't even mention the father but it brought the fact home to me that I'm never going to see him again.'

'It's okay, Eimear,' Starrett whispered, 'it's okay to talk about it.'

'No, I mean, yes, it's funny in a way. I just got the call last night from Father O'Leary, saying I needn't come up because sadly Father Matthew had passed. And then there was a bit on Highland Radio about it this morning, but, in a way it wasn't until Packie spoke to me there that it became...real, and I truly realised he'd passed.'

'I understand Father Matthew was close to you and your family?' Starrett offered, moving his apple and delicious ice cream to one side as he no longer had the stomach for it.

'Yes,' she replied, through a large sigh, 'he was a regular here. He'd join us quite a bit for food. The girls liked him; they even thought he was cool.'

She stopped talking and Starrett could tell that she'd been distracted with one of her own personal memories of the priest, a process that all who grieve must experience.

Starrett thought, for the first time, they were in a position where they might, just might, mind you, learn something important and *real* about Father Matthew. He just needed to find a way to get Eimear to continue talking naturally. Having Sgt Packie Garvey along side him, most certainly helped. Everyone was comfortable speaking to Packie; he was definitely a county treasure, if not a national one. Due to his exploits on the hurling field and his humble demeanour, everyone felt that they knew him already, and could talk to him as they would a family member or friend.

'You know,' she started back up again with renewed energy – she did tend to start her sentences in a louder voice than the one with which she completed them. 'He was with us when we moved into this house. Here, with us on our first day. I hadn't known him all that long at the time. We were due to flit on the Saturday, the first Saturday of this June, and I was getting into a bit of a panic. Gerry, my husband, wasn't much help either. He's an electrician – white appliances.'

'The only thing I've ever leaned about dishwashers and dryers,' Starrett admitted, 'is that it's always much better to close the door to said appliance from the outside.'

Garvey grinned largely. Eimear Robinson looked like she'd been caught unawares by Starrett's attempt at humour, which had kind of been his point, to throw her from her comfort zone a wee bit. After a few seconds' laugher she picked up her thread again.

'We were running late on the flit. Gerry was pulling double shifts to help pay for the move. So that meant it was just me and my girls and my sister, Mary, painting and then washing and cleaning everything behind us as we went along. Father Matthew volunteered to help me and he didn't have to volunteer twice. We roped him in, stuck a paint-brush in his hand and the five of us had a gas time. Ah jeez the craic was 90, all we'd have needed would have been Christy Moore in the corner of the room singing 'Listonvarna' to us and it would have been perfection.'

'Ye all did a great job,' Starrett offered, admiring their handiwork.

'Augh, I wanted it to be the business for my girls. It's our house, don't you see, well their house, and we had to struggle to change the mortgage from the last one to this. You know what it's like in the current climate but I said to Gerry, I said, "Gerry, if we don't break our backs and do this now we'll regret it for the rest of our lives. If we don't get this house now, we'll never be able to get it or one like it." Sure, once the property market takes off again, we'd never, ever have been able to put ourselves in a position to afford something like this. Gerry knew we needed to do this for the girls. Sure, they were in their late teens and still sharing a bedroom, but I'll tell you this gentlemen, they never once complained. Not once. Can you believe that? Not once did my girls complain. So I took extra jobs. I was on four at one time. Now I'm down to three, 'cause the pressure is off us a wee bit now, and Gerry took all the extra shifts and overtime he could get and you know what? We made it work.'

'Fair play to you,' Starrett offered in admiration, seeing a lot of similarities between Maggie Keane and Eimear Robinson in their total commitment to their children.

'Aye, thanks,' she said through a smile, 'and Father Matthew was here with us on our first day in our new house. He helped us move in and helped make it stress-free and great fun. There's something gas, something very special about the first day in your new house, isn't there? You want to run from room to room and just be in them all because they're all ours, all our rooms. I said to the girls, I said, "Julia and Jessica, these are all our rooms, this is our new house. For the love of God make sure you enjoy it." Since then Father Matthew was a regular visitor, he'd drop in for a chat or for dinner or Sunday lunch. And he'd always muck in.'

'Wasn't scared of rolling his sleeves up?' Starrett offered, in encouragement.

'Aye,' Eimear said quietly, sadly. 'He wasn't like a priest at all, more like a good mate. We'd work away together at St Ernan's, gossiping about everything under the sun. I'd talk to him about things I'd never talk to anyone else about. He was so understanding, so non-judgemental. He was always getting into trouble because when people came to him looking for advice he'd always say, you must do what you feel is right. You must listen to yourself not to others. Now, you should hear Bishop Freeman go absolutely beetroot when Father Matthew said something like that. I'd say to Father Matthew, "Father Matthew, you should be careful what you say around the bishop."'

'Huh,' Starrett chuckled, 'and what would Father Matthew say?'

'He'd say, "Oh don't worry about the bishop, he's never going to excommunicate me." And then he'd have a great old laugh, wouldn't he.'

'Did he ever explain what he meant by that?' Starrett asked hopefully.

'No he never did, Inspector.'

'Have you any idea what he meant by it?'

'I thought he meant that the bishop was okay and not a stickler for the rules, but I don't know,' Eimear said and stopped talking. She had a far-away look in her eyes.

'I just remembered another thing that Father Matthew said, in light of what has happened, is very…' she said, her sentence trailing off into silence.

'What was it he said, Eimear?' Starrett asked softly.

'He'd say, everyone wants to go to Heaven but no one wants to die.'

'Wow,' Starrett said, without realising he was saying so.

Garvey crossed himself.

'Did you know, when Father Matthew finished up here, he was going to the bishop's Diocese?' Starrett asked, ending the silence.

'Yes, we did as it happens.'

'How did he feel about that?'

'Well, it seemed the more he got to know us the more he felt that maybe he'd like to try to stay around here, but that could just be me being a bit big-headed, you know.'

'Was he happy in the priesthood?'

'That's not really for me to say,' Eimear said, saying a lot.

'No, sorry, yes,' Starrett said, immediately trying to regain his ground, 'I just wondered if he'd ever discussed with you…'

Starrett saw from the way the smile faded from her eyes that this wasn't a good approach either.

'Look Eimear,' he started, 'we believe someone took Father Matthew's life–'

'Oh my Go…' she gasped, 'I thought it was a natural passing. I said to my Gerry, I said, "Gerry, why Father Matthew? Why not some of the older priests?" I thought it was a tragedy he's been called back so young. But then…'

'But then?' Starrett prompted.

'Well I hate to bite the hand that feeds me but…Inspector, I find it difficult to support religion these days. All the suffering of those wee wains and then the Church trying to sweep it under the carpet and the state of the country and all…Oh jeez, you should hear my Gerry on the subject, don't get him started.'

Starrett made a mental note to do exactly that.

'So what I was going to say was,' Starrett said, 'I need to try and find out all about Father Matthew, all about his life, about things people would prefer we didn't find out.'

Eimear Robinson turned white at this point. Her mouth opened in an involuntary 'O' and she politely raised her hand to cover it.

'Are you okay?' Starrett asked. Clearly she wasn't, but it was an automatic reaction.

'I…I, ah…' she stuttered, 'I think I've just realised the enormity of what you've just told me…you know, that someone maybe killed Father Matthew.'

'Do you need to stop? We could come back?' Starrett offered reluctantly.

'No, no,' she protested, 'I want to help, it's just…'

'I know, it's very difficult.'

'Well, my girls are going to be very upset. Father Matthew was very good to them and they were always joking with each other. And then there's my sister, Mary. But please go on, I'll answer your questions as best I can.'

'Well, really the main thing I'm trying to discover is this: Was anything troubling Father Matthew, was he in any kind of trouble?'

'Well nothing definite, you know. Sometimes people look like they just need a bit of space and whereas my mum would always say, she'd say, "Come on in, sit yourself down and have a nice cup of tea and we'll have a wee chat." I'd just give them the space I thought they wanted.'

'But was there anything specific?'

'Well, Father Matthew was a great helper; he was more interested in helping others than asking for help himself. But sometimes you know – this could just be me reading something into something that wasn't there – he did look like he was far away, somewhere else, deep in his thoughts.'

Starrett tried a different tack, 'Did he get on okay with everyone at St Ernan's?'

'Yes, he did. He'd say they're all different and they need to be treated differently. He really liked Father Robert O'Leary, he said he

was always very helpful. God forgive me, Inspector, I hate to talk behind people's backs, but he thought Father McIntyre should be running Apple or Amazon or something similar, that his ukulele playing
and singing of Jim Reeves songs was all a cover and Father Matthew
also thought that Father McIntyre was very ambitious; he thought Father O'Connell should maybe get married–'

'Sorry?'

'I'm just saying, okay?'

'Okay.'

'I'm…God forgive me, I just hope it's useful.'

'Eimear, it's all useful, even stuff you don't think is useful could be
useful to us if we manage to put it in the correct context,' Starrett said,
by way of explanation, 'but can we go back to Father O'Connell for a
moment?'

'Yes,' Eimear said and then offered through a grimace, 'someone
needs to teach Father O'Connell how to keep his rooms a bit tidier.'

'Yes, I suppose you get to see a side of all the priests that no one else
does?'

'Well yes, I suppose.'

'You said that he should be married?' Starrett asked, accepting that
he'd most likely shut down that avenue of gossip, at least for the time
being.

'No, no,' she replied and smiled gently, 'I said that Father Matthew
said he should get married.'

'Right, good, so you did. Sorry about that. And what do you think
he meant?'

'He meant,' she started and then corrected herself with, 'I think he
meant that as Father O'Connell has so many widows as friends, and he
was always being taken out to lunch or dinner by one of them, that perhaps he should consider marrying one of them. I think he was joking
but then again, maybe not really.'

'Are all of his lady friends widows?'

'What, do you mean are some of them currently married?'

'Yes.'

'Well yes, as you've probably noticed from his girth, he does like
to have a full diary for lunches.'

'Okay, sorry I stopped you back there mid-flow; you were going to
tell me what Father Matthew thought about everyone up at St Ernan's?'

'Yes…Father Casey and Father Clerkin are hardly around. They're cousins I hear. Father Casey would be from the modern side of the family. They're always off doing Father Dugan's bidding.

'Father Dugan, I don't think Father Matthew had ever spoken to him. He's a bit of a gas though. He's meant to be this old recluse with his hair down to his knees, but he's always chatting away to me when I'm cleaning his rooms and for an old man he's very well preserved and clean and neat and tidy as a person, even though you couldn't swing a cat in his room with all his books and all his files, but he knows exactly where everything is and doesn't want anything tidied up or moved. I said to him, "Father Dugan," I said, "you should have all your books and papers filed away properly," and he said to me, he said, "Eimear, sure why would I want to do that. I have the best filing system in the world." I said, as I looked around his room, I said, "Really?" And he said, "Really, Fathers Casey and Clerkin know exactly where every last bit of paper is." And then he'd laugh away to himself as he shuffled some papers around or pretended to write.'

'Which leaves…?' Starrett asked when he stopped chuckling.

'Let me see now,' Eimear said, appearing happy for the distraction of trying to recall who she'd left out, 'Fathers Mulligan, McKenzie, and our temporary resident Bishop Cormac Freeman, whom we've already discussed. Apart from what Father Matthew told me, I don't really know much about The Bishop, excepting the fact that I'm not allowed to go into his room.'

'And the other two Fathers – Mulligan and McKenzie?'

'Well, Father Matthew joked that Father Fergus Mulligan's nose was the four master writers' link with the outside world.'

'You're talking about Fathers Dugan, Casey, and Clerkin, and Father Fergus himself?'

'Yes, you've got it. When I went to work there first, I thought I'd never be able to get a handle on all the fathers and their names. I eventually managed to do it, once I'd put them in their rooms, with their looks.'

'And Father McKenzie.'

'Ah the Ginger Beatle,' Eimear said, 'Father Matthew thought that Father Edward McKenzie was a hard worker, but that maybe he was being taken advantage of by Father McIntyre, or Tubsey, as he's called behind his back.'

'Did this cause any resentment from Father McKenzie?'

'I don't believe so. I believe he was happy to work in the garden – he'll tell anyone who'll listen that he's always worked on the land. You'll always find him in the outhouse closest to the garden, pottering away to his heart's content.'

* * *

As Starrett walked through the rough terrain of what would become the garden of the new build, he thought he might have learnt something, but not a lot, from his chat with Eimear. He would discover that his assessment wasn't as accurate as he first guessed and what she hadn't said was as important as what she had.

CHAPTER SEVENTEEN

Sergeant Packie Garvey and Romany Browne – were in constant phone contact with Garda Francis Casey in Ramelton as they tried to pick apart the untold history of Father Gene McCafferty.

Eventually they discovered that he had not been based at St John the Baptist in Cork because, as Casey pointed out, no such cathedral existed. Father McCafferty had, in fact, been serving at St Anne's in Cork.

Before that, Father McCafferty had been serving not at The Assumption of the Blessed Virgin Mary in Ennis because, again, no such cathedral existed. No, Father McCafferty had served at St Peter's in Ennis, which *was* in the Diocese of Killaloe.

So far so good.

Garda Casey's next move was to contact St Anne's Cathedral. The first priest he spoke to seemed interested but he insisted on phoning him back to make sure it was a legit garda call. Casey was growing impatient waiting for the return call and on the verge of believing all priests are corrupt and covering for each other.

When the Cork priest did finally return the call, his first question was, 'Is it true Father Matthew McKaye is dead?'

'Yes,' Casey replied.

He could hear the priest put his hand over the mouth piece on the other end and then he heard some mumbling. There was a bit of electronic noise down the line as the handset sounded like it was changing hands.

'Hello, this is Bishop Madden, how can I help you?' came a clear and English sounding voice.

'Oh, hello Bishop. I'm inquiring about a Father Gene McCafferty; I believe he served with you down at St Anne's before he moved to St Ernan's.'

'Yes, but he was retired to St Ernan's,' Bishop Madden said, sounding as though he was at great pains to clarify the situation.

Casey was about to ask his next question when Bishop Madden spoke again. 'Do you know yet what happened to Father McKaye?'

'At this stage we're looking into it but we're treating it as a suspicious death.'

'And how is Father McCafferty involved?'

'We don't know he is, this is just a routine call,' Casey felt the need to say. 'When one of my colleagues took a statement from Father McCafferty he told us he'd last served at John the Baptist in Cork.'

'I see,' Bishop Madden said, 'and you're sure this wasn't a genuine mistake because...?'

'He also gave us an incorrect cathedral for his Diocese before he served in Cork.'

'Ennis?'

'Correct,' Casey confirmed, 'but he said he was at the Blessed Virgin Mary in Ennis and again, the same situation as with you in Cork, no such cathedral exists.'

'No, of course not, Father McCafferty served at St Peter's.'

'Yes, so we've discovered,' Casey replied. 'Bishop Madden, can you tell me why Father McCafferty left your Diocese?'

'He retired – that's why he went to St Ernan's?'

'Why did he retire?' Casey asked, hoping that if only he asked the correct question the bishop wouldn't fib to him.

'His file is closed, Garda.'

Casey realised this might be the truth so he tried another approach.

'Do you personally know why he had to leave St Anne's?'

The reply took longer this time. Casey heard the phone being put down on the desk, he heard footsteps moving away from the phone and across a wooden floor, a door closing, footsteps back towards the phone and across a wooden floor, the phone being lifted again and then, 'Garda, what is your name again please?'

'I'm Garda Francis Casey.'

'And who is your senior?'

'Inspector Starrett, and he reports to Major Newtown Cunningham,' Casey replied, feeling certain this information was being written down.

'Okay, please sit by your phone and I'll ring you back in exactly ten minutes. If you're not there or your phone is engaged, I will not ring back again.'

Casey felt, hoped really, that he had been correct; Bishop Madden wouldn't volunteer the important information but when asked a direct question, he would not lie.

Twelve minutes later Casey was beginning to think he'd just been taken for a fool and Bishop Madden was busy making calls, helping to hide whatever it was Father McCafferty had been trying to hide with his own misinformation.

Just as Casey was about to ring Garvey's mobile number to get a message to Starrett, the phone on the desk in front of him sprang to life. He grabbed it after the second ring – just in case.

'Garda Casey?'

'Yes,' he confirmed.

'Okay, good. Well, here you have it: we believe that Father McCafferty was in the process of befriending some of the older, single members of our diocese.'

'But wouldn't that be normal?' Casey asked, and immediately realised he'd asked a 'wrong' question.

'Yes, indeed it would,' Bishop Madden replied, actually sounding a little relieved.

'But his befriending had nothing to do with the duties of a priest?'

'Correct,' the bishop replied, this time sounding disappointed.

'He was trying to befriend them so that he could…' Casey said.

He realised at once he sounded just like a man stepping though a conversation as though he was crossing a strange river, never sure of his footing or the stone upon which he might take his next step and even if he did manage to take a successful step, whether or not it would get him into trouble. He couldn't afford to be too hesitant because one wrong footing and he was in the river and the bishop would be free to sail away scot-free through the troubled waters.

'He was trying to befriend the older members of your congregation so they would will their wealth to him?' Casey offered, and crossed his fingers.

'Correct.'

'And not to the Church.'

'Correct,' the bishop replied.

'How did you discover what Father McCafferty was up to?'

'Well, it was very simple. The lady in question rang up to say she was just about to sign the paperwork Father Gene had left her but she wondered, shouldn't the beneficiary be St Anne's and not Father Gene McCafferty himself.'

'Were there other cases?'

'There are none in the file,' the bishop replied, as Casey realised he'd stepped on another sinking stone.

'Were any charges brought against him?' he then asked, hoping he was covering a multitude of sins.

'No.'

'No?' he repeated in disbelief.

'He hadn't actually broken the law.'

'Only because he'd been stopped,' Casey complained.

'Nonetheless, no law had been broken,' the bishop offered, 'besides, it is the Church's way.'

'But who's to say there weren't other times when he'd gotten away with it?'

'That's the difference between the Guards and the Church: you need to catch, punish, and, occasionally, try to prevent; we need to save souls and offer all who seek saving redemption.'

'Perhaps we could both have saved Father Matthew McKaye and no redemption would have been necessary,' Casey offered, and realised he'd most likely inadvertently slipped into the river. He waited for the fireworks.

But Bishop Madden offered only, 'Perhaps,' before hanging up his phone.

CHAPTER EIGHTEEN

The Ennis clergy were just as cautious as Bishop Madden, at St Anne's in Cork, but once they'd verified with Father Robert O'Leary that Sergeant Packie Garvey was who he said he was, they were more willing to offer up their full story on the comings and goings of a certain Father Gene McCafferty. In fact, Father O'Leary had received calls requesting background information on two separate members of Ramelton Garda, within minutes of each other.

In simple language, delivered with a French accent, Father Lepage (he didn't offer his Christian name, and neither did Packie push for it) delivered the following story.

Father Gene McCafferty had been assigned his first post at St Peter's in Ennis. He'd been there for nearly twenty years. It was thought the first years were scandal-free, in that his file for those years contained only praise. Father Lepage felt that McCafferty's fall from grace occurred shortly after he was passed over for a promotion and posting to Rome; McCafferty had been so critical of the successful candidate, he'd blotted his own proverbial copybook for eternity. When that particular penny had dropped, in that he'd realised that he would never rise above his station – in neither God nor his superior's eyes – Father McCafferty had started to plan an alternate pension plan, as it were.

As far as Father Lepage and his colleagues were aware, there were three instances on record of Father McCafferty 'feathering his own nest' at the expense of older, single parishioners.

1. Mrs Susan Harris
2. Mr Max Hall
3. Mr Ralf Clifford

Father Lepage believed, albeit privately, that Father McCafferty had succeeded at going undetected in one, or more, additional swindles. However, his only proof was that McCafferty was clearly living way beyond his (and his Church's) means. Father Lepage had tried to persuade his superiors at St Peter's to seek legal redress against Father McCafferty and freeze - and obtain first call on - any and all of his bank accounts. The Church, obviously feeling the pressure from all the bad press they were getting at the time, denied the request, preferring instead to organise a sideways 'promotion' for the problematic father. Cork was as far away from Ennis as they could get him.

At least for their part, the Diocese of Cork managed to take Father McCafferty out of circulation by putting him out to pasture at St Ernan's, probably, Garvey thought, reasoning that without a congregation, he'd be deprived of the fodder for his trademark swindles.

But had Father McCafferty been up to his old tricks again? And had Father Matthew not only discovered but maybe also caught him in the act?

CHAPTER NINETEEN

Starrett was feeling a bit peckish, so he and Gibson headed into Donegal Town, to the Blueberry Tea Room, to compare notes on the interview with Eimear Robinson. The popular tea room was Starrett's kind of place; it was packed and there was a great buzz about the place. The inspector had meant to go for the soup he'd spotted on another diner's table, but instead opted for a generous slice of carrot cake and a cup of coffee. Gibson had a coffee, but held off on the cake. They were just considering a second coffee and perhaps another wee bit of cake for Starrett when Gibson took a call on her mobile from Sergeant Packie Garvey, advising her of, 'an interesting development on the case'.

Twenty minutes later they were driving over the causeway, back on to St Ernan's. The minute they walked through the back door, Starrett clocked Bishop Cormac Freeman, his bullfrog eyes glaring at Packie Garvey, screaming at the top of his voice that he demanded to be allowed to leave St Ernan's to carry out 'important business for the Church'.

This was not the interesting development that Starrett had been expecting, much less hoping, for.

The ever reasonable and quietly spoken Father Robert O'Leary was finding that his usual sky-writing was having no effect, no effect whatsoever, on the bishop's demeanour. And when the bishop spotted Starrett at the back door, it was like a red rag to a bull and the hissy fit grew all the more preposterous. Starrett couldn't help but laugh at the bishop, the way you would a misbehaving child. This only served to further enrage the clergyman.

'Now you listen here, Starrett,' the bishop screamed, moving right up to the detective, so close he could smell his rancid breath. 'On whose authority are you detaining me?'

Starrett looked the bishop up and down, his disdain all too clear to those in attendance, namely Father O'Leary, Father Pat O'Connell – who had been assisting Father O'Leary in trying to restrain their very own bishop in a china shop – Sergeant Packie Garvey, Garda Romany Browne and Ban Garda Nuala Gibson.

The detective silenced the room, the same kitchen-cum-dining-cum-sitting room in which Father Matthew McKaye had been found dead nearly twenty-four hours earlier.

'I demand to know on whose authority you hold me, Starrett,' Freeman said again, attempting a more measured tone but failing miserably.

'You can call me by my first name if you like,' Starrett said in a calm voice, as though he was the bishop's best friend in the world, and the assembled couldn't hide their shock. All except one, they were oblivious to the fact that the detective even had a first name, let alone what it might be.

'Oh!' Freeman replied, equally surprised and losing his thread for a second, 'and what, pray tell, would your first name be?'

'Inspector,' Starrett replied, immediately and clearly, 'you can call me Inspector.'

The bishop looked to Father O'Leary as if to say 'Now do you see what I mean?'

'Garda Browne, could you please advise Father O'Leary of the instructions I gave you before I left St Ernan's last night?'

'Yes Sir,' Browne quickly answered. 'You told me to stand guard outside the bishop's room all night, and to get Sergeant Garvey to relieve me when necessary.'

'Thank you, Garda Browne,' Starrett continued, in his composed voice. 'And did I say why I wanted you to carry out this duty?'

'For the bishop's own safety, Sir.'

'One final question, Guard; did I at any point instruct you to detain Bishop Freeman?'

'No Sir,' Browne piped up immediately, like he was on the parade ground at the Garda Training School, back in Tipperary.

'But you just told me I couldn't leave my room?' Bishop Freeman said and then pleaded, 'Isn't that correct Father O'Leary?'

'In fairness, Bishop, the garda did say that he'd been instructed to remain outside your door. At no point did he say you had to stay inside.'

The bishop looked from O'Leary to Starrett to Browne to O'Leary and back to Starrett again.

'Oh right, well in that case, I'll be in my rooms,' he declared.

'That will be an excellent arrangement, Bishop,' Starrett started, 'now that your important business for the Church seems to have disappeared, I'd like you to make yourself available to me for questioning this afternoon.'

The bishop went to answer back, possibly even to go ballistic, but something – heavenly, even – seemed to restrain him and instead, he walked past the grand fireplace - the very same ancient fireplace that had been salvaged from the nearby Lough Eske Castle after the castle had been destroyed by the fire of 1938 – and disappeared up the old stair case.

The rest of them gave a great impersonation of a bunch of onlookers, casting aspersions from the beach as a captain launched the boat. All that was missing were their ice cream cones and handkerchief bonnets.

Speaking of important business, it was time to get back to the job in hand. Starrett thanked Fathers O'Leary and O'Connell, made excuses on behalf of the Gardaí team and soon they too passed the historic fireplace and climbed the grand staircase to their rooms above.

CHAPTER TWENTY

From somewhere in the bowels of St Ernan's the ever enterprising Packie Garvey had located a school blackboard, easel, and, believe it or not, a few virgin sticks of chalk. Not just that, but he'd already set it up in the boys' room. Garvey and Browne had rearranged the furniture in the already sparsely furnished main room to set the stage for the upcoming meetings-cum-briefings. Now, the pine dining table sat surrounded by four hard chairs, plus (in mixed styles and colours) two easy chairs and a seriously deflated mini-sofa (probably a Father Pat cast-off). On a separate small coffee table, Garvey had assembled a tea and coffee preparation area, complete with fresh milk and a generous supply of biscuits.

The first order of business was for Garvey and Browne to tell Starrett and Gibson the real reason for their urgent call to Donegal Town, which was to impart the information they'd recently discovered on Father Gene McCafferty.

Starrett was generous with his praise and asked Garvey to remind him to also thank Garda Francis Casey for his sterling work, a fact which seemed to make Gibson very happy.

'Right, let's recap,' the inspector announced, as he took a crisp stick of chalk to wrote 'St Ernan's' at the top left of the blackboard, underlining it with a squiggly wave. Beneath that – pausing every now and again to get the correct spelling or reminders from his daily updated notebook – he wrote, in his distinctive yet readable handwriting:

Fr. Matthew McKaye (deceased)
Fr. McIntyre (gossip, camp, Tubsey, blond, ukulele, Jim Reeves)
Fr. Fergus Mulligan (author of list, old choirboy, solid alibi)
Fr. Robert O'Leary (speaks with fingers, clever, oldest resident)
Fr. Gene McCafferty (thief, Cork & Ennis, elephant-ear elbows, newest res.)
Fr. Edward McKenzie (gardener and Ginger Beatle, farmer)
Fr. Patrick O'Connell (o.weight, ladies' man, snazzy dresser)
Fr. Peter Casey (researcher for Master Writer, V of silence, absent)
Fr. Michael Clerkin (researcher for Master Writer, V of silence, absent)
Fr. Peregrine Dugan (Master Writer, Methuselah, voice of God, in room)
Bishop Cormac Freeman

Then he took a space and added:

Eimear Robinson (St Ernan's housekeeper)
Gerry Robinson (Eimear's husband)
Mary Mooney (Eimear's sister)
Jessica Robinson (Eimear's 18-year-old daughter)
Julia Robinson (Eimear's 16-year-old daughter)

Starrett then made two chalk rectangular boxes and wrote 'Swindle/McCafferty' in one and 'Rare John Hamilton nibs/ Fr. McKaye' in the other. Then he set down the chalk, dusted the remnants from his hands and said, 'So…where do we begin?'

'What's Father Mulligan's solid alibi?' Gibson asked.

'Father O'Leary was looking out through the window of his room and he spotted Father Fergus leave St Ernan's around 3:30 and come back in again just after the 5:30 traffic report," Starrett replied as he drew a thick line through Father Fergus' name. "That's good enough for me. So, where do we begin?"

'Father McCafferty?' Browne offered.

'Yes,' Starrett agreed. 'We can't deny the potential motive developing.'

'I'd like to talk to Eimear's daughters,' Nuala Gibson volunteered.

'You know, they're closer in age to Father Matthew and if, as Eimear said, he was always around the Robinsons' house they might have been in a better position to pick up stuff the mother didn't.'

'Good. Good,' Starrett grunted. 'Maybe we should also include Eimear's sister as well at this stage – she seemed to be around the Robinson house a lot.'

'And should we really accept that the two "missing" writers-slash-researchers, Fathers Casey and Clerkin, *were* indeed missing yesterday?'

'Fair play to you, Packie,' Starrett said, rubbing his hands.

'You know, they could have pretended to leave on Tuesday, snuck into the house yesterday afternoon, murdered Father Matthew, snuck out again and disappeared to do the research?' Garvey continued. 'Do we know how he was actually murdered yet?'

'Dr Aljoe is still trying to figure that one out,' Starrett offered. He wasn't exactly lying but, at the same time, not exactly telling the whole truth. It wasn't that he didn't want his team to find out the exact details – he didn't even know the exact details yet – no, it was more that he didn't even want the subject discussed while they were in St Ernan's.

'Francis could track them down?' Gibson offered, betraying her distraction.

'Good idea, Ban Garda, and also get him to check on the world-wide web thingy for John Hamilton's pen nibs. See if he can find out for us how much they'd be worth?'

Gibson made a note to herself to instruct Francis accordingly.

'Okay,' Starrett said, 'now we have this new info on McCafferty, I'd like to have another chat with Father O'Leary on that subject – maybe he'll be a bit more forthcoming this time. Perhaps they all will.'

He circulated the chalk around between his fingers for a few seconds, using only one hand – the one with the permanently crooked finger – as he continued to stare at the names he'd written on the blackboard. He realised this was fast turning into one of those cases where the more you discovered, the more you didn't know.

Then an idea struck him.

'Packie,' he said, 'does anyone in St Ernan's know you requisitioned this blackboard?'

'I would imagine someone would have seen or heard me getting it up the stairs?' Garvey said.

'Yeah, you're right. Please, give us a hand here,' Starrett said and gestured to the blackboard and the main window on the other side of the room.

The two men hauled both blackboard and easel closer to the window, in fact so close that the tilted top nearly touched the wall. When the inspector had it in position, he moved to one side of the board, gripped it and instructed Packie to so the same, and together they flipped it over so that the clean side of the board was visible in the room. Starrett got the chalk again and wrote Father Matthew's full name and estimated time of death in one box. He finished it off by adding 'Potato Experiment'. In a second box he wrote 'Father Clerkin & Bishop Freeman', and, in a third, 'high tide and causeway'. Then he drew a wee boat and two men at the bottom right of the blackboard in some rippling circles and dusted his hands once more, satisfied with at least part of his morning's work.

CHAPTER TWENTY-ONE

Starrett couldn't be sure, but when he and Garda Romany Browne next visited Father Gene McCafferty in his room – next-door-but-one to the boys' room in which they'd just finished their meeting– the priest with the apparent desire for inclusion in the wills of Donegal's aged congregation was visibly tipsy.

Admittedly, the sun wasn't at its lunchtime high, but not exactly long since.

Father Gene McCafferty had his hands deep in his pockets, elbows flying wide and perpetually flapping like wings but, just like chicken wings, they never threatened to raise the subject from the floor. In fact, the priest seemed to have an aversion to the wooden floor; he looked as though it was either too hot for his soles or he was scared it was going to give way under him. In addition to all of this, he seemed to be having great difficulty retaining his balance.

'You know, I find that balance is all about confidence,' Starrett said, as he walked over to the priest and helped him back into his chair. 'Really, you know, the human body should not be able to move by the process of walking. We should all really fall over between each step – look at how thin our ankles are and how much weight they carry. But, as I say, the secret is that our confidence, and our natural momentum, not only keep us going but also keep us going in the re-quired vertical position.'

If Father Gene McCafferty was unsteady of foot, this was not the case with his mouth or his mind; he was mentally prepared for his meeting with Starrett and now that he was seated – tethered, albeit in-directly, to terra firma – his physical momentum had caught up.

Well, that was no doubt what he was hoping for, but if the opened bottle of poteen on his untidy table and his Buddy Holly glasses cranked on the bridge of his nose at a 120-degree angle were anything to go by, his brain was not orchestrating his body ballet to the full potential. Or, as Starrett succinctly put it, to himself mind you, 'The man's stocious, as pissed as a parrot!' Not that Starrett had ever seen a pissed parrot, which made him wonder, but only for a split second, where such a saying had originated.

Father McCafferty would have been well within his rights to cry foul, admit to his intoxication and request that the interview be conducted at a later date. But he did none of the above. Equally, Starrett realised that any information he did manage to obtain in the interview would not, or could not, be used in a court of law. But with the priest's guard down, information might flow freely and, at this stage, Starrett was hoping for a river.

'Why don't you and I just have a wee chat for now?' he started, nodding at Browne to put his pen and notebook away. 'We can do the interview when you're...well, we can do it at a later date.'

McCafferty gave one of his signature fade-out laughs. 'How should I put this?' he started off, steady enough.

Starrett waited some seconds for the priest to continue and eventually he did.

'No, I meant "How should I put this?" It was a question.'

'Oh, right I see,' Starrett smiled, 'I'd say, honestly.'

The priest stood up, looked in the mirror and straightened his glasses just in time before he fell back into his seat.

'Ehm, I don't think we need to worry about this now–' Starrett started.

'How should I put this?' This time the father did follow through with his thread. 'People need to worry, Inspector. Of course, people worry about stuff all the time, and it's good for them.'

'Really?'

'Yes, Inspector. They worry about their jobs, their health, their family, their money, their love...'

'Their love?' Starrett interrupted.

'Yes, Inspector. How should I put this? Yes, everyone needs to love.'

Starrett raised an eyebrow but decided to park the 'love' issue there for now.

'They also need to worry about their cars, their mortgage,' Father Gene continued, 'their kids' schooling, and then it all eventually starts over again when their kids grow up to have worries of their own. And the parents let their kids take up the worrying mantle.'

'Bejeepers, Father, that's a Hel...that's a heck of a lot of worrying,' Starrett offered.

'It sure is, Inspector.'

'And so tell me this, Father; when all of that's been resolved and they leave their kids to their own worries, then what do they worry about?'

'When, and if, they get through all of the above they are in grave danger of entering the "happy ever after phase", and they avoid that by sitting down and starting to worry about being run over by a dou-ble-decker bus.'

Starrett couldn't help it, he had to laugh at that. In his mind the de-tective kept going back to the priest's statement of everyone needing love. He began re-running his own emotions from around the time he'd considered joining the priesthood. Perhaps he'd been running away from love, the love for and of Maggie Keane? On the same night that he took her love for the first time, he'd already had a plan in place to leave the town and Maggie Keane the following morning. Since then, he'd never been able to come to terms with how he'd reacted to his feelings. He'd never even known before that night – all those times he'd acted like a cad – that he was capable of having such feelings. He'd never even believed it possible for a human being to act in a way that was so foreign to his or her own principles. And yet, he had done just that. And, while he accepted that his crime was merely a crime of the heart, could more serious crimes – maybe even murder – come from such a seed, planted way, way deep within a person's DNA? Star-rett was thinking about a seed that its host is not even aware of, let alone suspect that someday it might rise up and override one's in-stincts, with no respect whatsoever for its owner?

He thought of Bishop Cormac Freeman, but banished the thought immediately, unable to deal with its implications. He knew being un-able to deal with it must have something to do with the fact that he himself had a son, a son borne from the fruits of that initial night with Maggie Keane, that night when the needs of the seed within overrode, totally ignored, his undeclared plans.

He also accepted that he was wrong to continue this particular chat with Father Gene McCafferty, no matter how unofficial it was, no mat-ter that he would never want to, or be allowed to, use it as evidence. It would appear that Father McCafferty had been involved in taking advantage of the elderly, that much was true. Whatever that made him, the priest himself did not deserve to be treated with ill grace. And no matter how much Starrett might have right on his side when it came to dealing with Father McCafferty, due to his methods, he would be no better than the priest should he continue.

'I think, Father, that we need to leave this until you are in a better position to speak for yourself,' Starrett declared, as Romany Browne's mouth dropped open in shock.

Starrett arose, took up his conscience and walked. He was followed shortly thereafter by his shocked, but equally impressed, younger colleague.

'I think,' he continued to the bemused looking priest, 'that you should find one of your fellow priests and spend a couple of hours with a coffee pot and then we'll reconvene for a formal interview with one of the other priests in attendance.'

'With a priest you say,' Father McCafferty spluttered, 'ehm…how should I put this. Well, let's just say you should never put your trust in any one of us. Ehm…how should I put this, well let's just say priests, sure we're all the same: our dog-collar does not equal divinity. For instance, in here, in St Ernan's, I'm sure we have a gambler, at least one womaniser, a thief, a capitalist, a relative of Joe Kennedy, and a trio who are just too good to be true – God only knows what they're up to. And while we're on that particular subject, please tell me this, Inspector: Who pays their bills when they're away doing their research? Their fancy hotels and their travel and their per diems? Pray do tell me who pays for all of that, Inspector Starrett?'

CHAPTER TWENTY-TWO

Starrett was annoyed that the interviews seemed to be throwing up more questions than answers. Though he wasn't overly concerned. It was really just a matter of chipping away at that mountain of mystery and eventually – well, eventually assuming of course that they were tackling the correct mountain – it would crumble. Perhaps, though, they were going to require more assistance from Gabriel's Horns than what had been was necessary to bring down the walls of Jericho.

'So, tell me this,' Starrett began, as he sat down with Father Robert O'Leary in the elder priest's rooms ten minutes later. 'In St Ernan's, just who is the gambler?'

Father O'Leary looked over at Starrett from his coffee preparation routine, surprised enough by the question to pause in his endeavours.

'Thank you, thank you, thank you Father Gene McCafferty,' Starrett said under his breath.

'It's a gambler you're after now, is it?' Father O'Leary asked, momentary lapse of concentration gone as he continued to make the coffee.

'Well,' Starrett began, as he helped to carry cups, saucers, milk, coffee pot, spoon, sugar, and a packet of boring Rich Tea biscuits over to the priest's dining area, 'I've a few other catagories on my shopping list but unlike Maggie, my girlfriend, who can happily divert to another product, picking up her provisions as she passes Whoriskey's shelves, I need to collect everything in the order it appears on my list.'

'Right,' Father O'Leary said as he smiled, looking as though he'd regained his footing and his ability to air-write. 'Well, here's what I'd like to do, Starrett – I'll give you one guess and if you guess correctly I promise I'll confirm it for you but, if you guess incorrectly, we'll move on and you'll just have to discover the answer for yourself. Okay?'

'Seems fair, this way it won't be like you betrayed them?'

Father O'Leary neither confirmed nor denied the detective's assumption. He merely waited for the name.

'Okay,' Starrett said, 'I'd say that that our gambler is…' He paused and concentrated on Father O'Leary, the way The X Factor audience would a contestant waiting under the glaring spotlight to discover whether they'd been dumped from the show or made it through to the next round. In truth, the suspense was more imagined on his part, as the priest happily nibbled away on his second Rich Tea biscuit.

'…is Father…Pat O'Connell.'

Father O'Leary did not vocally acknowledge the admiration evident in his eyes. Rather he signed a tick with the forefinger and thumb of his right hand as if he had a pen between them.

'Are we talking of a serious gambling habit here or…' Starrett started when it became clear that the priest wasn't willingly going to betray his fellow priest any further.

'That wouldn't be for me to say,' the father claimed, 'however, if I was a detective, I'd be tempted to visit some of the bookies in Donegal Town. I'm sure they'd be much better equipped to answer such a question.'

Before Starrett had a chance to offer his sincere thanks, the priest continued, continuing with his rather amusing air-writing, 'and, ah, as it looks like it's going to be a sunny day, I'd most likely stay within the shadows of the castle tower if I were you.'

Starrett didn't want to chance his arm guessing the identity of any other souls on Father McCafferty's Judas list because, at this stage, they would be exactly that: guesses, and to continue to keep Father O'Leary's vital confidence, he'd need to get that air-tick every time. Although in one way he didn't mind: the more he got to speak with O'Leary and witness his unusual habit, the more he believed he could decipher the words from the signs, so visually arresting were they. He also (sadly) accepted the fact that should the spoken word not be present, the reality was that he wouldn't have the faintest clue what the priest was going on about.

CHAPTER TWENTY-THREE

Garda Romany Browne was quite excited to be on his first bit of solo detective work. The Potato Fork Test didn't really count. In his book – there was no initiative involved in that; he'd been told what to do and he'd done it. He didn't at all mind doing what Inspector Starrett asked of him; in fact, he found the inspector to be just like his mentor, Major Newton Cunningham, had said he would be: quirky; honest; bright; funny; fair; a team man; a great friend to have on your side in times of trouble and, on top of all of that, the best detective 'not just in the county', the Major had declared, 'but on the island of Ireland'.

Since the Major had been a true friend to his dearly departed father, remained a good friend to his mother and had been the only constant male presence in his young life so far, Browne had trusted the Major's assessment. Admittedly, it had taken a bit of time, but his boss finally seemed to be accepting him as a member of the team.

And he was also surprised by just how much he was enjoying the work. He hadn't thought much of the Major's suggestion that he join An Garda Síochána. Possibly early on he'd written off a career in any job that involved wearing a uniform after he'd witnessed how his mother had cried over that man in the uniform in the well-worn photograph. That man, she'd eventually explained to him, when she thought he was old enough, who was his father. That man, who had gone off to Cyprus with the Royal Ulster Rifles in order to protect his country and fellow men, and had never returned. 'But he might come back someday, Mam,' he'd naively offered, more in hopes of sparing her further tears. Eventually she had explained why his father would never return.

Browne had no memories whatsoever of his father, apart from the image on that well-worn photograph, but he remembered not being as resentful as he later thought he should have been when his mam started to 'spend quality time with other men'. He'd often wondered whether Starrett had ever gotten to 'spend quality time' with his mother, to the point where the Major had assured him that that just wasn't Starrett's style. 'Apart from which,' he'd said, 'Starrett has unresolved romantic issues with someone out on the Shore Road.'

Browne knew exactly what he meant: the 'unresolved romantic issues out on the Shore Road' involved a certain Maggie Keane, and Browne could see why his superior was so preoccupied with her. Besides, he was happy with both of Starrett's preoccupations: the first being crime solving, because Starrett was great at it and was an even better teacher, and the second being Maggie Keane because, pure and simple, it left him with a chance – a very slim chance, that much he knew – with the most beautiful creature he'd ever set eyes on: Dr Samantha Aljoe. But sadly, the pathologist seemed almost to swoon every time she came into contact with Starrett. At least her constant flirting with Starrett afforded him the chance to get to know her, more than he would under normal circumstance. And perhaps, if he played his cards right, it might also serve for her to get to know him better, and then someday maybe, just maybe, he might find himself in a position where he could ask her out.

Such were the pleasant thoughts that passed through his mind as he pedalled his way into Donegal Town on a bicycle he'd managed to borrow from Father McKenzie, who had insisted on personally fetching it from one of the ancient outhouses set between St Ernan's house and the island's treeline.

His task – in solo capacity, of course – was to find a bookie within the shadows of the castle tower, just as Father O'Leary had advised Starrett, and just as Starrett had passed on to him. Once he found the establishment in question, he was to enquire about their dealings with a certain Father Patrick O'Connell. Yes, O'Connell – the one who considered himself a bit of a ladies' man, the one he'd caught ogling Dr Samantha Aljoe on more than one occasion. Even so, surely there wasn't a man in the whole of Ireland less suited to the beautiful doctor than the purple-handed, grossly-overweight priest?

He turned his attention back to his detective work just in time to realise that he was hitting Donegal Town in the best weather – in the autumnal sunlight – to witness the shadows created by the castle tower. But as noon was fast approaching and the weak sun would move directly overhead, those shadows would become thin on the ground, not to mention insipid.

As luck would have it, there was but one bookmaker, EasiBet, within the shadows of the castle that autumn morning. Browne chained the bicycle, as instructed – and twice more reminded – by ginger-haired (and bearded) Father McKenzie. 'What does he care?' Browne wondered aloud, as he closed the clasp on the lock.

The bookies was a-buzz with excitement, as a dozen or so customers cheered at a TV screen broadcasting a horse race from somewhere or other, while two girls behind a safety grill busied themselves with paperwork. They looked up only briefly as he darkened their door. There's nothing like making a good impression, and that was nothing like a good impression, he thought, remembering one of Starrett's favourite sayings. But when the two of them glanced up again from their work, they became far more interested once they'd looked beyond the gardaí uniform.

Browne approached the older, more subtly made-up girl – again, a trick he thought he clocked Starrett use – and made his pitch to her.

'Good day,' he said, hearing in his voice a lack of confidence that he certainly didn't feel, 'I'm wondering if I could talk to you about one of your customers.'

'Oh, you'll want Mal, in the back office,' she offered sweetly, as a big cheer went up from the majority of the customers glued to the TV screen.

She swivelled her seat around so her back was to him, made a big drama of hopping off it and swaggered off towards a door. At least, that's how he saw her walk – his problem now was that he couldn't help but compare all girls to the graceful Dr Aljoe. The bookmaker's assistant disappeared behind the door and a minute later she appeared at another door in the shop, to Browne's right, and waved to him to follow her through it.

She introduced Browne to 'My boss, Mal' and swaggered off back to her highchair, whereupon Browne realised that her exaggerated walk was solely for the benefit of her boss.

'Aye right,' Mal said, barely looking up from his desk, 'and what can I do for you?'

'I'm Garda Romany Browne and I'd like to ask you a few questions about one of your customers.'

'Ask away,' Mal said, putting his pen down for the first time.

'Yes, the customer in question is Father Patrick O'Connell.'

'Aye right,' Mal said, 'yes, Father Pat. Now, you're not here to tell me he's the priest who was found dead over on St Ernan's, are you?'

'No, no,' Browne assured him, 'Father O'Connell is very much alive.'

'Aye right.'

'But I understand he owes you some money?'

'Aye, me and a few others, I reckon.'

'Really?' Browne said, involuntarily.

'Well, I can't tell you about the others – they're no concern of mine,' Mal said, taking a large leather-bound ledger out of the central desk drawer he'd just unlocked. He fast-flicked through the pages and then flicked through again, somewhat slower the second time. 'Yeah, here he is.'

Browne waited, and waited, as Mal slowly read down the page.

'Holy crap!' he shouted. 'I didn't realise…he must have been in again at the weekend.'

'How much does he owe?' Browne asked, growing impatient.

'I'll tell you that when you tell me what the Guards are going to do to help me get it paid.'

'You've the courts for that,' Browne offered and pulled out his notebook. 'What's the amount please?'

Mal remained silent, visibly in shock.

'How do you normally collect on bad debts?' Browne asked, gambling that the bookie, in his moment of shock, might be indiscreet.

Mal ignored the second question as he got around to answering the first, 'He owes us 17,651 euro!'

* * *

'Bejeepers,' Starrett gasped when Browne relayed this to him thirty minutes later in their temporary base in St Ernan's, '17,651 euro! How the feck does a priest run up a debt like that with a bookie?'

'Well, Mal said that he was only at nine grand–'

'Only at nine grand?' Starrett hissed. 'Since when is nine grand classed as "only?"'

'He was at nine grand, apparently,' Browne continued, 'and then, to try and get himself out of trouble, he laid on a lot of other bets, usually with different members of staff, which weren't marked to his account until they matured, meaning apparently he never reached the cut-off point of 10,000 euro.'

'Good to know they actually have a cut-off point,' Starrett moaned.

'He reckoned Father O'Connell played the odds "hoping, maybe even praying", were Mal's exact words, that the father would win at least one of his bets – they were all at high odds, you see – and that he'd cover all of his outstanding debts with one win, and maybe even have another one or two wins to keep him in–'

'…more money for gambling,' Starrett offered, closing down the topic. 'Good work, Garda.'

Starrett noted that, whereas some people – Packie Garvey, for instance – were uncomfortable taking compliments, others, such as Romany Browne, positively thrived on them.

'So how might his gambling be connected to the death of Father Matthew?' the aforementioned Packie Garvey asked.

'Well, what if the Hokey Cokey isn't what it's all about?' Starrett offered.

'Sorry?'

'What if it's just random? What if Father Pat O'Connell realised the trouble he was in, due to losing all that money on the gee-gees, and large lumps of the proverbial were just about to hit the spinning blades of the fan big time. So, perhaps he thinks if he can just find a way of creating a diversion, he could somehow find his way through the immediate patch of trouble, giving him a bit of breathing space so he could find another way of solving his problem?'

'You mean by murdering a fellow priest?' Sgt Packie Garvey offered. 'I don't think so.'

Browne looked like he was in line with Garvey but didn't want to go as far as vocally disagreeing with his superior.

'Okay, okay,' Starrett said, nodding to his sergeant and even appearing happy that his sergeant disagreed with him. 'Maybe you're right. But how about this; what if Father O'Connell was aware of the rare John Hamilton nibs hidden in the desk in Father Matthew's rooms? Maybe he'd discovered just how rare they were and he nicked the nibs in hopes they would pay off some, if not all, of his gambling debts.'

'That approach works better for me,' Garvey admitted.

'And then Father Matthew discovers the nibs are missing and he confronts Father Pat about them. Father Pat thinks the game is up un-less he gets rid of Father Matthew,' Starrett said, developing his theory but all the while never quite sounding like he'd totally committed to it.

Romany Browne made to say something, but Starrett unknow-ingly cut him off with, 'Before we go any further down this road I have two questions for ye: one, shouldn't we find out exactly what the nibs are worth? I'm with you, Packie, but I'm having great diffi-culty accepting that these nibs are worthy dying over. Two, could someone remind me what Father Pat was doing at the time Father Matthew was murdered?'

The ever trustworthy Sergeant Packie Garvey withdrew his note-book from deep inside his jacket, licked his forefinger and flicked through a few pages before announcing: 'He'd lunch with a Miss Ed-wina Uppleby, apparently a woman of independent means. She picked him up shortly after noon yesterday, outside the Craft Village shop, on the road to Ballyshannon. They had lunch at the Lough Eske Castle. They left the castle at 5:15, she dropped him off at the Abbey Hotel in Donegal Town where he ran into an old friend, they'd a drink, then he caught a taxi back and arrived here at 7:40 p.m.'

'Should be easy enough to check all that out,' Starrett said, to no one in particular. 'But, in theory, he could have had a quicker lunch than he claimed in order to establish his alibi; rushed back here to St Ernan's, murdered Father Matthew, nipped back into Donegal Town, "ran into" met up with his old friend – all just to re-establish his alibi, you understand – and then returned to St Ernan's.'

Yes, Starrett mused to himself, Father Pat O'Connell deserved the several lines of chalk he'd scratched under his name on the blackboard.

CHAPTER TWENTY-FOUR

Starrett sent Romany and Packie off to 'see a man about a horse'. And, as luck would have it, that very same man was resting in his rooms at the moment two members of the Ramelton Serious Crimes Unit of the Gardaí came calling.

'Oh, it's the boys in uniform,' Father Pat O'Connell said, as he rose from his chair and waddled over towards the door to invite the Gardaí officers into his room. For some reason or other he put his suit jacket on. 'Come on in. How's the case progressing?'

Packie thought there was a distinct whiff in the air; the whiff of an older man who didn't shower as much as he needed to. Perhaps, Packie guessed, that had been the reason for the priest putting on his jacket, particularly in a room that was already quite warm. The priest finger-combed his blue-black hair, but not to great effect.

'We're just collecting information.'

'What, no Ban Garda this time?' O'Connell offered, visibly upset, as the three men took seats at each apex of a triangle centred on a square, dark-blue patterned carpet.

'Not this time, no,' Packie volunteered, 'she's off with Inspector Starrett. Ehm, look…our investigation has thrown up a few more questions we'd like to ask you.'

'A few more questions is it?' the priest puffed. 'Fire away then!'

'It's come to our attention that you've got quite a slate going at EasiBet in Donegal Town?' Packie began, as Browne started writing in his notebook.

Father Pat looked indignant, distressed, annoyed, and then indignant again.

'I'm not sure what business that is of yours, Sir,' he said, shifting his large frame in his deflated seat, in the hope of finding a more comfortable position.

'Well, 17,000 odd euro is a lot of money to be in hock to your bookie for.'

'But hardly a criminal offence.'

'But with certain bookies it most certainly could be potentially detrimental to your health,' Packie said, sounding as considerate as he knew how to be.

'In my case,' the priest said, patting his protruding tummy with his purple and rough-skinned hand, 'they'll have to join the queue.'

'I must say that considering the size of your debt you seem re-markably relaxed about it.'

'As I said, I'm not breaking any laws.'

'But Father, you're a priest – we don't expect our priests to be gam-blers…to be…' Packie was going to leave it there but the obvious con-cern on his face was not going to allow it. 'Father, shouldn't you be an example to the community?' was the politest way he could find of dig-ging himself out of the hole.

'Should I be an example for the community?'

'Well, yes,' Packie said, slowly shaking his head in a disapproving way.

'Well, some might say that my time in the front-line of the Church's many battles would mean I deserve to be part of the community that I'd once taken care of, and now it is the community's turn to take care of me. I say, what do you say to that then?'

Packie was still shaking his head, but now he was smiling, trying to find a way to look less disapproving. 'Father Pat, all joking aside, 17 grand – that's a lot of money. That's a lot of money in anyone's book. What are you doing about paying it off?'

'What am I doing about paying it off, is it?'

'Yes.'

'And pray tell me, what business would that be of the Gardaí?'

Packie wondered how long it had been since the priest had last prayed, a thought he kept to himself as he ignored the question, choos-ing instead to ask, 'Have you ever had a debt to a bookie that high be-fore?'

'I…I just…' Father Pat started and then appeared to think better of where he was going to go with his answer, maybe even deciding to change tack altogether, Packie figured. 'Look, of course I've run up bills with my bookies before, but if you take it across the year, I'm al-ways, but always, ahead.'

'So you've been in hock to your bookie for over 17 grand before?' Packie asked, in disbelief.

'Well maybe not quite so high,' Father Pat chuckled, like a naughty ballooned version of Billy Bunter. 'But I repeat my earlier fact: taken across the year, I'm always up.'

'What's the most you've ever won on a horse?' Browne asked.

'What's the most I've ever won on a horse?' Father O'Connell said, his interest most definitely peaking. 'On a single horse or on an accumulative bet?'

'Both,' Browne replied immediately.

'Well, on one horse…the best I've ever done would be when I won four grand plus change. It was Cheltenham, St Patrick's Day, 2005. The horse was Another Rum, running at 40 to 1. Well, I just had to put a ton on the nose on that, didn't I? Then earlier this year, in January, I'd a handy wee accumulator and won thirteen grand on a one-euro stake.'

'You're kidding us?' Browne said, eyebrows rising in apparent disbelief.

'Please believe me, Sir, I most certainly am not kidding. First off there was Eye Of The Tiger at Lingfield. It was an evens favourite. The night before, it was 20 to 1,' the gambling priest offered, regretfully. 'Then there was Seven Summits at Catterick, that was at 7 to 4. The next one was Indus Valley at Kempton – that too was 20 to 1 the night before the race but by the time I placed my bet, it was down to 4 to 6, and then the final one of my fab quartet was Low Key, the 7 to 4 favourite, also at Kempton.'

'So how did you know which four to pick?' Browne asked.

Packie Garvey didn't know if the young guard was trying to stroke the priest's ego to get him talking or hr genuinely wanted to know. Either way, it worked.

'So how did I know which four?' Father Pat said, licking his lips voraciously. 'Well you pick up whispers, don't you. Word was that the betting activity started on some of these horses the night before the races. Then when you studied the form, you discovered that Eye Of The Tiger hadn't run for the best part of a year and a half, Indus Valley hadn't run for nearly two years and Low Key had last run in February 2013 – nearly a year before – and none of them had been showing great form. So clearly there was some kind of…something…behind the buzz. All four horses enjoyed some kind of current, or historical, link – directly or indirectly – to a former trainer by the name of Barney Curley. And a single euro bet, I mean, there's really no downside. I'll take a punt like that most times I go into the bookies. All you really need is for one, just one, of them to turn up trumps.'

'Was it all legit?' Browne asked.

'Well, I believe the stewards made comprehensive inquiries but everything must have been above board because I collected my winnings.'

'And tell me this, Father,' Garvey started, back in the driving seat again. 'In your career how many handy wee accumulator wins would you have had?'

'Three!' he replied immediately.

'So, do you see where we're going with this?'

'Ah yes, indeed I do, Packie, you're much quicker on the hurling field than you are at this auld questioning lark.'

'That's as may be,' Packie laughed, and refused to take the obvious cheap shot back at the priest, 'but either way, we're looking at a good bit of betting before you win that 17 grand back again and goodness knows how high your debt will rise before the wins start to emerge again.'

'You need a steady hand,' Father Pat cautioned the Gardaí, 'to guide you through troubled waters.'

Packie thought it was incredulous just how unbelievably blasé Father Patrick O'Connell was about his gambling – he was a priest, for heaven's sake! If he was a family man with a gambling problem he'd be at his wits end about where he'd find the money to pay off his debts. But here was this man of the cloth, a supposed example for the community in troubled times, and not only was he in debt to the tune of over 17 grand, he'd also admitted to having numerous affairs. And to top that, if that needed topping, he was acting as if he didn't give a shit.

'What recourse do EasiBet have against you?' Packie asked.

'What recourse do they have? How do you mean?'

'How do they get their money back?'

Father Pat raised the palms of both hands to the heavens in a 'Who knows?', if not a 'Who cares?' shrug.

'Do you think they could get you through the courts?' Packie asked, crossing the border from annoyance to amusement at the priest's attitude.

'As I said earlier,' he chuckled, 'they'd have to join the queue.'

'What, you were being serious?' Browne chipped in. 'You owe other people money?'

'No, most certainly not!' the priest snapped back. 'I just meant, with the state of the country, they're going to have to wait in the queue to get me into the courts.'

Again the priest shrugged, this time topping it with a smirk before continuing, 'And so they take me to court, what then? They win and get access to all my worldly possessions? Hey,' he said. He stood up cumbersomely, raised his palms up to the heavens again, turned around twice and said, through a laugh, 'they're welcome. This is it. You see what I stand up in? This is what I have to show for my life. Absolutely nothing. It's theirs. If they want to give me more credit on my account they can have it all now.'

'Are you aware of the John Hamilton nibs?' Packie asked, as the priest awkwardly sat down again.

'Am I aware of the Hamilton nibs?' Father Pat echoed, seeming relieved that the EasiBet questioning was behind him. 'You mean, the jewel in St Ernan's crown?'

'Yes.'

'Yes, of course I am. Everyone in the county is.'

'Do you know how muck they're worth?'

'I've been told they're not worth much more than 7,500 euro,' he replied in a whisper, as if he didn't want anyone to overhear that the nibs were most certainly not significant jewels in anyone's crown.

'Do you know where they're kept?'

'Do I know where they're kept? The Hamilton nibs?' The priest eyeballed Packie suspiciously. 'Funny you should ask me that question – Bishop Freeman asked me the same question, not more than a week ago.'

'And did you know the answer?'

'I told him exactly what I'm now telling you; I haven't a clue where John Hamilton's nibs are.'

CHAPTER TWENTY-FIVE

Meanwhile Inspector Starrett and Ban Garda Nuala Gibson were paying a visit to Father Gene McCafferty, the priest with the Buddy Holly glasses and the nickname, thanks to his flapping elbows, of Elephant Man. Starrett felt they now had enough evidence to confront the priest about the real reason he was moved 'sideways' from his previous two dioceses. The thing that troubled Starrett most about Father McCafferty was why he would tell two such obviously transparent lies. Could he really believe that the gardaí would refrain from, at the very least, doing a background check on the information he'd given them during the first interview? Surely the priest must realise that if he'd just given them the correct information in the first place, they'd have looked no further when they checked with the two cathedrals? Was he such an unsuitable priest that he thought the cathedrals' clergy would have greeted the gardaí with, 'Father McCafferty? You're checking up on Father McCafferty, are you? Well, let us tell you a thing or two about his dealings.' And then spill the beans?

Problem number one, Father McCafferty was not in either of his rooms. Problem number two, Starrett and Gibson – now assisted by the ever-helpful, not to mention broken-voiced, Father Fergus Mulligan – could not find Father McCafferty anywhere in St Ernan's house. Problem three, the same trio, the ranks of which had been swelled to a quintet with the arrival of Sergeant Packie Garvey and Garda Romany Browne, fresh from their recent interview with the larger than life Father Patrick O'Connell, couldn't find Father McCafferty anywhere on St Ernan's the island.

So, when McCafferty had lied to them about his past service, had escape been the end game? If the detective was concerned about this development, he didn't show it. He merely had Garvey contact Garda Francis Casey and have him put out an All-Points Bulletin (APB) on the missing member of the clergy. Then he announced to his team, in their temporary Operations Room on the first floor of St Ernan's, 'Okay, what next?'

'I think we need to pay another visit to the Robinson house, this time to have a chat with the rest of Eimear's family,' Gibson offered.

'Yes, the husband and the two daughters? What are the names of the two daughters? Don't tell me now, wait a minute…yes, she called them after two American actresses. What was it? Roberts, yes, Julia Roberts. Right, one of them was called Julia and the other one…wasn't she named after something Streep?'

'Meryl?' Browne offered helpfully.

'No, that wasn't it,' Starrett replied, deep in concentration.

Nuala Gibson went to make a suggestion.

'No, no, please don't help me, not even a clue,' Starrett protested. 'I nearly had it there, yes Lange, Meryl Lange? No…wait a second…Jessica, that's it Jessica Lange, or in our case, Jessica Robinson,' Starrett proudly announced.

He shouldn't have been too proud about remembering the names by heart, if only because Gibson had them written down in her notebook, along with the mother's, Eimear, and the father's, Gerry.

All well and good, but there was a fourth problem, potentially, and the biggest of them all: They couldn't for the life of them find the bishop with the bullfrog eyes. Starrett issued orders for another APB. Were the two disappearances connected? And if so, why? What was the link between Bishop Freeman and Father McCafferty? What did either, or both, of them have to do with the death of Father Matthew McKaye? Had Father Matthew discovered that Father McCafferty was up to his old tricks again? Had he found another widow to fleece? Had Father Matthew discovered this and was threatening to tell the Gardaí? Was Bishop Freeman involved and if so, how? Had the bishop made a pass at Father Matthew and if so, had Father McCafferty discovered it, and had he been blackmailing the bishop to force him into helping him stop Father Matthew from going to the Gardaí? Bejeepers, Starrett thought (thanks to Maggie Keane's daughter, he rarely allowed himself to say the word out loud these days), yes, bejeepers, could that really be it? Could that really be the motive for Father Matthew's murder?

Now he'd gotten himself on to the subject, how exactly was Father Matthew murdered? Dr Aljoe still hadn't figured out the riddle of the magic bullet and the mysterious missing exit wound. So, not only had he a murderer to find but he also needed to work out how the priest was murdered in the first place. He felt like another chat with Father Robert O'Leary, although he realised he didn't have enough new information for that. But when he did have, when he'd finally found the keys to this mystery, Father O'Leary would most certainly help him open all the doors.

* * *

Starrett knew time was fast running out on his second day on the case and he had too many things he needed to do before the day was as much a part of history as Father Matthew now was. He and Gibson needed to get to Eimear Robinson's house by six o'clock-ish, which is when Starrett thought the entire family might be gathered for their dinner. It would be the perfect time to interview the rest of Eimear's brood, as mother hen would be preoccupied with the evening meal. He also needed to visit Major Newton Cunningham before getting back to his own evening meal with Maggie Keane and her two daughters, Moya and Katie.

However, he still had something he needed to do before he addressed any of that.

When he, the various members of his team and Father Mulligan had been out searching the grounds for Father McCafferty, one of the places he'd checked was the closest stone outhouse to the main house. It seemed to be the domain of Father McKenzie, the supposed Ginger Beatle. Starrett still didn't get the Beatle connection. Okay, so the father was ginger haired (and ginger bearded) all right, but his hair most certainly wasn't styled after the Fab Four in their heyday. Surely Ginger Farmer would have been a better nickname? Even Ginger Beard or just Ginger would be more apt? Mind you, his was not the only nickname in St Ernan's that was a bit obscure. For instance, they called Father Gene McCafferty the Elephant Man just because he walked around with his hands in his pockets and elbows protruding to the left and right and flapping, supposedly just like elephant's ears. It was clearly a case of a group of old men hanging around all day, with nothing much to do except think up silly names for each other.

Anyway, he thought, back to the outhouse; during their search for McCafferty, Starrett had picked up a bit of a strange vibe from the Ginger Beatle when he'd briefly shown him around the ancient stone house, the one that was built directly into the steep hill behind the main house. At that point the detective had been preoccupied with finding the missing father, but not so preoccupied as to miss that something was out of sorts with Father McKenzie. And now he was ready to find out what, before he and Nuala Gibson left to fight the nightly, gridlocked traffic of Donegal Town en route to the Major's residence; en route to Maggie Keane. So, he bid Romany Browne goodbye before the young garda set off for the Station House in Ramelton, to catch up on his paperwork and offer whatever assistance he could to Garda Francis Casey in his endeavours at ground control.

* * *

As it turned out, there wasn't much call for Browne back at the station, apart from fielding the one and only call from the public that afternoon.

'Hello,' the caller said.

'Hello,' Romany Browne replied, 'how can I help you?'

'I'd like to make a complaint, please.'

'And what complaint would that be, Sir?' Browne continued, still upbeat.

'They've cut off my disability allowance.'

'Oh, I'm sorry to hear that, Sir. Which disability exactly is it that you suffer from?'

'Why I'm deaf of course,' the man replied, still so furious, his anger was seeping down the line.

Browne set the receiver down, knowing that if he ever relayed this conversation to any of his colleagues, not a single one of them would believe him.

CHAPTER TWENTY-SIX

When Father Edward McKenzie greeted Starrett – flanked by Gibson and Garvey – at the top of the steep and precarious stone steps that led to the stone out house, he looked as happy as a bulldog that had just eaten a wasp. He was attempting to speed lock the green wooden door behind him.

'Am…we'd like to talk to you inside Father, if you don't mind,' Starrett started, gesturing to the stone house, 'you know, a bit of a private chat, away from the house?'

Father McKenzie reluctantly reversed the direction of the key he'd just completed turning, and hesitantly led them back into the open-plan room.

The room itself was packed with odds and (gardening) sods, but all very cleanly and neatly stored in boxes and on the numerous racks, stacks and wall-hooks. The other end of the room was sectioned off with a large dirty-white floor-to-eaves and wall-to-wall tarpaulin. That sight, and his over-active nostrils, were the main reason for Starrett's quick return to the out house. He believed Father McKenzie when he'd claimed to have seen neither Father McCafferty nor Bishop Freeman, but something – maybe even Father McKenzie's unconscious behaviour – had demanded he take another look.

And as if to confirm his suspicions, Starrett noticed that the closer he got to the tarpaulin, the more antsy the priest became. Then, at the right-hand side of the room, just by the tarpaulin, and partially hidden in the folds, he spotted a couple of shallow wooden crates, stacked on top of each other, and full of potatoes. Behind the potatoes Starrett noticed some deeper crates filled with empty bottles.

'Tell me this, Father,' Starrett began, expansively, 'have you ever noticed that when you swat a fly and then dump it in a toilet the fec…

sorry, the darn germ-carrying insect only refuses to sink when you try to flush it down the toilet? And not only that, but the more you try to flush said fly, as you patiently wait until the cistern fills up again before you can re-flush, the more it hangs around, looking like it's having a great wee time swimming around in the bowl as it sneers up at you?'

'Aye,' Father McKenzie offered in agreement.

'Why do you think that is, Father?' Starrett asked.

'Has it to do with thingamabobs, trapped air, you know…whatsits?' Father McKenzie suggested, while looking very much like he'd have preferred to phone a friend.

'Well, I'm sure there might be some scientific explanation,' Starrett said, as he started to hoak around, looking for the edge of the canvas, 'but I much prefer the explanation that some things are just impossible to get rid of, do you know what I mean?

'Well yes, I think so.'

'Take for instance,' Starrett announced, in a Eureka! moment, 'the smell of the potatoes in your poteen still behind the auld canvas here…'

Father Edward McKenzie had the decency to smile largely before shrugging to imply, 'Well, you have to try, don't you?'

Starrett was not prepared for the industry he discovered behind the malleable partition. The space on the other side of the canvas was also a lot bigger than he'd been expecting, nearly as much again as on the potting shed side, in fact. And the floor on that side of the canvas benefited from a covering (mostly) of thick, dark-blue seagrass carpeting. The still and the bottling set-up was as elaborate and as big a plant as Starrett had ever seen.

'Bejeepers, Father,' Starrett started, thinking that no matter what his step-daughter thought, sometimes there was just no other word that worked for such situations, 'there's a lot of expensive hardware here just to keep the dozen of you in poteen.'

'Well, we do sell some of it to cover our costs,' Father McKenzie volunteered, looking every inch a man who was trying to prove that it's not so much what you say that gets you into trouble but more a case of what you don't say that keeps you out of trouble (he hoped).

'Really?' Starrett offered, 'how exactly does that work?'

'Ah, you'll have to chat to Father McCafferty about that,' Father McKenzie replied. 'He looks after the distribution of the drink,' he offered and then seemed to feel a need to add, 'and the vegetables,' and just when Starrett thought the priest was done he concluded with, 'aye, and I nearly forgot the what'sit's…yes that's them…the wee buns and the apple pies.'

'He does now, does he?' Starrett said, in a much louder voice, now realising he'd unearthed both the capitalist and the Joe Kennedy bootlegger-character in one fell swoop. 'All that must generate a fair bit of money?'

'My daddy always said that money is a lot like manure: it should always be spread around generously.'

'And you still have no idea where we might find him?'

'My father?' came the shocked but innocent reply, 'he's been dead a long time now.'

'No, no,' Starrett said, consciously pulling himself up short on impatience.

'Oh right, sorry, of course,' the priest smiled, his white teeth contrasting perfectly with their ginger frame. 'Father McCafferty. Yes, him. Well, I was going to say earlier, but you rushed off in a hurry so I didn't get a chance to tell you that it might be an idea to check Orla O'Connor's thingamajig…ah, you know?'

'House?' Gibson prompted.

'Yes that's it, house,' Father McKenzie enthused like he'd just invented the wheel. 'He goes over to Orla O'Connor's sometimes.'

'Would she be an older woman?'

'In fact, yes,' the father replied, looking slightly surprised that Starrett would know. 'She has prayer meetings over there as well, but Father McCafferty claims no one was saved.'

CHAPTER TWENTY-SEVEN

The first thing, the very first thing, Starrett noticed about Orla O'Connor was her hair. His first impression – albeit uncharitable, he admitted to himself – was old woman, young hair. The detective figured her approach must be, 'If I spend all my money on my hair, then no one will pay any attention to anything else.' Her healthy, full, light brown locks were long and straight and parted down the middle of her crown, with a single curl running all around the bottom, which, even though it casually flowed over her shoulder, appeared, to Starrett's eye at least, to remain static at all times, in the 'not a single hair out of place' cliché. Her nose had faded, though, and Starrett couldn't figure out whether it had been the result of the spectacularly dramatic but rough weather of the locale, or the spectacularly rough booze – maybe even, most likely, a combination of both. She had smoky, hooded eyes, which made her look like she was always about to yawn and her skin had that yellow-hue of an overly sweet dessert wine. And…well, Starrett had this theory that the majority of daughters start off looking like their fathers. The lucky ones, blossomed into wonderful creatures whose looks favoured their mother. Orla O'Connor wasn't one of the lucky ones. Yet even with all of the above afflictions, she had the confidence of one bestowed with beauty. Maybe it came from her smile, Starrett thought, because when she smiled you forgot about the rest. With her genuine smile, she made the three of them feel very, very welcome.

'Yes,' she replied, still within the sanctuary of the porch of her large neo-Georgian manse – which was straight from the pages of *Hidden Ireland* – on the outskirts of Rossnowlagh, 'I do know Father Gene McCafferty. He is a dear friend of mine. How can I help you? Please, come in.'

With one hand still on the door and the other deep in the pocket of her blue quilted Barbour, Orla O'Connor looked like she'd either just come in from attending to the chores or perhaps even just back from a brisk walk down on the beach, a quarter of a mile below her. Or, maybe around the house she liked to wear her red patterned silk scarf, fawn riding britches and a pair of black, patent-leather, slip-on shoes, after the male style favoured in the sixties by spivs, which kind of ruled out the walk on the beach or the out doing chores theories.

Orla led them down the main hallway and through the second door on the left, into the sitting room, which afforded them a magnificent view of the beach below and the dramatic countryside beyond. Starrett was so transfixed by this that he walked straight over to the oversized window to once again drink in one of Donegal's famous vistas. Packie also joined the inspector by the window, while Gibson hung back with Orla and made small-talk about how beautiful the house was and how expensive it must be to heat. The large windows, Orla claimed, as far as her oil bill was concerned, were nothing but major holes in the walls.

The house looked like it had been completely furnished with items rejected by the Antiques Roadshow, with a great deal of time and money lavished on both the curtains and carpets.

Two members of the gardaí were so engrossed by the view and the surfers on the famous beach, that they didn't notice one of their colleagues and the owner of the house, disappear from the room. An even bigger sin was that neither did they notice those two persons return five minutes later with two trays, laden with cups and saucers, plates and a teapot, coffee pot, milk jug, Paris buns, finger-sandwiches, and individually wrapped Jacob's orange flavoured chocolate-coated biscuits.

Social duties over and determined not to dampen his dinner time appetite with more than one Jacob's chocolate biscuit, Starrett got down to business as quickly as decently possible.

'So,' he began, 'you were telling us that Father McCafferty was a dear friend of yours.'

'Yes,' Orla replied, shadowing her mouth and chin with a napkin.

'How long have you known him?' Gibson asked.

'Let me see now, yes, it would be five years,' she replied. She spoke as though she had a hard boiled sweet permanently in her mouth.

'So just when he arrived at St Ernan's?' Starrett added.

'Yes, that would be it.'

'Just how did you meet him?' Starrett continued.

'I could not say for sure but I imagine he attended one of the in-terdenominational prayer meetings I hold here.'

'How often do these take place?' Gibson asked, as Garvey scribbled away in his notebook.

'At least once a month,' she replied. Starrett couldn't quite pick where her accent was from; it sounded slightly affected, but only very slightly, and it maybe had its roots in the North. He also accepted her accent could be the product of being away from her family home for a long time, perhaps starting at boarding school.

'So you hold one every month?' he asked.

'Mostly,' she replied, putting down her cup of tea and sandwich and looking like she couldn't possibly conduct a conversation and eat and drink at the same time, 'but in the summer, when we have some of our American friends visiting, we will throw in a few extras.'

'Are these prayer meetings always held here?' Gibson asked.

'Why yes, of course!'

'How long have they been going on?' Gibson asked again, Starrett looking like he was starting to flag a bit on this particular topic.

'Since my husband died, seven years ago.'

'Oh, I'm sorry,' Gibson offered.

'Do not fret, it was a long time ago and to be honest he was a wom-aniser for the majority of our marriage. We were not really suited. He was marrying my money – well, my family money, to be honest. I was blinded by this fast-talking, smooth, and handsome Donegal man with the gift of the gab.'

'I see,' Starrett said. 'I won–'

'I hasten to add neither of us got what we were after,' she said, cut-ting across Starrett and addressing Gibson directly. 'You were asking about how the prayer meetings started?'

'Well, yes,' Gibson agreed.

'So at the funeral, we had members of every religion, pretty much, in here. My husband was a Roman Catholic, but I did not want to of-fend any of our non-Roman Catholic friends. Neither did I want to in-sult the memory of my husband, so I asked a poet friend of mine to recite some of his more spiritual poems, just to mark what we were all feeling and thinking at the time.'

'Excellent idea,' Gibson offered. Even Starrett had to (silently) agree.

'Yes, indeed,' Orla O'Connor replied, straightening up her back even more. 'So it seemed natural to continue and it developed into what has now become a very popular prayer meeting.'

'How often do you have them?' Starrett asked, trying to get back into the conversation again.

'I have already said,' she said, slipping into annoyed school teacher mode, 'once a month and more–'

'…in the summer,' Starrett added, just to let her know he had been listening.

'I have a theory,' she continued, while smiling sweetly at Starrett, 'that modern-day religions do not work because each and every one excludes the other. For a true religion to work, it must include each and every person, no exclusion of colour, creed or religion, from any-where in the world.'

'But do you think that would be possible?' Gibson asked, appear-ing to see the logic.

'There would be no other way,' Starrett suggested, 'if only because the current system just doesn't work. Never did.'

'Yes, you are right,' Orla said, cheeks flushing as she grew visibly excited about the positive reaction. 'Each religion is bigoted towards its own, but you see, that is their biggest flaw, their biggest fault. For a religion to work it has to be pure. It has to be true to being something more than a preservation society. It needs to be universal; it would re-ally need to speak to each faith, to speak for every man, woman, and child. It needs to be self-critical to better itself. For a religion to be true it cannot, it just cannot be about Christians, Jews, Muslims, Buddhists, Members of the Second Federation Church, or whatever might be flavour of a particular generation or community.'

Starrett knew he should turn the conversation back to Father Mc-Cafferty, but, at the same time, there was nothing quite so inescapable as a zealot – male or female – on a mission to convert others to their vision.

'But won't all religions fall down when they adopt a leader?' Star-rett offered because a) that's what he felt, and b) he felt he needed to engage Orla O'Connor on her own terms.

'Why yes, of course!' she agreed enthusiastically. 'Do you not think that in this day and age if there was a true Messiah, his or her name would be on all of our lips and in all of our homes, quite literally, overnight, thanks to the speed of the internet and the accessibility of the television networks?'

Garvey looked a bit concerned at the recent direction if the interview.

'Of course, there is not one single spiritual leader out there,' Orla said, answering her own question, 'and the main reason for that is that there is no role for a Messiah in the modern world. There is nothing they could do; there is nothing that needs to be done that a Messiah could possibly do. For instance, even the United Nations is powerless to stop wars or to prevent human atrocities due to the complexities of world politics. So how could a mere Messiah possibly save us? And why would we need to be saved? We are nothing more than ants or bees preparing the way for the next generation of ants or bees. All we do really from the moment we are born is to form an orderly queue to meet our death. That is all there is, really, and only vanity and money-induced power suggest otherwise. The single thing that the Bible does teach us, the rare truth found in the Bible, is that the clergy (and I do mean the clergy of all religions) are the shepherds who tend the flocks who wait to die. The story of Jesus worked only because the world was as innocent as an infant back then. Mankind, perhaps, could end up a little more sophisticated, but basically it will still end up …as…well, as I have already said, as a queue for the end. And that is fine. If that is all we have to look forward to, then there is no point denying it or ignoring it. If there is a lesson we need to learn, then it is to follow the laws of the land – they do need some work, though. On top of that, all we really need is food to eat, clothes on our back, and a roof over our head because, when it really gets down to it, that is all that is really necessary. It is only our egos which dictate differently.'

Bejeepers, Starrett thought, and very uncharitably at that, Orla is ready to take this to the nation.

'Just one more very quick point and then we will get back to your questions, Inspector,' she continued, as if reading his mind. 'There is nothing wrong with the laws of the land – they were produced by well-meaning folk; the problem is rather with some of those who deliver them.'

Starrett allowed himself to appear distracted with the stunning views again in order to create a little space to think about Orla. In his mental absence, he got the mistaken view that Orla seemed to favour Packie Garvey over Nuala Gibson. Was this because of Packie's celebrity status or was she less threatened by him? Of Starrett's two colleagues, Garvey was the one who kept looking over to Starrett to see when he was going to re-join the interview.

In the end, it was the subject of the interview who pulled Starrett back in again. 'What religion do you favour, Inspector?' Orla asked, smiling again.

Starrett balked at giving her an answer; he had always believed that the secret to not upsetting anyone when it came to religion in a country never far from potential pious conflict, was to try to claim the same neutrality that had worked so well keeping Switzerland's nose clean. Still, pleading the Fifth rarely worked, and all fence-sitters enjoyed little more than sore arses, so Starrett always went with, 'You know what, I'm still trying to work that one out.' His answer never offended while at the same time, it gave the impression that here was a lost soul. Whether or not the other party felt Starrett was a soul worth saving was another matter altogether.

'Father Gene McCafferty...' Starrett offered, a few seconds later when it appeared that Orla O'Connor didn't, indeed, think he was a soul worth saving, 'did he ever have an official role at any of your prayer meetings?'

'No, Inspector, he knew not to try and impose his natural background on the proceedings, on top of which he had the good grace not to wear his clerical collar while in attendance.'

'Okay,' Starrett said, happy to be focusing on Father McCafferty again.

'He joined in with the *spirit* of our prayer meetings,' Orla continued. 'We tried to keep them light and joyous – a celebration, if you like.'

'So there was no weeping and gnashing of teeth,' Starrett suggested, 'no self-flagellation?'

'Ah, that would be a no to both of those,' she said, before smiling. 'We left all of that to the other houses of worship. I remembered how joyous the prayer meetings I used to go to as a girl were. I remember mostly the singing, where it did not really matter what we were singing, more how...how...heavenly, if you like, yes, how heavenly the singing sounded. Do you not see, that when you call it "a service", during the course of which you are going to be preached to, lectured to, and chastised over your sins, do you not see just how unappealing that actually is? And they wonder why the churches are emptying. I find people give themselves enough grief over their own sins, do you not?'

'Sadly, that's not something we find to be terribly true,' Starrett offered, falling off the symbolic fence so quickly you could have heard the thud.

'I did not say people repented their sins,' Orla said, through another of her wonderful smiles of forgiveness, 'I just said that they give themselves enough grief over their sins.'

'Did Father McCafferty do anything at all at your meetings?' Gibson asked.

Starrett got caught in the views out of the window again. This time, as the light was fading, he allowed his mind to roam freely, while still trying to monitor Orla's reply for tell-tale words. Was what she'd just said true? Did people really give themselves any grief, let alone 'enough grief', over their sins? He knew that out there somewhere, in the midst of this beautiful Donegal countryside, there was a person, a certain kind of person, who had stolen life away from Father Matthew McKaye. What was that person thinking at that exact moment, Starrett wondered, just as Orla was saying something about how bad Father McCafferty's singing voice was. If you murdered someone, would you think about it each and every day? Would you ponder deeply on it and is this the distance you are often seen looking off into? Would ghosts come to haunt you? Though Starrett had always figured a bigger nightmare would be to come upon a ghost in search of another ghost. But would you constantly agonise over the possibility of someone, such as himself or another member of the gardaí, tripping you up, catching you out? Would you want to be caught? Would you need to be caught? And would you ever think of the person you murdered? Would you obsess over how you had murdered them? Would you wonder what they had felt as they lay there, dying? Would you imagine they thought they were going to get through it? Do the victims always think they are going to survive their dance with death until the last possible micro-second of consciousness? Was a person, with that much emotional torment, capable of murdering someone and simply going about their daily business? Was Father Matthew McKaye's murderer happily going about his business right at this second? And was he happy now that Father McKaye was no longer around? Had the murder been worthwhile? Could they go on to live a good life? Or had they discovered that the little persistent voice in their head that kept repeating, 'if only you could get rid of Father McKaye, your life would be perfect,' hadn't been right at all? Was the little voice giving them grief now? Were they ready to repent to eradicate the voice? And if so, would they give themselves up easily? That last one was unlikely; if Dr Aljoe's findings were anything to go by, this had been quite a clever murder. It wasn't a crime of passion, and it clearly didn't happen on the spur of the moment. Or maybe it did, maybe it was just that the perpetrator was very lucky that–

'Father McCafferty was a lost soul and we came into each other's lives at the perfect time,' were the tell-tale words that drew Starrett out of his musings and back into the room again, mentally speaking.

'How often would you see him, Orla?' Starrett asked.

'Oh, two or three times a week,' she replied.

When she'd started off with 'two or three times', Starrett had expected her to say two or three times a month.

'That's quite a lot,' he offered, more as a statement than a question.

'Yes,' she said, 'we are very close; he has been a brick for me.'

'Do youse go to dinner and things?' Starrett asked, coming across perhaps more transparent than he'd intended.

Orla unleashed yet another of her smiles of chastisement and said, 'I know how these things work, you are the Guards and you are here to interview me, and I do know how tongues wag, so, in the spirit of full disclosure I would like to set the record straight here and say that Father Gene McCafferty and I do not now, and have never in the past, enjoyed an intimate relationship. And just so there is no doubt about this, what I am saying is that we have never had sex.'

'I wasn't suggesting–'

'Of course not,' Orla replied, 'but I felt it was time I just put that on the record. On top of which, I had more than enough of that auld carry-on with my husband to last me a lifetime.'

'I appreciate you being so candid with us,' Starrett replied gracefully, thinking that had been a strange thing for a lady to say, and an older lady at that. Was she perhaps trying just a little too hard to make this point? 'Tell me,' he said, drawing a line under her confession, 'does Father McCafferty help you organise the prayer meetings?'

'Well, yes he does, as it happens,' she replied, appearing to be happy of the opportunity to sing her friend's praises. 'Everyone who comes along brings something with them: a pie, some sandwiches, a quiche, wee buns, biscuits, drinks, what have you. Father McCafferty will invariably bring either one of the pies from St Ernan's or some fruit or vegetables from their gardens or, now and again, a bottle of their poteen. Horrible stuff, but he is very partial to it.'

'And do people make any donations or anything like that?'

'Well yes,' she replied, totally unruffled. 'When first-timers come over and they realise that it is the regulars that bring the food and drink, they feel the need to chip something into the pot. But Father McCafferty takes care of all of that. He collects it and tells me the amount, takes out enough for tea and coffee and pays the balance into one of St Ernan's charities.'

'This is truly a wonderful house you have here,' Starrett offered, hoping he wasn't being as transparent to the others, particularly Orla, as he was in his own mind.

'Why, thank you. When my husband and I were looking for a house all those years ago we wanted to be in this area and we wanted to have a Georgian styled house. The only problem was the majority of what we were after were manses, and were either in ruins or in service with the connected church. We wanted to put down some of our own history, our own roots, so we decided the only way to get that was to build our own version of an old house. I insisted we buy all the land around our original plot, as well, because I did not want people building dormer bungalows anywhere near us. The gardens have now matured and so I am very happy with it.'

'Have your children all left the fold now?'

'My husband never wanted any children,' she admitted, without the slightest sound of regret, 'and I never cared enough to argue.'

She looked at Starrett, then turned her shoulders away from him, put her head back and raised it slightly, just so she could look down her nose at him.

'Oh, I see where you are going with this,' she started, 'who will get the house?'

'Actually, it's a good question,' Gibson said, immediately springing to Starrett's support. 'We come across far too many cases where there's not a valid will and the property will fall into ruin before the estate eventually claims it.'

Even Garvey felt disposed to mutter, 'Yes, yes, that's right.'

'No need to worry about that,' Orla declared, 'Father McCafferty has gone to great pains to set it all up for me so that my house will become a retreat. They will continue with the prayer meetings, of course – we intend to step up that side of things next summer. We were going to do it this summer but then we did not really have a summer this year, did we?'

'Indeed,' Starrett said. 'It'll be very expensive to maintain, don't you know – a house this size, with no one living in it.'

'Well, Father McCafferty will remain here, of course. He will receive a stipend and humble accommodation. At the correct time, he will set up a trust to run the place. We have both discussed that it is vitally important that the place is not broken up, or sold off into small plots to build those wretched dormer bungalows the planners seem to favour. Father McCafferty has suggested that it should be called The Orla O'Connor House. He wanted to get a plaque made up for the front gate and carved into the stonework above the front door. I told him, "Can you please at least wait until I am gone?"' she said, before laughing.

'Father McCafferty is definitely a one-off,' Starrett couldn't help but mutter.

'As I was about to say, for this place to work, in order for it to be a real retreat and a true sanctuary, we need to keep the gardens as they are.'

'This is all going to be very expensive,' he mused. 'Are you going to go to the government for grants?'

'No,' Orla O'Connor said firmly, 'Father McCafferty explained that we can do that when we are up and running but they would want too much from us at this stage in return for a grant. He maintains that it is his priority to protect the house and the grounds and to do that properly we have to be self-managed.'

'So does he intend to charge for the retreat?'

'No, certainly not!' she said, as if she'd just noticed dog-doo on his shoes. 'I have sufficient funds for the project.'

'And so Father McCafferty will be your front-man for this project?'

'He will just be plain Gene McCafferty then,' she said. 'For the obvious reasons I have just explained, I cannot favour a certain denomination over another.'

'Did Father Gene McCafferty ever introduce you to one of his colleagues from St Ernan's, a priest by the name of Father Matthew McKaye?' Starrett asked.

'Yes, as a matter of fact he did. Father Matthew was a very nice man – well, more of a boy really. But very well-mannered, oh yes, very handsome. I would say that one such as he, without a clerical collar, would have broken quite a few hearts. He has been over here quite often, but a couple of weeks ago he stopped coming around. Father McCafferty said he did not know why.'

'Mrs O'Connor–'

'You can call me Orla, Inspector.'

'Orla,' Starrett started, beginning to feel sorry for her. 'Do you have a solicitor who looks after the legal side of all this for you?'

To all bar one in the room, it was blatantly transparent what was going on. Starrett accepted that, with their insider knowledge of why Father McCafferty had been moved on twice from his dioceses, it was obviously a lot easier for them to pick up on the scam. But, even with all of that, he still thought surely the poor woman should have at least a bit of an idea about what Donegal's Buddy Holly was attempting.

'Father McCafferty said that I need not worry about any of that. He is happy to take care of everything and he has promised that he will check all of the papers before I sign them.'

'So you haven't signed any of the papers yet?' Starrett said, with a bit of hope in his voice.

'Why no,' she replied, unsure and, for the first time since they met, appearing concerned. 'Gene has not finished checking them yet. He says you need to be very careful with solicitors these days.'

'Orla,' Starrett started, in his most kindly voice, 'by any chance do you have any good friends who live nearby?'

'Well there is…am…ah…of course Gene and…' She stopped talking and Starrett and his two colleagues realised immediately that she didn't really have a single true friend, which was, most likely, one of the real reasons behind why Father Gene McCafferty had almost been successful in pulling the wool over her bank account.

Starrett began the slow and painful process of explanation to Mrs Orla O'Connor, about the reasons why Father Gene McCafferty had been moved out of his previous two dioceses. He then continued with what he believed the priest had been trying to do with Mrs O'Connor's house and estate. Finally, he concluded his tale by informing her of Father Matthew's sad demise.

'Surely you are not saying that Gene was involved in Father McKaye's death, are you?'

'No Orla, we're not claiming that at all,' Starrett replied. 'At this stage all we can say is we're looking into the death of Father Matthew McKaye and during the course of our investigation we have uncovered certain facts about Father McCafferty. We have reason to believe that you were to be the next victim in one of his scams.'

'Oh, okay,' she replied, either not joining the dots or preferring not to.

'When are you due to see Father McCafferty again?'

'Well, he telephoned earlier today and said he was off for a few days on business for St Ernan's and he would most likely see me at the weekend or he would give me a call.'

'Do you remember what time he called you?' Gibson asked.

'Yes, I do, it was just after the Highland Radio one o'clock news bulletin.'

'Have you any idea where he might have gone?' Starrett asked.

'No, he did not say and I did not ask him.'

'One final question,' Starrett said, sitting upright and physically preparing to rise from the comfy sofa he shared with Ban Garda Nuala Gibson. 'Is there anywhere Father McCafferty would regularly go to? A hotel? Maybe a friend's house? Another retreat like the one he'd been planning to set up in your house?'

'Sorry, Inspector, I have no clue as to where Gene might be,' she confessed. 'It shows how little I really knew the man. In fact, I suppose this entire episode shows that there really is no fool like an old fool.'

CHAPTER TWENTY-EIGHT

Inspector Starrett and Sergeant Packie Garvey left Ban Garda Nuala Gibson at Orla O'Connor's grand house.

The plan was that Nuala would stay with Mrs O'Connor until a Mr Sean Clarke – an American living in the area who organised the music for Orla at her prayer meetings – could get over to Rossnowlagh, which was on the west coast of Ireland, just south of Donegal Town. Orla said she'd always found Sean easy to talk to.

The encouraging thing was, after talking to Starrett over the phone, Mr Clarke was prepared to drop everything and 'scoot across' (his exact words) 'to Orla's side. She's been there for so many of us who've taken so much joy from her prayer meetings; it's a pleasure to be able to return some of the support.'

Nuala Gibson made arrangements for Garda Francis Casey to drive over from Ramelton to Rossnowlagh to pick her up, once Mr Clarke had arrived. Before returning to Ramelton the two of them planned to have dinner at the nearby Smuggler's Creek which was dramatically set into the incredibly steep side of a hill overlooking the beach below.

* * *

Starrett and his trusted side-kick, Sergeant Packie Garvey, hopped into Starrett's car – a BMW, famous in Donegal for passing everything bar a petrol station – Garvey at the wheel as usual. They drove back up and into the congested Donegal Town and out the other side and onto the N15, along the Ballybofey & Letterkenny Road, intending to stop off just on the outskirts of town at Eimear Robinson's house. After checking his watch, the inspector discovered it was just after 7:30.

They were going to need at least two hours to interview Eimear's two daughters, Julia and Jessica, and her husband, Gerry, and, if they were very lucky, Eimear's sister, Mary, who was also, according to Eimear, quite fond of Father Matthew. Starrett did the maths. Along with the drive back to Ramelton, that would have them arriving at Major Newton Cunningham's house, out on the Rathmullen Road, no earlier than 11 p.m. That was just too late to go calling on a sick man, even in Donegal. So Starrett, very reluctantly, instructed Garvey to set the dials for the town land known as Ray, pronounced Rai, two- thirds the way along the Ramelton to Rathmullen hilly and ever-bending road.

Starrett could find nothing on the radio to distract him.

'Do we really think that there is a possibility that Father Matthew was murdered just because he somehow discovered what Father McCafferty was up to?' Garvey asked, using the 'royal' we.

'Well, it's most certainly an avenue worth investigating,' Starrett replied, 'but we've a long way to go yet, Packie.'

Packie looked like he wasn't sure whether Starrett meant in the case or on the road to Ray.

'Listen, Packie, I'm sorry for being a bit off recently, a bit crabbit, if you will.'

'Aye,' Packie replied, concentrating on the tricky dark road, 'you haven't been the same since they shut down Bakersville and you lost your supply of the cheesecakes you loved so much, you know, the ones without the cheese?'

'I wish you hadn't reminded me about just how good they were,' Starrett replied, and turned on the radio again without comment.

Before they knew it they were pulling up outside Packie's home in Coylin Court, Ramelton. Starrett bid farewell to Packie, took over the driver's seat, drove on out the road to Ray, and, just after the bridge, he took a turn to the right before heading off through a mini forest of dense trees. It was just before 9 p.m. and when he saw how weary Mrs Newton Cunningham was, he was very happy that he'd put off the Eimear Robinson family interviews until the next day, which would be the third day of the investigation into the death of Father McKaye.

When the Major's wife escorted him to her husband's bedroom, Starrett knew immediately that things were worse than he'd feared. He could never remember a time in his life when the Major was confined to bed.

'How are you doing?'

The Major looked to the door his wife had just departed through and signalled to Starrett to check that it was fully shut.

'Starrett, I'm bad,' he said, as the inspector sat down, 'and I'm not going to get better.'

Starrett's first temptation was to cajole the old soldier with the traditional, "Oh, you'll be back on your feet in next to no time." But the Major had never been one for either seeking sympathy or making grand sweeping statements about beating the dreaded enemy. No, instead the inspector resigned himself to the seriousness of the situation he had feared 'in his bones' just yesterday, when his boss had been too unwell to see him.

'What is it?' Starrett asked.

'Cancer,' the Major replied avoiding the cliché of 'the big C'.

'When did they discover it?'

'A few weeks ago. I'd this terrible pain in my back and it was so bad I thought I must have slipped a disc or something, so I went to my doctor. He examined me and when he was finished he looked at me, concern written all over his face. He said it wasn't a slipped disc and he wanted me to have to some tests, later that very afternoon, in fact. I went back to see him the next day for the results. He broke the bad news – cancer of the liver – but also explained to me that it had spread. He wanted me to go for immediate treatment.'

'So when do you start?' Starrett asked, as he remembered noticing the Major had recently been fastening his belt a hole or two tighter in the buckle.

'Starrett, I'm more prepared to meet my Maker than I'm prepared for the drama of surgery.'

The Major looked to the medicine on his bedside table.

'Morphine will get me through this battle, Starrett, this final fight.'

Silence.

'But what about your wife?' the inspector asked, without even realising he was going to ask that question.

'Starrett,' the Major said, growing visibly weaker before Starrett's eyes, 'the leaves on the chestnut tree in the autumn are certainly more beautiful than they are earlier in the year, but they still have to fall.'

'But–'

'And it's got little to do with gravity,' the Major whispered, signalling to his junior that the subject was closed.

There were so many things Starrett wanted to talk about with his old boss. There was so much he wanted to thank him for, so many things he needed to ask him. There were even a few things he needed to confess. He felt the urgency and need to get each and every one of these things off his chest and quickly at that, but he noted the Major's laboured breathing, The brave old soldier appeared to have fallen into a sleep. So Starrett sat in silence. None of this was about him. It was all about the Major.

Starrett stayed on to enjoy a cup of tea with Mrs Newton Cunningham. Unlike Mrs O'Connor, she had numerous friends and a few of them were rallying around the Major's resilient wife, offering tea and sympathy.

'You know,' she said, when she and Starrett found a private moment, 'the Major is trying really hard to put on a brave face for me, but I do know what's going on. It's important for him, though, important for us, for both of us really, that we continue this charade.'

'I fully understand.'

'You know, he is very fond of you Starrett,' she continued.

'And I him.'

'He was just as pleased as punch when you got back together with Maggie Keane,' she said, a smile creeping across her face. 'He said it would be the making of you.'

Starrett thought of Maggie Keane and mused as he did most days of his life about how incredible it was that, after all he'd been through, they'd ended up together again.

As if reading his mind she offered, 'You know, Starrett, the thing I've always found wonderful is that you can't make yourself love someone, nor can you make someone love you, but the most incredible thing of all is that you cannot make yourself not love someone you love.'

'I'm very lucky, Mrs Newton Cunningham,' Starrett said, and immediately regretted using the word 'luck' at a time like this.

'After all this time you're still calling me Mrs! You're a credit to your parents, Starrett, you were always very well-mannered but it really is time you started calling me Annette.'

Starrett knew it was important for both of them to be able to talk about mundane things when the Major was dying in the next room.

'He doesn't know I know this, but I did speak to his doctor and…' and she paused to bite her lip, 'he'll go very quickly. A week at the most.'

'But it's all so sudden,' Starrett gushed.

'As you well know, he's never liked going to the doctor, Starrett,' she started and then laughed. 'He claimed with all his ailments and war wounds he was held together with little more than a piece of string and a couple of staples anyway!'

The inspector made sounds of sympathy by clicking his tongue.

'Ah, Starrett, he's an old man – we're both old.'

'Aye, but there's been many a great tune played on an auld fiddle, Annette.'

'Now, now, Starrett, I need you to be strong for him, I need you to be strong for me,' she whispered, sounding like she would not trust herself to fully speak the words. 'We're not going to be of any use to him, any use at all if we start to grieve for him before he passes. You know what he's like as well as I do. He'll throw the both of us out on our ears. I need you to be with him the way you always are. Please, please, please Graham – never let him see pity in your eyes.'

Starrett wasn't aware that the Major's wife even knew his Christian name. The fact that she had used it in such a desperate plea meant he had to get out of the house before he totally broke down.

Before he did, he gave her frail frame a considerate hug. For her part, she hung on to him for dear life. Proof, if proof was needed, about how much she really needed him to be there - to be there for both herself and the Major.

Chapter Twenty-Nine

Starrett popped into the Bridge Bar on his way home to see if his friends, the other boys from the James gang, John and James, were in residence for a quick drink and a chat and the pick-me-up Starrett felt he really needed. But sadly, by their absence, they were both otherwise engaged on that particular evening. He zigzagged his way through the packed room, en route to his usual, quiet spot at the other end of the bar, the end furthest away from the street door, and ordered up a pint of Guinness. He was deep in thought about the Major when his rich and appetising drink arrived, and he couldn't help but overhear snippets of a conversation happening not too far to his right.

A woman, she sounded middle-aged, said, 'I've got self-esteem issues.'

'Does that mean you shag strangers?' a voice, Starrett thought he recognised, asked hopefully.

'Normally, yes,' she replied and added quickly, 'but in your case I'll make an exception.'

Starrett tuned out of the conversation. He was just about to savour his first sip when he felt someone sidling up beside him. But he didn't want to ruin this moment by acknowledging anything other than his pint. He could feel this presence beside him trying and trying and eventually, with a bit of shoulder shoving, getting just a wee bit closer. He tried to play the percentages by risking his solitude through interrupting it, albeit briefly, to fend off the unwanted attention.

'Ah, Moondance, it's yourself, bejeepers, I should have recognised the trainers!' Starrett offered the owner of the male voice he'd overheard several seconds ago, while never for a split second taking his eyes off his pint.

'The very man I'm looking for, I say, the very man I'm looking for, I thought I might find you in here!'

'Yeah, I find if I order a pint it helps me to mind my own business,' Starrett said, as though addressing his Guinness. 'Tell me this, Moon-dance, do you fancy one yourself?'

'Ah jeez, don't be like that, Inspector Starrett,' Moondance offered in his high-pitched whine while aping hurt, 'I've got a proposition for you that'll make money for us both.'

'Away with ye man so I can enjoy me pint.'

Starrett still hadn't looked up but he would have bet that Moon-dance, aka Bee Bee, aka Brian Boyce, would be dressed in his regular uniform of white flashed, electric-blue trousers and matching jacket with a white high-collar, zipped up (nearly to his chin) and crowned off with a Magic Johnson baseball cap pushed well back on his shaven head. He claimed his matching white Nike trainers -- with all their flashing lights – were worth more than Starrett's car, which wasn't say-ing much. The five foot four inch, light-framed, forty-plus-year-old managed to knock at least fifteen years off his spotty-faced age with his 'threads' and his 'bling' (Moondance's words).

'No listen, Starrett, just listen, it's a quick pitch and then I'll be gone,' Moondance continued, unperturbed, 'What do you know about Tom Dooley?'

'Go and fetch me a rope and I'll give you a practical demonstra-tion.'

'Jeez Starrett, man, you're a hard cat to...but look, you've proved my point, don't you see.'

'Okay Moondance, I'll make you a deal; you've got exactly three minutes to make your, your...what did you call it?'

'Pitch,' Moondance whined gleefully.

'Pitch, yes that's it, you got exactly two and a half minutes to make your pitch.

'But you said three minutes–'

'You've got exactly two minutes and fifteen seconds to...' Starrett paused to offer the bait again, but Moondance refused to bite so he continued, 'to make your pitch and then you're gone and I'll start my Guinness.'

'Okay, so my point is that the only reason you, me, and most of the people in here remember Tom Dooley is because someone bothered to write a song about him; that's why he's a legend. So my idea is that you collaborate with my artist Flanagan, the world's first trad rap artist. Flanagan – that's just the one name, Flanagan – do you remember him?'

'He's a cross between Christy Moore and Say Sneeze?'

'Close Inspector, very close – Jay Z, but at least it proves the auld marketing is having some traction–'

Starrett interrupted Moondance by glancing briefly at his watch.

'Yes, yes, so you and Flanagan write a song about one of the murderers you've caught. Right, I'm thinking...say, in the style of "Hang Down Your Head, Tom Dooley." Now, man, it would be much better for the song if this murderer died in the chase. But you have my word, there'll be no interfering, that's guaranteed, but I'm just saying it would be great for the promo boys if the murderer died in the song. My plan is for Flanagan to record the song, it'll be a massive hit and we'll split the royalties with you, sixty to us forty to you,' Moondance offered and then added in a somewhat quieter voice, 'after management commission.'

Starrett glared at him for the first time.

'Okay, okay! Jeez man, you drive a hard deal, fifty-fifty and no management commission?'

Starrett nodded his head up and down in a positive motion.

Moondance grew visibly excited, 'What? What...you agree? Inspector, you won't regret it, it'll be massive! Can I announce it tonight? I'll get you and Flanagan both on The Late Late Show. Tell me, Starrett, how good are you on the auld harmony vocals?' Moondance's excitement visibly dissipated somewhat. 'You did nod your head saying you'd do it, didn't you? That was you confirming, wasn't it? I just need to get you the paperwork, right?'

'Moondance, me auld mate, I was nodding to you to signify that you'd run over your allotted time and I was waiting for you to depart so I could start my pint.'

Moondance shook his head meekly as he disappeared into the crowd at the Bridge Bar. His way out was a lot easier than the zigzagging on the way in. That's always the way.

Starrett drank.

CHAPTER THIRTY

DAY THREE: FRIDAY

'You do know that the Norwegians claim the highest skies, but it's Donegal that actually has them?' Starrett declared to Gibson first thing the following morning.

Starrett's head and heart were heavy with Mrs Annette Newton Cunningham's words from the previous evening. So as far as he was concerned, Norway versus Donegal wasn't a debate, it was more a statement of fact. Gibson seemed to pick up on this because she did-n't contradict Starrett, but, equally, that could simply be because she also knew that Donegal's skies were the highest.

'How was Mrs Orla O'Connor when you left her yesterday evening?' Starrett asked the ban garda.

'She was quite upbeat actually,' Gibson started, 'Sean Clarke, the American, arrived long before Francis did and he's a very nice man. He and Orla were getting on like a house on fire.'

'I've never really got to grips with that one, Nuala,' Starrett mused.

'Sorry?'

'People getting on like a house on fire. I mean, really, think about it – that's one of the last things people should like to get on as, don't you think?

'Well, I've never really thought of it that way before, but now you come to mention it,' Gibson replied, clearly humouring her senior.

'Anyway, sorry,' Starrett offered, as though he'd just managed to solve the eighth Wonder of the World, 'you were telling me about the American.'

'Oh yes,' Gibson said, seeming happy to pick up her thread again, 'Sean is very talkative – maybe he was nervous, but he immediately went into a positive gear. Orla said she couldn't tell him what had happened, maybe she did, the moment I left the house, I don't know. He claimed he was happy to get out of the house and was up for a bit of good old chin-wagging. She talked a little about her husband.'

'Oh,' Starrett perked up, 'anything interesting?'

'Well, just that, in retrospect, she had to admire him in that he was totally transparent; what you saw was exactly what you got. Unlike someone she'd recently had dealings with. Apparently her husband was a womaniser and never tried to hide it from her. Sean confessed to Orla that his wife had been perfect, he just regretted that he'd never realised that when she was still alive.'

'So Orla was okay then?'

'Well, I thought I could see where it had all gone wrong,' Gibson said.

To her surprise Starrett nodded her on past Steve's Café, up to the right, past the Presbyterian church, which was on the left and badly needed its steeple cleaned due to the fact that the weather had in recent years taken a turn for the better and the current rainfall was no longer sufficient to cleanse the steeple. They drove on up Church Street and left at the fork by the Church of Ireland with its brand new roof, then up the hill a bit, bearing right and then a very quick left at the Cup and Saucer and onto the Letterkenny Road. 'I'd breakfast with Maggie and the kids and besides, Maggie says you're only humouring me by going into Steve's with me. But you were about to tell me how it had all been going wrong for Orla?'

'Well they, she and Sean were getting on so well, I could very easily imagine her asking him to run her Orla O'Connor House project.'

'Gullible?'

'I mean very gullible,' Gibson offered. 'At first, when we went into her house yesterday evening and she started to tell us about Father McCafferty's actions I was thinking to myself, how could you possibly have been taken in by such a transparent scam? But then I saw her with Sean and I thought, well I can see it clearly now.'

'Yeah, but don't you see, people like Father McCafferty are professional, they know exactly what they're doing, and equally, they know who to hit on and who to leave well alone. They're prepared to cultivate their victims over a long period of time, if they feel there is a need to. And then people like Orla, well, they are old and lonely and vulnerable and desperately feel the need for their lives not to have been in vain. They have their money, they have their grand house, their fine clothes, but they still need something more. They need their lasting testament not just to be their name on a headstone. They need a reason for them to have been here on this Earth and they will gladly spend every cent they have if they can find a way to be remembered after they're gone.'

'Oh yes, I nearly forgot,' Gibson gushed, nearly, but not quite, cutting him off. 'Francis wanted me to tell you that he'd tracked down the two priests from St Ernan's, you know, the two who are out on a research trip.'

'He found Fathers Clerkin and Casey?' Starrett shouted in excitement, bolting upright in his seat again, 'Where are they?'

'In Bandon Town in County Cork,' she said proudly.

'How on earth did he manage to track them down, Nuala?'

'It was Bishop Madden, the very man who told him the day before why Father McCafferty had been moved from St Anne's. They're aware of the movements of all visiting priests to their diocese.'

'Clever man, that Francis,' Starrett declared, thereby claiming some ownership for himself. 'You want to make sure you keep hold of him.'

'That's what Maggie is always telling me as well, but she says, "he's a keeper that one,"' Gibson admitted. 'Anyway, be that as it may, the research priests were actually basing themselves in Bandon Town. Apparently they made some important historical discovery in the Church of St Patrick and the Immaculate Conception. Francis contacted the church. The priests weren't there but apparently they were known to call into Warren Allen, (a local coffee shop about a three-minute walk away), now and again to update their notes over numerous cups of coffees and wee buns. Francis rang Warren Allen, spoke to the friendly manager, Sean Kennedy who said that, yes, they were there at that moment but, more importantly, they had been in there on Wednesday, from about three o'clock until they closed at six. He remembered it because it rained all afternoon and Michael and Peter had asked permission to stay there to work, until the rain had passed. He also said the priests tipped very heavily for the privilege.'

'So at long last we can remove two of the priests' names from our suspect list. Now that is good progress, Nuala.'

'Unfortunately, Francis has had no joy yet on the APBs he put out on both Father McCafferty and Bishop Freeman,' Gibson admitted to her superior, who was still so high on the news from Bandon Town, he'd ignored what he considered to be a temporary set-back.

Before he knew it, they were driving over the causeway leading to St Ernan's, and he noticed how much cheekier the army of rabbits were getting now they were growing accustomed to the gardaí and their vehicles' comings and goings. It was surprising that more of them didn't get run over, thereby saving the priests the bother of popping them off. The other thing he noticed was the stale smell he experienced now, every time he walked into St Ernan's House. Once he'd been in there for a while it always seemed to disappear, but that probably had something to do with his very keen nostrils growing accustomed to the less than pleasant smell. Could it have something to do with the absence of the St Ernan's housekeeper, Mrs Eimear Robinson? She hadn't been around since before the death of Father Matthew, and none of the priests seemed interested in taking up her mantel.

After the initial high, the first part of that Friday went downhill very quickly, with Garda Francis Casey's APBs continuing to produce zero results. Garda Romany Browne was busy working away on something, Starrett knew not what, but he seemed so industrious the inspector thought it best to leave him at it. Then he spoke at length with Father O'Leary, but learned nothing new. Garvey and Gibson, with Starrett and Father O'Leary's permission, searched both Bishop Freeman's and Father McCafferty's rooms, two long and unrewarding procedures, which produced no information apart from the facts that the bishop had enough gowns to clothe Ramelton's excellent pantomime cast and Father McCafferty must have another storage place, for he did not have a single personal item in any of his rooms. Surely there should be at least a paper-trail for the sale and distribution of the garden produce, pies, buns, and poteen, but then he remembered it was Father McIntyre, aka Tubsey, and not McCafferty who Father McKenzie had claimed was his front-man for St Ernan's commercial (and bootlegging) enterprise.

Starrett was less surprised by the lack of evidence – as in none – discovered in the bishop's rooms. St Ernan's was not the bishop's main residence, that was over in Sligo, and he figured that Father Patrick O'

Connell could very safely have bet all of his money on the fact that there would be no incriminating evidence found in Freeman's temporary quarters in the house.

Yes, after such a disappointing Friday, he was beginning to feel that his time might have been better spent popping off a few of those rabbits, to help St Ernan's with its vermin control. He was, of course, thinking about the other vermin outside of the house.

CHAPTER THIRTY-ONE

At just after 3:30, Starrett and Gibson left Garvey and Browne dili-gently working away and headed into Donegal Town, back out the other side and onto the hilly Balleyboffey Road, to Eimear Robin-son's house.

As luck would have it, Eimear, Julia, and Jessica were all at home. Gerry, the father and husband, was not.

'He's most likely working late,' Eimear offered.

'Or down the wine bar with Enya?' Julia, the youngest sniggered.

'Or snogging Beyoncé in the back field,' Jessica suggested, to chuck-les from Julia.

'Or giving Bono advise on how to dump his Facebook shares,' Julia offered to all-round laughter.

'Far be it from me to put words in anyone's mouth,' Eimear said, with a voice totally different to the one she'd used during her inter-view with Starrett a few days prior, in that this time she wasn't starting her sentences off loudly and then petering them out, 'but could some-one please say something nice about my husband, your father, and, by the way, just in case no-one has noticed, the bleedin' guards are here.'

'Dope,' Jessica said.

'Jessica, don't be so rude, what are you on about?'

'Mum, don't you remember Jessica explained it all to you,' Julia, acting as friendly translator said, '"dope" means "cool".'

'No,' Eimear said, in disbelief. 'Last night she clearly said that "sick" means "cool".'

'Mum,' Julia screeched, '"sick" is sooooo yesterday!'

Starrett and Gibson were getting into the spirit of the family hu-mour when something strange happened. The inspector was viewing the above scene by looking in the large mirror hanging above the fire-place. He found that, while interviewing, he frequently picked up more that way, because people behave differently when they think you're not looking directly at them. And all of a sudden he saw a vision of long blonde hair and shapely legs fly across the mirror. He immediately turned to look at the open door behind him and whatever, or whoever, it was had gone.

At the precise moment this was happening, Julia concluded her conversation with, 'At least you didn't say the dope was cool to call it sick,' which drew enough laughter, polite though it was, that Starrett couldn't hear whether or not the hallway door had opened and closed.

Jessica Robinson looked older than her reported 18 years of age, even though, on first impression, she was the least confident of the two sisters. She wore a large floppy, blue, woollen jumper, a pair of baggy white jeans and white trainer-liner sports socks. She wasn't exactly overweight but she looked like she was either just putting on some weight or just losing it. Starrett's mum always explained that particular syndrome as someone being 'on a cake diet'. Her hair was blonde, which didn't look her natural colour, and was straight, parted on the crown and very, very long, down way past her shoulders. She continuously played with it, flicking it around with her right hand and placing it behind her right shoulder. She didn't seem overly keen to make eye contact with Starrett.

Sixteen-year-old Julia, on the other hand, was a lot more engaging. She wore touches of make-up, noticeable about her eyes and her cheeks. She was kitted out in a black Nike tracksuit and expensive looking trainers, the ones with the wee wheels in the heels. Eimear repeatedly warned Jessica not to skate around the living room or, Jessica's preference, the wooden hallway. 'Watch my new floors!' she'd say to anyone who'd listen and even those (usually her daughters) who wouldn't.

'So, do you think my sister bears any resemblance to Jessica Lange?' Julia asked Starrett, as her mother disappeared into the kitchen to prepare the family dinner.

'Is that the actress who plays Mrs Brown in Mrs Brown's Boys?' Starrett asked as innocently as he knew how.

'Dope!' Julia screeched, 'totally dope!'

Starrett had found someone who shared his sense of humour. At least, that was if he was remembering the correct interpretation of 'dope' and he wasn't, in fact, being called one – a real dope, that was. This was all very confusing, he thought.

'So, are you meant to look like Julia Roberts?' Starrett said, chancing his arm.

'No,' Julia giggled, 'you'd never get a piano in my sister's mouth.'

Then the younger sister muttered something barely beneath her breath, which Starrett didn't pick up, apart from the word 'maybe'. Jessica clearly did because she hissed 'Julia!' and threw a cushion at her with all her might.

'You might be able to play a tune on her teeth, but could never get a piano in there,' Julia laughed, flinging the cushion back at her sister, who seemed a lot less concerned over this wise crack from her younger sibling.

'We'd like to talk to you a little bit about Father Matthew?' Gibson started as the laughter (mostly Jessica's) subsided.

Julia sat upright and Jessica shrunk slightly into the sofa, cradling the cushion her sister had recently thrown back at her.

'Now Father Matt, he was defo dope, sick, or whatever. He was all of them,' Julia declared, looking at her sister.

'As in cool?' Starrett asked, to ensure he was on the right page.

'Oh, as in most definitely cool,' Julia confirmed immediately.

Gibson and Starrett looked at Jessica who nodded a bright-eyed 'oh yes, I agree' look. Well, at least that's what Starrett took it to mean.

'You both got on well with him?' Gibson asked.

'Yes, we were like his adopted family,' Julia replied, as she got up from her seat by the window and skated her way across the room to join her sister on the sofa with a dramatic back-flop into the cushions.

'I hope you're not skating on my new floor!' Eimear shouted through from the kitchen.

'No mum, that's just the floor settling – it's a new house, Dad said it would creak like that for a few months,' Julia shouted back and then got up from the sofa again and skated across to close the door and return to her sister's side. 'Father Matt was one of us. He helped us move here, you know. He wasn't really like a priest.'

'What do you mean by that?' Starrett asked, '"He wasn't really like a priest".'

'Well, he wasn't old and wrinkly,' Julia said, through laughter.

'Anything else?' Gibson asked.

'He enjoyed a bit of fun, he was great craic,' Julia said.

'You could actually talk to him,' Jessica offered, 'he really listened to you.'

'Yeah, he didn't treat you like a kid,' Julia said.

'Do you think he was happy being a priest?' Gibson asked.

'Well, he said he thought he was joining the priesthood but all he seemed to be doing was washing dishes,' Julia said. 'To which my mum would reply, "Well if washing dishes gets you to Heaven then I'm already there."'

'Did he ever tell you if there was anything else he'd had preferred to do?' Starrett asked.

Both sisters looked at each other in a 'will you tell hi, or will I?' way.

'He told us that he wasn't cut out for it, that he wanted to leave,' Julia said.

'Julia!' Jessica said in protest.

'Well, it's true, Jessica, and the guards need to know what happened to Father Matt, so we have to help them by giving them as much information as possible!' Julia said, and in the absence of contribution from her sister she added, 'I'm just saying, Jessica, we need to find out what happened to Father Matt.'

'Okay,' Jessica said, quietly.

'You tell them, Jessica,' Julia said.

'No, you tell them!'

'He told you, he didn't tell me!' Julia said. 'That's hearsay, Inspector, isn't it? You know, when someone who didn't hear something tells someone else what was said?'

'That's correct, Julia,' Starrett confirmed.

'So it wouldn't stand up in court, would it?' she continued.

'Well there's no need to worry about that here,' Starrett replied, noticing that Jessica had grown a little nervy on hearing the word 'court'. 'At this stage we're really just concerned about gathering as much information as possi–'

'He told me he was going to leave the priesthood!' Jessica blurted out.

'When did he tell you that, Jessica?' Starrett asked gently, noting that Julia seemed proud of her sister.

'A couple of weeks ago,' Jessica replied.

'Where was your sister?' Gibson asked, looking a little concerned.

'She said, out with Bono.' Jessica was trying really hard to break the mood by going into one of her routines with her sister.

'Ugh!' Julia groaned, 'he's older than my dad! And nowhere near as fit,' she added proudly. She looked at her sister and moved closer to her, 'Just tell them Jess, eh?'

'Father Matt said that he realised he'd made a terrible mistake and he needed to fix it,' Jessica finally offered the sitting room.

'You mean he knew he didn't want to be a priest?' Starrett asked, trying hard not to put words into the girl's mouth. He was worried she wasn't far from breaking down and that would be the end of their interview.

'Something had happened to him and he knew he needed to get away from the priesthood before his time was up at St Ernan's. He was dreading leaving St Ernan's.'

'What was the something?' Starrett felt compelled to ask.

'That's all I know.'

'Was there another person involved?' the inspector asked, thinking immediately of Bishop Freeman.

'That's all I know,' Jessica repeated.

'I know he was devastated by the prospect of failing as a priest,' Julia said, diverting attention away from her sister again.

'Did youse discuss this a lot?'

'Well, when our parents weren't about,' Julia replied, 'Jess and I and Father Matt would get the newspapers out and trawl through them, looking for a new job for him.'

'Did youse ever find anything suitable for him?' Starrett had accepted that the interview was winding down with little more to be gained from the current session.

'Well, I found what I thought was a perfect job for him,' Julia said.

'Oh yeah?'

'Yeah, I thought he should replace Paul McGuinness as U2's manager,' Julia said and then waited a single heartbeat before adding her punch line, 'but Father Matt said now that they'd given their CD away for free he couldn't afford the cut in his wages.'

Starrett imagined that Julia's below par attempt at humour had been intended not to amuse but to draw attention away from her sister again.

* * *

As far as Ban Garda Gibson was concerned, it had been an unsuccessful attempt to draw attention away from the older sister.

Ten minutes later, Starrett politely declined Eimear's generous invitation to stay for dinner and he and Gibson started their journey to the Major's house. The offer was tempting though, if only because they would have had a chance to chat to Eimear's husband, Gerry, and her sister, Mary Mooney. Their interviews would have to wait until a later date.

The first thing the ban garda said when they'd successfully joined the quirky N15 northbound road was, 'Julia Robinson knows more, a lot more than she was telling us.'

'Perhaps next time you should interview her by herself?' Starrett suggested.

'I'd guess it's going to be very difficult to get her to even consider talking to us again without her sister,' Gibson said. 'Initially I agreed with you, that it should be a ban garda that interviews her. But now I'm not so sure – she seemed a lot more receptive to you.'

CHAPTER THIRTY-TWO

Starrett was happy they arrived at the Major's house at the more civil time of 7 p.m. that night. Maggie Keane was already there and so Nuala Gibson left after a few minutes' chat with Maggie, her friend, since she didn't feel comfortable accepting Annette Cunningham's offer to visit the Major in his bedroom.

Starrett, however, went straight in and, to his surprise, the Major seemed in better spirits than the night before. He said as much and the Major nodded in the direction of his medication.

'So,' Starrett continued immediately, 'I don't know if you're aware of this or not, but a young priest, a Father Matthew McKaye, was found dead up in St Ernan's – you know the house on the island, just outside Donegal Town?'

'Good on you, Starrett,' the Major said, getting Starrett to help him sit up a little more in the bed before elaborately tidying the bedding himself. 'That's exactly what I like to see, business as usual. So what do we know?'

Starrett briefed his superior on his progress so far.

'Do we know any of the cast?' the Major eventually asked.

'Well, that's why I really needed to talk to you, Major,' Starrett replied, hesitantly. 'I have a possible conflict of interest – with Bishop Cormac Freeman.'

'Never heard of him, Starrett, where do you know him from?'

'He was Father Freeman when I went to Armagh to join the priesthood,' Starrett admitted.

'Might he be behind the reason you left so quickly?'

'You got it in one, Major.'

'Have you any reason to believe he might be involved in the demise of young Father McKaye?'

'Well, Father McKaye was rather handsome. He was scheduled to move to Bishop Freeman's patch at the end of his final training. He told someone he wanted – needed – to leave the Church. He expressed a wish to do so before he left St Ernan's. He admitted to one of his colleagues that he'd lost his faith. Bishop Freeman disappeared a few hours before I was due to interview him. However, to be perfectly honest, at this stage there's nothing more circumstantial than that.'

'Okay Starrett,' the Major said, 'you've brought the matter to my attention. I know you well enough to know, no matter how much you might want to, you won't fit him up if he's not the one. Apart from which, if those were your true intentions, you certainly wouldn't have raised the possible conflict-of-interest issue with me in the first place. I'll have the current Mrs Cunningham type up my report; I'll sign it and have it included with my files in Gamble Square.'

'Perfect, as ever, just perfect,' Starrett said, a weight lifted off his mind.

'Tell me, Starrett, how's young Romany Browne doing?'

'Actually he's doing very well; he's gaining his confidence and, doesn't seem to take advantage of his looks, like I at first feared he might. I have a feeling he'll be a good member of the gardaí.'

'I have the same feeling, Starrett,' the Major said and then paused, looking deep in consideration. 'Look, Starrett, I really do promise I'm not going to get all maudlin on you with all the "after I'm gone" poppycock, but please keep an eye on him for me. His father was a good man, a decent soldier. Sadly, a bad end and all of that. Also you might keep a lookout on the current Mrs Newton Cunningham. I know your mum and dad will look out for her as well.'

'Of course.'

'Good, good.' The Major seemed relieved, looking as if he'd just ticked the last few items from his 'getting his house in order' list. 'Now, tell me this, Starrett, is there still a Father Peregrine Dugan down at St Ernan's?'

'As a matter of fact there is,' Starrett offered. 'How do you know Father Dugan?'

'Oh, he's got this tome he's been working on for...well, it must be over twenty years now, called The History of Ireland. I met him, oh, it would be well over ten years ago now since he came to see me to record my memories on Ireland's involvement in the Second World War.'

'Yeah, he's still stuck in his room, working on the same book.'

'I'd a feeling he might be.' The Major looked off into the distance. 'I remember we were talking, I forget the place, but I do remember the content. He asked me if I knew how many people had died in the War. I told him, as far as would be admitted by the various governments involved, it was over 60 million souls.'

Starrett gasped, even though he'd heard the figure before and most likely from the Major.

'And do you know what he did, Starrett? He started to weep. Not cry, but weep – the tears just streamed down his face and we had to stop. He said he just couldn't do any more work that day.'

The Major didn't dwell on the subject, and Starrett let it pass, fearing the subject might also bring down his boss. But it turned out the Major was happy to reminisce.

'The things we forget are how the memories we cherish most are memories of events, usually first-time experiences, that made such an impression on our lives,' he offered, seeming to benefit from a second wind. 'These memories are so important and precious to us, and make such a lasting impression on us, that we are incapable of forgetting them. In my case, all such memories have no monetary overtones.'

'For instance?' Starrett asked.

'I remember being around my house one evening after school, playing with my friend, Sixer Kelly, when Master Bailie, the headmaster of my school, pulled up in his maroon car and asked me to do him a favour.'

'Really?' Starrett said, concerned as to where this might be going.

'Yes, he'd just got a new Austin car and for some reason or other – I've never really been able to work out why, even after all these years – he couldn't drive it into his garage, which was just around the corner from our house. What he wanted to do was drive the car into the garage, leaving enough room to open the car door, and then turn the engine off, open said car door, get out of the car and then get someone – i.e. me – to steer the car, aiming for a centrally suspended fist-size sandbag near the back wall as a guide, and someone else – Sixer Kelly, in this case, to help him push the car the final five or six yards into the garage.

'I can remember sitting in the car, drinking in the rich aroma of the new leather seats and recently polished wooden dashboard, behind a massive steering wheel. I was both excited and scared, as was the case with all my favourite adventures, not to mention tremendously relieved when he shouted for me to put my foot on the brake about ten inches from the back wall and, thankfully, the pristine vehicle obeyed and ground to a halt.

'Then there was this girl, Lorna – she was the daughter of someone important in the town. They'd a big car and an appropriately sized detached house with huge, well-manicured gardens and stables around the back. I used to go for a dander around the village with no one but my thoughts to accompany me. I'd frequently come across Lorna dressed to the nines in her equine gear and riding a spectacular chestnut pony. Anyway, I soon worked out her route and her timetable and I would "accidentally" come across her on her route, and we fell into this routine of her up on her horse and me walking along beside her, and we'd rabbit away ten to the dozen to each other, like we were the best of friends.'

'Was she one of your earlier girlfriends?' Starrett asked in hope.

'No, no, not at all. It was the pony I was always keen on.'

They both laughed.

'Another of my precious perennial memories also involves a car,' the Major continued, quickly jumping back to the thread of his previous story.

'Go on,' Starrett encouraged.

'When a new local church brought a marquee to the outskirts of town as a way to drive the congregation up, the church council decided a good gimmick would be for the elders of the church to pick up the potential "new members" of the congregation in their expensive cars. Not only that, but they also offered to give them tea and cakes after the service and they'd drive them home again. It was the first time in my life I was ever in a motor car and the experience was totally earth-shattering for me. It was also the first time in my life I'd experienced the magic that is known as the floating voice, created by a group of men and women singing in natural harmonies. The first time my ears twigged something different – yes, maybe even spiritual – was happening, I looked all around the marquee to see if I could discover where the enchanting voice was coming from. I was looking so see who in our midst had this beautiful soulful voice. I soon realised that this floating voice was somewhere – physically and mystically –

above my fellow men and women. I soon stopped searching for the
source and settled down to bask in the glory of it.'

'Did the car collection gimmick work? Did you return on other
nights?

'A few times but then I stopped.'

'But why?'

'Well, Starrett, I'll tell you. They started to ask for people who
wanted to be saved, people young and old who want to, I believe the
exact words were "Take the Lord Jesus Christ into their heart, and ask
Him to forgive them their sins and to save them." But I just couldn't
make that kind of divine connection. Some of my mates did, but I always thought that might have had something to do with the stunning
girls strategically placed in the front row of the choir. On seeing the
choir girls, my mates readily raised their hands in confirmation of their
need, and agreement, to be saved.'

'Ever thought that might have been God's way of wanting to increase His congregation?' Starrett asked, before smiling.

'Yes, I'll give you that, it was certainly a consideration, Starrett, but
then as I looked at the elders one by one I realised they were some of
the biggest rogues in the village and I found it so much easier to follow my natural instincts. You see, my father was never a religious man,
no. But he was a good man. He always lived his life and taught me to
try to live my life treating others as I would like to be treated myself
and I've never needed anything more than that.'

'Even now, Newton?' Starrett asked, as he viewed the frail vessel
who seemed weary of the magic of life.

'Yes indeed, Starrett. Particularly now.'

The Major seemed to draw a definite line under that one. Starrett
would have liked to have gone a bit deeper, if only for his own spiritual understanding, but felt it inappropriate to do so.

The Major blinked his eyes furiously and then closed them. Starrett couldn't be sure if he was tuning into another of his memories or
if he'd fallen asleep. When eventually the Major's face lit up in an
enormous smile the puzzle was solved.

'Oh, let me see now,' he said, but it came out as a wheeze. He
coughed something into a tissue and wiped his lips. He smiled as he
caught the memory and continued, 'I'm thinking about my time on
the Lough Neagh shore one summer. My family were visiting my

uncle's farm for that summer. It was probably my fifteenth summer on Earth. Anyway, a bunch of us – boys and girls – were on the Lough shore, close to Ballyroan, and there were a couple of small canoes and people were taking turns going out in pairs in the canoes. Anyway, this beautiful girl, her name was Gillian Crawford, she would have been the older sister of a girl I'd taken a shine to. I can't even remember the younger sister's name now. So Gillian Crawford says to me, "Come on, Newton, you'll go out in the canoe with me, right?"

'Now, you have to remember that part of me was nervous, very nervous, because I couldn't swim, still can't, but the overwhelming feeling I was experiencing was excitement, of going out in a small canoe with this gorgeous older girl – a year was a lot at that age. She was such a beautiful looking girl and she'd asked for me to go with her, and you have to realise, this was even though we'd barely spoken but a few words. Mind you, the few words we had spoken were more than those I'd exchanged with her younger sister. I was always so tongue-tied around her.'

'First love,' Starrett said, but not as a question.

'That's as may be,' the Major continued, barely acknowledging Starrett's remark, 'she tucked her light, loose, white summer dress up into her knickers so that it wouldn't get wet and she climbed into the canoe, first sitting at the back and then using the paddle to steady the canoe before she invited me to join her. I had my back to her; I was going to be sitting between her shapely bare legs. I tried – unsuccessfully it has to be admitted – not to stare at her naked legs. I'd never seen so much bare leg before in real life! She helped me in, gave me the spare paddle, explained the process and, before I knew it, someone behind us had pushed us off from the shore line and we headed off in the general direction of the middle of the Lough.

'Starrett, the next twenty minutes were the most exciting twenty minutes of my life, maybe even including up to now, but please don't let the current Mrs Cunningham know I said that. Before long we were far enough away from the shore that we could no longer hear our friends' boisterous chatter. The only sound was that of the paddles through the water. Then she told me to stop paddling and for a while we just drifted in deceleration, until eventually we stopped.

'It was so quiet, oh so quiet. "This is so beautiful," I remember saying, not even realising I was saying those words. And then she very gently put her hand on my shoulder from behind. She squeezed her fingers softly into my skin, which sent an unprecedented shiver down my spine and into my nether regions. I don't know if she was agreeing with me or she wanted me not to talk, just to enjoy the natural beauty. But that's what we did. I can remember every single minute of my time in the canoe with Gillian Crawford. I can still recall it as if it happened just earlier this afternoon: blue sky; fluffy white clouds; gentle breeze; her scents; her bare legs touching mine on each side; her smiling voice when she broke the silence, telling me how much she too loved being on the Lough and drinking in the amazing scenes all around the water's edge. How she loved the peace and quiet. She said that's why she wanted me to come with her; she thought I would also appreciate the magic. When she spied something she wanted to share with me, she would gently squeeze my arm or my shoulder and point in the direction of what had caught her eye.

'"We better go back in," she eventually whispered, appearing to share my regret that we had to end this magic time together. But you know what, Starrett? I think it might have been my perfect time; just pure liquid perfection.'

'And did you and this girl–'

'Gillian Crawford…'

'Did you and Gillian Crawford–'

'No, never,' the Major replied, as though he thought that if he allowed Starrett to conclude his question it would spoil the memory. 'Never, Starrett, but don't you see? That just might be why it's my perfect memory. The fact that there are no other associated memories to tarnish it, no rows or arguments, no nights of being stood up, no jealousy, nor other boyfriends or girlfriends to ruin it. Yes, Starrett, that is probably why I've never been as much in love as I was for those precious twenty minutes.'

The Major closed his eyes. This time he did not smile. Perhaps Starrett had worn his old friend and superior out this time. He watched as the breathing grew uneven and imbalanced, until it fell into a rhythm, which let Starrett know that, this time, the Major had definitely fallen into a sleep.

CHAPTER THIRTY-THREE

'You know, Starrett,' Maggie Keane said as she drove the inspector back to her house after bidding goodnight to the Major's wife, 'I've been thinking about this a lot since we got back together and I want you to promise me something.'

'Okay,' Starrett replied immediately.

'But you don't know what I'm going to ask you to do?' she said, trying to keep her eyes on the road while removing some of the loose hair out of her eyes. It was proving to be a difficult task because a few wild-cat strands were misbehaving and ended up entangled in her eyelashes, so every time she blinked she set off a chain reaction in her hair. Starrett thought it endearing.

'Well, you're not going to ask for it if it's not important,' he replied, after he carefully freed the hair trapped in her eyelashes, carrying out the manoeuvre as carefully as if he was a bomb disposal expert, halfway through the task.

'Starrett, I don't know what's gotten into me but I've developed this great phobia about being buried when I die.'

'Augh, Maggie.'

'No, no, Starrett! Don't put me off! Please, hear me out – I could never forgive myself if I died and hadn't told you.'

'You won't need forgiveness then, Maggie.'

'That's a point,' she said, through her lopsided grin that exposed her crooked teeth to Starrett in the rear-view mirror, 'what I should have said was: I won't forgive myself if I don't tell you now when I have a chance to.'

'That works,' Starrett said, turning around to face her.

When they arrived in Ramelton she didn't take the left onto the bridge over the Leannon River but drove straight on up to the Bridge Bar. It was packed right out onto the street.

'It's too crowded for the way I'm feeling tonight,' she said, 'do you mind if we go somewhere else?'

'I'm just as happy to go home,' Starrett said.

'I'd like to go somewhere,' she replied, quietly, as she did an illegal Hughie Green – a.k.a a U-turn – on the forecourt of Whoriskey's petrol station. They drove down past the heaving Bridge Bar again. 'You're a garda, Starrett. You work late and you leave our house early. If we're not careful, we'll end up as ships that pass in the night.'

'Well, we do occasionally bump into each other during the night,' he offered playfully.

She brushed her hand through his hair and was distracted again by the crowds outside the Bridge Bar.

'It only gets that packed when Henry McCullough is playing,' she said, requiring both hands to turn right over the bridge.

'Sadly it's not Henry,' Starrett said, remorse clear in his voice. 'He's very ill; I doubt he'll ever grace another stage.'

'Agh no,' she sympathised as they pulled into Gamble Square and parked midway between the gardaí station and McDaid's Wine Bar.

'Why can't things just remain as they were?' Starrett said, his mind shifting from the soulful Henry McCullough to the Major.

'That's the problem with bachelors,' Maggie Keane said, as she turned off the ignition and turned to face the inspector, implying that she was happy just to sit there. 'They get too set in their ways. They grow very selfish, thinking too much about themselves and their lives and not having to bother to consider any others.'

'Whoops!'

'The bottom line, Starrett, is that nothing, absolutely nothing, remains the same. That is a physical impossibility and so we just have to accept that change is inevitable and move on. If you're going to be any good to me, in my role as a mother, Starrett, you're going to have to learn that little lesson and adapt your life to help me get on with things.'

Starrett accepted that Maggie Keane, like a few other mothers he knew, would always put her children above everything else, including herself. But the most incredible thing of all was that none of them ever considered it a sacrifice.

'You were going to ask me a favour?'

'Yes, I was. I don't want to be buried, Starrett, I really don't,' she pleaded. 'I know it's stupid but I just don't want to be eaten by worms. Will you please promise me that you won't bury me?

He started to laugh.

'Starrett, I'm serious.'

'No, sorry, I was just laughing at something else; there was this Donegal criminal and he once said "I really want to be buried beside my wife, and I'll pay ten thousand punts to the first man who buries my wife – just tell her I'll be joining her later".'

'He wanted her dead?' she gushed, 'or is that just another of the Starrett bejeepers stories?'

'No, it's 100 per cent true!'

'Well, it's just that our Moya has been telling me some of the tales you tell her.'

'Bejeepers, sorry about that,' he said, hamming it up.

'Well, actually this one was a good one and it really worked. So I have to thank you.'

'All sexual favours gratefully accepted,' he offered, knowing he was chancing his arm.

She leaned over towards him and seductively nuzzled her lips in very close to his ear and whispered breathlessly, 'Ah, shame about that, you were doing really great up until then.' She leaned back into her side of the car and continued, 'As I was saying, Moya asked me permission to put on make-up. I said most definitely not.'

'So that's why she came to me?' Starrett said, and smiled largely.

'So she went to you and you said…' Maggie, clearly moved by the story, ruffled his hair again with her fingers, 'you told Moya there once was this wee girl in Milford and from an early age her mother trained her how to apply make-up. But the mother actually taught her to apply the make-up on to her image on the surface of the mirror and she grew up to be one of the most beautiful girls in Donegal and that was just because she hadn't contaminated her skin.'

Starrett smiled at the memory.

'Where do you get these stories from, Starrett?'

'There're all out there, they're all true,' he claimed.

'Really?'

'You just couldn't make them up, Maggie.'

'Well, Moya loves you for them,' she said, 'Katie loves you, too, of course but it's always the youngest girl who befriends the cuckoo.'

'Cuckoo?'

'You know, the stranger in the nest?'

'So that's what I am, is it, a cuckoo?!'

'Only to Katie and me,' she joked, 'Moya's totally on your team and she's still at an age when she thinks your stories and lines are a hoot.'

'She'll grow out of them, that's why I'm betting on you, Maggie,' Starrett said. He'd something else on his mind he'd been wanting to discuss with her for ages and he accepted this was most likely his best chance. 'Maggie, I've something I need to talk to you about.'

'That sounds ominous,' she replied, grimacing slightly.

'I'm not getting on with Joe as well as I imagined I would,' he admitted. 'You know, with us all being reconciled and all.'

'Starrett,' she said gently, 'you have to realise that you're content to sit around all night in the Bridge Bar with the James Gang. There's another thing, the James Gang, how old are youse? And it's not even as if any of you have James as a last name,' she laughed out loud. 'But youse are content to sit around all night in the Bridge Bar, drinking your Guinness and chewing the fat, imagining you're all going to leave the bar, get on your trusty steeds and ride off to your hole in the wall up in Loughsalt Mountain.'

'Maggie, whist, won't you? Our hiding place is meant to be top secret.'

'Yes, exactly!' she said through a large stage sigh. 'Whereas on the other hand, Joe and his friends, they're not like that, thank God – he and his friends are out there, they're on the road just to be on the run. Your gang…well, you've all reached the stage in your life where you've started to be scared of dying; Joe and his friends are just as scared of not living.'

'Aye, they don't know it yet, but soon they'll realise that all they're really out there for is to look for someone just to stay in with,' he offered and before she could reply, he thought of something else he wanted to admit to her. 'You know, when we got back together again, that was the first time in my life that I started to consider…you know, how much time I'd left? Maybe as well, how much time I'd wasted, how much time we'd wasted?'

'You big oaf, Starrett,' she said, glaring at him. 'You're considering how much time we wasted because we didn't stay together from the first time right through?'

Starrett nodded to her that she'd been correct in her assumption.

'Listen to me carefully, Starrett; I'm here to tell you that, quite simply it just would never have happened. Furthermore, we are together today purely and simply due to the fact that we did split up.'

Starrett could sense the thought-bubble rise above her head so he kept quiet until she was comfortable enough to speak what was on her mind.

'I'm not the girl you thought I was,' she eventually said. 'I don't want you to be in love with the girl you thought I was.'

'I'm not, Maggie, please believe me, I'm not.'

'The girl you knew, Starrett,' Maggie Keane continued, as if she hadn't heard him, 'was a wee country girl, who thought the way to keep her boy was to sleep with him, only to discover that he'd left the very next morning to join the priesthood. And then…and then discover she was pregnant and young and alone. Then I met Niall and I was too mixed up to even think of love. But he was patient with me, he saved me, helped me grow, Starrett.'

'I know, Maggie.' He was now regretting he'd ever opened up this avenue of conversation. Occasionally life was just like driving along a motorway, and you're coming up to your turnoff but the flow of heavy traffic just sucks you along with it, way beyond your turnoff point, and although you can see it happening there's nothing you can do about it without potentially causing an accident. So, the only thing you can do is to go along with the flow of traffic, hoping for the best in your new circumstances and your new destination.

'Don't read it wrong, Starrett; I need you to know that I really loved Niall. I mean, he's the father to my daughters. He took on Joe. If it hadn't been for his cancer,' she said, quietly and without regret, 'you and I would mostly likely never ever have passed the time of day again.'

Was she trying to hurt him with her words for some reason or other? More likely she was just tipping him off that he better wake up and shape up.

'But then Niall did die of cancer and you and I did meet again,' Maggie Keane continued, on a more hopeful note, 'and even though you'd changed as much as I had, there was still a part of me, if only because of all the baggage and complications, there was still a part of me that would have preferred that we didn't get together again.

But, you see, my reality was that I didn't really have any say in the matter. Initially I was intrigued by you, and most certainly I was amused by you. I liked being with you. Then, in spite of myself, I fell in love with you. So we met again, we fell in love and either we deal with that or we fall out of love. And if that happened, then that's when we'd have to learn to deal with not being with the person we love and, believe you me, that's a lot harder to deal with.'

Starrett knew Maggie was referring to her dead husband.

'Starrett, maybe being out at the Major's tonight has reminded me once again about our lives and how precious they are, you know? You and the other members of the James Gang better stop worrying about how bad things are today compared to yesterday. You need to forget about the past as if it never existed. You really have to enjoy today because you know what, Inspector, no matter how bad you look and feel today, always remember that by tomorrow you'll look and feel just that wee bit worse than you did today.'

'But not as bad as you'll feel and look the day after?'

'Now you're getting it, Starrett,' she said, ruffling his hair again.

'And just remind me again how you would look if I let the worms ea—'

'Starrett! Ah! Don't! – now that you've put that image into my mind I'll be thinking about it all night!'

She sidled up to him again and moved her head so close he could feel her breath around his ear. Then she whispered, 'but if you're really nice to me and buy me a glass of wine in McDaid's, I'll allow you to distract me later when we get home.'

'Bejeepers mam, I'm your man,' Inspector Starrett boasted.

CHAPTER THIRTY-FOUR

Being a Saturday, Starrett had arranged to meet Gibson and the gang at the gardaí station, which, coincidently, was dangerously close to the aforementioned McDaid's Wine Bar, down on Gamble Square. Starrett, tea cooling on his desk, summoned Romany Browne, who sat at the inspector's desk with a small bottle of still mineral water, an apple and a banana. The banana he kept secure in a creased brown paper bag, the apple he kept free, looking like he didn't know whether to juggle the three items or start to eat one or drink from the other. Either way, the apple was clearly the poor cousin and perhaps a sacrifice to be offered up to his senior.

'Did you know, Garda,' Starrett started, forcing Browne to, a) pay attention to him, and b) place the three items on his desk, 'that when penguins are migrating, mostly, they make it to their destination only if they stick with their waddle. However, if they are solo they invariably get lost.'

Browne looked first at Starrett and then at his apple and finally at his bagged banana. Starrett looked at Browne, then the apple and then the banana shape in the brown bag and then back to the apple and then back to the banana shape. He nodded to himself, signalling that he'd made his choice, but not before finishing his story to Garda Romany Browne, the guard, formerly, briefly, known as Pips O'Toole.

'And my point?' Starrett asked but didn't wait for an answer, 'well, my point is that it's vitally important to stay in the waddle and work as part of the team.'

'Okay,' Browne said, half relieved but still visibly worried in case his banana was at risk.

Starrett lifted his right hand to make his move but he diverted it at the last possible second into the top right-hand drawer of his desk, where he blindly futtered around for a few seconds before he removed a brand new KitKat from his stash.

'So,' he declared, following a swig of his cooling tea and his first stick of KitKat, 'what were you up to yesterday, Garda Browne?'

'I was trying to track down Father Gene McCafferty.'

'What about the bishop?'

'I figured I'd a better chance of success if I concentrated on one of the two missing members of clergy.'

'And why did you decide to chase Father McCafferty over Bishop Freeman?'

'I thought it would be easier to find the father rather than the bishop,' Browne replied immediately.

'And why was that?' Starrett was now intrigued as to what the logic might be.

'I figured that if Father McCafferty was prepared to tell such obvious lies – about where he'd served before he was sent to St Ernan's – then there was an equal chance he wasn't going to be very good at covering his tracks this time either. Bishop Freeman is another matter altogether – he looks like he could be very devious, on top of which, I don't much like the way he looks at people.'

'By people you mean yourself.'

'Well yes,' Browne admitted.

'Sound logic,' Starrett said, 'very sound logic. So how are you progressing?'

'Well, Father McCafferty doesn't have a car and none of the bicycles are missing. So he obviously had to walk away. The nearest easy rendezvous point seems to be the Craft Village Centre, back out on the main Donegal Town to Ballyshannon road, so I checked there to see if a priest was met there by anyone, including taxis.'

'No joy?'

'No joy,' Browne conceded. 'Then I realised that Father McCafferty just might have twigged that was too obvious and traceable an escape route.'

'O-kay.'

'So then I checked all the taxi companies in Donegal Town to see if any of them had been booked to pick up a priest from this side of the bay.

Once again there was no joy with that line, just a lot of complaints about how bad business is at the moment. Then I checked the mini cabs outside of Donegal Town, mostly they were the driver-owner type companies and again no luck. So then I drove around the locale to see if there were any other wee petrol stations or shops he might have called in with or been picked up from. Again…nothing. Next, I checked small hotels and guest houses in the area. Finally, I did a door to door of all the houses in the immediate vicinity.'

'Again nothing?'

'Correct, Sir.'

'Maybe he just bummed a lift?'

'Someone would have seen him, Sir, I checked all the houses along the nearby road. No-one saw a priest, walking, talking or hitching a lift. You're pretty noticeable Sir if you're a priest walking along the roadside.'

'So he just disappeared off the face of the Earth?'

'Impossible,' Browne replied, matter of fact. 'No, I think I've worked out where he is, Sir.'

'Really, Garda Browne? Colour me impressed.'

For a split second Browne looked like he might have regretted his boast.

'You know, Romany,' Starrett said, 'it really isn't important to be right all of the time. But it's vitally important to keep coming up with ideas, because, at some point one of them is going to be on the right track.'

Browne nodded to show he'd understood Starrett's logic.

'So where is it you think Father McCafferty is, Garda Browne?'

'I believe he's still in St Ernan's, Sir?'

'But we searched St Ernan's.'

'I know Sir, but I think there must be some secret space or room in there. Father McCafferty doesn't look to me to be the kind of man who could either walk a long way or be capable of sleeping it rough, so the only other option is that he's still on St Ernan's.'

'Okay, that makes sense. So what is your next move?'

'Well, that's as far as I got really. I've been on the internet most of the night checking out the history of St Ernan's. There's talk of a secret tunnel. I don't know where it starts or where it leads to, but it's been mentioned in too many different articles for it not to exist.'

'You know, Garda Browne,' Starrett started off, 'I should point out that every now and then one of the penguins that breaks off from the waddle does make it to the destination, eventually.'

'Are the priests going to allow us to search St Ernan's again, to look for secret compartments and trap-doors and tunnels and what-have-you?' Browne asked, taking silently what he felt just might have been a compliment.

'Why don't we just scoot up there and check it out for ourselves?'

'Just the two of us?' Browne replied in disbelief.

'Well, Ban Garda Nuala Gibson is busy writing up her reports and she and Francis Casey and Sergeant Garvey will be busy today check-ing up the alibis and trying to get a lead on the whereabouts of the bishop. So that just leaves the two of us.'

'But it's a very big house?'

'I think I know a wee shortcut,' Starrett said as they took off, him at the wheel, in the direction of Letterkenny.

CHAPTER THIRTY-FIVE

The first part of that wee shortcut to St Ernan's - and the house's mysterious potential trapdoors and tunnels that lay beneath - turned out to be a detour by the Letterkenny General Hospital and, in particular, the offices of Dr Samantha Aljoe. The doctor had received a request from Father O'Leary to release the remains of Father Matthew McKaye for burial.

'So you made it quicker than you thought,' was Aljoe's greeting to Starrett and then, on noticing Garda Browne, 'ah, you've got a new sidekick.'

'Yes indeed,' Starrett said, taking the one free chair in her office. 'So have you managed to solve the mystery of the magic bullet?'

'No, Starrett,' she said, taking a few photos out of a green file on her desk, 'but I can show you in detail–'

'Ah jeez woman,' he protested, 'I'll never have the stomach to look at that! Please, just explain it to me.'

Garda Browne lifted the photos that Starrett had replaced on the desk. He seemed to be examining them very carefully.

'So this is the track of the bullet?' he offered, using a pen to demonstrate his line.

'Yes,' Aljoe replied, leaning over the photos beside Browne and putting her arm on his shoulder, 'but the only problem is: there is no bullet.'

'Still no exit wound?' Starrett asked, looking at the ceiling.

'Just the entry wound, the tract, the damage and then…nothing.'

'Incredible!' Browne said.

'There's no chance that, you know, due to gravity it could simply have dropped out again after having done the damage?' Starrett ventured.

'Quite impossible,' Aljoe replied immediately, 'it, whatever it was, left just too much damage in its wake for there to be a clean tunnel for it to drop out from again. On top of all of that, after the projectile hit and destroyed its target, Father Matthew would have slumped over.'

'Could someone, you know, with knowledge have extracted the…the projectile?'

'Not without leaving a much larger hole than the one created by the entry point.'

'How about if they'd used a magnet?' the inspector said, always ploughing onwards.

'That's getting a bit Sherlock Holmes, Starrett,' the doctor replied, raising her eyebrows. 'But yes, it would be possible, assuming we're talking about the remains of a bullet, but you'd need a very strong magnet and it would bring a lot of blood and brain tissue with it.'

'I wish I hadn't asked you that now, your answer was much too vivid for my stomach,' he said, noting that Garda Browne was hanging on to the doctor's every word and every move.

'What other weapon could have caused this amount of damage?' Browne asked, proving he wasn't too much in awe of the company, or on second thoughts, perhaps his question was exactly for the benefit of the female in their midst.

'Now that's a good question!' Aljoe replied, turning around to face Starrett's junior. 'What are you thinking of?'

'A spear? The arrow of a cross bow? The arrow of a bow? An ice pick? An iron spike?'

The light went on in Starrett's head at that moment.

'The only problem with all of them is there would have been no element of surprise,' he said. 'Father Matthew would have put up some efforts in self-defence and there is no evidence about his person to suggest he'd done that.'

'Correct,' Dr Aljoe offered, 'and if any of the aforementioned had been used, there would have been some trace, some contamination. Whatever killed Father Matthew, it left no trace whatsoever.'

'Have you ever seen anything like this before?' Browne asked hopefully.

'No,' she said, with a tone of certainty that visibly deflated Garda Browne.

'Is there any reason you can think of why we shouldn't release Father Matthew's remains to the priests at St Ernan's?'

'None whatsoever, Starrett – I'm 100 per cent covered from my side.'

'Okay, let's do that then, Doctor, let them have the body. Have you any idea when they want to bury him?'

'They're talking about Monday. I believe they have an undertaker on standby.'

Starrett immediately thought about the Major and he didn't stop thinking about him the entire way to Donegal Town.

CHAPTER THIRTY-SIX

The next stop on Starrett's wee shortcut became apparent to Garda Romany Browne the minute the detective walked into Father Robert O'Leary's rooms, right by the top of the staircase in St Ernan's.

'Tell me,' Starrett started off, 'you know you said that you didn't feel comfortable volunteering information to me...'

'Yes,' O'Leary replied, tentatively.

'But if I ask you a specific question, i.e. I'm not fishing, you said you'll give me a correct answer?'

'Or words to that effect. But yes that sums up our deal,' he replied, putting the book he was reading down on his desk before sign-writing 'that's our deal' with his forefinger and thumb.

'Okay. Then can you please show me where the secret rooms are in St Ernan's?'

Father O'Leary grinned.

'So you've been doing your homework.' He both spoke the words and wrote them in the air.

'Actually, it was Garda Romany Browne here who did my home-work for me,' Starrett admitted. Then he looked down at Father O'Leary's book –not quite the light reading he'd imagined, it was The Private Life of Chairman Mao by Li Zhisui. The father flipped off his red tartan carpet slippers and left them neatly by his sofa, as though guarding his open book from the observant detective. He took a sheep-skin jacket from his bedroom and pulled a black beanie hat from the pocket, and put both of them on. He walked out of the room without saying a word.

Browne and Starrett followed him as he crossed the landing, straight to the stairwell. The old priest then went down the staircase, past the antique fireplace, along the large hallway with the strange yet effective honeycombed ceiling, out through the front door, into the conservatory styled entrance hall and down one flight of stairs, which took them to the ground level by the same front door Starrett had knocked on exactly four days ago.

Instead of going out into the cold fresh air, as Starrett had thought they might, the priest opened a door on the side of the staircase and walked through it. From beyond the doorway, the detective noticed a light being switched on. He and Browne stooped slightly to enter by the same door. An immediate right took them down fourteen steps and into a large window-less basement, part of which had been cut into the side of the hill into which St Ernan's House nestled.

Father O'Leary still hadn't said a word, bar confirming the inspector's understanding of their arrangement. He turned and walked back out of the basement area, leaving both gardaí standing with their arms the same length.

Starrett found the basement area, with its catacombs, comfortably warmer than he'd been expecting; it clearly benefited from a heating system or furnace somewhere, or maybe it was some kind of by-product of the heating system upstairs. Either way, everything down there was very dry, if badly lit with reacting lights, which sprung to dim life as he travelled closer to them, following him as he continued to plunge into the darkness ahead. He thought he heard a noise behind him but after a few seconds' pause he assured himself it was nothing more than heat either expanding pipes or wooden floorboards in their wake, or maybe both.

Parts of the basement were packed, wooden floor to concrete ceiling with old furniture and uniformly sealed cardboard boxes. Starrett knew from experience that the furniture was in a holding pattern, for either a skip or a bonfire. Every twelve feet they passed through an open doorway of a roughly four-foot thick wall that clearly supported the solid concrete beams, which in turn supported St Ernan's House above them. The concrete beams were obviously a modern addition to the original work, most likely replacing wooden beams that were ravaged by the damp.

Browne lagged a wee bit behind Starrett, seemingly distracted by something or other, so the detective soldiered on before seeing a door, where there had been openings in the previous support walls.

There was a light shining underneath and he thought he could hear several voices from the other side – they certainly weren't coming from above. The space behind the closed door must be directly under the living-cum-kitchen-cum-fireplace sitting area.

He decided that he needed Browne with him before he went beyond the door so, in the half-light, he retraced his steps. He'd come back through two of the thick wall openings when he had a flash of Garda Romany Browne being in danger. He didn't know where it came from but he felt it as sharply as any of the premonitions he'd ever felt before.

Starrett's mother, the seventh daughter of a seventh daughter, had a gift, a gift of vision and of healing. During his life people were forever calling at the house to have his mother 'attend to them'. Starrett's memories were of how physically and mentally drained his mother was after all of these sessions, to the point that, when Starrett returned to Ramelton to join the gardaí, his father had insisted his mother retire, if only to protect her own health.

At first, Starrett didn't think he'd been blessed with his mother's gift. But then there were a few times too many where he'd experienced flashes – like the one he just had – which had so saved his bacon that it had started to become difficult for him not to believe she'd passed on some of her powers to him.

He didn't panic. He needed to find Garda Browne, and quickly. He was caught between the points of not wanting to embarrass himself by seeking help from upstairs, when there was possibly nothing wrong, but, equally, that help might be warranted, before something terrible happened to either Browne or himself, or both of them.

Searching in one of the side storage areas, he found a lampshade-free metallic lamp, which he lifted, removed the bulb which he placed carefully on a box beside him. He wrapped the cable around the bulb end several times, tied the end in a knot so that it wouldn't get in his way, took a couple of trial swipes to judge the weight, tried to gauge exactly how hard he'd need to hit someone to render them helpless and, finally, set off in search of Browne.

He thought he saw some light from the hallway through which they'd entered the basement, but then it disappeared. Could Father O'Leary have left them down in the basement and then set someone on them because they were getting too close to the truth? If that were true, what exactly were they getting close to?

As Starrett searched, he began to focus on possible theories – he found it helped him deal with the situation, down there, in the stale dry air of the basement. Could the reason for Father Matthew's murder simply be that he'd uncovered Father McCafferty's plan to swindle Mrs Orla O'Connor out of her house and possibly her inheritance? At the peak of the market, a few years ago, Mrs O'Connor's house and land would have been worth between 1 and 1.3 million euro. These days she'd be lucky, very lucky, to be able to sell for half that. But then people had been murdered for a lot less than half a million – plus her inheritance, of course. Was that it? Had Father Matthew discovered Father McCafferty's plan? Had he threatened to tell Orla or maybe Father O'Leary? Had he already told Father O'Leary and perhaps Father O'Leary was in cahoots with Father McCafferty and that was the reason why he'd led Browne and Starrett down into the basement and left the others involved in the scam to deal with them? It would certainly be a sure bet for Father Patrick 'Please, Call Me Pat' O'Connell. If he could put all he could raise on Father O'Leary not being involved in the scam, that, in Starrett's book, would be as safe as going all in on Seabiscuit. Yes that certainly would go a long way to dissolving his money troubles.

Through the final wall opening, towards the entrance, he thought he saw a shape slumped on the floor. He ran across to it, thinking it must be Browne and fearing the worst.

It was Browne.

He was alive, unconscious and bleeding from his forehead.

While he examined his garda with one hand, he retained his tight grip on the lamp with the other. As this realisation was developing he suddenly became aware of this mass of darkness hurling at him, at vast speed from his right, from deep in the shadows of where the support wall joined the external wall. He was processing how to swing his lamp when out of the corner of his other eye he clocked another mass, this time definitely a figure – a plump figure –rushing at him from the opposite side. He jumped up, took a back-hand swing to his right and totally failed to connect, but the energy of his swing kept him turning and the lamp connected – and forcefully – with the figure coming at him from his left. Starrett floored the attacker with a single, but lucky, blow.

At which point the mass approaching him from the right, who Starrett now recognised from the Buddy Holly glasses as being none other than Father Gene McCafferty, aka the Elephant Man, was upon him and battering him furiously with his fists, swearing profanely to assist himself with his efforts.

A couple of the thumps connected solidly about Starrett's chest. They didn't hurt him, the adrenalin was seeing to that. He needed to keep Father McCafferty from landing one on his glass chin though, so he tried to keep the ball of fury at bay with his left hand, while taking aim with his right.

Once again he totally missed his mark and immediately decided that next time he'd be less ambitious with his aim. This time he aimed at the weapons, which were doing the most damage to his upper body, that is to say Father McCafferty's fists, particularly his left fist. Starrett went with all his might for another back-hand and he could hear the sound of bone cracking as his lamp connected with the priest's left wrist. Father McCafferty screamed in agony but showed no signs of stopping. His tongue, if not his strength, was getting stronger by the second and he tried in vain to wrestle Starrett to the ground with one hand, knocking the detective over in the process. Grazed, bruised, winded, Starrett could think of nothing else to do but to shout at his opponent.

'Stop man!' he ordered.

On and on the Elephant Man came, thumping and kicking for all his worth, one fist then two feet.

'Right, feck this for a game of soldiers!' Starrett shouted at the top of his voice, and, taking aim again, he screamed his favourite war cry. 'This one is for all the marbles!'

He swung his trusted lamp with all his might and it connected better now, this time with Father McCafferty's right wrist, producing a crack so loud McCafferty's startled eyes and open mouth reacted a split second before the resultant pain actually registered.

CHAPTER THIRTY-SEVEN

The Cavalry arrived in the form of Father O'Leary and Father McIntyre. Starrett realised it wasn't so much a re-enactment of the Battle of Little Big Horn, but more a tag-team wrestling match.

It turned out that Father O'Leary had sent Father McKenzie, the other mass of darkness who had hurtled towards Starrett in the chaos, down to the basement after the two gardaí, in case they needed assistance. In fact, Father McKenzie had actually been in the process of setting into Father McCafferty as he – having already successfully felled one member of the gardaí – was clearly just about to get stuck into the other.

Father O'Leary apologised to Starrett about the confusion of the fighting priests.

'A bald man should never, ever fight over a comb – particularly with another bald man,' was all Starrett would offer in comment.

He helped Romany Browne to his feet. The blood on his forehead was not from an instrument of violence, but from scraping his forehead on the floorboards.

'How many of me do you see?' Starrett asked.

'Just the one,' Browne replied, as he dusted himself off.

'You're perfect then.'

On the one hand, Father McCafferty had a broken wrist, and on the other hand he'd a broken wrist as well.

Father O'Leary did the best he could to make Father McCafferty as comfortable as possible, instructing McKenzie to run upstairs and grab a couple of ice packs from the kitchen, which he then placed on McCafferty's wrists. Browne looked on while his boss used the time to nip into the room behind the door where Father McCafferty had obviously been hiding. What he found there was a very cozy arrangement, which looked more like student accommodation than the basement of a priest's retreat. It was obvious that Father McCafferty had decamped into the basement room, as he seemed to have all of his worldly possessions down there. Starrett dumped all that he thought was important, including a fat brown envelope containing hundreds, if not thousands, of euro, into two box files.

An hour and a half later the detective was back in the ancient Garda Station House, in historic Gamble Square in Ramelton. He dumped the two box files on Francis Casey's desk and as the garda with the afro hairstyle tore into them, Starrett figured he couldn't have been more excited were the boxes filled with the sadly lamented Bakersville cheeseless cheesecakes. Francis admitted that he still had no joy locating Bishop Freeman.

Starrett returned to his own office and the work of updating his notes and awaiting the arrival of Father McCafferty, who he'd left in Letterkenny General Hospital under the watchful eye of Garda Romany Browne. There was a wee bit of a buzz about the Station House, with some of the gardaí obviously feeling they'd got their man –it certainly looked that way, anyway. If not, why on earth would McCafferty hide in the basement for over a day? And why would he want to attack two members of the gardaí if, indeed, he was innocent? Yes, Starrett had to admit, being caught red-handed trying to swindle Mrs Orla O'Connor out of both her grand house and her inheritance, was a crime the priest with the elephant-ear elbows most certainly would do time for. Then he chastised himself: here he was doing what he always cautioned his team not to do: put the cart before the horse. 'Deal only with the facts you have,' he said to himself. And he turned to the page in his notebook reserved for McCafferty to refresh his memory of the priest's alibi.

He ran his finger down the page until, yes, there it was – Father Gene McCafferty had claimed to have been with one of the most beautiful women in County Donegal at the time of Father Matthew McKaye's untimely demise. He had point-blank refused to offer any more information than that to Nuala Gibson when she had originally questioned him. Had that merely been bravado, purely for the benefit of Miss Gibson? Either way, there were just too many beautiful women in County Donegal for the gardaí to be able to find the one Father Mc-

Cafferty was referring to. Perhaps they should start with the blind ones, he reasoned, and then immediately dismissed the uncharitable thought.

McCafferty eventually arrived in Ramelton just after two o'clock where he was processed and taken straight to the interview-room in the basement of the gardaí station. There he was confronted by Starrett and Nuala Gibson, fresh from a quick pit stop for coffee and raring to go. The priest looked pitiful, with both wrists bound in casts and resting just by his belt, either side of his stomach. For the foreseeable future, the priest would have to be spoon-fed, and that would be the least embarrassing of his worries.

Before they'd a chance to even think of asking their first question, Father McCafferty started up with: 'Don't you realise that I've got a heart condition? You could've killed me!'

'From where I was standing you were the one doing all the attacking,' Starrett rightfully claimed.

'Well, I thought I was being attacked by thieves,' McCafferty protested, 'I'd a right to be down there, you didn't!'

'Okay,' Starrett said barely, just barely, managing to restrain himself from saying, "Whist! Would you give me head peace?" Instead he said, 'Okay, let's get started here,' and went on to announce, for the benefit of the tape recorder, the time, the date, the fact that the priest did not want a solicitor present and the names and ranks of all those present. 'So far so good,' he said to himself, off microphone. 'So,' he continued, opening a file in front of him, 'we know all about the activities in your previous two dioceses, before St Ernan's. You admitted to Ban Garda Nuala Gibson that you had acquired some money. Now we know how.'

'We're sure, when we go through your files and all of your bank statements,' Gibson added, 'we'll find just how much we're talking about.'

'How should I put this…' Father McCafferty started, using one of his signature start-up lines.

'Oh, you might like to try, "I'm totally fecked!"', Starrett suggested to the crestfallen priest.

'I was thinking more along the lines of: I didn't break any laws,' the priest replied.

'Really?' Gibson shot back.

'Look, I never forced any of them to give me anything; they were all willing participants in our agreements.'

'That's an interesting approach, Father Gene,' Starrett said, 'very interesting approach. I think you'll find the authorities will take a completely different view on you and your scams. We've just recently visited Mrs Orla Robinson and I think you'll have a lot of trouble persuading her that she was a "willing participant in your agreement". But we can leave all of that to the fraud squad. In the meantime, we'd like to talk to you some more about the death of Father McKaye.'

Father McCafferty didn't show the slightest bit of concern apart, that was, from his usual ability to leak from all of his pores.

'So listen, Father,' Starrett said, not sure if he was amused or concerned about the 'willing participant approach', 'here's how I see it. You took Father Matt over to Mrs Robinson's, you figured all the women were impressed by him, so Orla would take to him as well and that could only help your cause. And she did take to him. But then, bit by bit, didn't he only go and discover what you were up to. My guess is that he either threatened to turn you over to the authorities or he tried to blackmail you into giving him a piece of the action. Either way, Father Matt ended up dead in St Ernan's for his proposal.'

'Okay, how should I put this, Inspector,' McCafferty said, wincing in pain as he tried to rest his arm on the wing of his chair, 'it would have been impossible for me to murder Father Matthew because I was elsewhere at the time of the murder.'

'Yes, very interesting,' Starrett said, hoping his waning patience was transparent. He read through Gibson's report of the first interview with McCafferty.

'Yes,' he eventually continued, 'here is it. You said during your interview with the Ban Garda that at the time of Father Matt's death you were with the most beautiful woman in Donegal?'

'It's the same difference, but I actually said "the most beautiful woman in the county".'

'Sorry, I stand corrected,' Starrett apologised, 'you were with "the most beautiful woman in the county".'

'Yes,' McCafferty grunted. His sunken eyes appeared to sink even further into his skull, most likely as a result of the painkillers starting to wear off. His Buddy Holly glasses certainly didn't help, serving only to magnify the various shades of darkness around his eyes.

'And do you want to give us any more clues to her actual identity?' Starrett coaxed.

'As I said before, a gentleman never tells.'

'Well, we're okay then, you'll be free to talk,' Starrett offered, but McCafferty didn't take up on the slight. 'You see that convinces me even more that you're guilty, the fact that you created this fictional character you were supposedly with when Father Matt was murdered. And really if you were innocent, all you would need to do is give us the details of this mystery beauty and then we could check with her.'

McCafferty tried a grin that didn't really come off, as he was clearly now in bad need of some more medication.

Starrett noticed McCafferty attempting to see if his thumbs would move through the cast, only for him to be rewarded with what looked like another lightning bolt of pain.

'Augh, I wouldn't bother if I was you,' he offered compassionately, 'thumbs are so overrated. Why do you think we need thumbs? Just think of how absolutely amazing it would be if we'd a fifth finger instead of a thumb!'

'Well, we wouldn't be able to shake hands,' Gibson offered, looking and sounding like she was genuinely interested in the topic.

'Think of all the germs we'd save ourselves from,' Starrett replied, unable to avoid staring at McCafferty. He wished, for just a split second, that he was the kind of garda who would go to the lengths of putting pressure on one of McCafferty's wrist to torture a confession out of him. But only for a split second.

'So are you ashamed of this woman?' he continued.

'I bet she's a hooker,' Gibson volunteered barely under her breath.

'Or perhaps a woman you're setting up as the victim for your next scam?' Starrett pushed.

McCafferty was now sweating profusely and tears had started to fall down his face. He looked desperate. A full confession probably wasn't too far away. The tape would show that it would be a fair confession.

The priest's eyes were now pleading with the inspector. But the inspector couldn't work out if he was looking for forgiveness or painkillers. Come on man, you know you want to, Starrett said under his breath, as Gibson asked, 'Look Father, do you want us to get one of the priests to sit in with you when you make your statement?'

Clearly she too felt they were very close to the point of a full confession to the murder of Father Matthew McKaye. And he did make a confession. To the name of the woman, the most beautiful in all of the county – his alibi for where he was as Father Matthew McKaye lay dying in the kitchen at St Ernan's. Yes, the beauty was a certain lady by the name Aoife Sweeney.

Fifteen minutes later, Garda Francis Casey had uncovered an address in Donegal Town centre to fit the woman who owned the mobile number McCafferty had passed to his interviewers. Fifteen minutes after that, Romany Browne, who'd now made a full recovery, and Sergeant Packie Garvey were on their way to the very same address.

In the meantime, the interview with Father Gene McCafferty was suspended until as such time as they reached Aoife Sweeney. The logic being, that when the alibi turned out to be a lie, as both Starrett and Gibson suspected, they could then use it as leverage to extract a full confession from the priest.

That, at least, was Starrett's theory.

He would clear this case up today, which would allow him some quality time with the Major.

He checked his notes again. There were still some leads he and his team could follow, and Casey and Gibson were diligently working on them, but he really felt in limbo as they waited for the news from this Aoife Sweeney. Could this woman really be as beautiful as Father McCafferty claimed? If so, surely the next question had to be, what was she doing with Father McCafferty?

What was it that a man saw in a woman vice versa that made the magnetic connection for them? Did it go beyond looks, perhaps to the spirit – was that the force beyond the physical attraction that sealed the connection? Starrett often noticed women going about their daily business and the way they'd unconsciously, adopt a harder 'outdoor face'; a face well capable of cutting the ice of the worst mornings. But the minute they'd bump into someone they knew, the hard face would crack and melt into a friendly greeting and a large smile and in that moment their appearance would totally change, and they'd transform into a much more attractive being. Yes, there was nothing like a warm smile to make a woman glow – Starrett would have to put a smile high on the list of things he was attracted to. Even with Maggie Keane's crooked front tooth, which gave her that unique lopsided grin when she tried to smile, it was based on an imperfection but it was still so very endearing. Maybe it was the impish wink with which her smile took its bow that made it work, well at least as far as Starrett was concerned it was.

On the other hand, there were few things quite as unattractive as a woman crying. Crying ruined the lines of a woman's face. He reckoned that was why so many actresses got crying so wrong in the movies; they were just never prepared to look so ugly on the big screen. And there were few things quite as sad, or unforgivable, as a man making a woman cry in public. It wasn't so much the humiliation of physically crying in public, as the blatant display of force some people like to have over others, inflicted merely by the power of words.

Starrett thought all these things - or maybe re-thought them, because through his daily study of human beings, he often happened upon such thoughts – just like now as he wondered about exactly how Aoife Sweeney would look.

* * *

Meanwhile, down in Donegal Town, Romany Browne and Packie Garvey were about to discover the secret of exactly how Aoife Sweeney looked, if indeed maybe even discover if such a person ever existed, or she wasn't merely a figment of Father McCafferty's desperate imagination.

The address Garda Francis Casey had pinned down led them up a traffic-free alleyway and directly across from the Diamond (more like a rectangle someone had forced out of shape than a diamond) from Magees, producers of not just some of the best tweed jackets in the world, but also a line in some very eye-catching hats as well. The alleyway led to a courtyard surrounded with what looked more like offices than domestic dwellings. Surely not a brothel, Garvey wondered? The brass plate by the side of the address they were seeking proclaimed 'The Freedom Practice (2nd floor)'. They walked up the narrow, but clean, staircase and through a door, also marked 'The Freedom Practice'.

There was a small-ish waiting room with three men and two women sitting, pretending to read papers or magazines. If this is a brothel, Garvey thought, it must be quite liberal. Either the women can wait for their husbands, or maybe they were awaiting their own turn.

Strangely, none of the five people in the waiting room seemed particularly concerned with Garvey and Browne's uniform. Another man, clearly past his peak, entered through the door just after them and he scrutinised the room like a man who'd just boarded a train and was hoping to spot the friendly face of a regular fellow-traveller.

Garvey marched up to the receptionist and introduced himself and Browne.

'I'd like to speak to Aoife Sweeney please?'

'Right,' the friendly, middle-aged receptionist replied, 'you mean Dr Sweeney, of course?'

Both Browne and Garvey clocked the large lettering on the wall behind her at the same time. 'The Freedom Practice' was once again written in large brass letters and then underneath in smaller, gentler, joined-up lettering: 'Good health gives you freedom.'

'Sorry,' Garvey whispered, 'yes, of course.'

'Is this official gardaí business or do I need to get youse to fill out two forms with your medical history?'

'It'll be gardaí business,' Garvey replied, trying to sound as official as possible.

Even though it was gardaí business, Sergeant Packie Garvey and Garda Romany Browne were kept idling in the waiting room for nearly twenty minutes until Dr Sweeney's next break between patients. They, too, pretended to read magazines, if only to protect the space around them. Packie got a few nods of acknowledgement, acknowledgement, no doubt, of his skills on the hurling field.

The first time Packie Garvey saw Dr Aoife Sweeney's face his heart skipped a beat. The first time Romany Browne saw Dr Sweeney's face he was distracted by the clock on the wall behind her as it busily chipped away at his Saturday.

'Packie, it's such a pleasure to actually meet you in person,' she said, as she refused to stop shaking his hand and fluttering her eyelashes. 'Sure, it's the first time I've seen you with all your clothes on....'

This totally threw Romany Browne, who didn't immediately twig what it was she was going on about.

'...and caked in mud!' she added, giving a further clue. 'What can I do for the gardaí today?'

'We're here to talk to you about Father Gene McCafferty,' Garvey said, moving along swiftly to the official business.

'Ah yes, Gene,' she sighed, 'what's he been up to this time?'

'Sorry?' Garvey said.

'Well, I've never met any man so rich, either in monetary terms or

in credits-in-Heaven terms, who could eat as many chocolates, burgers, steaks, chips, crisps, sweets, desserts, cakes, biscuits, fry-ups, and
ice cream cones as he does, and not drop down dead. It's dangerous,
gentlemen,' she said, as she swung around in her seat to nod in the direction of the wall behind her, and a blow-up drawing of the human
heart and its servicing system. 'The arteries are so easily blocked, but
not quite so easy to repair.'

Garvey shuddered at the thought, promising himself to swap his
daily fry-up at Steve's for porridge.

'Yes, we're aware of his heart-condition,' Garvey said, 'we just
wanted to ask you if you saw him this Wednesday past?'

Dr Sweeney quick-flicked back one page of her diary. 'Yes,' she
said, 'he was in for his bi-annual MOT.' She paused to laugh. 'The full
service, as it were! We started,' again she looked at her diary, 'just after
3:15 and I'd given him the news just after 5:30. I had to keep him waiting a bit as I over-ran with another patient.'

'How was he?' Garvey felt obliged to ask, even though he realised
Starrett's case had come crashing down around his feet.

'I said to him, "Gene, I've never met a man so rich they can afford
to eat all the chocolate, burgers, steaks, chips, sweets, desserts, fry-ups,
and ice cream cones they want to and not drop down dead."'

They got the picture, and pretty vividly at that.

CHAPTER THIRTY-EIGHT

When Starrett received the phone call from Sergeant Garvey informing him that the McCafferty alibi had checked out, he was pretty upbeat about the news. He'd always felt it was just as important to let the innocent go free as it was to catch the guilty.

For his part, Starrett was happy that he would no longer have to deal with Father Gene McCafferty. The Gardaí Fraud Squad would now take responsibility for the priest. They wouldn't have much to do, as Starrett and his team had pretty much piled up the details of all of his scams on a plate for them. However, they still had a whole other plate to fill. 'Sometimes I'd like to be able to take my eyeballs out of their sockets and give them a proper cleaning, just so I can go back to the case with fresh eyes,' was how he had put it.

The inspector had instructed Garvey and Browne to remain in Donegal Town to see if they could finally grab an interview with Eimear Robinson's husband, Gerry. He and Gibson would head back there themselves after making a quick stop at the Major's, to see how he was doing.

As they drove to Ray Bridge with the rain literally bouncing off his windscreen, Starrett said, 'It feels like it's been raining for forty days and forty nights.'

'What about Thursday afternoon, that was a wonderful autumnal afternoon,' Gibson offered.

'Yes, yes of course,' he conceded and then added, 'but I just said it felt like it had been raining for forty days and forty nights and I wanted to say something religious and that was all I could think of at the time.'

'How long have you known Major Newton Cunningham?' she asked.

'He's a good friend of my father's so he's been around for as long as I can remember,' Starrett answered, regretting the fact that he'd been too transparent. 'When I was growing up, he'd always be around the house and he and my father would reminisce about the war...' Starrett said before stopping in a smile. 'I remember this one story in particular that the Major had a habit of telling when there'd be a group of people around for dinner and he and my father were in their entertaining mood, reminiscing away.'

Then he paused as though he wasn't going to continue.

'Well, you can't very well stop there,' Gibson encouraged, 'you have to tell me the rest of the story!'

'Well, when they were in occupied territory trying to "take" somewhere or other,' Starrett started up again enthusiastically, 'that's how they'd always start – "and then we had to take Caen Woods, so we..." – and off they'd go. Anyway, when they were on the march they'd always have to carry everything with them, on their person, as it were. They discovered that the driest place to store tea leaves was in fact in their underpants...'

'This isn't going to be rude is it?' Gibson asked, as she tried to find a gear low enough to get Starrett's trusted BMW up a precipitous hill.

'Bejeepers, no!' he replied, backsliding once again in his promise to avoid using that word. He figured trying to give up using a favoured word was a bit like trying to give up cigarettes; you're bound to indulge from time to time. 'Where was I?'

'You were just telling me that the Major used to carry his tea leaves in his underpants,' she said. 'Goodness, I don't think I'm ever going to get that image out of my mind.'

'Right, so the Major and his troop were walking along, about to "take" somewhere or other, and they happened upon this deserted farm where they found a lot of chickens. They were chasing them around the farmyard, in search of eggs, and all of a sudden they came under a heavy mortar attack from the enemy. The Major would say "One minute we were chasing chickens about the beautiful farmland and the next we were being bombarded by heavy artillery and didn't they only go and blow the hens to kingdom come. Through the force of one of the explosions", he would say "I found myself flying through the air and landing safely in a haystack." That's when he really thought his number was up. Apparently, he quickly felt around for all his limbs to make sure everything was okay and apart from one little accident of nature he was a-okay. Then, he says, he remembered the tea so he shouted to the chaps "Has anyone got any milk? I've just wet the tea!"'

Starrett couldn't help laughing as he'd often done at that story.

He looked at Gibson who looked like she was still processing the joke.

'Ah jeez, no Starrett,' she said. 'Surely you don't mean that he like…actually…wet the tea as in…ah, that's gross…! Really?' She burst into a fit of uncontrollable giggles.

They sat in silence for the remainder of the journey – silence, that was, apart from the rattle of Starrett's engine.

When they arrived at the Major's tree-protected property, he was in a medication-induced sleep. His wife reported that he'd had an okay night and a good morning.

'He said he needed to speak to you about something,' she said. Starrett studied Annette's face; she looked weary while at the same time trying to remain upbeat for the people who came visiting her ailing husband.

'Did he say what it was about?' he asked quietly, as they both looked on at the Major sleeping peacefully.

'No,' she whispered back, 'he was a bit delusional, asking if the people had taken to the streets yet. Saying it was only a matter of time; people weren't going to put up with what the government, Irish Water, and the bankers had thrown at them. He figured the water rates would be the last straw. He felt it was only a matter of time before the people rose up and took to the streets, which he said he wasn't sure would be a bad thing. He was worried about the Guards being in the front line. Then he asked about you, asked when you were coming again, said he really needed to speak to you. He told me to wake him up when you arrived. But you know, Starrett, he's getting so little rest, I just can't do that to him.'

'Of course you mustn't,' Starrett whispered, raising his bent forefinger and shaking it from side to side to emphasise his point.

'Your mum and dad were here this morning,' Annette said, in a louder voice, after she'd gently closed the bedroom door behind them. 'Maggie Keane was here, too. She's so good, Starrett – she's coming back later today to help me with the visitors. It's funny, Starrett, most people who call don't even get a chance to see him. He's a proud man, but he doesn't want to have visitors. But he's right isn't he? I can't let people see him like this, can I?'

'People understand, Annette,' Starrett replied, thinking of Nuala Gibson. 'They're happy if they come into the house and support you.'

'And then when he's feeling better, all he wants to do is see you, your mum and dad and a few of our dear friends, but not someone he once bought a car off. He doesn't particularly want…that's not being snobby is it, Starrett?'

'Not at all, Annette. I'll put a garda on the end of your lane, help keep the proceedings respectful.'

'Yes, that would be very helpful,' she replied, noticeably relieved. 'I hadn't thought of that. It's very sad that all his old cronies are long since passed, but he'd have liked nothing better than to have a bunch of them in with him, get the poteen out and have a good old chin-wag about their war adventures.'

Starrett was going to comment on how great a gang the Major and his mates were, but he stopped himself short for fear that he may sound like he was speaking about his boss in the past tense.

'He had a good chat this morning with your father about the arrangements,' Annette continued. 'He seemed very relieved to get all of that off his chest.'

'Ah good.'

'You know, he still hasn't acknowledged to me how bad he is, Starrett.'

'He's an old soldier, Annette, so he can deal with everything – everything, that is, apart from leaving you. You've got to be strong for him.'

'He's not going to get better, Starrett,' she said, most likely forgetting that they'd discussed this before, or maybe she just needed someone to voice all her thoughts to.

'I know, Annette, I know.'

'I worry I'm being selfish now and I just want to keep him around for selfish reasons,' she admitted, 'but he's not suffering.'

'Please take this time with him,' he offered in encouragement, leaving so much unsaid but hopefully understood.

'There's just never enough of it, of time, is there.'

CHAPTER THIRTY-NINE

'You'll never guess what happened back at St Ernan's!' Gibson said, a split second after they were back in the privacy of Starrett's car.

Starrett was still trying to process his conversation with the Major's wife, so he didn't initially respond to the ban garda.

'It's the bishop, Sir, he just turned up out of the blue at St Ernan's, half an hour ago,' she said, reporting the news she'd heard from Garvey, via mobile phone, just a few minutes before Starrett had left the Major's house.

'Did he say where he'd been?' the inspector eventually asked when his brain clicked into gear.

'Said he hadn't been anywhere, he'd just been going about his business. Said he still had enough friends on the gardaí to ensure the APB Starrett had put out on him was ineffective.'

'It never rains but it snows,' Starrett said, as he belted himself into the passenger seat and they set off in the general direction of Donegal Town, if only because that's where all the action seemed to be.

* * *

Garvey had taken it upon himself not to interview Eimear's husband, Gerry. He figured Starrett would never forgive him if they let Bishop Freeman slip through their fingers again. So he and Garda Romany Browne remained at St Ernan's, in effect to 'guard' the disappearing bishop.

As Starrett and Gibson came to the end of the spectacular Blue Stack mountains on their right, Starrett started to feel uneasy about confronting Freeman. He put it down mostly to the mood he was in, having just left the ailing Major. Then he wondered, not for the first time in his life, why all people couldn't be like the Major, or like his father, or the James Gang, or his Bridge Bar drinking buddies, or even like the very decent and upstanding Packie Garvey. Surely, Starrett thought, as they passed through the magnificent creation that is the rugged Donegal countryside, the world would be a much better place if all men were like them and not like Bishop Freeman? Yes, so he still hadn't proven that the bishop had any direct involvement in the death of Father Matthew McKaye, but he knew from first-hand experience that there was evil in that man's very soul.

Starrett wondered, and not for the first time, that if there was indeed a higher special being, a spiritual force, a God if you will, how on the one hand He could create countryside as inspiring as the Donegal landscape while at the same time claiming authorship of the likes of Bishop Cormac Freeman?

Packie Garvey rang through on Gibson's mobile to check how long it would be until they'd arrive at St Ernan's. Starrett took the phone and said he now felt that his priority should be to talk to the members of Eimear Gibson's family, namely her sister, Mary Mooney, and her husband, Gerry. In the meantime, Garvey should take Bishop Freeman into custody and transfer him to Ramelton Gardaí Station for questioning.

'If he seeks any clarification,' he continued, 'tell him he's assisting us with our inquiries. Please tell him he's entitled to have his solicitor present.'

Packie, as ever, didn't question the order, he acted on it.

'Are you not just exposing yourself to a hornet's nest there?' Gibson said, showing that whereas she would never, ever disobey Starrett's orders, or his requests, as the inspector preferred to refer to them, she might, on occasions such as this one, see if there wasn't maybe a better way of going about things.

'That's as may be, Nuala,' Starrett said, perking up a bit, 'but I've found that while on your life path, sometimes, just sometimes mind you, what you choose to avoid is just as important as what you aim for. The former can certainly do you a lot more damage than the latter.'

Gibson, for her part, very subtly chose to avoid any further conversation on this matter.

'Should we head back to Ramelton?'

'Let's head to Eimear's house,' Starrett said, 'we're very close.'

Exactly three minutes later they pulled up outside Mrs Robinson's house, a new place with bare earth banked all around and hints of some fresh planting. In five years' time the house and its surrounds would look natural and perfect, or as near enough perfect as it was ever going to be. Then they'd need to find another project to pique their interest. We always put ourselves in a position where we're five years away from perfection, so, in practice, it's always the point we never reach.

'I'll tell you what, Nuala, drive up close to the house so they can't see us from the front window,' Starrett said, slipping way down into his seat, remembering the blonde, long-legged reflection who had dashed across the sitting room mirror the last time he was in the house. 'Then, you go to the front door and I'll slip around the back.'

On the back porch, the detective enjoyed a collision with the star of the scene he ever so briefly caught in the mirror. The girl with the very long blonde hair was so preoccupied about getting out of the house while simultaneously buckling up the belt on her blood red, military-style jacket, that she quite literally collided with the person of Inspector Starrett. The inspector came off the worse the wear as her industrial styled, black leather boots connected full on with his shin. Yet he didn't exactly mind because the vision of female perfection who helped him up from the ground near nullified the sharp pain growing in his shin.

In that moment, his mind jumped from the X-rated scene by his knee to the one of Dr Samantha Aljoe carefully removing, if his memory wasn't playing tricks on him, an equally long blonde hair from the body of father Matthew McKaye and placing it delicately in one of her translucent evidence bags.

'Eimear's sister, I presume?' he offered, as he made sure the woman had recovered her land-legs before letting go of her.

'Eimear's sister,' she confirmed, her smile disappearing as quickly as it would have from Rooney's face if he'd been awarded a penalty only to then go and miss it.

'Ah perfect,' Starrett said, producing his warrant card, 'I'm Inspector Starrett and you're the very person I was hoping to have a natter with.'

'Off to visit friends,' she said. 'Meet later?'

'Ah no,' he said, re-opening Eimear's back door. 'We won't detain you for too long.'

The woman looked like she was going to defy him and walk away but then obviously thought better of it, so she meekly walked through the door he'd been holding open for her, looked at her watch, took out her mobile and started to text away on it, ten to the dozen.

'Ah, I see you've met our Mary!' Eimear said, when Starrett and the leggy blonde walked through to the kitchen. 'I was just saying to the ban garda here, I said, "Ban Garda, you only just missed my sister."'

'Yes,' Starrett agreed. 'We had a meeting of sorts, I think me shin came off the worse. Eimear, Mary is in a bit of a hurry – by any chance, is there a wee room where Ban Garda Nuala Gibson and myself could have a quick chat with her so we don't put too much of a dent into her Saturday afternoon?'

Mary was meanwhile rolling her eyes and her thumb was flicking up and down on her telephone screen.

'Oh yes,' Eimear declared proudly, 'I was just saying to Jessica recently, I said, "Jessica, we're not getting much use out of our sitting-room, are we?. I suppose we're going to have to wait until you and Julia are bringing boys ho–"'

'Yes Mum,' Jessica said, 'I'm sure the guards don't need to hear that. Aunty Mary is in a hurry.'

'I'm not your Aunty!' Aunty Mary snapped.

'Mum,' Jessica called out, 'is she disowning you or me or both of us?'

'Jessica, you know our Mary doesn't like to be called Aunty. She feels it ages her.'

'Whatever,' Jessica said.

'Whatever,' Mary echoed, but not quite carrying it off.

'Mary, take them through to the sitting room,' Eimear ordered as if she was commanding a troublesome child. 'I'll bring you through some tea and coffee shortly.'

'Eimear!' Mary hissed, rolling her eyes.

Mary Mooney looked like she'd personally modelled for Johannes Vermeer's masterpiece, The Girl with the Pearl Earring. She'd applied her makeup so perfectly that it appeared as though it just might have been painted on her face by the Dutch Master himself – there wasn't a single spot of make-up free skin about her face. And, if anything, her lips were so perfect, with their razor-sharp lines and their vibrant red lipstick, they looked like they quite possibly could have been tattooed on.

She was clearly conscious of just how much lipstick she'd applied because every few minutes she would open her mouth slightly and run her tongue across her teeth from left to right, wiping off any offending smudges. Only the way she did it, as far as Starrett was concerned, was pretty X-rated itself.

The other area Mary had concentrated on was her fingernails. Each nail was varnished in a different vivid colour and then on top of that colour, she'd painted ten different patterns, ranging from a star to an attempt at a rainbow.

She sat down on the sofa, seemingly unconcerned that her tartan, pleated micro-skirt rode up to expose the little of what remained un-exposed of her tanned, bare legs. It wasn't so much that Mary Mooney had long legs, it was just that she was showing a lot of them. Maggie Keane would frequently tell her daughters that girls only wore short skirts to distract boys from looking at their inferior lower legs. Mind you, Starrett wasn't sure that there would be an imperfect feature on Mary Mooney's body. He noted that she didn't seem to like to smile like other women he could think of, though. And, despite all that sup-posed temptation, the inspector found it easy to avert his eyes from Mary Mooney's lower limbs because, having already, very nearly, seen everything she had, including what she'd eaten for breakfast, he came to the conclusion that he much preferred the look of mystery. He could tell the initial effect of her beauty was quickly wearing off on him, if only because his shin was starting to throb again, like someone had just tried to saw through it with a rusted hacksaw.

'We'd like to talk to you about Father Matthew, if you don't mind,' Starrett started, finally taking control of his faculties.

'I do mind. A lot. Won't do me much good though.'

'Your sister said you and Father Matt got on very well.'

'How well?' she asked, very nearly pronouncing the question mark.

'Mary,' Starrett said, changing gear, and pausing.

He thought he realised the subtext of her two-word reply, i.e. how much of what I did, did she tell you? In other words, there was possi-ble information here to be learned.

'Mary,' he started again.

'You're sounding like a nursery rhyme,' she quipped.

Starrett was going to finish her line with 'quite contrary' but decided not to risk rattling her.

'I understand you and Father Matt were quite close.'

'For a priest he was okay.'

'Did you only meet him around here?'

Mary Mooney looked at both of them slowly, as though she was trying to decide how much to tell them. He wondered if Gibson wasn't there, would this young lady be more open to his questioning?

'At first,' she admitted, 'Eimear liked him. Decent sort. Looked good. Looked great, in fact. Well fit. Became friends. We'd talk about everything. Asked him if he missed sex. He said "of course". Said it was like not being able to quenching a great thirst. I shifted him.'

'But he was a priest?' Gibson complained.

'Meet a thirsty man in the desert you just gotta give him a drink,' she replied through a smirk, 'don't you.'

'Where did youse go?' Starrett asked, happy that it appeared, at least, that Gibson's involuntary comment hadn't derailed Mary's candidness.

'Round my house, when Callum, my husband, was out.'

'How often?' Starrett asked.

She took up her mobile again and scrolled through it, pausing every now and again.

'Seventeen times,' she admitted.

'Always at your house?'

'Few times here when Gerry and Eimear were out at the flicks and Julia and Jessica were being moody teenagers in their room.'

'Were you, you know, not scared of being caught?'

'He was a priest, no one suspected.'

'Did Eimear know?'

'Didn't she tell you?' Mary replied in disbelief.

'Who else knew?' Starrett continued quickly, so she wouldn't get preoccupied by the fact he'd duped her.

'Not many.'

'How many?'

'I don't know.'

'You don't seem to care,' Gibson chipped in again. 'Weren't you scared that your husband would come back and discover you?'

'He's always out. He's what you guards would call a "boy racer". But never let him know I said that. They just hate to be called that.

He's only concerned about his car. Now if his car cheated, well, then he really would be pissed. Really pissed. Can cars cheat?'

'Were youse in a relationship at the time of his death?' Starrett asked.

She laughed.

'What?'

'We weren't in a relationship. Sure, I'm married. We were just shagging.'

'Okay were you...' Starrett struggled to use that word in mixed company. 'Were youse enjoying a sexual relationship at the time of his death?'

'No, we stopped a month ago,' she admitted, after a bit of sniggering.

'Did you stop it or did he?' Gibson asked.

'He did.'

'Was he torn by his religion?'

'He found someone else–'

'But–' Gibson interrupted.

'I know, I know...' Mary in turn interrupted, '...but he was a priest.'

'Do you know who he started seeing after you?'

'Haven't a clue.'

'So how do you know for sure?' Starrett asked.

'He needed it. I tried to shift him after we stopped and he turned me down. He needed sex. Father Matt really needed sex. The only reason he'd turn me down,' Mary claimed proudly, 'would be due to the fact he was being shifted by someone else.'

Starrett was glad Gibson was taking notes. He imagined they'd probably pick up more when they'd a chance to review the notes afterwards, and with Mary Mooney's (mostly) text-length sentences, this was one set of interview notes it wouldn't take them long to get through.

'So, after you and Father Matt split up...' Starrett started, wanting to move the interview on to other, hopefully equally revealing topics.

'We weren't having an affair, no need to break up,' Mary hissed.

'Okay, sorry, after you and Father Matt stopped having sexual intercourse, did you still see him at Eimear's house?'

'Yes, loads.'

'Were you still friendly to each other?'

'Not much in common, but still civil,' Mary said.

'Did youse fight? Argue?'

'No, we weren't married; we weren't even a couple, so no need to argue.'

'You don't know who he saw after you?'

'No,' she said firmly, her tongue darting across her teeth again.

'Do you know if he was seeing one girl or several girls?' Starrett asked, ploughing away at his list of questions. He occasionally made up a list of questions under the title 'Questions I should have asked but forgot to'. His last question, which had seen Mary shake her head to the negative, wouldn't have been on such a list, but his next question quite possibly might have.

'Did Father Matt ever discuss with you if anything was troubling him?'

'The only thing that appeared to be troubling him, we got fixed within a few minutes of us meeting up,' she replied.

'And what was that?' Starrett asked, drawing a strange look from Gibson.

'That he needed shifting and I shifted him,' Mary replied, confident enough not to be caught beating about the bush.

'Right, right, I see, but I was thinking more of you know…if he was in financial trouble?'

'For a priest he seemed well off – expensive clothes and underclothes, well groomed, he was very clean, nice smell,' she replied, now looking like she was really trying to concentrate on his question. 'He never tried to tap me for a few euro, the way my husband does.'

'Does your husband not work?'

'Yes he works, it's just every cent he has goes into his only true love, his car, a Nissan Skyline GTR.'

'What does he do for a living?' Starrett asked, very impressed by Mary's husband's choice in wheels.

'He's installs computer systems in hotels,' she said, in a lower voice.

'What do you do?' Gibson asked.

'I'm a beautician.'

Starrett banished all judgemental thoughts from his mind.

'Did youse talk about your work?' Starrett asked.

'Really? Is that really your question?' Mary replied disdainfully, 'Callum and I rarely talk about anything.'

'And Callum is?' Gibson asked for the record.

'My husband!'

'No, sorry, it's my fault, Mary,' Starrett laughed, 'I was asking you if you and Father Matt ever talked about your work?'

'No.'

'Did you talk about his beliefs?'

'He would have a whole lot of those deep and meaningful conversations with our Eimear.'

'Were Eimear and Father Matt having a physical relationship?' Starrett asked.

Mary looked like she wasn't as much upset that he would ask her such a question, as that he would think Father Matt could possibly be with her sister after having been, in her mind, with the better one.

'That's just not possible,' were the words she used.

'Why not? They seemed to get on well together, they seemed genuinely fond of each other?' Starrett stated, remembering Eimear Robinson was the first person he'd met on this case who seemed sincerely upset about Father Matt's demise.

'Our Eimear lives her life for Julia and Jessica,' Mary began. 'She wouldn't do anything, and I really mean anything, to directly or indirectly jeopardise their wellbeing.'

Starrett was surprised by her answer in that she'd gone beyond the confines of a text message for the first time since they'd started the interview. She seemed aware of this herself and even appeared quite proud of her mini achievement.

'It just wouldn't have been possible,' she reiterated, maybe because Starrett looked like he wasn't sure whether Eimear and the priest hadn't shared a moment.

'Okay, if it wasn't Eimear–'

'It wasn't our Eimear,' Mary said, flatly, flashing her speedy tongue across her teeth.

'Okay, it wasn't Eimear,' he agreed, for the sake of the interview. 'Do you think he might have discussed this other woman with Eimear?'

Mary Mooney looked like she was considering this possibility for the first time. 'He might have done,' she agreed.

'Priests often seem to be attracted to older women,' Starrett mused.

'Older woman, def not,' she declared on his behalf. 'Father Matt wouldn't be interested in anything other than a young thing. He said that's why he'd never be able to be a priest, having to deal with the older women.'

'So what did youse talk about when youse were alone?' Starrett asked, picking up her thread.

Mary Mooney looked shocked by the inspector's question. Starrett and Gibson were, in turn, shocked by her gesture and reply. She raised both hands up to either side of her head and she moved them down her body slowly, about six inches away from contact. She paused and then said, 'Talk? Do you really think so?'

Starrett had to accept the fact that Mary Mooney knew absolutely nothing whatsoever about Father Matthew McKaye, apart from the fact that, apparently, he liked to be shifted.

He had one final question for the one who was still basking in the glory of her recent flaunt.

'Mary, what were you doing on Wednesday afternoon, between 3:30 and 5:30?'

'Lucky for me I was still at work in the salon in town until about 7.'

CHAPTER FORTY

Starrett and Gibson rose from their seats in Eimear Robinson's lounge after Mary Mooney had more elaborately completed the same task, only she encored her performance by giving a quick twirl, which allowed her pleated tartan skirt, short and all as it was, to umbrella out, exposing even more skin.

She then walked over to Starrett, shook his hand and kissed the air on either side of his face, offered her first smile of the proceedings and whispered, 'Eimear has my number, call me.'

Starrett had been so intent in interviewing Mary Mooney that neither he nor Nuala Gibson had advised Gerry Robinson that they wanted to interview him next. When they returned to the living area in the kitchen, Julia informed them that Gerry had gone out for a walk with Jessica, who wanted to clear her head to avoid another migraine. Eimear was nowhere to be seen, but Starrett could hear noises coming from upstairs, which he assumed were from her domestic chores. He didn't want to hang around in case Gerry and his daughter were out for ages so he asked Julia to tell him they'd be back around six o'clock for the interview.

Donegal Town was gridlocked with vehicles circling and circling the Diamond, scouting for precious parking spaces. Pedestrians circled the Diamond in the opposite direction, all seeming very amused by the drivers' inability to find parking spaces. He wondered aloud to Gibson if the pedestrians looked kind of out of sorts because that they would all have to travel over to Letterkenny for their entertainment and recreation (as Donegal Town did not have it's own cinema or swimming pool) and were worried that when they returned they too would end up circling the Diamond in search of a parking space.

Just like a couple who had long since known each other's lines and routines, Gibson chose to just ignore Starrett.

Starrett wondered in silence if any of the people currently circling the Diamond were decendants of the original 42 people who were involuntarily transported from Donegal Town to the United States of America in the period from April 1737 to August 1743. Then he wondered if any of the 40 men and 2 women who had been banished to the States for either being a vagabond or a thief, had "made good" or if any of their decendents had "made good".

'So who do you think our Father Matt was having an affair with after he and Mary Mooney broke up?' Gibson asked, interrupting Starrett's distractions to the grid lock nightmare.

'It had to be someone who didn't mind that they wouldn't be on a traditional date, someone who didn't mind that it wasn't going to go somewhere.'

'Someone like another married woman?' Gibson suggested. 'Maybe even a protective mother?'

'What the eye doesn't see, the stomach doesn't miss!' Starrett exclaimed. 'Stop the car here.'

'But we'll be double parked,' she complained.

'What shall it profit a man if he shall gain the whole world and not be able to park his car wherever he wants to? On top of which, we're the gardaí.'

Starrett had hopped out before Gibson had even a chance to pull up. He actually ran into the home bakery, and if Gibson's eyes weren't deceiving her, he jumped the queue and came running back with a white bag nestled securely between his hand and his chest.

'However,' he said, when he was settled back in, secured by his seat belt, 'what the eye does see,' he continued, patting the bag he was now holding on to for dear life, 'that is to say half a dozen freshly baked wee cheesecakes, then the stomach most definitely misses.'

When Starrett walked back into St Ernan's, the first thing he noticed was the strength of the stale smell he'd experienced on previous visits. To expel the staleness from his nostrils, he stole a quick whiff from within his cheesecake bag as he rushed up the stairs. He knocked on Father Robert O'Leary's door, directly across the landing from where the stairwell emerged into the bright light from the large window. The beam was breaking through the clouds for the first time in days and it was so sharp, he felt it should be spiritually empowered, like the torch of God.

Father O'Leary welcomed the two of them and seemed as equally tickled as the inspector about the prospect of the cheesecakes. Starrett felt as though he'd just been to the tuck shop and now he was about to share his spoils.

'We'll save them to have with a fresh cup of tea,' Father O'Leary insisted, and Starrett couldn't have been happier. Full stop, he just couldn't have been happier.

'How are you progressing on the case?' the father asked as they settled down to their tea and cheesecakes.

'Well, we've managed to rule Father McCafferty out; his alibi is solid,' Starrett admitted.

'Okay,' Father O'Leary replied. 'What about the Mrs Orla O'Connor business – will you do anything about that?'

'Father McCafferty is in the hands of the Fraud Squad now, they'll take care of all that,' Starrett offered, stopping for the final bite of his first cheesecake and a swig of his strong tea before breaking the pause with, 'I've been thinking about your own investigative work and I was wondering if you'd had a chance to see if there could be any connection between some of that work and Father McKaye's death.'

'As I mentioned last time, those under scrutiny themselves don't even know we carry out the investigations.'

'Yeah,' Starrett said, 'I hear you, but at the same time, I know certain members of the ministry who, should they be investigated, wouldn't just allow it to stop there. They'd use their considerable clout to discover who was behind their potential downfall.'

'For some of the same reasons of confidentiality I mentioned earlier, I can't explain to you why I know this, but I can tell you: there is no reason to even suspect Father Matthew's loss of life was due to my investigations,' O'Leary said, with such a degree of finality that Starrett felt it would be counter-productive to continue with this thread. 'So where does that leave you?' he said, offering Starrett at least a bit of a lifeline.

'Okay, Father O'Leary, I will take you into my confidence in the hope you'll take me into yours,' Starrett said, noting that even though the priest didn't seem all that impressed, his Ban Garda definitely seemed to be. 'Earlier today I discovered that Father Matthew was having an affair with a married woman.'

The priest didn't bat an eyelid.

This fact threw Starrett completely off his stride. If Father O'Leary knew all about the affair, and he clearly did, why hadn't he told him?

Then the detective remembered their earlier conversation, when the priest had pretty much admitted he wouldn't shop anyone, but if Starrett came to him with legitimate information, he would confirm it to be true.

'I did try to drop you a little hint that Father Matthew was not exactly what we'd consider perfect material for the priesthood.'

Taking all this in, the inspector became convinced that if he'd managed to film the priest for the last minute or so, and he re-ran said film several times over, he'd have been able to confirm that Father O'Leary spelt out his last sentence in its entirety, and word perfect, with his thumb and forefinger acting as a fountain pen nib. Next, the word 'nib' served to remind him of the stolen John Hamilton antiques.

'Well, that was a little bit too subtle for me,' Starrett admitted. 'Anyway, this lady said she felt that Father Matthew stopped having relations with her because he'd met someone else.'

'So, now you know more than me, Inspector, and that's as it should be,' O'Leary said, contentedly.

'Have you any idea who this other woman might have been?'

'I could tell you who she wasn't, but that mightn't be of any assistance to you,' the father said.

'You just never know, and don't be too worried about disappointing me. I always find it's equally important to be able to rule people out rather than try to find evidence to add them to a suspect list.'

'Well, all I can tell you is that Father Matthew and our cleaner, Eimear Robinson, did get on very well. Perhaps some naysayers may suggest there was a liaison, but I don't believe you need to speculate on anything deeper than friendship.'

'Have you discovered the whereabouts of the Hamilton nibs yet?' Starrett asked, not wishing to push any further on the Father Matthew and Eimear relationship because he realised he would get nowhere with it in this interview.

'Sorry, nothing on that front,' he replied spelling out the words 'that front' with his finger.

'It was suggested to me earlier that Father Matthew was not short of funds.'

'You think he might have taken them and sold them himself?'

'Perhaps,' Starrett replied, shrugging his shoulders.

'Perhaps. But I only say "perhaps" because I don't know otherwise, although I admit to you that I would very much doubt that possibility.'

Gibson refreshed their teas and Starrett and Father O'Leary helped themselves to their second cheesecake. Starrett imagined he and the priest, if only because he himself had thought so, would've split the sixth cheesecake between the two of them. Gibson was having none of that, which meant she was having all of her entitled second cheesecake intact, albeit temporarily. He went to ask several questions but in the end asked none, hiding behind his tea and enjoying the last bite of his cheesecake.

'How is your young garda, Romany Browne?'

'Yes,' Starrett offered, finding his voice again, 'he was very lucky; he managed to jump back on the horse quickly and is back into the investigation.'

'Ah yes, the speedy revitalisation process of youth,' Father O'Leary said, pensively. 'Now you come to mention it, there didn't seem much wrong with him when he and the sergeant took Bishop Freeman away for questioning.'

'Listen,' Starrett said, standing up, 'we need to get back into town to talk to a few more persons of interest.'

'Yes of course,' the priest said, showing them to the door. When Gibson had walked through it, he put his hand out to stop Starrett from following her. Waiting for Gibson to move from earshot, the priest continued, 'Please be very, very careful in your dealings with Bishop Freeman. He's a very, very powerful man, Starrett, and like most men of great power he has no preference to wield it justly. I've always found it's good to look at those who have gone before.'

Father O'Leary air-wrote the last sentence in the smallest letters he'd used so far.

Chapter Forty-One

'Let's head back to Eimear Robinson's house,' Starrett said, as he and Gibson hopped back in his car, 'I want another chat with her and you can interview Gerry at the same time.'

Just then the ban garda's mobile rang. It was Browne, saying he was on his way back to Donegal Town. Starrett told Gibson to tell Browne to meet them at Eimear Robinson's house.

Garda Romany Browne was already waiting for them by the time they got there, and Starrett got right down to the business of their visit, and invited Eimear to join him for a quiet chat in the privacy of her own lounge.

Eimear seemed upbeat – if her rosy cheeks were anything to go by, it looked like she might have been out in the blustery afternoon air for a clearing-of-the-head walk of her own.

'So, you got to meet our Mary at last?' Mrs Robinson said, as she proudly settled into her pale sofa in the lounge she'd never used before she'd met the Ramelton detective. Starrett was worried that if he didn't solve the case in a hurry, he might wear that sofa out.

'Yes, and quite an interesting chat at that, Eimear,' Starrett said, as he removed his notebook from inside his windbreaker. Starrett was a fan of windbreakers – you didn't have to worry about them. You could just toss them in the back of the car and they wouldn't complain by producing creases. But the main problem with windbreakers, as far as he could tell, was they didn't, for some reason or another, have inside pockets where a member of the garda, such as himself for instance, could store his notebook and pens. Trouser back pockets didn't work for Starrett either because while in there, his black leather notebook tended to get badly bent out of shape quite quickly and he'd more than a couple of pairs of trousers ruined by a leaking pen. But now, after all these years, he'd managed to find a Burberry windbreaker with an inside pocket, just the one mind you – but then that was all he needed to get by.

As Eimear gushed about her new house, Starrett began to wonder how well her husband was getting on with the ban garda.

'Surely,' Eimear said, proving her mind wasn't too far from that very same matter, 'in this day and age of political correctness, she should have interviewed me and you should have interviewed Gerry.'

'It's just an interview, not an interrogation,' Starrett explained, trying to bluff his way around her correct assumption.

She seemed to relax a bit with that reply.

'So,' he offered up, his notebook and pen at the ready, 'Mary confessed to me that she'd a relationship with Father Matthew McKaye.'

'Sure, he was friends with all the family,' Eimear replied, now not as relaxed as she had been a few moments ago while enjoying the comforts and newness of her lounge. 'Didn't I tell you that he'd often come up and eat with us, or sometimes he'd even just have a cup of tea? In the early days he'd come up just to watch TV with the girls – sure, he was nearly one of the family.'

'Yes, I believe you told me most of that, Eimear,' Starrett replied, writing something down in his notebook in his neat handwriting. 'But what you didn't tell me was that he was also coming up to enjoy sexual relations with your sister, Mary.'

Eimear Robinson crossed herself. 'That's no way to speak of the dead, Inspector,' she said.

'Mary's words were even more to the point,' he sighed. 'Tell me this, Eimear: Were you aware that Mary and Father Matt were sleeping together?'

'Yes,' she replied.

'Why didn't you tell me?'

'I tried to stop her; I said to her, "Mary," I said, "you can't be sleeping with a priest." And do you know what she said back to me, she said, "I wouldn't normally, they're all much too old and ugly for me, but he's young and cool and well fit."'

'You still haven't told me why you didn't tell me?'

'I was ashamed,' she admitted. 'But listen, Inspector, what you have to realise about our Mary is that, from a very early age she felt, she felt that...'

'Go on?'

'I feel embarrassed talking to a man about this.'

'Think of me as you would your doctor,' Starrett said softly, trying to encourage her. But Eimear Robinson seemed to grow so self-conscious by his remark that he started to wonder what she got up to with her doctor.

'Okay,' she said, 'I'll try. The thing about our Mary is…she is very well meaning and all and she…she…well, she's never really taken on board the whole emotional side of making love. So to her it's like the same as you or I would think or feel over having a kiss.'

'You're saying she was generous with her favours?'

'Yes, but not in a bad way!' Eimear said. 'To her it was her way of making a connection with people. But she's really very nice; she spends more money than anyone I know on her appearance. Make-up, clothes, you know, she has the best of everything, absolutely the best.'

'So she spends a lot of money on her make-up and clothes?'

'A lot?' Eimear laughed, 'I keep saying to her, "Mary," I'd say, "it's not Callum you should have married, it's Sir Richard Branson!"'

Starrett had a bit of a chuckle at that.

'Then she'll say,' Eimear continued, appearing happier on this topic, '"Eimear," she'll say, "I know you think I'm not picky over who I shift, but I would draw the line at your man Branson, he's much too in love with himself to give anyone else a look in."'

'You see,' Starrett said, revealing he'd already moved on from this topic, 'when someone is murdered, jealous husbands of unfaithful wives would automatically appear on our suspect lists.'

'Well, I can see how Callum's family would be on your list,' Eimear said.

'Is Callum aware that his wife has other relationships?' Starrett asked, as he remembered Mary's discreet message suggesting he get her number from Eimear and give her a ring. Initially he felt she was just coming on to him but he wondered if she'd a piece of information she wanted to give him about Father Matthew, away from Nuala Gibson.

'Inspector, my sister is generous with her favours but she doesn't think she's cheating.'

Starrett raised his eyebrows without even knowing he was doing so.

'No, no, listen to me, Callum is her husband and she's very fond of him and she'll always go home to Callum.'

'Was Callum aware that Mary had a relationship with Father Matthew?'

'Did he know?' she started, 'or did he turn a blind eye? I wouldn't be the one to ask.'

'Did Mary have other men she saw regularly?'

'My father had a saying he'd often use, "Eimear," he'd say, "I'm not my brother's keeper." Well, I'd like to say to you that I'm not my sister's keeper.'

'But youse get on well?'

'Of course,' she smiled, 'we're sisters, but my priority is my daughters.'

'So Mary…?'

'So Mary has another family now, Callum and his brother, Mark, and their family unit. They'll take care of her the same way I'll take care of Julia, Jessica, and my Gerry.'

'Okay, Eimear, but I just want to ask you this one more time because it might be vitally important to this case,' Starrett said, speaking as slowly as he knew how, in the hope he was making his point, 'could Mary have been having an affair–'

'No, no, no,' Eimear protested, 'our Mary would go out of her way to tell you this herself, she does not have affairs!'

'But she sleeps with other men?' Starrett in turn protested.

'Yes, but she's never seen out with them in public, never runs around with them, or goes away with them for dirty weekends, or out for cosy romantic dinners to rub her husband's nose in it. Our Mary loves sex, she loves having a beautiful body and she loves displaying her beautiful body – she really does. Callum …well, Mary herself has often said, "Callum," she'd say, "he's only a three-quarters man: he looks like a man, he eats like a man, he sleeps like a man, but he's absolutely no use at all to me in the bedroom."'

Starrett felt just then - during the three-quarters man line - Eimear looked like she'd just let herself down. That she'd started off trying to say something funny to lighten the mood of the interview but it had backfired, and she'd ended up doing her sister, and her sister's husband, a disservice.

'Okay, let's leave your sister for now,' Starrett offered, to Eimear's visible relief. 'After Mary and Father Matthew stopped enjoying their physical relationship, he started seeing someone else. That's what Mary claimed.'

Eimear looked like totally deflated and Starrett couldn't work out if it was because, even though he claimed he was going to draw a line under the Mary topic, here he was talking about her again.

'I'm interested in who Father Matt was seeing after Mary,' Starrett declared, hoping to let Eimear see he really was moving on. Once again she didn't seem to take any comfort from his words.

'Have you any idea who it was he was seeing?' she asked.

'I was hoping you might tell me.'

'Sure, how would I know? Did our Mary not tell you who it was?'

'She said she didn't know. And you've no idea?'

'If our Mary didn't know I doubt anyone would know,' Eimear claimed.

'Eimear, I have to ask you a very sensitive question now and I want you to realise that there is nothing personal behind this question,' Starrett offered, trying to soften the inevitable blow.

'Fire away,' Eimear said half-heartedly.

'Did you…did you and Father Matthew ever have a physical relationship?'

Eimear appeared to breathe a large sigh of relief, before laughing openly, yet defensively, at Starrett and then nudging him in the arm a few times before saying, 'Sure, Father Matt and me were good mates, you should never ever mess around with a mate.'

'Especially when he's a priest,' Starrett felt obliged to add.

'Especially when he's a priest,' she confirmed.

CHAPTER FORTY-TWO

Ban Garda Nuala Gibson was still interviewing Gerry Robinson when Starrett and Eimear emerged from the lounge, so he and Romany Browne headed off in the gardaí car to pay a visit to The Three-Quarters Man, Mary Mooney's husband, Callum. He asked Eimear to tell Gibson to take his car and meet them back at St Ernan's when she was done.

Starrett arrived outside Callum Mooney's house to find him polishing away at his boy-racer type-car, a midnight blue Nissan Skyline GTR, as though it was the family jewels.

'He seems too happy with his new car to me to be much interested in crime,' Browne said.

'Looks can be deceptive. People don't buy a classic car because they're happy,' Starrett started, remembering a former avenue of employment, 'but they most certainly will buy one when they're sad.'

'Surely you're not suggesting his car is a classic?' Browne offered.

'Oh, don't you see, to him it's much, much more valuable than our interpretation of a classic car.'

Callum Mooney was as clean-cut as his prized possession. He was dressed in dark-blue denim jeans with a very small turn-up, Timberland fawn boots and, even with the approaching Donegal winter, he wore a fresh, white T-shirt, covered only by a red, V-neck woollen jumper. He'd a healthy thick head of brown hair, symmetrically cropped to half an inch all over. He didn't look confident but he did look content. Starrett figured he must be in his later thirties, which would have surely put him at a ways over the age of the average 'boy racer' but still, at that, a bit younger than his wife.

He seemed to engage more with Browne than Starrett, as the two members of the gardaí walked over to him. He was working on his car parked outside his bungalow at the far corner, from the main road, of a fairly new estate, Porter Terraces, only a five-minute drive from Eimear's house on the other, and more hilly, side of Donegal Town.

Starrett and Browne flashed their warrant cards and introduced themselves.

'Mary's not here at the moment,' he volunteered.

'It's yourself we've come to visit,' Starrett said, before smiling.

'Oh and why's that?'

Starrett looked around the street and said, 'Would you not prefer to go indoors before we have our chat?'

'Am I in trouble or something?'

'You'd know that a lot better than we would,' Starrett offered, wondering what, if anything, Callum Mooney was feeling guilty about. 'Listen Callum, there's nothing for you to be alarmed about, we've just got a few routine questions for you.'

Callum motioned for Starrett and Browne to head to the rear of his bungalow, but instead of taking them inside, he took them to a makeshift shed. It was small and windowless and packed with rows and rows of tools, all neat and clean, aside from the few car bits and tyres scattered around; on the back of the door hung a pair of dark blue, oil-stained overalls.

'So how can I help you?' he asked.

Starrett quickly glanced around the shed, searching in vain for somewhere to sit. The smell of oil and petrol was quite overpowering, especially in such a confined space.

'We're investigating the death of a friend of Eimear Robinson,' Starrett said, electing to start off with the indirect approach.

'Father Matt?'

'Yes, did you know him?'

'Well, I didn't really know him, I mean, he was friendly with Eimear, Julia, Jessica, and my Mary, and I met him a few times up at Eimear's.'

'So the only time you'd have seen him would have been up at Eimear's?'

'I believe so, yes.'

'Did you ever chat to him up at Eimear's?'

'Not really, just generally,' he replied, and then seemed troubled. 'Look, Inspector, can I be very frank with you?' he continued, as he turned his back on Browne.

'I wish you would,' Starrett said, as Browne stepped out of the shed on a nod from Starrett.

'Mary had a thing with the priest,' he almost whispered. 'It's really hard to understand and even more difficult to explain, but it really doesn't mean anything to her. She has her needs.'

Starrett was finding it difficult to understand a husband condoning his wife sleeping with another man.

'Don't you feel–'

'I had the measles when I was young,' Callum continued, 'and I took a long time to get better. But I got better. Then, after I married Mary I had some vascular problems. My weight was flying up and down. I'm still not exactly sure about the connection but I was assured that it was all to do with my original bout of measles, and the long and short of it is that all of me didn't get better.'

Starrett nodded sympathetically.

'Mary and I are very close in other ways. Right?'

'Okay,' Starrett said. He wondered if that meant that Callum found it impossible to be jealous. The fumes in the small shed were starting to distract him too much. 'Do you mind if we step outside?' and he left the place without waiting for an answer.

Callum Mooney didn't seem upset, more like settled. In fact, the word that Starrett had first thought of when he and Browne had first come upon Callum out front working on his car came back into his mind, and that word was content; he seemed content, very content. Was it an act? Had Mary really started sleeping with other men only after her husband's illness?

With most other men in a situation like this, he'd try to rile them, make them mad, see if there was a jealousy lurking deep down, see if the right spark was ignited, could they, would they be capable of murder. From the look in Callum's Mooney's eyes Starrett didn't get any such indication. So why piss him off just for the sake of pissing him off? Sure, the man had more than enough to live with. How much more could God punish a man than to put him with a woman such as Mary Mooney but not give him the wherewithal to do anything about it?

'Callum,' he said, after he'd drank in a few large dollops of fresh air, 'what kind of work do you do?'

'I set computer systems up in hotels.'

'Locally?'

'Across Ireland,' Callum replied. 'I get to travel all over. The firm has contracts with most of the hotel chains and whenever a new hotel is opening or an older hotel is installing a new computer system, I move in for three or four days to get their computer system up and running.'

'And are you busy?'

'Yes, and I get as much overtime as I want.'

'So no sign of the recession in your business then.'

'Actually, it's been to our advantage in that a lot of the hotels have been using the slowing down of their businesses to install new systems, for when business picks up again.'

'Great to see that at least someone is expecting things to get better,' Starrett said, and then added as an apparent afterthought, 'What were you doing on Wednesday last between the hours of 3:30 and 5:30?'

'I was on my way back from a hotel in Wexford. I left there around about 3, and I'd normally manage to get back here around 8 ish but I pulled in, in Athlone, for an hour or so for a kip because I felt my eyes get a bit heavy.'

'Right Callum, that'll do us for now,' the inspector said. 'We'll be in touch.'

'That sounded a bit feeble to me, Sir,' Browne said, as he turned on the ignition.

'What?' Starrett said, still distracted.

'His alibi.'

'The truth, you'll find,' Starrett began, more friendly than re-proachful, 'does tend to always sound just that little bit feeble. It's important to remember: it's mostly the lies that need the security of drama.'

* * *

The two gardaí left Callum Mooney to his beloved car and scooted back out in theirs to St Ernan's, and as they were walking along the corridor and passing Father McKenzie's room, they saw the door was open.

'Look at him working,' Browne whispered to Starrett, 'darning his socks in the night when there's nobody there.'

They were on their way to the boys' room for their meeting with Nuala Gibson. When they got there, Starrett pulled the blackboard out from the wall and flipped it over to the side they were really using for their case study.

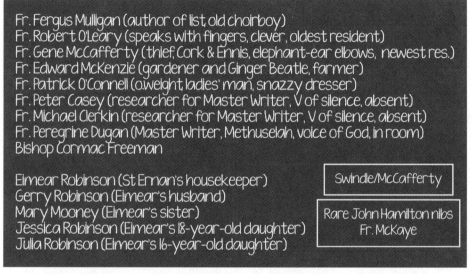

Fr. Fergus Mulligan (author of list, old choirboy)
Fr. Robert O'Leary (speaks with fingers, clever, oldest resident)
Fr. Gene McCafferty (thief, Cork & Ennis, elephant-ear elbows, newest res.)
Fr. Edward McKenzie (gardener and Ginger Beatle, farmer)
Fr. Patrick O'Connell (o.weight, ladies' man, snazzy dresser)
Fr. Peter Casey (researcher for Master Writer, V of silence, absent)
Fr. Michael Clerkin (researcher for Master Writer, V of silence, absent)
Fr. Peregrine Dugan (Master Writer, Methuselah, voice of God, in room)
Bishop Cormac Freeman

Eimear Robinson (St Ernan's housekeeper)
Gerry Robinson (Eimear's husband)
Mary Mooney (Eimear's sister)
Jessica Robinson (Eimear's 18-year-old daughter)
Julia Robinson (Eimear's 16-year-old daughter)

Swindle/McCafferty

Rare John Hamilton nibs
Fr. McKaye

Starrett then took the chalk and wrote 'At work' after Mary's line.

'Can you please check in with her place of work to confirm she was actually there at the relevant hours?' he said, looking at Garda Browne.

Next he added 'Callum Mooney' and 'travelling' after Julia's line.

'Can you please check where he was travelling from in Wexford and see if you can get confirmation on what time he left?'

Browne nodded his agreement to both orders, or requests, as Starrett had a habit of calling them.

Chalk still in hand, the inspector then asked Nuala Gibson how she got on with Gerry Robinson.

'Very well, actually,' she said, taking out her notebook. 'He seemed quite straightforward to me. Eimear clearly wears the trousers in the house; he kept saying "What did Eimear say when you asked her that?"'

Starrett seemed to be growing a little impatient, so she flicked a few pages on and said, 'I suppose the really important points would be: one, he admitted he knew about Mary and Father Matt and when I asked him did he not think that Mary's husband would be very upset about that he said,' and she checked her notes again to get it exact. 'He said, "No. It's Callum's brother, Mark, who'd be more upset about that. He'd be the one getting the sloppy seconds."'

'No!' Starrett said, drawing it out to at least three syllables.

Sergeant Packie Garvey, by no means a prude, looked very sick on Callum's behalf.

'If Mary was a lad, we'd all be applauding her,' Browne offered.

'I wouldn't!' Gibson said, a little put out. 'I most certainly wouldn't.'

They all sat in shock for about thirty seconds.

'Now that I think about it,' Starrett said, looking like he was miles away, 'when I was talking to Eimear earlier and we were discussing Mary cheating with Father Matt, she said something along the lines that Mary had her family, Callum and Mark, to protect her in the same way she would protect her daughters, Julia and Jessica.'

Again silence ruled the room.

'So, what else?'

'Ah,' Gibson said, flicking and flicking through her pages again.

'You see, Ban Garda Gibson, it's true – you really do have to save your best for last,' Starrett jested. 'You're struggling there to try and find something to top your Mark Mooney revelation.'

'Well…nothing much really, apart from the fact that Gerry doesn't really like Mark,' Gibson said, alternately tapping her notebook with her pen and putting her pen in her mouth. 'Gerry feels he's an ugly piece of work and he might even be a little intimidated by him. He also told me that he was working - in company - all Monday afternoon on a big job at Donegal Estuary Holiday Homes. I've got Donegal Estuary Holiday Homes details so I can check his alibi.'

'Okay, good,' Starrett offered, smiling largely. 'Beejeepers, Nuala, now that's a recovery Packie would have been proud to have pulled off on the hurling field.'

CHAPTER FORTY-THREE

Starrett knew it would make him late to visit the Major, but equally he just had to drop in on his next witness, and right away.

He'd always cautioned his team to be careful about getting into a fight with a man with scars. Equally, he'd constantly advised them never to tackle a man with more tattoos than teeth. Their next witness certainly had more tattoos than teeth, but that might have been, quite simply, because he had more tattoos about his body than you'd find in a tattooist's sample book. Their next witness also looked like he might have more scars around his shaven head than would be discovered on the heads of Colonel George Armstrong Custer's last-standing troops.

Starrett and Gibson's next witness was also podgy, red-faced, with glaring eyes, which mostly glared skywards. He wore an off-white, armless vest, a very tight-fitting pair of white jeans and a pair of black Camper trainers. There was an emblem of symmetrical thorn branches woven into a complex circle, dead centre of his vest. This theme was also prevalent in the numerous red and black tattoos about his hands, upper and lower arms, neck, and disappearing on his chest beneath the low neckline of his vest. His shaved head was crowned with a pair of Bono-style wrap-around sunglasses.

He had a black-blue, ground-scraping mutt with matching glaring eyes to those of his owner. Starrett checked the ugly dog for tattoos; he couldn't see any, but he wouldn't have been surprised if he had.

This next witness was, at least on first appearances, an ugly piece of work. This next witness was Mark Mooney.

Starrett had been sure that Mary's cheating with Father Matt was going to produce jealousy somewhere along the lines, but he never could have guessed that it wouldn't be from the husband, but the brother-in-law. And now they were about to confront that jealousy head-on.

But for all of the above, he was frightfully well-spoken and he'd the decency to put the mutt on a lead as the three members of the gardaí approached him in his immaculate front garden. The lead only served to annoy the mongrel who barked, growled, and dribbled as if they were all sports in a Canine Olympics.

'Shut it, Judas!' Mooney barked, and Judas whined to a dribbling silence.

Starrett introduced himself and his team and they each produced their warrant cards.

'Yeah, Callum rang me earlier to say you'd been around to have a chat with him,' Mooney claimed. 'I figured it wouldn't be too long until you arrived at my door.'

He removed an iPhone from his pocket, checked it, rubbed the screen around his vest a few circles, and checked he'd cleaned the screen enough before returning the phone to his pocket.

'Shall we go inside?' Starrett suggested.

'Certainly not,' Mooney laughed. 'This show of force on my doorstep will keep the local tea-leafs away from my house for ages, maybe even years. It's all good!'

Starrett looked around the site, with its forty shades of white-washed, pebble-dashed, mismatched houses; Gore Gardens was definitely a lot older an estate than Mark's brother Callum's estate. The detective clocked from the condition of Mooney's windows, doors, paintwork, blinds, and garden, that his house was, by far, the best on show in this particular estate.

'Okay,' Starrett said, realising how spot-on Mooney was with his assessment. If you're a wise thief, you never ever steal from another. 'We're here to talk about Father Matthew McKaye.'

'Yes, Eimear's friend who was bonking my brother's wife.'

Mooney dropped his eyes from the skies to Ban Garda Gibson for this reply. She acknowledged him only by writing something in her notebook.

'Right,' Starrett said, 'now at least we know you know who we're talking about.'

'So the fact you're here means you've already talked to Gerry Robinson,' Mooney said.

'How so?'

'It figures,' he said. 'It's all good; he's never forgiven me for bonking Eimear all those years ago. I did tell him it was just the once, but I don't think he believed me. They say that not every woman cheats,' Mooney paused for effect, 'but the woman who cheats will, more than likely, cheat more than once.'

'You're claiming you had an affair, not just with your brother's wife, but also with your brother's wife's sister?' Gibson asked, looking skywards herself, as though she was trying to concentrate on pinning down the ever-growing list of illicit partners.

'I was basically balancing up the cosmic ball of energy,' Mooney claimed, pointing to the emblem printed on the centre of his off-white vest. He pulled his iPhone from his pocket once again and completed the exact same routine he'd not long since finished.

Now he was up close, Starrett realised that Mooney's T-shirt wasn't a dirty shade of white, as he'd first suspected, but the actual colour of the vest, and it looked as though he was wearing it for the first time.

'Sorry?' Starrett said, feeling he needed to be enlightened, for the record, on that one.

'In this ball there is no beginning and no end. It's made up of lots of thorn branches and they just weave in and out of each other, the way lives do. Where one branch or life finishes, another starts, and on and on it goes until it gets to the end, or to the beginning again.'

'And this is relevant how?'

'Okay. When Mary and Callum first started to have their problems – well, Callum's problems really – Mary turned to Gerry–'

'No!' Gibson said in disbelief.

Jeez, Starrett thought, you'd never read this in a book, people just wouldn't believe it. 'So Mary and Gerry slept together?'

Mooney, clearly loving the shockwaves he was generating, said, 'Yes, but just the once.' He ran through his mobile phone routine yet again before adding, 'The big chump. He went on a guilt trip, started to act really strange – he wouldn't admit it to Eimear, so Mary did. Eimear had been thinking Gerry's bad mood had something to do with her. So Mary told her. Told her it wasn't her fault, told her it wasn't even Gerry's fault, and took all the blame herself, so she did. Okay so far?'

'Yep.'

'But the cosmic circle was out of kilter at that point. Eimear needed to balance up her circle of power again. But she didn't have it in her to take revenge on her sister by sleeping with her sister's husband, Callum, because she truly loves her sister. So she took her revenge by doing the next best thing – sleeping with her sister's husband's brother. Moi!'

Starrett couldn't believe he was actually hearing all of this. Gibson looked like she really wished she wasn't hearing all of this.

'So Eimear and I got it together one night when we were all around at Mary and Callum's for a barbeque and she'd a few drinks and no one noticed us nip into the field at the other end of Callum's garden and–'

'Okay, Okay,' Starrett interrupted, hoping to spare Gibson her blushes.

'Mary has had the complete set of the three of us, Callum, Father Matt, and me,' Mooney boasted, on her behalf. 'So it's all good.'

Where exactly did this leave everything Starrett wondered? Clearly Mark Mooney, Mary Mooney and Father Matthew, were the three he felt he needed to concentrate on.

Mary Mooney was sleeping with her husband's brother, Mark. Mary Mooney then slept with Father Matthew. Had she still been sleeping with Mark at the same time? Father Matthew was then murdered. Was Father Matthew murdered because he'd been sleeping with Mary Mooney? Mary Mooney's husband would have been the most likely suspect except for the fact that he was (apparently) incapable of…jealousy. On top of which, he appeared to have a genuine alibi. Mary Mooney's husband's brother, on the other hand, was the jealous type and he was sleeping with Mary Mooney, so he would appear, by the processes of elimination and deduction, to be the prime suspect.

Unless of course, as Mary Mooney herself had suggested, Father Matt had indeed started to sleep with someone else; the mystery woman he gave up Mary Mooney for. So could Mary Mooney have been capable of murdering Father Matt, perhaps because she was jealous? But she claimed she loved her husband – yes, she occasionally 'shifted' other men, as she so politely put it, but it really didn't seem to mean anything to her. Aside from which, she too, had a cast-iron alibi for the time of Father Matt's demise.

All this, this cosmic circle, only served to bring Starrett back to trying to discover Mary's successor in Father Matt's arms.

'You know Mary and Father Matthew stopped sleeping together before he died?' Starrett started, formulating the question in his mind as he felt his way along it.

'Yes, and I can also confirm that they certainly haven't slept together since he died,' Mooney said and laughed, then noticing Gibson's disdain added, 'don't worry sister, I'm not religious.'

Starrett was convinced had Gibson not been present the godless Mooney would no doubt have included some kind of tactless rigor mortis gag.

'Mary reckoned Father Matt stopped sleeping with her because he was seeing someone else,' Starrett suggested, trying to get back on track again.

'Yes, she mentioned that to me as well,' Mooney agreed, returning to a more respectful mood. He gave his phone yet another serious clean. He pretty much ignored them as he concentrated until the imaginary stubborn piece of dirt would surrender.

'Do you have any idea who he might have been sleeping with after Mary?'

'You know, Mary and I discussed it a lot and neither of us had a clue.'

'Does your brother know about you and Mary?'

'I know how Mary comes across, maybe even a wee bit slutty,' Mooney started, 'but really, please believe me, she's got a heart of gold and she cares about Callum. She really does love him; she's respectful of him. She goes out of her way to be discreet about her needs. But to answer your question: I think he knows, but I don't know for sure. We once had a very oblique conversation when he said if Mary needs to be with someone, he'd prefer it was me rather than some tube. I don't know if that was him discreetly giving us his blessing. I never even acknowledged that I knew what he'd been talking about.'

'Can I ask you what you do for a living?' Starrett asked, being careful he didn't side-step into the path of the mutt's salivating jaws.

'I work as a Risk Officer for PayPal.'

If Starrett had drawn up a list of jobs suitable for Mark Mooney, a Risk Officer for PayPal wouldn't have been in the Top 10, nor even the Top 100 for that matter.

'Listen,' Mooney said, proving it wasn't the first time he'd received such a reaction. If anything he seemed pleased by it. 'You should see me in my suit.'

'So, a Risk Officer,' Starrett said, genuinely interested, 'what exactly does that entail?'

'Well, I get to check out the viability of the projects PayPal are offered.'

'That sounds like it could be interesting?'

'Yeah sometimes, and sometimes it's just corporate stuff you have to do,' Mooney deadpanned, as he unconsciously slipped into his phone routine.

'Would a job like that pay well?'

'On paper, the salary is good but when you factor in all your travel time and time away from home, which you don't get paid for, not as richly as rewarding as you originally think, aye, not quite so good. But no complaints from me. All good.'

'Are you married?'

He replied immediately in what sounded like his standard answer: 'Never needed to.'

'Do you have a partner?'

'Ditto, see above,' Mooney wise-cracked.

'Have you ever had a serious relationship?'

'Now you're just being nosy,' Mooney said, but not sounding upset. 'But if you must know, yes, I had a very, very serious relationship with a German lady called Bernadette Atinka and…it just didn't work out for us. So rather than keep on trying, I stayed true to my feelings for her. I genuinely believed Bernie was the one and when that didn't work out, I knew that no one else could be the one, so I never bothered to seek further.'

'But Mary?'

'I believe our American cousins would call it "friends with benefits".'

Starrett and Gibson sighed in unison.

Judas had now started to chew on his leather lead. Mooney seemed either to not to notice or not care. How long would it take the mutt to chew himself free, Starrett wondered? Now might be a good time to ask his final question.

'Mr Mooney, could you please tell us what you were doing on Wednesday past between the hours of 3:30 p.m. and 5:30 p.m.?'

'That's simple, I was mid-air, between here and Geneva, or should I say mid-air between Geneva and here. I landed in Dublin about five and with one thing and another it was just before eight o'clock before I got back home.'

Gibson wrote away in her notebook, seemingly disappointed. No doubt she would be intrigued to see if this alibi actually checked out.

Just as they were about to return to the gardaí car, Mooney looked like something was troubling him, like he was feeling something had been left unresolved.

'I hope you understood what I meant about the strength of the cosmic circle,' he said.

'Sorry?' Starrett felt obliged to say.

'Okay, I'll spell it out for you, because I feel it's very important,' Mooney said, giving Judas a playful nudge with his foot and only getting a shoe covered in dribble for his efforts. 'Remember when I told you that whenever Gerry cheated on Eimear with Mary, things were out of sorts, and Eimear had to balance them up again by sleeping with me?'

'Yes,' Starrett replied, dragging it out so that it sounded more like 'no, I don't'.

'Okay. Then the priest slept with Mary, breaking the cosmic link between her and Callum and I.'

'And me,' Gibson felt compelled to say in correction.

'If you had been there as well, sister, I'm sure I would have noticed,' Mooney said, to Gibson's clear disdain.

'I was just saying that it should be "Callum and me", not "Callum and I",' Gibson said, looking like she now wished she hadn't bothered.

'But you were saying?' Starrett coached Mooney, wondering if he was going to fall into a trap of his own making.

'Yes,' Mooney replied, also happy to be getting back on track again. 'So then someone had to play a cheat card on the priest.'

'So are you saying that either you or Callum had to cheat with someone behind Father Matthew's back?'

'No not us, well, yes, it could've been us for the cosmic circle to work but it wasn't us. For this to work it could have been anyone else in the universe. And as the priest wasn't married, the cheat card had to be against something he loved.'

'God?' Gibson suggested.

'Close, sister, close,' Mooney said, sneering, as he achieved another quick check and clean of his mobile. 'Something, or maybe more accurately, someone he loved even more than God.'

'Okay, you've got our undivided attention?' Starrett prompted.

'Himself!' Mooney said, gleefully.

'Really?' Starrett muttered, while he thought: absolute poppycock.

'Yes! And so when someone took the priest's life, the cosmic circle was realigned so the universe could roll on again.'

* * *

'Bejeepers, isn't it just great for the universe to be rolling on again,' Starrett said, when he and Gibson were back in the car and heading up north again.

'I'll certainly sleep a lot better tonight.'

'Do you think he actually believes all that crap?' Starrett asked, to the universe in general and Ban Garda Nuala Gibson in particular.

'Well, it probably sounds good to Mary,' Gibson suggested, 'and it clearly works.'

'How do some women end up taking excuses-for-men to their bed?'

'I'll tell you better than that Starrett, some women I know are better friends with their dinner dates than the men they're prepared to go to bed with,' Gibson added.

'Perhaps they feel so gutted about their actions that someone – their dinner dates, for instance – will have to pay,' Starrett suggested, before adding, 'in more ways than one.'

Just then the Don Williams song 'Lay Down Beside Me' came onto Highland Radio. Starrett mentally tuned into it for the few remaining minutes of the song. As he listened to Don's soulful delivery, he began to think that all the great songs must be about love. But then the penny finally dropped when he realised that all the really great love songs are in fact about the lack of love.

'So have you figured out the answer to my question yet?' he asked Gibson, who'd appeared to go into her own wee world during Don's record.

'You mean, how do some women end up taking men like Mooney to their bed?'

'Yes, but I was being a little more general than that.' Starrett replied, feeling he needed to clarify.

'Maybe because they can't find anyone else?'

'Really?' Starrett said, wondering where all those women were when he was smack-bang in the middle of his wilderness years.

'Either that,' she continued, 'or they just don't feel they're entitled to anyone better.'

Chapter Forty-Four

By the time Gibson dropped Starrett off at the Major's house, it was, as he had feared, just too late in the day for a visit. Maggie Keane's car was still in the driveway so Starrett told Gibson to scoot off home. He also asked her to have whoever was on duty at the Station House in Ramelton advise the bishop and his solicitor that Starrett and Gibson would interview him the following morning, Sunday, at 10 a.m.

It turned out the Major had enjoyed quite an improvement during the day. There were hardly any visitors, just Starrett's parents and Maggie Keane. Maggie had insisted that the Major be left alone to rest. Her philosophy was that the body is the best healer of itself, you just need to allow it the luxury of rest so its powers could be most effective. The Major even felt like getting up the following day. 'We'll see?' his wife had responded.

'There you go,' the Major had said before releasing a huge sigh, 'the official acceding of power has happened. Now I'm reduced to waiting around to see if my wife will allow me to get up out of my own bed. Things are definitely on the slide.'

'Oh aye, and I can remember well the times you were just as happy to stay in bed all day.'

When the Major eventually realised what she was getting at, all he did was look at her, blush, and smile knowingly at the memories. Maggie reported that it had been a beautiful moment for all of them.

So as to make the most of the moment, Starrett quietly crept over to the Major's bedside to say a silent good night.

Then, on the way back home, the detective and Maggie nipped into McDaid's Wine Bar for the heat of the fire, the warmth of the wine, and, for his part, the need to put Bishop Cormac Freeman out of his mind. One bottle later, Maggie drove them home, claiming Starrett had drank most it, and what she had needed was just a nightcap.

When they got to Maggie's fine house, he'd a Guinness and she'd another glass of red wine. They retired to bed about midnight, enjoyed half an hour of delightful naughtiness and fell from consciousness into an alcohol- and post-coital, bliss-induced sleep.

A few hours later Starrett inadvertently woke Maggie. She explained to him afterwards that he'd been moaning on and on and thrashing about like he was physically fighting demons or monsters or something in his dreams.

And Maggie Keane had been right. There had been a monster in Starrett's nightmare. It was a monster in priest's clothing and he'd returned to disturb Starrett's sleep just as he'd done all those years ago and just as he'd done in his nightmares several times over in the intervening years.

As Starrett thrashed about in Maggie Keane's bed, his reality was that he was in his dormitory, in a church building somewhere in Armagh, where he'd gone in his youth to study to become a priest.

The monster on the other side of Starrett's dormitory door was bullish, arrogant, red-flushed, and high on sexual power. He was someone who subscribed to the theory that a person was never in question when God was on his side. In the melee, the handle had come off the door and Starrett grabbed the door with both hands, fingers on the outside. He could see through the widening and closing of the door as he and the monster fought for their ground and, far from being stressed by the seminarian's efforts to keep him at bay, the monster seemed to enjoy the tussle. Starrett realised that to the monster it was some kind of bizarre foreplay and he was clearly aroused. The monster grabbed Starrett by the fingertips and surprised him by making to close the door, in Starrett's favour. By the time Starrett realised what was happening it was too late and the door was being slammed against its frame. By a microsecond, and only a microsecond, Starrett managed to free his left hand and three of the fingers of his right, but…the forefinger of his right hand was trapped by the monster's razor-sharp fingernails and was slammed in the vice that the door made with its frame. Starrett could feel the lightning pain mainlining its way to his brain and immediately back down to his poor forefinger, where the shattered metacarpal would forever remind Starrett of this ordeal.

He sank to the cold chess-board-tiled floor and the leering monster tugged the door open. Starrett's energy was all spent and he could feel himself at the mercy of his nemesis. Starrett's right index finger was a full 90 degrees to the normal and limply folded over the back of his hand. The monster seemed magnetised to the battle wound and he dragged his victim from the floor. Starrett could barely stand but he noticed now that the monster was so aroused, he was uncomfortable in his trousers. The monster awkwardly attempted to free himself, looking to Starrett every inch the Devil he was meant to protect his flock from. Starrett thought about his parents, preoccupied by the idea that he might be letting them down. He mustered all of his reserve and ran at the monster, going for the plural, at 29 inches above floor level, and kicking with all his might. The monster sounded like a pig squealing when conscious of the knacker approaching with a captive bolt stunner. He squirmed eel-like on the floor, still emitting an ear-piercing scream as his amorous intent wilted.

As Starrett was cautiously shaken from his nightmare by Maggie Keane, he saw the face one final time, and he shuddered, now in sweat-drenched consciousness, at the memory of that visage.

'Jeez, what was that, Starrett?' Maggie whispered, 'I've never seen you like that before!'

They got out of bed, even though it was still only 2:50 a.m.; Starrett had a quick shower and joined her in the kitchen. Over a tea and a couple of the cheesecakes her daughter Moya has made especially for Starrett, he told her the full story, the story behind his nightmare.

Even the re-telling of it, he shuddered uncontrollably at the memory of that monster's face, the priest who all these years later had come back into Starrett's life again, only this time dressed in the purple robes of a bishop.

'I caught my breath,' Starrett said to Maggie Keane across her kitchen table as he concluded his retelling, 'and I gathered up a few clothes from around the room, which I hastily stuffed in my father's army rucksack. I'd time only to pause, gingerly wrap a tie around my pathetic excuse for a forefinger, and I ran out into the night, and didn't stop until I reached London a couple of lifts, a lot of pain, and two days later.'

'You poor man, well boy, really,' Maggie said as she went around to his side of the table, sat on his knee and gave him a hug, holding his bent forefinger very carefully in her hand.

'But you know, Maggie,' he started up again, 'earlier on today, Nuala and I were questioning a suspect and he spouted on about this cosmic theory of his, where he maintains that when someone is wronged there has to be a price paid and if there's not, then something very bad happens.'

'And so you think because you did a runner, leaving me with child, you were punished for it?' she offered unsympathetically.

'Well yes, don't you see–'

'For goodness sake, Starrett, don't go all bleedin' feckin' hippie on me!' she sighed, cutting him off but yet still managing to flash him her lopsided grin. 'I keep telling you, and I keep telling you because it's true, that if you hadn't done a midnight flit–'

'Morning, actually,' he said, 'I scarpered in the morning.'

'Right, good to see your momentary lapse of humour hasn't disappeared. But as I was about to say, and will say again because it's so important: If you hadn't left me, I'd never had met Niall and have my two wonderful daughters. So the next time you meet your suspect, please tell him that sometimes something bad happening actually produces wonderful things in the world. On top of which, sometimes there are truly evil men about, as is the case with your Bishop Cormac Freeman, and my theory would be that, eventually, someway, somehow they get their just desserts. Maybe that should be just rewards, but I think you know what I'm on about.'

CHAPTER FORTY-FIVE

DAY FIVE: SUNDAY

Maybe it was because Starrett had, for the first time ever, told someone about the incident he'd been hiding all his life, or maybe it was due to the fact that for the first time in his life, he had someone he could finally share the horrific and traumatic memory with. Either way, he felt very differently now, in the presence of the bishop. Starrett reckoned he'd now beaten him twice. The first time he'd suffered no more than a broken finger. The second time – that was to say, during the nightmare, and thanks to Maggie Keane's down-to-earth approach – he'd come away totally unscathed.

For the bishop's part, however, he didn't look quite as comfortable, having endured his recent incarceration in Ramelton's very humble gardaí station. He'd exchanged his usual regal attire for a sober grey suit and a collarless white shirt, and robe-free, the majesty of his office gave way to the sight of an overweight man.

Yes, but although Bishop Cormac Freeman was down, he most certainly wasn't out.

'You realise you're over, you're through, you're all mine and I'm going to stamp on your pathetic life until it's dust,' was the bishop's opening gambit.

'That sounds suitably pious,' Starrett said calmly. He knew, as he always knew, that everything was official now and on tape and if he'd a chance of extracting a confession from the bishop, he was only going to succeed if he remained calm, the voice of reason.

'Quite simply, you can't throw a bishop in jail, Starrett,' the bishop continued with his bellicose rant.

'The law of the land pays no heed to how humble or mighty those before it think they are,' Starrett said, before announcing to the already running tape the date, time, and names of those present - Freeman, Russell Leslie (Freeman's very dapper local solicitor), Gibson, and himself.

'I demand you let me go now, this very moment!' Freeman barked, his bullfrog eyes straining to pop from their sockets. 'Leslie, get me out of here immediately!'

'Okay, Bishop Freeman and Mr Leslie,' Starrett started evenly, 'there are two issues here. The first is that, as you know and have been officially informed, I'm here to question you regarding the murder of Father Matthew McKaye.'

'Are you charging me?' the bishop roared, the veins in his neck visible and working overtime to supply blood to his brain. 'Please, charge me Starrett, oh please do, then I'll really have you where I want you.'

'The inspector has advised you that he wishes only to question you about this matter,' Russell Leslie offered, taking great pains to calm his client. 'Let's settle down and hear his questions.'

'The second issue is that you absconded like a thief in the night just before we were due to meet for an interview down in St Ernan's. That is why you were detained. That is why you will most likely be charged, at the very least, with being a fugitive.'

Russell Leslie raised his eyebrows but didn't say anything.

Starrett also realised he was on a very sticky wicket on that one and that if the Major had been well and up and about, he'd probably have warned Starrett about detaining the bishop overnight. But that wasn't the point, the point was to try and get to the bottom of the bishop and Father Matthew's relationship.

'I understand you've already admitted Father Matthew was going to join you in your diocese?'

The bishop remained noiseless for the first time since the proceedings commenced.

'All you need do is answer yes or no to confirm or deny the inspector's information.'

'Yes,' the bishop barked, now appearing to grow as annoyed with his own solicitor as with Starrett.

'Can you tell me how the system works please?' Starrett asked.

'What system?'

'How it's decided which diocese a young priest will serve in?'

'It's decided by the Church,' Freeman snapped.

'And you wouldn't normally be involved in the process?'

'Of course I wouldn't,' he said, through laughter. 'The Church has dedicated secretarial staff for all of that.'

'But in this instance, you intervened–' Starrett continued.

Bishop Freeman cut him off with, 'I've no need to answer that question; it has no relevance.'

'Well, here's the thing, Bishop Freeman,' Starrett started, 'I have reason to believe that you did intervene, and so if you won't confirm or deny it, I'll have to detain you and go and visit your diocese tomorrow to confirm or deny those facts there.' The bishop was about to reply when Starrett added, 'I should also point out that tomorrow I have to attend the funeral of Father Matthew McKaye, so it could be late tomorrow or even early Tuesday morning before I get back to Ramelton.'

'As a bishop I have the discretion to make such recommendations,' Bishop Freeman eventually admitted, through gritted teeth.

'And why did you make such a recommendation?'

'I thought the young priest would be a fine addition to our diocese.'

'You thought the young priest would be a fine addition to your diocese?'

'Yes, that's what I said,' the bishop replied before looking at his solicitor as if to suggest 'What's this guy on?'

'And how many times in the past would you have found a young priest who would have been "a fine addition to your diocese"?'

'How on earth would I know?'

Starrett paused here for a time and made a big deal of it, intending to imply to the bishop that the earth he was treading wasn't altogether solid. He had been taken by something Father O'Leary had said to him in their previous meeting: 'I find it's good to look at those who have gone before.' So much so, in fact, he'd set his top researcher on to that very task.

'Well, funny you should say that, Bishop, you see because I have a young garda, by the name of Francis Casey,' Starrett began, now looking like he was clearly enjoying himself, 'and Francis Casey, to quote some of your own words, is, "a fine addition to my diocese", if you'll forgive me a wee bit of poetic licence. You see, I give him a project and bejeepers if his research isn't only second to none. Isn't that correct, Ban Garda?'

'Yes,' Gibson replied, proudly opening the brown file in front of her.

'So I asked our Garda Casey if he could find out for me just how many young priests you'd personally recommended for your diocese.'

'I thought we were here to discuss the death of Father McKaye,' Bishop Freeman said, addressing his solicitor with a flicker of concern.

'Oh, but we are,' Starrett replied immediately. 'Please, just bear with me. Ban Garda Gibson, how many young priests did Garda Casey discover?'

'Seventeen.'

'Seventeen, eh? And over what period of time are we talking?'

'Eleven and a half years.'

'Seventeen over eleven and a half years, eh, surely not?' Starrett said, taking the file and hamming it up as if in disbelief at the stats. 'Why, you're 100 per cent correct!'

He returned the file to her, setting up his next question. 'I know there's a lot of research there in Garda Casey's file, so could you please confirm how many of the seventeen young men would have been considered, considered...how's the best way to put this...not pretty, well ...maybe pretty, but probably better we describe them as...handsome?'

Bishop Freeman rose to his feet in an attempted proceedings-stopping protest. But without his robes, he didn't have the majesty to pull it off.

Starrett merely held up his hand in a stop sign. A stop sign greatly emphasised by his crooked finger. 'Just a few moments please, then we'll most certainly want to hear from you, Bishop Freeman.' Starrett nodded again to Ban Garda Nuala Gibson, who was in her Sunday civvies rather than her uniform.

'Well,' she started, 'of course, it's all very relative isn't it, but by and large we could say that out of the seventeen young priests Garda Francis Casey found, all seventeen of them of could be described as handsome.'

'You're kidding?' Starrett protested.

'I'm not,' Gibson offered, 'and neither was Garda Casey.'

'So that's, let's just count them, one – two – three – four – five – six – seven – eight – nine – ten – eleven – twelve – thirteen – fourteen – fifteen – sixteen – and seventeen!' Starrett grandstanded. In fact, he'd had to speak over the bishop's protests from number eight until seventeen.

But he wasn't quite finished yet.

'Ban Garda, there's one other stat I need you to pull from Garda Casey's file.'

'Okay,' Gibson said, looking like she was primed to jump back into Casey's fact-findings, which were not as multi-paged a file as Starrett and Gibson were trying to make out. Basically they'd placed Casey's neatly typed foolscap page in the middle of a file containing Donegal's RTA (Road Traffic Accident) reports for the previous two years.

'How many of the original seventeen are still with the diocese they were, in Bishop Freeman's own words, "going to be a fine addition to", or for?'

'Ah, that would be zero,' Gibson advised those around the table.

'Okay, and I promise this is my final question for you Ban Garda: How many of the seventeen young, pretty…sorry, not pretty but handsome, additions to Bishop Freeman's diocese lodged a complaint, either official or verbal, about said Bishop?'

'Twelve.'

'Twelve, eh, just like the twelve apostles?'

'Yes, but there might be more, Sir,' Gibson offered. 'But that's as far as Garda Casey has managed to get with his research.'

Starrett now focused on Bishop Cormac Freeman. He searched his face, his eyes, his body language for a sign, even just a flicker of regret. Nothing. He found nothing – Bishop Freeman was indignant to the end.

'So you see, Bishop Freeman–'

'You see what?' the bishop barked. 'This is nothing; you've got nothing, not a single thing! There are always trouble-makers among the young priests. I seem to remember you were one such priest yourself. I just never seem to remember you being one of the handsome or pretty ones, as you have a habit of calling them. You must have caught me in a weaker moment,' he smirked.

Starrett looked in disbelief at the tape on the wall edge of the table between them. If he'd jumped across the table and smashed the bishop to a purple pulp, he wouldn't have gotten anywhere close to the satisfaction he now felt. Bishop Cormac Freeman had near enough admitted on the garda tape his physical attack of Starrett. The lights and magic eyes confirmed that the tape had been in perfect working order at the time of the remark. Yes, it was quite possibly just an oblique reference, but it was still a reference, nonetheless. He couldn't believe how transparent a man the bishop was, and how blasé he was being about the whole affair.

Then, as on the fateful night all those years ago, Starrett was scared. He was scared because he knew people like Bishop Cormac Freeman, or Father Cormac Freeman, as he then was, felt it there absolute God-given right to satisfy their lust by feeding on the fresh pickings of their juniors, and heaven help anyone, including their current victim, who got in their way.

'You see, Bishop Freeman, we know that you'd personally intervened in the case of Father Matthew, as you had with the previous seventeen cases, to ensure he'd come within your control – and therefore your grasp – at your diocese. Father Matthew had mentioned to several witnesses that he didn't want to go to your diocese. He had admitted to some that he was losing his faith. You were the sole reason he was losing his faith. I believe he discovered what had happened to some of his predecessors. If Garda Francis Casey could uncover this information then so could Father Matthew. In fact, if anything, as a priest, it would have been easier for him to do so. We all know you don't like to be turned down, Father Freeman.'

'Bishop Freeman!' he snapped.

'Sorry, yes, of course,' Starrett apologised. 'I just reverted there, for a few seconds, to your earlier life. So, when he turned you down, you grew incensed and killed him.'

'Really?' the bishop said, mocking Starrett.

The inspector was now so close to cracking this case he felt if he could only push the correct button, he could get the bishop to confess. This would allow him to tie this terrible mess up and he'd be able to spend less time with this devil and more precious time with one of the good guys, Major Newton Cunningham.

'Did Father Matthew come to you and try to blackmail you? Did he tell you that unless you got him out of going to your diocese, he'd go to the authorities with what he'd discovered?'

If Bishop Freeman's reaction was anything to go by, that stab in the dark looked like it had hit the target dead centre.

Starrett decided to play a final bluff.

'Bishop Freeman I am charging you–' Starrett started, slowly and deliberately.

'What! What! You can't possibly,' the bishop protested. 'But my alibi, my alibi, what about my alibi?'

'You mean the alibi of you walking about the streets of Donegal Town?' Starrett said. 'We checked and not one person claimed to have seen you. No one saw a bishop, in all his finery, wandering around Donegal Town.'

'Of course I wasn't in my robes!' the bishop complained. 'I was in a grey suit, such as this!'

'None of the staff at the Donegal castle saw you wandering around the castle grounds. Oh, and by the way, just for the record, the roof still hasn't been returned.'

'Starrett will be blaming me for that as well if we're not careful,' Bishop Freeman said as an aside to Russell Leslie.

'We also checked in with the bookshop you claimed to have visited?' Gibson continued.

The bishop clocked her, hopefully hoping for a break in his luck.

'They were in fact closed all Wednesday afternoon for stock-taking,' Gibson advised a visibly crestfallen Freeman.

Russell Leslie seemed unemotional about the walls falling in around his client. Was that because the solicitor had started to consider how much more the case would be worth to him if the bishop turned out to be guilty?

'So,' Starrett continued his earlier thread, 'Bishop Freeman I am charging you–'

'Okay, okay,' Bishop Freeman pleaded, raising his hands up towards the heavens in an apparent, yet unspoken, plea, 'my Father, my Father, why hast Thou forsaken me?'

In that instant the bishop reminded Starrett not of one of God's disciples but of a character from a Leonard Cohen song who was 'reaching for the sky only to surrender.'

In the second part of the same elaborate gesture, the bishop lowered his hands. He put his left hand inside his inside right-hand pocket and withdrew a pen and a micro-notebook. He scribbled something down, tore out the tiny page and passed it across the table to Starrett, who was delivering a running commentary for the benefit of the tape.

'The note from Bishop Freeman says "Vincent Wickham" and lists a mobile telephone number.' Starrett recited the number again for the benefit of the tape. 'And who is Vincent Wickham?'

'Am, an associate of mine,' Bishop Freeman admitted.

'Yes…and?'

'He will confirm to you,' the bishop started off in a very quiet voice, 'that he and I were with…with a rent boy…'

That wee bit of information certainly piqued the interest of the already piqued solicitor.

'Go on,' Starrett prompted, accepting that his pride - in tying up the case - had most certainly come before the inevitable fall.

'We occasionally take a room in a well-known hotel. It's always booked in his name. Can I assume you will be discreet with this information? You know you could ruin me with it?'

'You've already ruined yourself,' Starrett said, without a trace of pride. 'I'm going to leave the room now. Ban Garda Nuala Gibson, will you please get a few clean sheets of paper for the bishop here. When I return, I want not only to see your written statement, but your written resignation, too, effective immediately. This Church has enough to deal with without enduring yet another scandal. But I swear to you, and just as sure as my right forefinger is permanently bent, if you don't write your resignation I'll take all this information straight to the papers.'

'Are you not taking a bit of a risk, threatening me?' the bishop moaned. 'Sure, I haven't even written my confession yet.'

'Of course that's true,' Starrett himself confessed, hoping he was carrying off the look of someone who'd just been caught out. 'But, bejeepers, isn't that where the auld tape recorder comes in very handy.'

CHAPTER FORTY-SIX

Starrett was back in the arms of his adopted family, the Keanes, just in time for Sunday lunch.

Maggie Keane had also invited Starrett's parents, Nuala Gibson, and Francis Casey. She made Starrett promise before he left her house (it was always referred to as her house) that very morning, no matter how he was getting on with his interview, he would take a break at lunchtime to return home for a family lunch. Starrett was unconditionally happy to commit to this lunch and was totally prepared to take a break from interviewing Bishop Freeman if he needed to. Luckily the interview had reached its natural (successful to a degree, for Starrett) conclusion just after 12:30. And with Gibson at the controls, the detective even had time to stop off at Whoriskey's to buy a couple of newspapers and a bunch of flowers for Maggie (she just loved her flowers) and could still be wiping his feet on Maggie's back-door mat (literally) just before her clock rang out its one and only daylight chime.

The lunch was a great success and Starrett even managed to restrain Gibson, Casey, and himself from discussing gardaí business. The only exception being that when Francis Casey arrived, Starrett lavished praise on him for his research into the bishop's methods for grooming his fodder. It was his research and the information he'd uncovered, Starrett admitted, that had been the catalyst for bringing the bishop to justice. The fact that the bishop hadn't murdered Father Matthew or, more exactly, where he'd been when the young priest was murdered, was ultimately what would lead to his downfall.

Was Starrett disappointed that Bishop Freeman wasn't the murderer? Not in the slightest. Would he have liked to have returned to

Tower House to get stuck back into the case? Certainly not. He knew his team had been working flat out since Wednesday, on top of which they'd all been subjected to all the travelling to and from Donegal Town. So, a break would benefit everyone, including himself, and they'd all be back (relatively) fresh on the Monday morning, raring to go. The break would also afford him some quality time with Maggie, Katie, and Moya, and he'd be able to fit in a bit of his favourite leisure time activity of walking on the beach at Rathmullan. However, he reminded himself that he was talking about Donegal, where people made plans and God laughed at them so much, the resultant tears took the form of torrential rain.

The plan itself was a solid one in principle but then it turned out that Katie had decided she had to go visit her friends in Letterkenny. She was now of an age where hanging out with her select group of friends was much more appealing than quality family time. But she wasn't yet of an age where she could drive, so her mum would have to deliver her up to Letterkenny and collect her later. Maggie Keane didn't consider such trips a chore, for she much preferred to be the one in charge of her daughter's safety while on the roads. Too many times she'd visibly shuddered when the news of yet another car – over-packed with teenagers of Katie's age, with one older (and sometimes barely old enough) driver fresh from passing their driving test, at the wheel –involved in a horrific and fatal crash. Those worries were years (but in reality, maybe even only several months) away.

Moya was also disappointed that she had to go to Letterkenny, as Starrett had planned to visit the Major at the same time, and no matter how much Moya protested it, Maggie didn't want her in the house by herself. The trade-off was Maggie's promise that they'd go see a movie in Letterkenny while Katie hung out with her friends, and Katie better – 'No excuses acceptable!' – be ready to return to Ramelton with her sister and her mother after the movies. Moya scooted off to find out what was on, and the times.

Moya teased Starrett about him still using 'bejeepers' in so many of his sentences. He seriously thought he'd cut down on it but then she patiently explained to him that he wasn't even aware of just how much he was using the word.

In a harmless duel over the dinner table, Starrett teased Moya about getting some shopping for him while she was up in Letterkenny.

'What do you need then?'

'Am, let's see now,' he started, 'how many bananas are there in a bunch of grapes?'

Maggie rolled her eyes but looked on proudly.

'I don't know,' Moya replied, totally bewildered.

'Well, then you'd be a fine one to send to the green-grocers, wouldn't you?' Starrett said and they both fell into a fit of laughing, Moya so much so that tears started to roll down her face.

'I don't know which of youse is the silliest,' Maggie began, reluctantly drawn into the laugher, 'you for thinking it's funny, or our Moya for encouraging you!'

Perhaps Maggie thought he was indulging her daughter but the reality was that Starrett loved the chance to jest as much as Moya. Although, perhaps what she really loved was the fact these jokes were delivered by an adult, and a forty-plus-year-old gardaí inspector at that.

Starrett bid them goodbye late that afternoon and the house which had been buzzing seconds before was silent in their wake. About thirty minutes later he headed down to the Major's.

Just as he was crossing Ray Bridge the rain stopped, the clouds lifted, the sun came out, and so Starrett drove straight past the gate to the Major's house and on into Rathmullan.

A few minutes later he was off on a brisk walk along the beach.

Every time he took to Rathmullan beach he resolved to do so every remaining day of his life. He only lived seven miles away, the views were stunning, in a life-affirming way, the beach was never what you could really call crowded and frequently he was the only soul on the beach, it was free and it was the second most enjoyable thing he did in his life.

But for some reason or other, things never really worked out that way and there'd always be an excuse to keep him away from the beach; he'd get distracted by work, there'd always be tomorrow to have a walk on the beach. When you're in the thick of life, he thought, you never really ever accept that tomorrow just might not come. Starrett also reckoned that even as you grow older and you have to accept that your days are numbered, yes, even then you still believed you had the right to a tomorrow. Time passes so quickly, it really does, he thought to himself. Sure, it was a cliché, but clichés only become clichés because they are true, maybe even painfully true.

He strolled along as the sun was starting to say goodbye for the day, its rays breaking on the fast moving clouds and creating the magnificent beams of light known as God's torch. It was getting cooler and he realised that it had been over a month since he'd last been on the beach. How quickly that month had flown by.

He thought of the Major and figured that no matter how quickly the last month had passed for Starrett, it would pale in comparison to the Major's last month, possibly the last month of his life. Starrett did a complete U-turn on the beach, quickened his pace and headed straight back to the car park at the start of the pier where he'd parked just minutes before.

* * *

The Major was indeed in great spirits and, as Maggie Keane had suggested the previous evening, he'd looked and acted like he might be enjoying a remission. He was extremely pleased to see Starrett. He was indeed up and out of bed, but he was wrapped up snugly in his dressing gown and several other throws and blankets. Even though night had fallen outside, he was still sitting out in the conservatory, looking out at the darkness. It seemed to Starrett as if the Major could see beyond the Donegal blackness and the old soldier was studying another version of the views Starrett had just been enjoying down on the beach. It was as though he had X-ray eyes and could see the lapping water, the rich patchwork quilt of autumnal fields, the mighty mountains and the even mightier heavens above. Maybe he was recalling it all from memory.

He had a chair beside his own, ready and waiting for Starrett.

As they drank their tea, the Major's generously laced with poteen, Starrett filled him in on the recent developments of his case. He then told him the story of his own previous run-in with Bishop Cormac Freeman.

'You know, Starrett,' the Major said, when the detective had concluded his story, 'we all have to realise that in this world some people are just downright bad! We have to accept this fact and learn to work with it.'

'But where do people find the right to not only do these things, then think they can get away with it?'

'I remember when I was very young,' the Major began. 'My father was also in the army and I remember I asked him why the First World

War had started and he studied me as if to consider how much he should tell me. And do you know what he told me?'

Starrett shook his head to show that he didn't.

'He said that two strangers met on a pathway, and there wasn't room for both of them to pass on this path at the same time and neither of them would step back and let the other pass, so they physically fought for the right of way.'

Starrett nodded.

'And that was as simple or as complicated a start to the Great War as I ever heard. One man, feeling he had a God-given right over another. And that is where badness comes from – one man believing he is better than his fellow man.'

The Major took another sip of his poteen-flavoured tea.

'And that's where we come in, Starrett. People have to be held to account for their actions. Yes, of course, the people who feel they are better than their neighbours are always someone's father, someone's son, someone's husband, someone's wife. Sadly, all these people become secondary casualties. But the criminals clearly weren't too worried about those relationships when they were committing their crimes or, as of late, when they were caught raiding the country's larder and banks. This man, Freeman – is he the reason you've lost your faith in God?'

'God? Bejeepers, now there's a big concept,' Starrett mused, not entirely comfortable with the direction of the conversation but at the same time happy to avoid the subject of the Major's health and its consequences. 'If such a concept really existed, then surely there would be no need whatsoever for the likes of Freeman because all our lives would be better if we all lived in harmony with the world and man - and womankind - rather than in constant conflict with it?'

'Too simplistic a concept for mankind.'

Starrett accepted, of course, that his was a very simplistic view, but, nonetheless, he believed it a valid one.

'The main problem I have with Freeman's type is the fact that they bring out only the worst in their fellow men,' Starrett added. 'They make their fellow men, to a certain degree, want and need vengeance, if only to redress the balance of the badness they have created.'

'Because bad men have the power to make good men bad?' the Major mused.

'Perhaps?'

'Yes, that's a very simplistic view,' the Major repeated, 'but valid, nonetheless, due the purity of its genesis.'

Starrett hoped that was that subject parked; he never felt any use came from these types of thoughts.

'Sometimes I used to think that we, as in the gardaí, we were chipping away at Mount Errigal with a toothpick,' the Major said, offering Starrett a new topic, perhaps realising that the detective wasn't entirely comfortable with the first. 'Yes, while at the mountain-face we felt we were doing something, but when we stepped back and looked at the big picture we realised, on consideration, our work was useless.'

Starrett went to protest.

'But then,' the Major grandstanded, 'when you're in the family homes of those wronged and you look into their eyes and you see the hope therein, the desperate hope of what they need you to do for them, if only to validate the importance of the lives of their recently departed loved ones, that's when you realise just how important our work is, how important your work is.'

Starrett tutted his agreement.

'Starrett, I wanted to talk to you about this. You know when I'm gone things will change.'

'Yep,' the detective agreed because he was long since resigned to this fact.

'What will you do?'

'You know, Major, I think I just might retire. I've got Maggie and the kids now and–'

'Balderdash,' the Major wheezed, 'absolute balderdash. Do you really think a woman such as Maggie Keane is going to stand to have you under her feet all day long?'

'It won't be like that, I've lots of things I can do when I retire.'

'Retirement,' the Major grunted, 'aye, that was what I thought might be on your mind. Can I just tell you that the biggest misapprehension of mankind is that when we retire our days will be longer. WRONG! Oh so wrong. If anything, they go quicker. The biggest secret in life is that retirement is not all we were promised. Believe you me, Starrett, and I've witnessed this around all my cronies, the retirement years are not the Golden Years.'

'Major,' Starrett started off slowly, 'are you scared?'

He really hadn't wanted to ask the question but he felt this might be something the Major wanted to discuss. It might have been the reason the Major had sent the message via Maggie that he needed to talk to Starrett. What with all of the Major's old cronies having passed away, he wouldn't have anyone he could discuss this with.

Without looking at the detective, the Major put his hand across to grab Starrett's hand.

Starrett thought that might just be the sum total of their shared moment, so he squeezed the Major's frail hand back.

'In our younger years, we will fear a new ailment or illness when we suffer from it for the first time. But that fear only lasts until we master the art of surviving it,' the Major said, still staring ahead of him out of his cosy conservatory window into the blackness. 'The next time that same illness comes along, experience tells us that we're going to be okay. We know we're going to beat it. Experience convinces us that it's not going to kill us, because we are now fully equipped to deal with it.'

The Major clearly wasn't finished so Starrett continued to yield the floor to his superior.

'You start to worry,' the Major eventually offered, 'only when the death, which was always the enemy of your youth, gradually becomes your friend.'

'Are you prepared, Major?' Starrett whispered, because he really wanted to know, he really needed to know.

'Starrett,' Major Newton Cunningham said, pausing to look around at the detective as if to see if he was ready for the answer, 'we spend our lives trying to learn the rules of life. And then don't we only go and discover that there really are no rules to life and we start to realise that when you think you have it sussed, that's really when you're proving you haven't.'

Starrett felt disappointed. It wasn't that he'd been expecting the Major to reveal the secrets of alchemy or how to get a number one album, but finding out you think you've got it sussed only to realise that you haven't; surely that's nothing more than small cheese.

But then the Major smacked Starrett straight between the eyes with, 'We've got to get a hook on the end and realise that it's not a relief, it's not for the better – it's not even for the worse – it's not part of the journey, it's not us passing over to something greater.'

Again the Major looked at Starrett and studied him for a few seconds.

'But you've never believed in more anyway have you, Starrett?'

'Well, here's the thing, Major. Years ago, when I found myself thinking a lot more on this subject and I started to consider the concept of Heaven, you know, the place where we all get to go, but only if we're good?'

'I've heard of such a place.'

'Well, when I was young and my grandmother died I asked my mum if I'd meet up with my grandmother someday in Heaven. And like all good mothers she replied, "Of course you will." Then my friends would say that they were also going to meet not only their grandparents but, bejeepers, if they didn't think they were also going to meet up with some of their dead pets up there, as well. Then I started to think of all the people and pets who had once walked this Earth since the beginning of time. I started to realise that this place called Heaven was going to be so fecking crowded it was going to look more like my personal definition of Hell.'

'Aye, Starrett, the priesthood's loss was most definitely An Garda Síochána's gain,' the Major said, looking anything but depressed. 'We don't pass to the other side. Even if we should find the secret of how to pass over to the other side, there is nothing there. It's the end of the journey. It's not just the end of the journey, mind you, it's just the end and you know what, Starrett? I take a lot more comfort from accepting that than I do from thinking about this place called Heaven.'

'Then why are we here, Major?' Starrett asked, in clear frustration.

'Only to ensure, for our children's sake, that we leave the world in a better state than we found it.'

'That's really all there is?'

'Bejeepers, Starrett,' the Major offered, with a smile so large it nearly drained all his reserves, 'that's the sum total of what our duty is. But never think of it as only "all", it's not an insignificant task Starrett. That's why I need you to promise me you'll continue our work.'

'Chipping away at Mount Errigal with our toothpick?'

'Aye Starrett, that's all I need you to do.'

'I've one question before I commit,' Starrett said, while of course realising that it didn't matter what the Major said or did. Once he was gone, the bureaucrats would make all the changes they'd been trying to enforce the Major into for the last seven years.

'And your question?' the Major wheezed as he studied his protégé hopefully.

'Can you tell me, will we have a wooden toothpick or one of your fancy silver ones?'

The Major just chuckled and dozed off again.

They sat in that conservatory, talking on into the night, between the Major's cat-naps, until the Major needed his morphine and physical assistance to get back to his bedroom.'

When Starrett and Annette Cunningham had helped the old warrior back to his bed and she'd administered his medication, it wasn't long before he fell into a troubled asleep. As he stood at the back of the bedroom and watched his superior, his breathing laboured – laboured in that it appeared to rattle his cranium – Starrett wondered why the Major had to come through the wars, mainly his 1950s tour of duty with The Royal Ulster Rifles in Cyprus, with all his valour and medals, only to be caught in the cross-hairs of the sniper known as the Big C. Although still alive, his body was totally destroyed and the havoc created and the damage done was way, way beyond what the old enemy had ever attempted to do, even at its very worst.

CHAPTER FORTY-SEVEN

The remains of Father Matthew McKaye were removed to St Ernan's.

By the time Starrett and his team arrived at 9:30 on the Monday morning, the priests and the local undertaker had prepared Father Matt for his final journey.

In the intervening days since the body was discovered they had lost two of their number: Father Gene McCafferty and Bishop Cormac Freeman.

Fathers Patrick O'Connell, McIntyre, Fergus Mulligan, Edward McKenzie, and Robert O'Leary were all in attendance and decked out in their Sunday best. Fathers Michael Clerkin and Peter Casey were still missing in action in Bandon town and the fourth Master, Father Peregrine Dugan, was in his rooms, no doubt still working away on his masterwork, The History of Ireland.

Father O'Leary advised Starrett and his team to go in, one by one, to pay their last respects. The remains were in the little-used first room on the left-hand side as you entered through the front door. Unlike previous visits, St Ernan's now smelled of scented candles burning and heather-infused air freshener. The shutters were closed and Starrett noticed how they inadvertently created two crosses of light as the sun broke through the folding breaks.

The light from neither cross reached the coffin.

When it came to Starrett's turn to pay his last respects, he was really amazed by the work the undertaker had done. He looked at Father Matthew, so still and so peaceful, but yet he didn't look like he was sleeping. Starrett remembered, that when he was young and growing up and he went to the cinema, or when he saw a Western on the TV, he would always study the 'extras' who'd been shot and were meant to be dead, which obviously meant showing no visible signs of life. Actors can't hold their breath forever and it was his little game to see which of them stole a breath or two, when they thought the camera wasn't on them.

What was once the body of Father Matthew McKaye offered none of those signs.

Starrett thought of the Major's words from the previous night and he had to leave the candle-lit room.

Later, when Father O'Leary was presiding over the prayers, Starrett stood outside the door, looking in. Father O'Leary had decided that as there was no family, other than his fellow priests, he would officiate over the burial service in St Ernan's, but as decorum dictated, in the presence of the local priest. It was, therefore, brief and the only thing Starrett could remember of it was Father O'Leary concluding by saying, 'We have to try to ignore what we cannot change in the hope that we will enjoy a better chance of changing that which we can.'

Starrett got directions to the graveyard from Father Fergus Mulligan. He kind of wished he hadn't because the priest's permanently breaking voice sounded like every single word pained him.

Starrett and Ban Garda Nuala Gibson drove straight over to the nearby picturesque graveyard. Starrett figured that most of the funerals he'd attended seemed to have been held on stunningly beautiful days. What cosmic reason could be behind that statistic? That thought only served to bring him back to Mark Mooney. He couldn't help but wonder what Mooney looked like when he was at work, all decked out in his suit jacket and trousers. No doubt it would certainly make a big statement in contrast to the Mooney he'd interviewed. And what did PayPal think of Mooney's tattoos?

As he waited for the funeral procession to arrive, Starrett's thoughts drifted to Mary Mooney, and her sleeping with her husband's brother, the aforementioned Mark Mooney and her sleeping with her sister's husband, Gerry Robinson, and her sleeping with Father Matthew McKaye. Then he remembered the very same Mary Mooney whispering to him to give her a call. Had she also been trying to sleep with him? He laughed at himself, not at her, for the ridiculousness of such a thought. Would she be at the funeral in this very steep graveyard?

And just why were graveyards invariably on such difficult terrain, terrain so awkward that six men had to struggle to keep their footing as they carried the coffin upon their shoulders to the grave? Was it because in the old days, when farmers would be 'asked' to donate some of their land to the Church for such purposes as graveyards or building a church, would they invariably pass on their poorest land? (Perhaps he was being a wee bit too uncharitable with that one). And when was the last time a coffin had been carried on the shoulders of six priests? He ticked the priests off on his fingers: the ukulele playing capitalist McIntyre; Mulligan, with the still breaking voice; the kind O'Leary; O'Connell, the gambler; and the Ginger Beatle, McKenzie. By Starrett's count, that left them one short. Would the ageing father O'Leary be fit to support one-sixth the weight of the body and the coffin? If he wasn't up to the task, they'd be two men short. Would the undertaker's two assistants act as stand-ins?

The sun was out, but nonetheless the wind rustling through the withering leaves of the graveyard's perimeter of trees was chilling Starrett's cheeks and ears. He stooped back into the car and rescued his seldom-used hat. The problem was that it was now so battered, it looked more like he was off to the races himself, to put on a few bets. Perhaps he should check in with Father Pat O'Connell as to the safest nags to carry his money.

He and Gibson hadn't spoken since they arrived at the graveyard. It didn't seem right to discuss the case at that moment. Starrett scoured the graveyard and eventually, at the far end and down a difficult slope, he found what he was looking for: the freshly dug grave. They strolled in that direction to discover the grave was neatly dressed with boards and tailor-made sections of green, astroturf covered, tarpaulin.

Another car pulled up and was abandoned at the main gate. The Irish Family Robinson slowly climbed out of their battered Ford. Starrett remembered Eimear Robinson's genuine tears when he'd first spoken to her about Father Matthew. He was heartened that someone other than the St Ernan's priests had turned out to acknowledge Father Matthew's life.

As a male exited the driver's seat, Gibson said, 'That's Eimear's husband, Gerry.'

Mr Robinson wasn't exactly dressed for a funeral. In fact, he wasn't dressed for a funeral at all. His overalls testified to the fact that he'd most likely been forced to leave his work to attend the funeral with the rest of the family. As the Robinsons made their way over to the graveyard, Julia walked beside her mum whereas Jessica seemed to favour her father.

Before Starrett had enough time to study the Robinsons any further, the hearse pulled up at the main gate, which was still partially blocked by the Robinson's family vehicle. Gerry ran down the graveyard and moved his car to the car park, on the opposite side of the road, as Eimear was heard tutting after him.

Within seconds of the hearse the St Ernan's priests all arrived in a six-seater people carrier. Luckily enough for the ancient priests, the hearse was able to drive right up beside the open grave. In her father's absence, Jessica Robinson stood in the graveyard by herself until Nuala Gibson went and joined her. Eventually her father made it back and Gibson returned to Starrett's side of the grave.

Starrett had been correct in that the undertaker, now known as the 'burial director', had supplemented the five priest's shoulders with one of his assistants. A second assistant steadied and directed the coffin to its final resting place.

Father Robert O'Leary conducted the graveside proceedings, once again in the company of the local priest, and it was difficult to make out what he was saying as a result of the wind gathering strength and pace. Should Father O'Leary resort to air-writing, would Starrett have been able to understand the priest from the combination of sounds and signs, he wondered?

As the coffin was lowered into the ground, it appeared that Jessica Robinson was the funeral attendee most visibly upset. Her sister seemed upset as well, but Starrett figured she was more upset on her sister's behalf. Eimear looked like she was getting upset on behalf of both her daughters, while Gerry, who kept gawking at his watch, looked like he really needed to get back to work.

All the priests threw a fistful of dirt into the grave on top of the coffin. When Father O'Leary invited Eimear, with a nod of his head, to do the same, she shook her head to the negative. Jessica stood away from her father and threw the handful of soil she'd been grasping in her fist, down into the grave and quickly returned to her father's side.

She stood biting her bottom lip, seemingly preoccupied with Father McKenzie, wiping the dirt from his hands as he walks from the grave.

CHAPTER FORTY-EIGHT

After the remains of Father Matthew McKaye were finally laid to rest in the picturesque graveyard, the small group started to break up. Starrett didn't feel it appropriate to doorstep anyone in the actual graveyard, An Garda Síochána business or not. Eimear had a quick chat with Father O'Leary out of Starrett's earshot. She made a detour, from her exit to join her waiting husband and daughter, to say good-bye to Starrett.

'I need to check a few other things with you,' Starrett said, as they shook hands.

'Yes, yes of course,' she replied, once again starting her sentence loud and letting if fade down to half volume. It was as if when she started speaking she didn't realise just how loud her voice would be so she had to pull back on the volume. 'We just need to leave quickly now as Gerry has to get back to work.'

'We could give you and the girls a lift back if it helps?'

Eimear looked like she was going to accept and then thought better of it, 'No, it's fine, Gerry will drop us off at the house. Why don't I meet you in town for a quick coffee, say half an hour at the Blueberry?'

* * *

Twenty-eight minutes later Eimear was rushing into the Blueberry as though she was half an hour late. She searched all around the busy restaurant like a chicken searching for food and Starrett was convinced that she actually looked through him a couple of times. He stood up and the second he did she finally spotted him and Gibson.

Gibson went off to the counter to order an additional coffee.

'Very sad wasn't it?' she whispered.

'Yes, very sad.'

'Poor turn-out, particularly for a Donegal funeral,' she said, still whispering in the reverential tones reserved for funerals. 'I don't think I've ever been to a funeral with so few people turning up.'

'Because of all the recent publicity, the St Ernan's priests didn't want it to become a public spectacle, so they kept the arrangements private,' Starrett offered, by way of explanation.

Eimear just nodded.

By which point Gibson had returned with the café latte for Eimear and three pieces of carrot cake, at Starrett's request.

'So,' the inspector said, as Eimear took two packs of sweetener from the sugar bowl resting centre table, 'you didn't tell me that you'd an affair with your brother-in-law, Mark.'

Eimear looked up from the sweetener to Starrett, as though he'd just betrayed a friend. At first he thought she was going to cry. 'So you know all about the whole sordid mess by now I reckon,' she said, as she neatly lined the two packs of sweetener together and then tore the corner off them simultaneously, pouring the contents into her coffee in one go. The thing that caught Starrett's attention was not so much this trick, but rather why was someone who was trying to wean themselves off sugar doubling up on the sweetener?

'I said to our Mary, I said, "Mary, let that be a lesson to you. A shot over your bow, a warning if you will; the next time you sleep with Gerry or even look at him that way, I'll sleep with Callum."'

Starrett nodded and was about to speak when she continued.

'And that's not all I told her,' Eimear said, looking around the neighbouring tables to see if anyone could overhear them. 'I said, "Mary, and I'll tell you this for nothing, once your Callum has slept with me, he'll never ever sleep with you again."'

Eimear Robinson was still dressed in her funeral clothes: white shirt; long, belt-less black dress; black boots. With her straight black hair, subtle hints of make-up, and verbal claims that she could transform from a worried mother of two into a proud vamp who'll stop at nothing to keep her man, she was making it look quite convincing.

'The thing about our Mary,' she continued, as she cut off a good chunk of the cake with her fork, 'is that she seems to believe that the only way she can justify her existence is by knowing that men

– all men – are attracted to her in a carnal manner. And you know what, Inspector? I'm not even sure that our Mary even enjoys sex!'

She forked the piece of cake she'd cut off and popped it into her mouth, delicately munching on it and glaring at Starrett in a semi-suggestive way.

Or at least that's what Starrett thought. This woman had morphed from the mousey, butter-wouldn't-melt-in-her-mouth mother he'd met the first time round, to a supposed temptress, a predator even.

'And then, didn't poor Callum only go and get ill,' Eimear continued, without the slightest sign of sympathy, 'and so Mary needed to play away from home all the more.'

'We spoke to Callum,' Starrett started, 'you know you suggested he might be the one who was most upset with Father Matthew?'

'Starrett,' she protested, so loud that she drew the attention of several of their fellow diners, so she made sure to drop her voice back to a whisper to continue, 'I said to you, "Starrett," I said, "Mary has her family to protect her." I was trying to be subtle. Fat lot of good it did me. By saying "family to protect her" and not "Callum to protect her", I was trying to discreetly tell you that it was Mark you should be checking out as the one with the motive, the motive of jealously.'

'Sadly, Mark has an alibi,' Starrett admitted.

'Really?' Eimear said, almost suggesting it rather than asking.

'Yes,' Gibson confirmed.

'Does his alibi 100 per cent check out?' Eimear Robinson inquired, again as though butter wouldn't melt. Butter maybe not, but all that remained of her tasty carrot cake were crumbs so few, even birds would give them a miss. Birds might, but Eimear couldn't; she moistened her forefinger and moved it around the plate to pick them up, totally cleaning its surface.

Neither Starrett nor Gibson had answered her.

'Does his alibi 100 per cent check out?' she asked again.

'Mark Mooney claimed he flew into Dublin airport and drove up to Donegal,' Starrett said. 'He said he stopped for a rest. I suppose if he had caught an earlier flight?'

Starrett and Gibson looked at each other in a Keystone Cops kind of moment. As in: Did you check that out? No, I thought you were checking it out? Well, I thought you were checking it out.

'I'll ring Garda Casey, get him to check it out,' Gibson eventually said.

When Starrett asked Eimear for Mary's phone number she looked at him with a disappointed, definitely judgemental, 'What, you too?' kind of look.

With Gibson absent from the table at that moment, Starrett realised what was behind Eimear's disappointment, but he decided against confirming it. He didn't want to reveal that Mary had asked him to ring her.

'Have you had a chance to think of anyone else who Father Matt was seeing after Mary?' he asked.

'Does there need to be anyone? What I mean to say is, he was a priest, maybe he just saw the light, realised what he was doing was wrong and returned to the celibate ways of a priest.'

'Mary reckons the only reason Father Matt stopped seeing her was because he was seeing someone else. She implied that he needed to be with someone.'

'That would be our Mary, everything starts and ends with sex. Every part of her life is focused on that one thing,' Eimear said, before glancing around the dining room, either to check if anyone could overhear them or if Gibson was returning. Appearing content her conversation was private, she continued, 'Look, Inspector, I'm a woman – I'm a fine woman, believe you me – and I have my needs...' she left it hanging there for a few seconds before continuing '...but my children also have their needs and my children's needs are more important than my own. And I'm not moaning, I'm not begrudging anyone, nor saying "I've made my bed and I've got to lie in it." I'm happy to put my children first. Children are the making of a person. Perhaps our Mary would have turned out differently if she and Callum would have had kids when they'd the chance, but she said to me, "Eimear," she said, when I was eight months pregnant with our Jessica, "God, I'm never going to do that to my body!"'

Starrett wondered if there was a chance that Mary could be so body proud and sex-conscious that she might have murdered Father Matt just because he shunned her. Yes, she claimed to have been working in the salon, and her alibi had checked out. But could she, would she, have hired a hit-man? Starrett had heard of a woman in Navan offering her lover a thousand euro to kill her husband, and when he'd said no, she'd continued searching for another man to do the job. Could that possibly explain the mysterious circumstances of

Father Matt's death? Dr Samantha Aljoe still hadn't fully explained the method of murder. Was there a possibility that this was some new Eastern European method of assassination? Why hadn't he thought of that before? Yet another item of research to set Francis Casey upon.

'And Gerry and me,' Eimear continued, 'we steal whatever special moments we can. Some wise man once said, or maybe it was printed on a beer mat or something, I don't remember, but anyway this wise man said, "Where there is no love," he said, "put love, and you'll find love."'

Starrett was basking in these words of wisdom when she hissed, 'Absolute bollox, love, if you ask me.'

The detective couldn't work out if the love referred to was a term of endearment for him, or if love was itself 'absolute bollox'. He decided not to ask for clarification, just in case.

'But as I said,' Eimear offered, draining the remainder of her coffee, 'it's all about our kids and it matters not a lot about whether or not Gerry and I are in love.' As usual, Eimear's voice was fading. 'We can deal with all of that when the girls have left home to start up their own families.' By now Starrett was straining to hear her, 'I just hope they don't make the same mistakes I did.'

When Gibson returned, Eimear said, 'Right, I need to go off and do a bit of shopping for my girls for their dinner tonight, and Gerry too, of course.'

As she walked out the door, Starrett nodded in her direction and said as much to himself as to Gibson, 'Another fine example of what the lack of love has done.'

CHAPTER FORTY-NINE

By the time Starrett and Gibson had returned to St Ernan's there was a still eeriness about the historic house. A collective feeling of resignation, of 'Okay, that's that, let's try and get on with it.' The smell of scented candles and air freshener had all but disappeared and the stale odour had returned. The priests of St Ernan's were still missing the woman's touch of Eimear Robinson. Starrett wondered when she'd be coming back. Was that perhaps what she and Father O'Leary had been chatting about up at the graveyard?

Sergeant Packie Garvey and Garda Romany Browne were kicking their heels up in the boys' room. Garvey reported that they had checked out Mark Mooney's alibi and he had definitely been on the flight from Geneva that had landed in Dublin at 17:00, and Garvey reckoned Mooney's claimed 8 p.m. arrival in Donegal Town was the earliest possible.

'So what are we missing here?' Starrett asked, of the blackboard as much as his fellow colleagues.

'Eimear Robinson seemed to think Mark Mooney is to blame,' Gibson started slowly. 'Perhaps things hadn't been the same between him and Mary since she'd taken up with Father Matt. Perhaps when Father Matt dumped her she didn't want to go back to cheating on her husband with his own brother.'

'We've been told a few times that Father Matt had made a decision, a big decision,' Starrett mused, still looking at the blackboard as if he was expecting the hand of God, or even the fingers of Father O'Leary, to write the name of the culprit for him. 'What if that decision involved leaving the priesthood and settling down with Mary and Mary was totally committed to that and then Father Matt fell in love with someone else and dumped her?'

'But she still has a cast-iron alibi,' Garvey suggested.

'But didn't Eimear say that she had her family – meaning Callum and Mark – to protect her, the way Eimear protected her daughters?' Browne offered, now following Starrett's stare to the blackboard.

'Yes, and?' Starrett said in encouragement.

'And so Mary went crying to Mark, saying, "Look what he's done to me, it's not fair–"'. Browne stumbled a wee bit, sounding as though he was unsure how to develop his theory.

'As in, "Bring me the head of John the Baptist"?' Starrett suggested.

'Sorry?' Gibson said, shaking her head as if she was lost in all of this.

'Okay, long story short; John the Baptist, the man who baptised Jesus, criticised Herod for marrying Herodias, his brother's ex-wife.'

That in itself was enough to stop the gardaí trio in their tracks. It was even enough to make Starrett think twice.

'Not only that, but Herodias was also Herod's niece,' the detective continued, starting to realise once again exactly how bizarre a story it was. 'So Herodias' daughter, Salome, dances a very seductive dance for Herod and he is so impressed, or turned on by her dance, that he promises her she can have anything she wants. Her mother – still pissed at John the Baptist for criticising her for marrying her brother-in-law – persuades Salome to ask Herod for the head of John the Baptist, to be delivered to her, on a plate.'

'And all that just because John the Baptist had denounced Herod and Herodias over their union?' Gibson asked.

'Exactly,' Starrett said, looking a bit embarrassed that it might appear he still knew the Scriptures so well, or at least reasonably well – well maybe not even reasonably well, but well enough that he still had a few quotes up his sleeve.

'Yeah, I think I saw that movie as well,' Browne claimed, taking some of the wind out of Starrett's sail.

'So let's see now…' Starrett said, starting to scribble on the blackboard again, 'Mary Mooney is Herodias (the wife), Mark Mooney is Herod (the husband), Callum Mooney is Philip (the cuckolded brother), and Father Matt is John the Baptist.'

'So who is Salome?' Browne asked.

'I don't think she appears until the sequel,' Gibson chipped in.

Starrett smiled.

'So, Mary Mooney asks her brother-in-law, Mark Mooney, to bring her the head of Father Matt,' Starrett said, completing his version of the parable; but in this case, not an earthly story with a heavenly meaning, but more one in which a Bible story begat a crime novel.

'But Mark also has a cast-iron alibi,' Garvey stated, for the record.

'Yes, but what if he hired someone else to do it?' Browne suggested, his momentum and enthusiasm growing by the second. 'I mean, surely Herod wouldn't have chopped off John the Baptist's head himself?'

Starrett nodded his agreement.

'And so he only went to Geneva on that particular day to ensure he'd be away and have that cast-iron alibi?' Browne continued, on a roll.

'Nagh, I don't buy it with Mooney,' Gibson said, shaking her head very positively and very slowly, 'he's too intelligent–'

'Too intelligent?' Browne cut in, 'He was shag...sorry, I meant of course that he was sleeping with his brother's wife! That's hardly someone who's too intelligent!'

Starrett, Gibson and Garvey all looked surprised and impressed by Browne's moralistic statement.

'I still think he's too smart to expose himself by hiring someone to murder Father Matt,' Gibson concluded.

'He did suggest that Father Matt's murder completed the "cosmic circle" and "balanced up" the right and wrong,' Starrett added. 'But I'm with the ban garda on this one; he wouldn't have hired someone else to do it.'

'Okay, okay, I can live with that,' Browne said. 'However, we still don't know 100 per cent how Father McKaye was murdered. Right?'

Garvey said, 'Right.'

'Correct,' said Gibson.

Starrett said, 'Yeah?'

'And you're saying this guy is clever?' Browne offered, still pushing onwards.

Starrett and Gibson nodded positively in unison.

'So what if Mark Mooney was so clever that he could have figured out some kind of system and set it up, whereby Father Matt could be killed remotely while he was in Geneva?'

'On first glance,' Starrett started slowly, 'that sounds fanciful at best...however, on second consideration it sounds...even more fanciful.'

They all laughed.

'Phew, that was close,' Browne said, when the laughter had finished. 'I thought you were going to ask me to work out exactly how he'd managed to get that to work.'

'Ah, that would be more a case for Inspector Christy Kennedy,' Starrett said, remembering the case he'd worked on with the London-based Portrush detective.

'I don't think the garda has ever seen that movie,' Gibson offered.

'Which all leaves us…where?' Starrett continued, happy to see his team at least pushing together in good humour to try and resolve this case.

'Low on suspects,' Garvey replied.

'So, exactly how many suspects do we have left at this stage?'

They all looked at their blackboard and Browne was the first to offer 'None?', even though they were all thinking the very same.

'What are we not considering?' Starrett asked, thinking again about the bizarre method of murder.

'Who of those that knew Father Matthew have we not yet considered?' Sergeant Packie Garvey asked, displaying he was as good with a bit of fancy footwork off the field as he (most definitely) was on it.

'Father Robert O'Leary,' Starrett said, without even thinking about it.

'Father Peregrine Dugan,' Ban Garda Nuala Gibson offered, a split second later.

CHAPTER FIFTY

At the very least Starrett still had his trusted brown-green hat. It was a good hat from Christy's of London and of the shabby chic look and style as favoured at the Curragh. It had served him well on numerous occasions, this time proving to be very handy against the bleak winds circling the graveyard..

'I find it's not so much about swimming,' he said, as he picked up his hat from the chair beside the blackboard and left the makeshift meeting room by himself, 'it's more about how long you can hold your breath.'

As the detective disappeared out the door, Garvey, Browne, and Gibson looked at each other.

'Did you get that one?' Gibson quietly asked her two colleagues.

'You mean you got any of them?' Browne said, in clear amazement.

'The important thing,' Sergeant Garvey volunteered, scratching the crown of his head, 'is that Inspector Starrett knows exactly what he means.'

A few seconds later, Starrett tapped on Father O'Leary's door.

A few seconds after that Starrett and Father O'Leary were making their way to, and tapping on, Father Dugan's door.

And before they knew it, wasn't the old and supposedly decrepit Father Dugan brewing them up a pot of tea and sending O'Leary down to the kitchen to heat up some fresh apple pie for the three of them. Starrett reckoned that, so far, he was holding his breath pretty well.

'So Father Matthew's remains are buried,' the old priest said, by way of starting up the conversation, so much so that Starrett reckoned he was totally transparent. Better than being so old and settled that he was going to be happy to sit there in silence with his own thoughts and ignore the detective altogether.

'Aye, that's him off now, poor soul,' Starrett said, and realised, and accepted the fact, that he was really saying nothing. He knew he was reacting to some form of post-funeral, St Ernan's blues.

He dreaded the conversation might head down the 'old man viewing the death of someone he knew and starting to get preoccupied with his own demise' route, if he wasn't careful. But no, that was not where Father Dugan was heading, not at all in fact.

'You know,' Dugan said, swishing some warm water around his rose-smattered white tea-pot, 'I look at him and I'm astounded by how happy I am that it's not me. That I've been spared for another day, I'm still alive.'

'Aye, you've got your book to complete,' Starrett said, as the old priest took his still swishing teapot to the sink to dump its contents.

'I've been working on it so long I don't know anything else,' he replied, shuffling back to the table and adding three spoonful's of tealeaves and then the just peaking boiling water, the steam of which rose quickly and disappeared into his hanging grey hair. 'Sometimes I believe I'll never finish it, and maybe not because I can't, but because I don't want to.'

His voice was so loud, Starrett imagined that Father O'Leary, in his apple-pie warming absence, was missing only a little of the conversation.

'But do you not feel having worked this long and hard on your book,' Starrett started, stopping to observe the room around him, which was packed with books and files, all neatly stored in every available nook and cranny and on top of all the floorboards not required to support something or be walked on, 'it would better to top and tail it with your own words?'

'Oh, I don't know, Inspector.' The priest broke into a large smile and bobbled around the room, picking up cups and saucers from a cupboard here, a drawer there, and a teaspoon from just about everywhere. 'If I agreed with you, would that make me guilty of the sin of vanity?'

'Bejeepers, not at all, Father,' Starrett said immediately. 'If a scholar is going to invest his energy and time using your book for reference, they're going to want to ensure that no Tom, Dick, or Paddy added to it after your death.'

Father Dugan seemed to have stopped mid-floor to consider this very point when Father O'Leary returned to the room with the hot apple pie. All pretence of polite conversation ended there and then, as the three men got down to the serious issue of their afternoon tea.

Father O'Leary was the first one to break the silence.

'I heard you and your boys and girl discussing King Herod and John the Baptist,' he started, as ever accompanied by his very finest air writing. 'And while it's a conversation which shouldn't be alien to these rooms, I was somewhat surprised to hear it being discussed by the gardaí.'

'Very interesting,' Father Dugan added seamlessly, as Starrett wondered how much more, and how many, of the gardaí's conversations had been overheard.

'Does it tie in with this case?' Father O'Leary said.

Starrett hesitated; his hesitation was picked up immediately by both priests.

'Okay,' Father O'Leary started, 'let's reverse the situation: I'll tell you what I know or suspect and you can confirm it when I'm right, just like I've been doing with you. And maybe, just maybe I'll be able to give you a few hints.'

'That seems only fair,' Starrett replied, feeling he'd little left to lose.

'Good,' the father said, rubbing his hands together as if to warm them. Or perhaps he was just warming up his invisible nib. 'So, at the hub of this story we have a man, Herod, who took his brother's wife,' Father O'Leary said, voice and nib in full flow. 'The wife (assisted by her beautiful daughter) tricked Herod into beheading a man called John the Baptist.'

'Important point of order here,' Father Dugan's voice boomed out all around his room.

'Yes?' Father O'Leary said, conceding the floor.

'We're not talking about any other common garden man here, are we? Point of fact, there are some who would say that at the time of the death of Yochanan Ben Zechariah–'

'Sorry,' Starrett said, interrupting the old priest, 'who?'

'Yochanan Ben Zechariah was John the Baptist's Jewish birth name,' Father O'Leary offered, smiling at Father Dugan.

'Yes,' the older priest confirmed, 'sorry, what I should have said was, at the time of John the Baptist's death, he was not just a contemporary of Jesus, not just an equal of Jesus, but, some would say, maybe he was even better than Jesus.'

'Agreed,' his colleague said, and did an air-tick to the positive.

'There are some who would say that John the Baptist had to die in order for Jesus to emerge,' Father Dugan continued, before nodding at Father O'Leary.

Right, right, Starrett thought, I've already been around this house with my team and it didn't lead us anywhere, anywhere that was apart from right smack-bang back where we'd started. Then he thought how there didn't seem to be anything this priest didn't know, so perhaps he should just shut up, pretend he knew more than he really did and see what he could learn from this lecture.

'So, we know that Eimear Robinson has a sister called Mary – she would be Mooney by marriage – and Mary cheated with her sister's husband,' Father O'Leary said, not as much taking the floor again but more totally flooring Starrett with what he knew. 'Another way to put that would be that Mark Mooney cheated with his brother's wife.'

'Good so far,' Father Dugan more graciously conceded.

'Now, in your little domestic drama, Inspector, you have one additional twist – or that maybe should be one extra twist that we know of, or we think we know of. In this scenario we're suggesting that John the Baptist, Heaven forbid, also lay with Herod's wife, or, in our case, Father Matthew lay with Mary Mooney.'

Father Dugan just rolled his eyes as if to suggest, 'Ah, the kids today.'

'Father McKaye, aka John the Baptist, lost his life, if not his head,' O'Leary said.

'So we need to work out who insulted Herod enough–' Starrett started, only to be cut short.

'Don't be afraid to look back to the original story,' Father O'Leary offered very seriously. He also did his air-writing version of his sentence, but he did something else, something he'd never done before. He underlined it and not just once, but several times.

The meeting broke up several minutes later, Starrett making elaborate excuses when he'd decided the priests had started repeating themselves.

He slowly and carefully closed the door, but not all of the way – he walked away from it, waited at the top of the stairs for a few minutes, tip-toed back to the door to Father Dugan's suite of rooms, gently knocked on it once and walked right in to catch Father O'Leary saying: '...yes, but Herod wasn't really all that bad, his only problem was that he was too easily led by his append–'

'Ah sorry, I must have left my hat in here somewhere,' Starrett offered, as Father O'Leary pulled up on his sentence very quickly.

Starrett eventually spotted it exactly where he'd planted it. 'Bejeepers, here it is,' he said, pointing to it and grabbing his favourite clothing accessory, before looking on the inside and adding very innocently, 'Yes, this is mine, look, I've got my name tag sewn into the inside.'

'Yes, I'm sure it is,' the voice of God boomed, knowingly. 'Is that a trick you learnt at boarding school?'

Starrett wasn't sure if the old priest, who'd been born on the same day as Mickey Mouse, was referring to the trick of marking his clothing, or the trick of trying to catch persons (or priests) of interest totally unawares.

CHAPTER FIFTY-ONE

Gibson took a call on her mobile from Maggie Keane. She immediately passed the phone to Starrett without saying a word.

'Starrett, it's the Major,' Maggie gushed breathlessly, 'Annette just rang to say he's slipping away, he's just received the Last Rites and she thought you'd want to be there.'

'I'm on my way,' Starrett replied, before disconnecting and saying to Gibson, 'the Major's please, Nuala, I don't think we have much time.'

Starrett tried to pass the time of the journey by reminiscing about the Major and their times together, but his stomach was fighting with him so violently for his breath, he was unable to do so. Forty-seven minutes and ten white knuckles later they were pulling into the Major's drive.

Annette Cunningham looked so relieved to see him. For the first time in his life, Starrett realised that he was just as important a presence in their lives as they were in his.

As he walked into the Major's dimly lit room he knew immediately to prepare himself for the worst. The reality was that the split second Nuala Gibson's phone had rung, he knew it was the call he had been dreading. His time with the Major on the previous evening had lulled Starrett into a false sense of security. So much so in fact that he'd really wanted to conclude work on the Father McKaye case so that he could spend some more real time with the Major.

As he stood there looking at his friend, his breathing laboured, Starrett also realised for the first time in his life that he only feared death when he was younger because he didn't understand it. He feared it a lot more now that he was older because he'd grown to understand it that bit more.

Annette sat on the bed beside the Major. 'Darling,' she said, her
voice steady, 'Starrett's here to say goodbye – you don't need to hang
on any longer.'

The Major opened his eyes, smiled lovingly at his wife and at Starrett, who'd walked over to the bedside. The old soldier didn't resist
the weight on his eyelids, which was slowly forcing them shut again

Starrett quite literally saw the passing.

It started before the last breath, when the colour started to fade and
the breathing gently fell. He thought the Major was gone because he
looked so peaceful. But then he noticed the clear pulse in the vein in
the left-hand side of the neck (the Major's right). Starrett focused on the
pulse in the vein in the neck, willing it on. Then the pulse stopped and
he could actually feel the Major slipping away. Starrett marvelled that
in its own way, the passing was maybe just as miraculous as birth, because the body knows instinctively how to protect you against the con-
tinuous stresses, strains, and pains, by releasing you.

Then the body, for the very first time in 73 years, 6 months, 2
weeks, 1 day, 7 hours and 5 minutes, was totally motionless.

Starrett noticed the remainder of the colour drain quickly, very
quickly, from the corpse. Sadly it was now most certainly a corpse,
and the colour of life slowing was replaced with the viral efficiency of
the death hue.

People believe that clothes, shoes, hats, blankets, centrally heated
houses all keep them warm, but it's none of those things: it's the heart.
Because the very second the heart packs in, and even though the body
is still protected, comforted by those clothes, blankets or central heating, the body is stone cold to the touch within minutes.

Usually death is not this close to life, but Starrett could feel them
both still lingering. He wondered, were these the sensations his mother
had to deal with all of her life? And yet for all his knowing it was near,
even still in the room, death still froze him in life. It was like death was
looking for yet another body (perhaps his?) to draw breath from. Despite everything, in that moment he was still so unprepared for death's
presence and the single thing that cut him to the quick was how perfectly still the Major was. There were no more gentle rises and falls
generated by the heart and lungs. There was nothing, because where
there is no life, there is only death, and death is as still as sadness.

CHAPTER FIFTY-TWO

Starrett was surprised by how little recent events had distracted him from his case. No, in point of fact, he was actually quite shocked. He wasn't to know that the death of a loved one frequently does this to a person. In an average day he would see the Major once...maybe even twice, if mitigating circumstances dictated so. There were also days, possibly even two or three in a row, where he wouldn't see the Major at all. On such days, mostly one would contact the other by phone, just to check in. So it was going to take a week, and possibly even as long as a month, before Starrett would really start to miss the Major's towering presence in his life. That's when the real hurt and emptiness would kick in, and kick in with venom. By then, he'd be thinking of their meetings, their chats by the riverside stone wall just across the road from Tower House, the Gardaí Station House in Ramelton. Starrett swore that the Major had used a section of the wall he so enjoyed sitting on as a seat for so many years that he had worn it down into the saddle-like shape.

In a way, Major Newton Cunningham's current absence from Starrett's life was more akin to a friend who'd just gone away on holiday or business for a few days. When the cruel reality set in, then Starrett would start to miss his good friend the way a junkie misses his fix.

Maggie Keane could have described the intensity of such a pain to him but she knew it was much better to let it creep up on him, silently and slowly.

For now his preoccupation was with Father Matthew McKaye, and solving the case of his murder.

* * *

'I know who Father Matt left me for,' spoke Mary Mooney.

It was Tuesday, mid-morning, and on reaching St Ernan's and set-ting up in the boys' room, Starrett had braced himself and made the call, mainly because he'd nothing else to work on.

Mary had insisted they meet in person – 'I could never do this on the phone,' she'd said. They had to meet alone, 'I couldn't do this if one of the real guards is with you.' Starrett wondered if that meant Mary Mooney didn't consider him to be a real garda; most likely something to do with the uniform, he thought, or his lack of one. She'd wanted to meet in a strange place, 'I need to meet you where they don't know me,' she'd said.

Starrett's imagination had run away with him and he was half ex-pecting her to say, 'You book a room in the Abbey Hotel, ring me on my mobile, give me the room number, and I'll come up.' He was so half expecting her to say this, that he'd started to work up a reply and the only one he could come up with was, 'I don't cheat,' because he didn't. Never had.

'I'll meet you in the lounge of the Abbey in half an hour,' she'd said, 'I'll already be there, I'll find somewhere private, there's lots of little nooks and crannies, you come looking for me. But Starrett...'

'Yes?'

'Just make sure you come alone,' she'd said.

That is how, thirty-three minutes later, Starrett happened, by acci-dent, upon the very glamorous Mary Mooney, so discreetly hidden in the lobby of the hotel that he nearly didn't find her there. In fact, he couldn't find her and he'd only done so when she'd peeked out from behind a half-closed door and, quite literally shouted out to him, 'Star-rett, I'm over here!'

Which kind of made the whole cloak and dagger approach a bit of a farce.

'Would you like a drink, Starrett?' she said, wiping her teeth with her tongue and then without waiting for a reply added, 'God, I need a drink to steady me nerves. Be a wee pet and go and get us some wine.'

'It's only 11 a.m., Mary,' he protested.

'I need a drink,' she hissed.

Five minutes later he returned with two small bottles of Jacob's Creek white wine for her and a bottle of sparkling mineral water for himself.

Mary Mooney quickly unscrewed the top and emptied most of the contents of the bottle into her glass in one plop, some of it spilling onto the beer mat underneath. As she was pouring the wine, Starrett noticed the latest edition to her canon of beauty: She'd each and every finger nail painted a different colour from when they'd last met, but not only that, she'd a totally new set of nail art, again in contrasting colours. A circle of white dots on a blue background on one, a small green diamond on a red background on another, and so on. She was clearly going for the Benetton Colours of the World look. Her long, bare legs were tanned to perfection, which was strange when you consider that the last time that the sun broke the cloud with any degree of anger, or heat, in Donegal would have been a weekend way, way back in July, back when summer arrived late and disappeared early. Starrett figured from the little he knew of these things that it must have taken Mary Mooney at least, at the very least, an hour and an half to turn herself out in such a flawless state.

'Cheeky little nail varnish remover,' she said, as she gulped down half of her wine.

Starrett raised his eyebrows.

'Jeez, Starrett,' she said, after studying him intently for a few seconds, 'you look like you could do with a drink yourself. What are you so nervous about?'

'I, ah…' Starrett stumbled.

She patted his hand before he'd a chance to formulate a reply, 'Be a wee pet and go and get me a couple of ham toasties. There're great in here – I'll suffer if I drink all of this on an empty stomach.'

The inspector did as he was bid and when he returned five minutes later, she was deep in conversation with a couple of female friends. So much for being discreet.

He arrived just in time to hear one of the friends saying, 'He didn't! No! Shut up! Behave!' All delivered like rapid fire from a machine gun.

She introduced Starrett as a friend of Callum and hers.

When they eventually left, nearly bumping into a pillar they were eyeballing Starrett so much, he said, 'Okay, Mary, you said you'd discovered who Father Matt was seeing after he left you.'

'Yes,' she gasped, 'un-fecking-believable!'

She looked all around them, checking this way and that, and when she was sure there was no one within hearing distance she said, 'You won't believe who it was, Starrett.'

Starrett waited and waited for the punchline. Mary kept glaring at him, daring him to make a suggestion just so she could say, 'No!' He didn't fall for it verbally but he fell for it mentally, and it was doing his head in. Inside he was screaming, 'Who the feck is it?', while outwardly he stared at her as though examining every inch of her face in search of the secret of beauty.

'Why are you so nervous, Starrett?' she said.

'Mary, who was Father Matt's girlfriend after you?

'Jessica Robinson,' she hissed.

'No!' said Starrett. 'Get away!'

'Yes,' Mary said proudly, proud in the way that only a revealer of a secret can be. At the same time she must have been thinking, 'You wee bitch, you, nicking my man,' while simultaneously feeling guilty for not hosting the thought, 'Oh, my poor wee niece, defiled by that horrible, wicked priest.'

Whatever she was thinking, a whole maelstrom of emotions were most certainly, and visibly, charging up Mrs Mary Mooney. Starrett, for his part, breathed a huge sigh of relief. He really had feared that she was going to ask him to get them a room.

'So how did you discover that?' he said, hoping to diffuse the situation.

'Our Julia told me.'

'Julia knows?'

'Yes, she thinks her sister is about to lose it big time. Apparently she nearly did lose it at the funeral yesterday.'

Suddenly the penny dropped. He remembered Maggie telling him that it was usually the younger daughter who takes to the mother's new man, or cuckoo, the way Moya had taken to Starrett. Of course, Eimear Robinson and Father Matt weren't lovers. Starrett's second thought was: But in this case, who even knew for sure? When it came down to it though, Starrett believed Eimear when she said she'd never slept with the priest. So Eimear and Father Matt would have been good friends and he would have been around the house, so often as a friend, a friendly cuckoo, that there would have been that attachment but it should have been with the younger sister, Julia. But it wasn't, it was the older sister, Jessica. Starrett had already noted Jessica was the one who was most upset by the priest's passing and when he'd inter-viewed the two of them, Julia had said something that only Jessica could hear but it had obviously been something suggestive or crude, by the way Jessica had reacted to it.

Yes, he'd noticed these things but he hadn't put them together.

'Have you spoken to Jessica about this?'

'No,' Mary admitted, 'but it's her mum I'm really worried about – she worships those girls, she just lives for them.'

'Do you think there is any chance Gerry knows about this?'

'Are ye fecking kidding me?' she shouted out loud, and then whispered, 'sure if he found out, there wouldn't be a priest in St Ernan's who would be safe. Scrap St Ernan's, there wouldn't be a priest in the whole of the fecking county who would be safe!'

'Did Julia know about you and Father Matt?'

'I don't think so. I'd like to think that if Jessica had known, she'd never have gotten involved with him. I've always gotten on great with my nieces. I like to think they can talk to me about anything.'

'Did Julia know much about the relationship?'

'Not really, I think she just knew there had been one and she was at her wits end, she was really worried about how to help her sister.'

'Okay,' Starrett said, 'look Mary thanks for this–'

'I'm sorry I couldn't tell you earlier,' she confessed. 'I just couldn't utter those words in my sister's house.'

She toyed with her wine and half of her sandwich.

'Look at me, I don't know whether I'm coming or going. But I just knew I had to tell you,' she said and then she looked like she was considering something else. 'I was surprised you didn't ring me sooner…'

'I–' Starrett started.

'You didn't! Shut up! Behave!' she semi-screeched, doing a double wipe of her teeth with her tongue.

'What? What?'

'I've got it, you auld dog you,' she whispered, checking her position on the seat as though conscious of her decency. 'You thought I was going to try and shift you!'

'No, no!' Starrett lied, in relief.

'Behave! Starrett, you're much too high profile for me,' she said, and smiled, placing her hand on his arm, the way one would do affectionately with an uncle or a grandparent. 'On top of which, everyone in the county knows you're Maggie Keane's man.'

CHAPTER FIFTY-THREE

'I know who Salome is,' Starrett declared, as he walked into the gardaí temporary quarters in St Ernan's.

'Who?' the gardaí trio asked in unison.

'Jessica Robinson.'

'Eimear's daughter?'

'The very same, Gibson' Starrett replied, immediately and upbeat, very upbeat.

'So, okay,' Browne said, appearing to be concentrating for all his might, 'so are we now thinking Jessica Robinson was Father Matt's girlfriend at the time of his death?'

'Yes,' Starrett replied.

'And what exactly does that mean?'

'Good question,' Starrett said. 'That's what we need to find out. I think the Ban Garda and I need to go and have a chat with her.'

As it happened, Starrett and Gibson, in Starrett's BMW, passed Eimear Robinson, in a battered VW Golf, on her way to St Ernan's on the mainland side of the causeway. They acknowledged each other with brief waves. With benefit of hindsight, Starrett realised just how important that sighting was, in that the mother hen wouldn't be fussing around the house while Starrett and Gibson tried to interview her eldest daughter.

At first, for comfort or support – or maybe even both – her sister, Julia, joined them. After Jessica seemed comfortable with the gentle, caring tone of the interview, she told her sister she was okay and she could leave her to finish the rest of the meeting on her own.

'No!' Julia protested, 'I don't mind staying.'

'I want you to go,' Jessica said, quietly but firmly.

'Dope,' Julia said, as she glided out of the room on her wheels.

'Jools,' Jessica cried out after her, 'mum's floors! We're not even meant to be in here!'

Jessica was dressed once again in her blue, floppy shapeless jumper, but this time she had paired it with loose black tracksuit bottoms and dark blue canvas tennis shoes.

'We understand you and Father Matt were close?' Starrett started, deciding the best way into this interview was to treat Jessica as the adult she was.

'Very close,' Gibson added.

Jessica eyed them both. She didn't appear to be as uncomfortable as she had looked during their last chat, nor did she seem as upset as she had been up in the graveyard. She still played with her long blonde hair though, flicking it around her finger and then placing it behind her shoulder. Starrett reckoned she most likely didn't even realise she was doing it. He remembered the long strand of blonde hair Dr Aljoe had discovered on Father Matt on the first day. Jessica was most definitely more relaxed with them on this visit. Perhaps she was happy to finally have the chance to get whatever was upsetting her off her chest. Perhaps she was happy Starrett and Gibson were now going to help her bring the subject out into the open and she wouldn't have to continue living with guilt while at the same time trying to secretly mourn the man she loved.

'You know Jools and I told you he was unhappy in the priesthood?'

'Yes, I remember that Jessica,' Starrett replied.

'And you know we told you that he was going to leave the priesthood?'

'Yes,' Gibson replied.

'Well, he was going to leave the priesthood so we could be together,' she said, as she stopped playing with her hair and cradled both palms of her hands gently on her stomach.

Starrett was impressed Jessica was addressing the topic head on, rather than circling around it.

'Had Father Matt told your parents about this?' Starrett asked.

'We didn't need to.'

'Sorry?' Starrett started, not really following her.

'My mam caught us down here late one night, making out,' Jessica volunteered freely.

Gibson looked shocked but managed to restrain herself. Starrett knew he had to go with the flow and not appear too judgemental.

'Sorry, Jessica, I'm not entirely sure I understand exactly what "making out" is,' Starrett said, as casual as he knew how to be. 'You see, from what I can gather from my girlfriend–'

'Maggie Keane?' Jessica asked immediately, as if she was seizing this golden opportunity to confirm a piece of gossip.

'As it happens, yes,' Starrett replied, openly confused as to why people in Donegal Town seemed to know so much about Maggie. 'You see, Maggie also has two daughters and when they're kidding around, the younger one thinks that "making out" is kissing, which apparently is what it means in America, whereas the older sister, Katie, well, she seems to think that "making out" is–'

'Making love?' Jessica offered thoughtfully.

'Well, yes,' Starrett replied.

'Katie is correct,' the elder Robinson sister confirmed. 'And, yes, my mam caught Matt and me making love.'

'How did she react?' Gibson asked.

'Well, all things considered,' Jessica said scrunching up her face, 'she was pretty civilised about it.'

'What happened?' Starrett asked.

Jessica looked confused, and perhaps a little embarrassed. 'Oh you mean when she discovered us?'

Starrett nodded.

A huge grin of relief spread across her face. 'I thought for a moment there you were asking me to explain exactly what we were doing.'

Gibson couldn't help giggling, which started Jessica off in a fit of giggles as well. In that one second she was no longer an adult discussing an adult encounter but a wee girl enjoying a naughty moment with one of her mates. The interlude served to settle the proceedings down a bit by relaxing everyone.

'So, my mam,' Jessica started again, once she'd managed to regain her composure, 'well, she could have been…she could have blown her top. Well, maybe she didn't…maybe because my dad was upstairs asleep and if she'd woken him there really would have been hell to pay. Or maybe it could have been she just wanted to manage the situation by getting my Matthew out of the house immediately.'

'Did your dad find out?' Starrett asked.

'Goodness, no way!' Jessica said, physically looking like a kid again, one who'd just been caught eating directly from the sugar bowl. 'I really felt for mam. I couldn't work out if she was more disappointed in me or with Matt. She didn't make a fuss; she covered me with her dressing gown, whispered to Matt to see himself out and led me upstairs.'

'When did this happen?' Starrett asked.

'A bit over two weeks before Matt died,' she said quietly.

'Did your mum discuss it with you after Father Matt had left?'

'No, that's the funny thing,' Jessica said. 'She never even acknowledged that the incident had ever happened, that's why this has been a very difficult time for me, no one is allowing me to grieve and I'm the one who has lost the most. You're the first people I've really discussed this with…'

She looked like she was very close to tears again. Starrett was hit hard by the impact of this young woman crossing the emotional lines from woman to child and then back again, and sometimes within the same sentence.

'…and it's…this is really helping me. We really did love each other, you know.'

'We know,' Gibson said, going over to join her on the sofa and putting a comforting arm around her.

'I'm sorry,' Jessica sobbed. 'I don't want to be babbling here like a kid. I need to be strong – Matt always said I was the stronger of the two of us. He said I'd given him the courage to leave the priesthood.'

'Had he told anyone he was leaving?' Starrett asked.

'He told that old letchy bishop that he wasn't going to be going to his diocese. Matt said the bishop was seriously pissed. He told Father O'Leary that he was having serious reservations about whether he really wanted to continue on with it all. Father O'Leary was so caring and considerate with Matt. He didn't throw a hissy fit. He's such a nice man, Father O'Leary, such a sweet man. He's how all priests should be. He calmly told Matt now was the right time to consider his doubts. He advised him to listen to his heart and follow it, and not listen to what his head felt he should do. He said, "It's your life and you've only got one and whereas mistakes are your own to make, life's so much easier if you can avoid the buggers."'

'Yes, Father O'Leary really is a decent man,' Starrett agreed.

'Do you think…' Jessica started and then stopped and then started again, 'do you think the bishop murdered my Matt?'

'Jessica, Bishop Freeman has an alibi for the time of Father Matt's passing,' Starrett said.

She nodded her acceptance.

'Did you and Father Matt see each other after the night your mum caught you together?'

'Why yes,' she said, smiling again before sitting up and gently disentangling herself from the ban garda's comforting arm. 'I mean, we spoke a lot, we met a few times, but we never made love again.'

When neither of the gardai commented, she continued, 'Matt said he would leave the priesthood and get everything set up, and then we should start "dating" and take it from there, as a normal couple, rather than getting caught up in the stigma of me being a priest's lover.'

'Makes sense,' Starrett offered, in encouragement.

'Made sense at the time,' she said barely above a whisper.

'Did Father Matt ever tell you about anyone he'd a falling out with?'

'Nope.'

'Did he ever tell you about anything or anyone troubling him?'

'No,' she replied quickly, 'and we discussed everything. He was a very happy boy. You know, he was just a few years older than me? He'd always say that by the time he was forty, people wouldn't even notice the difference in our ages, let alone be preoccupied with them.'

'Jessica, we have to ask you this question, so please don't be upset by it,' the detective started.

'Okay,' she replied plainly.

'Could you just tell us what you were doing last Wednesday afternoon between the hours of, say, 3:30 and 5:30?'

'Oh, that's easy! I know why you're asking, you have to ask the question just to rule people out.'

'That's correct,' Gibson confirmed.

'In my case, it's simple,' she said proudly. 'I was with a bunch of my mates all that afternoon and early evening. We were at Aoife and Maeve's house, we'd all great fun. Then I got back here and my mum told me the awful news from St Ernan's.'

As Jessica recounted to Gibson the details of Aoife and Maeve's address, Starrett looked troubled. He had a question which had been floating around his head for a good few minutes now and he was 50/50 on whether or not he was going to ask it. Before he had a chance to consider the subject any further, the words just slipped from his tongue by their own accord:

'Did Father Matthew know you were pregnant?'

'No, but my mum did!'

CHAPTER FIFTY-FOUR

Starrett returned to St Ernan's with a heavy heart. Gibson was at the wheel, as usual.

'As soon as I drop you off at St Ernan's I'll scoot back into town and check her alibi with Aoife and Maeve,' she said.

'Let the boys do that,' Starrett said, shaking his head to try and remove something from it. 'You and I will have a wee chat with Eimear.'

As they entered the back door of St Ernan's, the detective could hear someone, probably Father Ginger Beatle, close by in the trees and popping away on the air rifle, most likely trying to score another rabbit or two for the evening's dinner.

Eimear Robinson was immediately back at the sink, busying herself with the dishes. Father O'Leary was sitting by the roaring fire, holding a newspaper up, which he didn't appear to really be reading. From some far corner of the house Starrett could hear a couple of voices, most likely Father Mulligan discussing some writing project with the Master Writer, Father Dugan. Starrett concentrated on the voices for a little while until he was sure he recognised the breaking voice of Father Mulligan.

To all intents and purposes it looked like just another day at St. Ernan's. Starrett figured it was both shocking and heartening how quickly life had returned to 'normal' following a death in the midst.

Still, for all of that, there was something troubling Starrett about the scene. He couldn't quite put his finger on it but he knew in his gut that something was wrong, something was missing.

Eimear, who'd acknowledged Starrett briefly when he'd entered the room went on with her work. Father O'Leary folded his newspaper elaborately, put it down and invited the inspector to sit with him by the fire. Gibson went upstairs on a nod from Starrett to ask

Sergeant Packie Garvey and Garda Romany Browne to check out Jessica Robinson's alibi.

'Any further progress?' Father Robert O'Leary asked.

'Yes, as a matter of fact,' Starrett replied, still distracted by what could have been missing from the scene.

'Anything you wish to share?' the priest continued, minus his usual air-writing.

Starrett looked at him and smiled and shook his head slowly from side to side.

'Can I make youse a cup of tea?' Eimear asked, once again her opening words a lot louder than her closing ones.

Just then Browne, Garvey, and Gibson came down the stairs. Gibson broke off towards Starrett and the other two continued out the back door.

'I think we'll skip the tea for now, thanks,' Starrett started, 'but Eimear, I'd like another wee chat with you.'

'That's okay,' she said, wiping her hands in a crisp-clean dish cloth.

'We'll nip upstairs,' he added, rising from the comfy chair. 'Leave Father O'Leary here to his peace and quiet and his morning paper.'

Father O'Leary made polite protests but seemed much happier with the arrangement. Eimear walked over to the table where she had her coat on the back of the chair and her handbag on the floor nearby, both of which she collected before following Gibson up the stairs.

Starrett brought up the rear of the trio and as he was breaking the ground-floor ceiling and first floor, he realised exactly what he'd been missing from the scene earlier. The foul smell was gone. And it wasn't that is was being hidden behind scented candles and air freshener – no, it was quite simply gone.

Eimear Robinson had a good gawk around the room Starrett and his team had commandeered as their site office. She was trying really hard to study the writing on the blackboard, unaware that the crafty ban garda had already swung it around to the red herring side.

'Youse have settled in here very cosily,' she said, as the inspector offered her the seat that he placed in front of the blackboard. 'How can I help you? I mean, I don't want to rush you or anything, but I haven't been here for nearly a week now, so I'm way behind on my work. I said to the father down there, "Father Robert," I said, "just give me a couple of days and I'll have St Ernan's looking as good as new."

He said we're 186 years too late for that. He's so dry, so funny, most people don't pick up on it.'

'Eimear,' Starrett said, 'we need to talk to you about Jessica's relationship with Father Matthew.'

'Sure, I've told you already,' she protested mildly, 'he was just a good friend of our family and he was around at our house at lot. He was a great friend of all of us.'

'Eimear, we've just questioned Jessica...' Starrett said.

'You'd no right to, you know!' she protested again, more vigorously this time, 'I had a right to be present when you were talking to my daughters! I might be just a housekeeper, but I know my rights, Inspector.'

'We know Jessica and Father Matthew were in a relationship,' Starrett said, knowing there was no other way to get through this phase but tackle the issue head on.

'A relationship?' Eimear said loudly. 'Sweet Jesus, Mary, and Joseph, what are you on about?! Sure, she's only a child and with a child's imagination. You see, Inspector, that's why it's the law of the land that an adult has to be with a child when the guards want to question them.'

'She's just over eighteen, Eimear,' Gibson sympathised. 'In the eyes of the law, she's an adult.'

'Augh, just listen to yourself woman, she's no adult, she's our wee Jessica! I was just saying to our Gerry last night, "Gerry," I said, "it seems like just yesterday when I was pregnant with our Jessica and look at her now, just look at her now?"'

Eimear sounded and looked like she had forgotten the point she was going to make; either that or she just didn't want to shut down that particular thread. By the time she had muttered her way to the second 'look at her now', she was barely audible.

Starrett was just going to ask his next question when there was a low knock on the door. Gibson went to open it and in wheezed Father O'Leary, performing his old man shuffle where his feet barely left the floor as if he was skating on an ice rink for the first time in his life. He arrived bearing a tray laden with a teapot, three cups, saucers, milk, sugar and a plate, quite literally loaded with plain Rich Tea biscuits.

Eimear Robinson looked relieved.

Three minutes later, when Father O'Leary shuffled back out of the room, Gibson poured all their teas and Eimear said, 'Now listen, Starrett, please believe me when I tell you there was no relationship between Jessica and Father Matt, apart from perhaps in her imagination.'

Then she started to hoak around in her handbag. Handbag? It was more like a malleable suitcase and she seemed to have everything in it bar the kitchen sink, and if the amount of hoaking around that went on was anything to go by, a Belfast sink might have even been in there, too. Starrett was surprised that his over-active nostrils seemed to detect a bit of a whiff of a stale-ish smell coming from the inside of that bag. In fact, he was very surprised by that, what with everything about Eimear and her house and her daughters being clean, very clean. He tried, without being rude, to steal a look as she continued digging around. There was a white plastic bag, knotted at the top, but apart from that the contents looked normal for a woman's handbag. Eventually she got what she was after; a couple of packets of sweetener. She placed one on top of the other and when she was sure that all the corners were lined up symmetrically she tore the corners of both packets simultaneously and poured the total contents into her tea.

Starrett set down his own tea and walked over to the large lockable cupboard the gardai had commandeered for safe-keeping of evidence. With his back to Eimear and Gibson, he eventually found what he was looking for: a small evidence bag with the two packets of Sweetex sweetener, which Starrett had discovered deserted on the kitchen table the previous Wednesday evening. Starrett carefully examined the two discarded packets of sweetener and turned to Eimear. At that moment he remembered Father O'Leary's suggestion that he shouldn't be scared about looking back to the original story of King Herod and John the Baptist.

'Eimear,' he said, 'how many spoonful's of sugar did Father Matt take with his tea or coffee?'

'Sugar,' she laughed, 'you should have seen his teeth! I've never seen a man with such perfect teeth, he'd never let anything like sugar near them.'

'What about sweetener?' Starrett asked, replacing his valuable piece of evidence in the cupboard, locking the door and returning to Gibson and Eimear for a final sip of his tea.

Once again Eimear laughed, this time shaking her head in a large 'no'. 'He couldn't abide the stuff, said he'd never needed it, said he felt it was just as important to avoid the substitutes.'

'Eimear,' Starrett said, returning his cup to its saucer very naturally, 'when we've finished our tea we need you to come with us to the gardai station in Ramelton.'

'Will I need a solicitor?'

'I think you might,' Starrett replied, 'I think you might.'

CHAPTER FIFTY-FIVE

Two hours later, Starrett, Gibson, Eimear Robinson, and her solicitor, coincidentally the same solicitor Bishop Cormac Freeman had retained, a Mr Russell Leslie, sat down together in the basement of Tower House, the gardaí base in Ramelton and the centre for Starrett's Serious Crimes Unit.

It was, in a way, a bizarre room in which to conduct an interview, due to the fact that the windows were only eighteen inches deep and all at the top of the wall, and because the room was 85 per cent subterranean, all you got to see were people from the knees down and cars from the top of wheels down.

Starrett announced the details of the proceedings for the benefit of the tape recorder. His problem with the proceedings, however, was that although he felt he knew who had murdered Father Matthew, he still didn't have a clue how the murder was carried out. He knew he needed to be very careful, because Eimear's solicitor Russell Leslie was cute enough not to allow his client to incriminate herself.

'Okay,' he said, it sounding more like a large sigh, and him feeling like he didn't have much heart for the proceedings. 'This is a right old mess, isn't it?' He then had to announce, for the benefit of the tape recorder, that proceedings were temporarily interrupted as Garda Romany Browne entered the room with a tray of teas, coffees, and Jacob's chocolate-coated, orange-flavoured biscuits (a personal favourite of Starrett's – a point he did not note for the benefit of the tape recorder), milk and sugar.

Once again, Eimear spent quite a bit of time hoaking around in her bag until she produced two more packets of Sweetex. And once again she lined them up and tore the top right-hand corner simultaneously off the packets before pouring the contents into her tea.

Browne's interruption had been planned in advance by Starrett for this very moment. He quickly pulled a new pair of evidence gloves from his pocket and put them on and then very cautiously picked up the four pieces of the two Sweetex packets from the table between them and placed them in an evidence bag.

Eimear Robinson smiled at Starrett as though she first thought the detective's actions were amusing and then the smile disappeared when she slowly came to the conclusion that they were not.

'Eimear,' Starrett said, as he peeled open one of the small Jacob's bars, 'when did you discover that your daughter had been made pregnant by Father Matthew?'

Eimear blinked but barely once more than normal. Apart from that single indiscretion, there was no other reaction to Starrett's question. This, in its own way, and all things considered, was quite an over-reaction.

'Starrett, we just discussed this up at St Ernan's,' she replied, slowly and firmly. 'Father Matt was a friend of my family, nothing more, just that. And God forgive me for saying "just that" because he was a good friend to all of us, a good friend. Who's got it in for my family? Who's been telling you lies, Starrett?'

'Eimear, Jessica has received confirmation from her doctor that she's pregnant,' Gibson offered sympathetically, and when Eimear didn't react positively to the fact, she added, 'It won't take very long to prove Father Matt is the father of the child.'

'You can't do a test,' Eimear snapped back at the ban garda in shock, 'Father Matthew is in the ground!'

Those last five words proved to Starrett, if proof were needed, that he was correct.

'Mrs Robinson, the pathologist will have kept samples when she carried out the autopsy,' Russell Leslie offered, clearly hoping that his client would be guided to a safer route.

'Okay,' Starrett announced, feeling this wasn't fair anymore, 'Eimear, shall I tell you what you did?'

Eimear turned to her solicitor who was very slowly mouthing a 'no' to her. She kept quiet.

'You came across your daughter, Jessica, and Father Matt making love on the sofa in your sitting room just over a month ago. Your husband, Gerry, was asleep upstairs so you very quietly sent Father Matt off into the night and you took your daughter up to her room, and not another word was said about it. That was that, until two weeks later you discovered that your daughter was pregnant.'

This time Eimear Robinson did not complain, although Starrett reckoned she was far from giving up the fight.

'Everyone I've spoken to has told me the same thing: Eimear Robinson lives for her daughters – you even told me yourself how much you struggled with a few jobs to push yourself beyond your comfort zone to get the house, mainly for your daughters. Eimear, I'm not saying that's a bad thing. But it did lead me to start to think of you and examine the fact that you were prepared to do anything for your daughters.

'Wednesday is usually your day off and so when Father Dugan said that he didn't see you come across the causeway that fatal Wednesday, I'd already counted you out. Not that I even felt I needed to do a check on you in the first place. I didn't suspect you in the slightest; out of all the people I met, you were the one who seemed most moved to genuine tears by the death of the young priest.

'But then earlier today I realised you'd been in the dining area with Father Matthew on the afternoon he died. You told me he was meticulously clean and kept the kitchen perfect, cleaning up after himself as he went along.

'When I was searching the kitchen-cum-dining area in St Ernan's last Wednesday, I discovered four pieces of Sweetex packets on the seat of the chair, beside where Father Matthew was found. Clearly, if you'd dropped the Sweetex packets when you were in St Ernan's the previous day, Father Matt would have cleaned them away.

'But the most incriminating thing is that we're not just discussing the discovery of any auld Sweetex packets, are we?' Starrett posed. 'Bejeepers, no we're not. We're discussing Sweetex packets that have identical tears, tears which betrayed your unique way of opening two packets at once. We've got the original Sweetex packets from last Wednesday and I'm sure Eimear's prints will be on them,' he said, directing that last statement to the solicitor.

Russell Leslie scrunched up his face as if to suggest, 'Is that it, is that all you've got?' Well, he was paid to really, wasn't he?

'So how did Eimear get on to St Ernan's?' was what the solicitor actually asked.

'Easy,' Starrett replied, using the pause to open another Jacob's orange chocolate bar. 'She simply wore trousers, most likely a pair of tracksuit bottoms and a top and hid her hair up under a baseball cap, and from that distance Father Dugan would have most certainly pegged her as a man.'

Starrett guessed as much, only because that's exactly what he would have done if he'd been a female trying to overcome the same obstacle.

'Then what?' Starrett asked, voicing the question on everyone's mind, including his own. 'Eimear discreetly made her way into the dining area, where she knew Father Matt would be hard at work, preparing the evening meal. She'd be aware of Father Mulligan's afternoon walking habits – he habitually goes out at 3:30 and returns at 5:30. She knew that volunteers to help with the cooking would be as rare as hen's teeth. Eimear, you then sat down in Father Matt's kitchen. He made you a cup of tea as he was getting ready to boil the potatoes. Then he joined you and you chatted.

'There were no marks about Father Matt's body, no signs of a struggle, which suggests to me that he knew his murderer. When the father was still sitting at the table, Eimear, you got up and quietly went behind him and you killed him.'

'And killed him?' Russell Leslie shouted, incredulous at the very insinuation, 'Inspector Starrett, really?'

Starrett had two more cards to play but his fear was, he really needed three. The good news, though, was that Eimear hadn't uttered a peep.

'Okay Russell, fair point, fair point,' Starrett admitted, 'I've got one more piece of incriminating evidence.'

'Oh yeah?' the solicitor tutted.

'Yes,' Starrett said and paused, 'after Eimear murdered Father Matt, she grabbed a damp tea towel and used it to clean away the discharge from the small wound found above the hair line on the back of Father Matt's neck. There would have been a considerable discharge of blood and brain and body tissue, possibly a lot more than she'd been expecting. Her second mistake was that she tried to hide the tea towel in the back of the cupboard, under the sink, the exact same place we all dump stuff we don't know what to do with. For this last week, that soiled teatowel has progressively stank out the kitchen-cum-dining area of St Ernan's. That was until Eimear – earlier today, in fact, on her first time back in the building since the murder – rescued the incriminating evidence, placed it in a white plastic bag, and attempted to seal it by knotting the top of the bag.'

Eimear merely shrugged as if to say, 'Really, me?'

'And,' Starrett started, drawing the word out for as long as he possibly could get away with it, 'that white plastic bag is currently in Mrs Robinson's handbag.'

Gibson looked like she was impressed. Well, Starrett figured, she either thought that or she thought her boss was crazy.

'Can I have that bag please, Eimear?' Starrett asked, politely. 'We have to send the contents to the lab for testing but I'd bet you my trusted BMW that we're going to find Father Matt's DNA all over it.'

'Do I have to?' Eimear asked Russell Leslie.

'Before you answer that question, Mr Leslie, can I just say that said tea towel is the property of St Ernan's; what's more, the bag the towel is contained in was also purchased by a member of St Ernan's to transport groceries back to the house from Donegal Town.'

On hearing that, Russell Leslie advised his client that as neither the towel, plastic bag, nor the premises said towel and plastic bag were discovered on, were her property, she would have to comply with the inspector's request.

Eimear reluctantly and unhurriedly did so. She still didn't look like she was going to admit to anything though.

Starrett crossed his fingers inside his trouser pocket and played his final card.

'Eimear, of one thing I am certain,' Starrett said, 'if it wasn't you who murdered Father Matt, it must have been Jessica.'

At first she just glared at Starrett for close to a minute.

'You can't hurt the dead,' Eimear Robinson eventually said calmly and quietly, 'but if you could I'd be happy to dig him up, just so I could kill him all over again.'

Starrett checked the tape was still rolling. The room was surreally quiet. If you allowed yourself to be distracted, there were still sounds of a normal Tuesday in the garda station, still sounds of Ramelton working its way slowly up through the gears of the day. But for the four in the basement interview room of Tower House, there was nothing, nothing apart from the sound of their own breathing, which was just about to be interrupted by the sound of Eimear Robinson's voice rising at the beginning of her sentences and trailing off towards the end, trailing off to the extent that sometimes she was barely audible and Gibson kept having to ask her to repeat parts of her confession.

'When I walked into our new lounge and saw them...well, actually, I heard them before I saw them, they were suppressing their animal sounds of pleasure so that they wouldn't be discovered. Then, as my eyes grew accustomed to the darkness, I started to be able to make out their forms. Our Jessica, God forgive her, naked as the day she was born, riding him like she was on a horse. They were so preoccupied with their pleasure they didn't even notice me enter the room.

'He'd still his priest's black shirt on, but opened all the way down. His trousers and underpants were down around his ankles. But he'd still his black leather shoes on. Of all the things that could have run through my mind at that moment, the one that annoyed me the most was that that fecker was on my new sofa with his fecking shoes on!

'I remember thinking about my poor Gerry, upstairs, asleep, and all the overtime he'd had to work just so we could buy that sofa and here was this…this pric…this priest, defiling our eldest daughter on it with his fecking shoes on. Gerry and I have had our differences and we've had our problems, and I'll admit I'm responsible for as many of our problems as he is, but for all of that he was – he is – a good father and a good provider for our children and this is the way Jessica thanks him?

'Jessica was a child, she'd an excuse, but he should have known better. He was an adult; adults are not meant to take advantage of children. But on top of being an adult, he was a PRIEST, for heaven's sake. A priest, a disciple of the Holy Father. How could God let that happen? You answer me that, Inspector Starrett, how could God let one of his priests defile my daughter?'

Starrett didn't have an answer to the question that had most troubled the island of Ireland for the last hundred years.

'I watched them for a good few minutes and then I started to realise Jessica knew what she was doing, she knew how to take her pleasure. She'd clearly done it before. Was she as bad as he was? No, of course not, at least he should have known better!

'I waited until I thought they were about to climax and then I walked up to them out of the shadows. I half hoped that I'd scare them both to death, particularly Father Matt. Sadly, yet another of my prayers bit the dust. I started whispering to them, shaking them, and they stopped in shock. I remember being so happy at the fact that I'd been able to prevent their climax – a small victory, I know, but a victory for me nonetheless. I wrapped her dressing gown around her, stuffed her jimjams into one of her arms while I held on to her other firmly, and I just kept pushing my other hand into his chest, little punches, but as strong as I could muster, whispering at him to get his clothes on and get out and never come back.

'Once he'd gone I led her up to her bedroom. I didn't say a word to her, I didn't trust myself. I just shoved her into her room and closed the door.

'I went downstairs again, but by now I was weeping so much I could hardly see what I was doing. I took all the covers off the cushions on our sofa and I put them straight into the washing machine and I sat up crying until the cycle had finished and I moved them to the drier.

'There was still a smell of their sex in the lounge so I sprayed the room a few times with air freshener and finally went to bed. I got up first the next morning and I was surprised by my resolve, how un-upset I was feeling.

'A few days later our Julia was a bit off – she'd been very upset for a wee while – so I took her out on one of our walks and eventually I got it out of her, what had been upsetting her. She dropped the bombshell. Jessica was pregnant. Father Matt's name wasn't mentioned. I still don't even know if Julia knew about her sister and the priest.

'Later that day I realised that Father Matt was just downright evil. I knew the Church would never ever do anything about him fornicating with my daughter. All they'd do is to try to manage the situation. This incident, my beautiful daughter being defiled by that priest, would become just another part of their permanent and ongoing damage control. This was totally unacceptable to me and so I resolved to find a way of ridding the world of him.'

Eimear finished talking like she'd concluded all she needed to say.

'Eimear,' Starrett started, 'talk us through what happened last Wednesday afternoon at St Ernan's, please.'

'It was easy,' she began, 'I mean, it was so easy it was untrue. I decided Father Matt was evil. I decided that he needed to die. The next night, I was watching late-night TV – I put myself to sleep most nights watching TV. So I miss most of the stuff. but for some reason I was awake for this one programme, you know, the one where they take some subject and try and prove if it's true or false. On this particular night, the night I was watching, the topic was: Is it possible to kill someone using an ice pellet?'

'Sorry?' Starrett said, confused.

'You know,' she said, from the benefit of knowledge gained from watching a fifty-minute documentary, 'instead of using a lead pellet or a bullet, is it possible to kill someone with an ice slug?'

'Really?' Starrett said, totally amazed.

'Yes,' she said, bemused at Starrett's reaction, 'it was on the History Channel. It's a great programme. Most of the subjects they tackle, though, I'd go "why would you even want to bother to try that?" But this particular one was, as I say, of growing interest to me.'

'And did they prove that they could? Kill someone with an ice pellet?' Starrett asked.

'In theory, yes,' Eimear Robinson claimed, 'but I proved it in practice.'

'How?' Gibson asked, appearing to want to keep the confession on track.

'Don't you see? It's the way to commit the perfect murder,' she continued, 'the man in the programme said, "This way," he said, "there would be no tell-tale bullet left behind to forensically incriminate the suspect."'

'I experimented a bit at home, making the ice pellets in the icebox of our new freezer. Up at St Ernan's, we all have a go with the air rifle, trying to rid the island of the rabbits and making a bit of rabbit stew as a by-product.

'Using a biro pen top as a cast, I perfected my slug. I used a nail file to trim it down to the perfect size. I tried a few times until I got it just right.'

'But how did you manage to get them to St Ernan's without them melting?' Starrett felt obliged to ask.

'Simple, I just popped them in a small thermal flask of Gerry's,' she replied and then added proudly, 'I'd been thinking I'd have to cart an icebox to St Ernan's until I came up with that part of the plan.'

'And the ice slugs don't melt in the barrel?' Starrett asked, realising how bizarre this whole thing was becoming.

'The man on the telly explained that the secret with the air rifle is that it uses compressed air rather than explosives. And if there are no explosives, there is no heat.

'So, last Wednesday, on my day off, I headed up to St Ernan's, but instead of driving or getting a lift with our Mary, as I would normally do,

I parked my car in the driveway of one of the holiday homes, which are never used this time of the year. As you guessed, I dressed in trousers and put my hair up into one of Gerry's old black cloth caps. I knew Father Dugan would clock me crossing the causeway but because of the clothes I was wearing, he would put me down to be one of the priests returning. I got there just after 3:30, knowing that's when Father Mulligan goes off for his constitutional around the island, his daily intake of fresh air.

'Father Matthew was surprised to see me on my day off,' Eimear continued, now appearing to move into a different gear. 'I was immediately friendly to him, which seemed to please him. Obviously things had been very frosty between both of us since the night I'd discovered him with Jessica.

'He made me a coffee and we talked at the table like we'd done hundreds of times before. He pulled his chair around to face the fire and we must have been there for an hour and he said, "I'll better get back to my chores," he said, "the potatoes will soon be boiled." I told him to sit where he was in the heat of the fire and I'd bring him over another fresh cup of coffee.

'I nipped over to the sink, turned on the water to hide the sound of me getting the air rifle from beside the back door, and I took one of the ice pellets from my thermos flask. I broke the barrel, placed the pellet in, shut the barrel, and crept over to Father Matt. I placed the barrel of the air rifle as close as I could to the back of his neck, placed it just above his hair line with the barrel pointing upwards,' she said, and then turned her head slowly away from Starrett and Gibson and used her index finger to demonstrate the point on her neck and the direction of the barrel.

'I pulled the trigger. There was a pop, as usual. The priest started to speak, "Eimear…" he said, but before he'd managed another breath the ice pellet was destroying his brain. I checked his neck for a pulse. He was dead. There was, as you've already suggested, quite a discharge from his neck. I quickly grabbed the tea towel he'd left on the table earlier and held it to the wound until the discharge was complete. I wiped his neck clean. My idea had been to kill him because he was evil. At the same time, I didn't feel my daughter should lose a mother. So, my plan was that one of the priests would discover him there and think that he'd died a natural death and that would be it.

'I heard some shuffling upstairs. I thought Father O'Leary was on the way down to satisfy his sweet tooth once again before mealtime. So I threw the soiled tea towel under the sink, as you do, as we all do, and I got out of there. I forgot my empty Sweetex packets, of course. Most people would have just thrown them in the bin as rubbish, but not you Starrett, no, not you. Because the bishop was in residence and Father Matt was so young, the guards were called. And here we all are, not even a week later.'

Starrett was amazed by how normal Eimear appeared. She looked like and sounded like she was taking everything in her stride. She had a week to come to terms with Father Matt's death and she had just under a month to come to terms with her daughter and Father Matt's relationship. Would there come a time when Eimear would start to think if only she'd bit her lip, counted slowly to ten and instead of acting the way she had, that is to say, trying to sweep the incident under the carpet like it had never happened, it might have, just might have been better for her to behave like a mature mother? That is to say, she could have, should have, given guidance to Father Matt and Jessica. Told them that if they were really serious about their relationship, to just slow it down a wee bit? Maybe she could have advised him to leave the priesthood, get an ordinary job, settle down and go about it all the right way? Would Eimear ever think that if she had just done all of the above, then maybe Jessica and Matt McKaye would have, could have, lived happily ever after?

But Eimear's main problem had been that she was doing all she knew how to do: trying to totally block the incident from her mind. She wanted to ignore it. She'd even refused to discuss the late-night rendezvous with Jessica. It was as if she was trying to pretend that it had never happened. However as soon as she found out her daughter was pregnant, there was no longer a possibility of ignoring it. The evidence was there, growing inside her daughter, and soon all the world would be capable of witnessing it and the family she'd dedicated her entire life to would be shamed.

Someone had to pay for that and that someone was Father Matthew McKaye.

CHAPTER FIFTY-SIX

DAY ONE: WEDNESDAY

The very next day, in another graveyard, in yet another beautiful Donegal landscape, Starrett was attending another funeral, this time the funeral of his lifelong friend, Major Newton Cunningham.

In Starrett's experience, funerals usually took place on beautiful autumnal mornings. The thing about beautiful autumnal mornings in Donegal is that the sun, as it lights up every corner of the rich tapestry of fields; hills; mountains; trees; rugged hedges; blue heavenly skies; faint white clouds and all creatures great and small, does tend to show off our creator's magic in all its spiritual glory. Starrett wondered was this meant to be a reminder for the survivors, just as himself, of exactly what they were going to miss when they too passed.

Just after the burial, a man came up to Starrett and asked if they could have a private word. Starrett agreed and led the man to a quieter part of the graveyard, by an old oak tree. The man had a Dublin accent and introduced himself as Superintendent John Connolly. The superintendent gave the detective a speech about a conversation he'd recently shared with the Major. Basically, the Major had advised the superintendent that the only way Ramelton's Serious Crimes Unit could continue would be if it was allowed to continue to run the way it was currently run. The superintendent wanted to honour the Major's wishes, and he realised that the Major could not be replaced, so he was volunteering to deal with the gardai politics on Starrett's behalf. He suggested that Starrett might even want to increase his team, only by two, but he could pick whomever he wanted.

Starrett wasn't really in the mood for either the chat or the thoughts it might provoke, if he was honest, but he could hear the Major's voice in his ear, 'Just be open to some of the proposals that will be made to you and remember, not all the seniors are bad people.'

'I'll think about it,' Starrett had offered as a concession to the Major. In Starrett's language 'I'll think about it' didn't mean 'No, but I don't want to tell you "no" right now.' It meant he would think about it.

'But that leaves us with a bit of a problem,' Superintendent John Connolly confessed.

'Sorry?' Starrett said, distracted by the fact that he thought the conversation had already reached its natural conclusion.

'Earlier this morning the body of Bishop Cormac Freeman was found–'

'But I thought he was in custody?' Starrett said, his already confused feelings now running a new riot.

'He got out on bail and, as far as Dr Samantha Aljoe can determine he was murdered yesterday evening, between the hours of nine and eleven.'

'And you think I–' Starrett said, now too confused and troubled to even try to think straight.

'No, no, of course not! Otherwise it would have been premature of me to have that conversation with you. Besides which, Dr Aljoe confirms that during the time of the bishop's death she and half the county were with you, at the Major's wake.'

A few minutes later, when the superintendent had gone on his way, Starrett walked across to Maggie Keane and explained the full situation.

'I could leave here with you now, leave the guards for good, Maggie,' Starrett offered, and meant it.

'I know you would, Starrett, that's exactly why you don't have to. Go and do your work, we'll see you later today,' she said, as she gave him a big hug before winking at him as they broke off. Both Moya and Katie gave him a big heart-warming hug, too.

He and Gibson were just about to leave the graveyard when a thought seemed to hit him, and it was a troubling one.

'Hault your horses, Nuala,' he said, 'please, wait in the car -- I've two important bits of work to do to tie up the case.'

The detective strolled up to Father Robert O'Leary, who was in attendance at the funeral in order to be of assistance to the frail Father Peregrine Dugan, who was taking a rare day off from his work on The History of Ireland to make an even rarer public appearance.

'Fathers, sad day, a very sad day,' an emotional Starrett offered them.

They both offered the detective their condolences.

'So, you solved the case on the seventh day,' Father O'Leary said, 'I always knew you would.'

'And it was Herodias' sister (if she even had one) and not her daughter, Salome, after all?' Father Dugan said.

'Sadly, yes,' Starrett replied, really meaning it.

'You've heard about Bishop Freeman?' Father O'Leary asked, while still shaking the detective's hand.

'Just,' he replied, looking back to the vacated place in the graveyard by the old oak tree where he'd recently had the conversation with the Major's replacement. 'I'm off there now, but I've solved another of St Ernan's mysteries.'

'Oh really?' Father O'Leary asked looking a little concerned.

Starrett futtered around in his inside pocket for a few seconds and produced an envelope which he handed over to Father O'Leary.

'The packet of Hamilton Nibs?' O'Leary guessed with as much enthusiasm as Starrett had seen from him in the last week.

Starrett nodded yes.

Where? Father O'Leary spelt out in the cold air with his forefinger and thumb.

'We found it down in your basement in the room Father Gene McCafferty was holed up in,' Starrett offered. 'I've one question for you before I go.'

'And your question?'

'Why,' Starrett asked Father O'Leary, 'do they call Father Edward the Ginger Beatle? I get the ginger bit,' he added, trying to show he was not above plying his trade to work out domestic puzzles as well as criminal ones.

'Apparently,' Father O'Leary replied, 'The Beatles had a song called 'Eleanor Rigby'. I believe, during the course of the song they sing about a certain Father McKenzie.'

'Yes, right, right, of course,' Starrett boasted, avoiding eye contact with the priests, 'the obvious connection.'

THE END